GOBLIN MARKET

RICHARD BOWES

POPULAR LIBRARY

An Imprint of Warner Books, Inc.

A Warner Communications Company

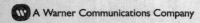

GOBLIN MARKET

Everyone in the City, slave and free, telepath and not, mortal and God, was captive to Goblin Market.

Out in the north where it was summer, Garvin strode in time. Holding the room in the mirror of his mind, he shuffled worlds before it like a deck of cards, looking for the one his advance scouts had described.

He passed by worlds that had never supported human life, other worlds emptied of all but small garrisons, worlds subjugated and still being exploited: all the dull grinding horror, the cringing slaves and systematic looters of his father's universe. Behind him in the infinite emptiness, the hundreds of members of Warchild Cluster whom he towed were no more than a faint murmur.

Until recently, he had loved Time, had swum in it like a fish, spun worlds like toys. Now he waited for the vision he knew was coming.

Then the Oracle was upon him . . .

Also by Richard Bowes

WARCHILD

Published by
POPULAR LIBRARY

For Brian Thomsen. And now I know why authors thank editors for their patience and understanding.

PROLOGUE

Father

The City Out Of Time pulsed like a heart at the center of the Gods' creation. Each of the twenty thousand worlds of Time was separated from the next by a few minutes. Together they formed a year. At the center of the City lay the Palace of the Gods and at the top of the Palace, in the Crystal Chamber, the War Cabinet met to discuss the rebellion of the Warchild.

Around one-half of an oval table, wearing court dress, sat chamberlains and comptrollers, managers and madams, the human servants of the Gods. One of them, Coli, the Chancellor, a black man cautious and loyal enough to have grown old in service, formed a careful mental image of a kid in a Mohawk telling a mob which screamed approval, WE ARE GOING TO THE CITY OUT OF TIME AND TEAR THE PLACE DOWN! Coli cleared his throat and addressed the God, "Your son made certain this message would be delivered to us, ever victorious one."

Deferentially, their eyes turned toward the throne where their God sat dressed in the scarred leather cuirass of the Master of Battle. WHERE? The God reached out for the information. A spy master displayed a mental map which showed in red the areas of Time held by the rebels. At least a third of the worlds of Time were touched. A long dark splotch spread toward the City itself. On a world where it was summer in the northern hemisphere near the Baltic Sea, the spy affixed a black dot. THERE, ALL-CUNNING WARRIOR, NOT MORE THAN A FEW DAYS IN TIME FROM ECHBATTAN'S WORLD.

The God squinted hard blue eyes under iron-gray brows, bit down on the stub of an unlighted cigar. "Excellent," he muttered.

The God let his mind reach out over the City into which the wealth of Time flowed. He felt the half million inhabitants, free and slave, all beholden to him, found them in their shops and homes, working in hydroponic greenhouses and operating the systems which kept the City heated and supplied with oxygen and water. He touched them as they bought and sold sex and drugs in Night Town and human bodies and minds in Goblin Market. He reached out to the four great gates, Amber, Silver, Onyx and Gold, which stood ninety degrees apart on the giant circumference of the City.

All the great trade routes, the Time Lanes, led to the portals in those gates. Through them came the supplies, human and otherwise, to feed the hunger of the City and the Goblins. In the great days there had been a flood of booty. Now, with the rebellion, the torrent had slowed but the City itself still had to live.

The ceiling and walls of the Crystal Chamber were made entirely of glass. The people of the City, feeling their God's touch and turning instinctively toward the Palace, saw one of his favorite manifestations. The grizzled Master of Battle sat facing the Goblins over the heads of his servants and theirs.

Those in the Chamber could look out behind the God's throne and see lights bright as midmorning sun shining down on half the City from the mile-high ceiling. Facing the God were the windows overlooking the soft dark of Night Town. In front of that dark sat a half dozen green figures with yellow eyes, their minds closed to human contact. Seated before them were a dozen Steeds, each controlled by a Rider. At the table itself were Zombies, telepaths who served the Riders. Steeds and Riders were all deference to the God. But the

Goblins seemed not to react to anything that was thought and said in the room.

It was known in Time that the Gods reigned in the City and the Goblins governed in the outer worlds. No mere mortal understood the exact terms of the agreement between them. It involved the care and feeding of the Winds, that much was clear. The crowd in the square before the Palace saw the Master of Battle look over the heads of his counselors, past the Steeds and Zombies, to stare significantly at his Goblin partners.

Gesturing across the City to Goblin Market, sweeping the crowd with his powerful telepathy, the God told his people, BEHOLD THE WIND. Turning their attention as commanded, the crowd felt Goblins guide a Wind onto the vast floor of the Market. Scramblers and electronic restraints had been turned off in the slave pits where telepaths, mostly children caught and brought to the City, were held.

The people of the City shuddered as a hundred young lives were snuffed out like candles, absorbed into the Wind. The Goblins then guided it to the machinery under the Goblin Market and hooked it to the transformers that converted telepathic energy to power. Lights flickered for a moment as the Wind which had powered the City Out Of Time for the last few days was disconnected. Small and depleted, that Wind was led away by the Goblins. The lights returned, the crowd cheered, the God nodded, and the meeting resumed.

Some of the Steeds seated in front of the Goblins on stools were beautiful, some terrifying. An exquisite black woman wore jeweled robes; a tall young man had half his face tattooed bright red. All had the same eyes, observant but not alive, telepaths controlled by Riders inside their brains.

The black woman, responding to the command of her Rider, who in turn was obeying its masters the Goblins, rose from her stool and bowed low to ask, OUR GRASP OF THE SITUATION IS NOT AS PERFECT AS YOURS, ALL-CONQUERING CAPTAIN.

CORRECT, replied the God, looking away.

INDULGE US, the tattooed Steed was spurred by his Rider to beg. SHOW, O MINE OF PATIENCE, HOW YOUR SON, THE WARCHILD, IS TO BE STOPPED.

THOUSANDS OF WORLDS HAVE FALLEN, the first Steed said. ALL THOSE WORLDS WHERE IT IS SUMMER IN THE NORTH ARE IN DANGER OF FALLING. ECHBATTAN'S WORLD IS NEXT ON HIS PATH. IT LIES ONLY TWO DAYS FROM THE ONYX GATE OF THIS CITY. The God's advisors turned to stare, amazed at the impudence of the Steeds.

GOBLIN MARKET IS HALF EMPTY OF SLAVES. SOON THE WINDS THEMSELVES WILL GO HUNGRY, another Steed, impelled by his Rider to fall on his knees, reached out telepathically to implore the God. WORLDS TURN AWAY FROM WORSHIP OF YOUR DIVINITY AND CEASE TO YIELD THEIR TRIBUTE TO THE CITY. DO US THE HONOR OF GIVING SOME SMALL GLIMPSE OF YOUR PLAN TO STOP THE REBELLION OF YOUR SON, WHO CALLS HIMSELF WARCHILD.

The advisors flinched and looked away, waiting for the Master of Battle to strike down Steed and Rider. Nothing happened. In the long moment it took for that to register, several in the room reflected on the divine patience of the God with the Steeds. They wondered if it was because his own son had a Rider implanted in his skull.

"Don't worry about my special plan." The voice from the throne was young and hoarse. "Take it from me, this City ain't falling to rebel assault," it sneered. "If the Warchild attacks Echbattan's world, he and his army are gonna be dead meat. And I expect to see his head on the table here."

All eyes returned to the throne. The leather cuirass lay on the floor. Without anyone seeing him do it, the God had changed his form. He who had created so much rarely kept the same identity for long. With the unlighted cigar still in his mouth, the Perpetual Urchin, one of the less pleasant manifestations of the God, looked at them with contempt.

The Urchin, with a face smudged with soot, wearing tattered clothes, his eyes bright and old as city streets, said in a taunting tone, "I just like to see you guys squirm." Then he lighted the cigar with a match he struck on the seat of his pants.

And Son

Garvin tumbled out of a portal in a fury. Beyond a thin line of his own troops was an enemy host. Reaching toward them, he broadcast, LET'S SEE YOUR LEADER DANCE.

Something Garvin had seen in Time had scared him. Now he wanted to take risks to forget. Garvin Warchild stood on a hillock in plain sight of the enemy. Darrel and Maji, soldiers who had known Garvin since before his rebellion, were right next to him. Other telepaths and soldiers of his elite guard, the Warchild Cluster, poured out of the portal behind him. They formed up around Garvin, happy to be out of the horrible emptiness of Time.

Troopers in the small rebel army already on the world roared, "Warchild! Warchild!" Companion telepaths relayed the image of their leader. Like him they were very young. With his Mohawk, black jeans, and leather jacket, the Warchild could have been one of them. The army watched through the eyes of those nearest Garvin as he stood staring at the enemy host. Altogether, he had only a few thousand troops with him. The enemy numbered at least one hundred and fifty thousand. It was no contest. COME ON OUT, KARL! Garvin broadcast.

The presence inside the Warchild's mind looked through his eyes, heard with his ears. 'this world is a key to echbattan's outermost defenses,' his Rider told him. It recalled for the Warchild a map of the worlds under Echbattan control, showed him their own location up near the Baltic on a world where it was early summer in the north. 'we can take it out with a single coup. but that is not worth dying for.'

Garvin was breathing hard. Automatically, whenever he felt his Rider, the Warchild touched the gold razor at his throat. Originally that had been a reminder to the mind parasite that he could kill them both. Now the Warchild wasn't even aware he did it. At the age of seventeen, he had just seen a prophecy of his own death. I AM WAITING FOR YOU, KARL, Garvin called the enemy leader.

'you mustn't let something as foolish as the oracle distract you,' his Rider advised.

YOU'RE SCARED SHITLESS, Garvin replied.

'a single rifle shot could end us.'

IF THEY HAVE A RIFLE.

The telepaths of his army formed a heroic image of Garvin standing over the body of a giant Steed he had killed, covered with his enemy's blood and his own. They let that just touch the consciousness of the nontelepathic army which faced them.

The enemy was spread out over low hills just beyond bow range, armored cavalry and phalanxes of foot soldiers, massed archers behind them: the host of the Absolute Ruler Karl, Emperor of Europe and as much of Asia as he could lay hands on. The rebel troops were all from off-world and were armed with rifles and automatic weapons but had used them very sparingly. Their leader didn't want any slaughter. Some thought the Warchild's aversion to bloodshed was his biggest weakness.

Their job had been to bait Karl into appearing where Garvin could get at him. As instructed, the advance guard had appeared on the Polish plains and sat there until the Absolute Ruler lumbered up to them.

The Warchild's telepathic officers, the Companions, linked minds and included the soldiers under them in a relay. Garvin grasped that relay casually. ROUTINE, he told the troops. OLD KARL CHASED YOU TILL YOU CAUGHT HIM. He formed the image of an elephant brought down by a thin trip wire, and his troops cheered.

Only a few half-trained minds resisted as Garvin scanned the enemy. 'i would estimate that they have only one fully functioning telepath,' his Rider remarked as Garvin sifted through their consciousness. For them it was 1314 A.D., the tenth year of the reign of Karl, an obscure duke who, by grace of the Gods and the Goblins, had conquered everything from London to Muscovy. Divine grace enabled Karl to see into men's souls. Karl's host stirred at the touch of the Warchild, and his relay. 'hurry,' his Rider urged.

IS OLD KARL TRYING TO GIVE US THE SLIP? Garvin sorted through nervous foot soldiers, knights anxious to be at the enemy, priests converted to worship of Goblins. Then he caught an image of himself, blond and tanned, his Mohawk like a helmet crest, ponytail blowing in the summer wind.

Karl the Over Ruler stared through the magic weapon given him by Angels. Garvin recognized them as Zombies.

'he has you in telescopic sights,' his Rider screamed inside Garvin as Karl took aim and touched the trigger. The Absolute Ruler had quite a bit of crude natural ability and his Angels had given him some training. But the Warchild got inside his mind, tore at his memories, twisted his fears. Karl felt rats chew his testicles.

The air went out of the Over Ruler and he fired into the air. He fell from his horse, crying, got up, and began dancing clumsily, singing aloud, "Where Warchild rules/The Goblins die."

Karl's army stood stunned as their leader pirouetted out of their ranks and knelt at Garvin's feet. Then the Companion relay swept over them with an image of the Warchild triumphant, and all of them fell to their knees.

YOU DID THAT NEATLY, a Companion told Garvin and smiled. She was cute, with a silver Mohawk ridge on a head of short black hair.

He smiled back, feeling the exultation that came from tempting danger. She was an aide newly assigned to the Cluster. He knew he hadn't slept with her. But she was familiar enough to make him wonder if somewhere in Time he might have hooked up with her near double. The Companion's name was Blaze and Garvin made a point of having her nearby when he went to inspect the Over Ruler's tent.

It stank of horses and musk oil. But it was fairly clean and looked comfortable. Darrel and Maji knew without being told to stay outside. Discreetly, Warchild Cluster dispersed from around the tent. Inside, Garvin at first just wanted to hold Blaze, to run his hands over her. Then he got them both undressed and comfortable on a pile of silk pillows. While he moved with the young woman, Garvin was able to forget the prophecy of his own death.

He prolonged the pleasure as much as he could. But there came a moment when she looked at him and even without telepathy Garvin could read the absolute faith she had in the Warchild. Blaze was beautiful and loving, and that was as scary as what the Oracle had shown him.

Garvin thought of the vast, high-strung army she was part

of. He knew that he could show none of them how a short while before, tumbling in Time, he had smelled an electric hum and heard the red of roses. It was fainter than he remembered but he recognized the Oracle. The first thing the Oracle showed Garvin was a large public plaza. 'that looks like echbattan's world. . . .' his Rider had started to tell him.

Then it had seen what was in the center of the plaza and shut up. A pyre had stood under a blood-red sun. Again and again in the Oracle's vision Warchild and Rider had seen a pile of naked bodies starting to burn. Some were alive enough to writhe. But hanging upside down on top of the heap, Garvin had seen himself motionless, bleeding.

LIKE A BARBECUE, he reminded his Rider and felt it wince. Garvin put his arms around Blaze again. Without his rebellion she might have died in Goblin Market. With him dead she was sure to. He had to believe that somewhere in Time there was a way to block that fate.

CHAPTER

One

As Garvin thought about the Oracle, a girl named Alexis, called Lex, caught an image of the Warchild. She awoke on the first chilly morning, months away from him in Time, felt him tell her, RISE UP! Half asleep, staring at the ceiling, Lex tried to connect the boy, with his ridge of blond hair and slightly flattened nose, to something in her dreams or memories.

Before calling on her to rebel, the mind which showed her the image told her a name. But that had faded as Alexis, groping for an explanation, decided she had seen a member of some new band. What stayed strongly with her was a trace of hope, of purpose, things she hadn't known how much she needed.

ALEXIS, AWAKE! a mind told her abruptly, and Lex felt a pinpoint of fear at the touch of Vasa, the Zombie. The woman's mind probed as Lex woke up all the way and remembered that there were no more new bands and, since Time and the Goblins had found her world, not an awful lot of hope. HOPE IS THE BREAD OF THE STARVING, the Zombie announced.

Vasa quickly found Lex's memory of the image of the boy and broke contact. Lying quietly, Lex reached out and felt her teacher probe the minds of the ten other apprentice Zombies in the Bates Motel. Each of them had been taught a mental pattern, a mantra of numbers and letters and words that spun almost constantly. It was a barrier, a way of keeping one's thoughts and dreams to oneself. Vasa now unlocked each effortlessly and at the same time blocked the students from her own mind.

Then Vasa broke contact and Lex felt her start to scan the neighborhood. She understood that Vasa, having searched their minds for traces of the message, was looking for the telepath who had sent it.

WHAT? Lex felt others first ask the ones sleeping in their rooms, then the apprentices of the Bates Motel in general. WHAT IS SHE LOOKING FOR? Stretching under a down comforter, Lex concentrated on the feel of that, filled her mind with the sight of her breath puffing out into the light of the frosty morning. She shut out fellow apprentices asking, LEX, WHAT IS IT? WHAT IS VASA DOING?

Lex could block any one of them separately and even most of them together. That was not always polite, nor wise nor politically correct for those who served the Goblins and the Riders. But she also suspected what she had seen was treason and that some of the kids would try to use it against her if they found out.

So instead of blocking, Lex let them feel the cold as she threw off the covers and put her bare feet on the floor of the motel bedroom. She heard Johnny and Sandy next door give little screeches. From rooms farther away she felt resentment, even hate. BITCH THINKS SHE IS SO CHILL, Brent told Amy, forming the thought carefully for everyone to share.

The cold brought Lex unwelcome memories of her family on the morning in April when she had left home. That was a short while after the Goblins and Riders captured her world and remembering wasn't wise or politic either. But even a hint of those thoughts was enough to keep the rest of the Bates Motel crew at bay.

Besides, as she shivered in a thick robe and waited for the shower water to heat up, Lex couldn't stop remembering them squatting in the kitchen in front of the electric stove. Mandy, her little sister, was occupied with memorizing the Goblin Chain, the litany taught to kids with no telepathic potential. "The child obeys the teacher, the teacher obeys the soldier, the soldier obeys the Zombie, the Zombie obeys the Rider, the Rider obeys the Goblin, the Goblin serves the Gods of the City." Being seven had advantages: if Mandy could say that aloud for her teacher, she would get a candy bar at lunchtime.

In the mind of her brother Bobby, Lex had touched pure pain. Every morning he felt his losses like new wounds. Some surgery, some implants, some drugs and he was half lobotomized and totally neutered. Lex recalled him shivering not so much with cold as with delayed shock, pressing his hands against his chest to see if at the age of fourteen he had begun sprouting tits.

Her mother had been the hardest to take. She and Lex stared at each other after Mandy and Bobby mumbled, "Bye," without looking up and left for school and forced labor. Her mother had gotten assigned as a truck driver, a position of trust. "You need a lift?" she had asked Lex, standing there wearing no makeup and no expression on her face. Lex, unable to speak aloud, had formed an image of the brightly colored jitney that was going to take her away.

At that moment her mother saw Lex as a Zombie, a figure with whom there were no secrets or trust. Something ripped inside Lex. Her mother had said to her, "All we can do is survive however we can. Remember that." Then she thought of her husband and Lex got hit by twenty-three years of memories, old and recent, angry and tender, mundane and erotic.

Six months later, feeling the first steam of the shower water, stepping into the warm spray, Lex could block minds but not memories. She thought of the father who had never returned from his job at the UN on the day when everything changed. She remembered not so much the way he looked or sounded as the calm way his presence felt. She remembered how he and she would both KNOW something at the same moment, how ideas would crackle in the air between them. From him, Lex had inherited telepathy, the only thing of any value in Time.

Her family faded in the steam as Alexis toweled herself off, looked in the mirror, faced the big fashion question: What to wear on a conquered world? The answer at the Bates Motel was, anything you ever saw anyone else wear and wanted to have.

Lex combed her hair in the mirror and remembered the hours she had spent hating the dark brown her mother wouldn't let her change. Now she saw how it softened a face that had gotten very pale and thin. Before Time and the Goblins found her world, the mirror had brought news good or bad, depending on her mood.

In the months at Zombie school, days passed in which she didn't think of her looks. Lex had turned seventeen without fanfare as her body began rearranging itself, trading baby fat for curves. At moments she could actually see herself becoming beautiful. Ironic, since anyone she would have wanted to impress was either dead or terrified of her.

Pulling her hair into a ponytail, Lex turned away from the mirror and put on a sweater, white sneakers, and jeans. Mostly now when she drew clothes out of supply she was just interested in fit and anonymity. It didn't do to think where those clothes had come from.

Lex opened the door of her room and felt the welter of erratic, half-trained minds vie for Vasa's attention. HEY, TEACH, I DID IT! Brent broadcast.

WHAT DO YOU MEAN YOU DID IT? I DID IT, Amy cut in.

ENOUGH! Vasa was a distance away from the motel and seemed distracted. Lex caught a trace of worry. I AM SURE THE GOBLINS AND RIDERS CONGRATULATE AMY AND HOPE FOR A HEALTHY BABY. DO YOUR MORNING EXERCISES. I WILL RETURN SHORTLY. And Vasa broke contact.

Lex cast her mind after Vasa. Her last six months had been spent learning to turn flashes of intuition and fragments of insight into disciplined telepathy. But probing the older woman was still almost like grabbing smoke.

As she stepped into the hall, a tiny kid in an oversize sweater looked out a door down the way. "Lex, I did it," the girl told her, happy but apprehensive, patting the nonexistent bulge on her belly. "One of the servants just brought the test results."

CONGRATULATIONS, AMY. Lex put as much light and warmth into her thoughts as she could. "I hope the baby makes you happy," she added. A woman in a gray coverall hurried down the hall past them, carrying a pile of towels. Other kids treated it more casually, but the servants embarrassed Lex.

A big, pudgy kid with acne, wearing only a cowboy hat and plaid boxer shorts, appeared in the doorway behind Amy. NUMBER THREE FOR ME, Brent told her. THAT LEAVES ONLY YOU, BITCH. He formed the thought slowly, projected it crudely for all of the Bates Motel to share. Groans came from other rooms.

The woman with the towels suddenly dropped them and began clapping her hands, doing a shuffle dance and singing "Congratulations!" over and over. The look of despair in her eyes made her celebration grotesque. Lex reached out and broke Brent's hold on the servant's mind. She caught fragments of the woman's memories: her name was Dee; she had been a paralegal before everything changed.

"I'm just trying to show happiness. You got something against happiness?" Brent asked Lex. The servant, Dee, finding their attention diverted, grabbed the towels and scuttled away. Brent projected his image of himself: big, heroic, a harem behind him, the last jock in the last high school on Long Island.

Brent was a fool too extreme to deal with. Lex turned her back and went down the hall. Brent probed but she evaded his thoughts. He called out, "You don't let me do it, teacher will knock you up herself." He showed her a crude image of Vasa doing just that and gave a phony laugh. Brent still didn't understand that it was his stupidity, not his joke, that made her cringe and that Vasa was going to see the cartoon on every mind, including his own.

Downstairs in the motel restaurant, now the dining hall, U-2 played. Dinah and Samantha, Brent's first two conquests, four and three months into pregnancy, sat near the door and barely nodded to Lex. Johnny and Sandy, sitting at the back, had their hair dyed the same shade and wore identical jackets with shirts hanging out. They watched quietly as she got coffee and orange juice from the counter. KILLER STUD GET TO YOU, LEX? Johnny asked and motioned for her to sit with them.

Lex and Johnny had gone to the same high school. When they found that making telepathic babies was a sure way of pleasing the Riders and Goblins, he suggested they try it. When Lex wasn't interested, it turned out that Johnny and Sandy thought and even looked so much alike that they made a cute couple. Sandy had gotten pregnant the month before.

Johnny stared into his bowl of cereal. Making sure no one else was probing them, he showed Lex an image of the boy with the Mohawk. I CAUGHT THAT THIS MORNING. VASA DID TOO AND TOOK OFF AFTER THE ONE WHO SENT THAT THOUGHT.

AND IS STILL OUT LOOKING, Lex added. By concentrating hard, they could communicate with each other and at the same time block other students' minds. The exercise was Inhale and Block: Exhale and Send, like rubbing your stomach and patting your head. WHO IS HE?

"What are you two showing each other?" Sandy asked and reached for a cigarette. Johnny took it out of her hand and crumpled it.

WARCHILD. Johnny formed the image of the face for Lex. She could tell it scared him. THE MIND THAT SENT THAT IMAGE SAID THIS IS THE WARCHILD, he told her. VASA INTERRUPTED BEFORE I CAUGHT THE REST. They broke contact before they had to share a treasonous thought: the telepath who had shown that image wasn't a servant of the Goblins.

At that moment, the rest of the Zombie school came in the door. Brent and Amy, followed by two other teenage couples, Joel and Carrie, Fred and Nancy, all still half awake. AMY IS NUMBER THREE! AMY IS NUMBER THREE! THE RIDERS ARE GOING TO SEND ME FROM COUNTRY TO COUNTRY, WORLD TO WORLD, MAKING TELEPATHS! Brent chanted, slapping hands with Joel and Fred, who looked bored.

ASSHOLE! every student in the school, including the three he had made pregnant, told Brent. But Lex recognized it as an automatic response. Most of the others weren't struck again and again by the guilt and horror of being a favored survivor. All their stories were similar and they all tried not to remember them.

AND LEX WILL BE NUMBER FOUR. Everyone knew Brent was pathetic, that he lied about his jock past, that his telepathic control was erratic. He never seemed to realize that they had all seen his real memories. Brent had been a couch potato with few friends and no future before the Zombies discovered a spark of ability.

Now he could think of himself as a stud. Lex guessed that's how Vasa saw him too: as an instrument that helped fulfill some kind of quota. She could visualize the report: "Long Island, New York, North Shore District, autumn 1988. Yield 600 tons of scrap metal, 6,000 miles of electrical wiring, six telepathic babies." Lex had learned enough to know how Zombies stayed alive and got promoted.

She looked around the restaurant walls at the posters of movie stars, listened to the taped music. DO YOU THINK U-2 DIED IN A DITCH SOMEWHERE? she asked Johnny, who flinched. A servant entered carrying Brent's plate stacked with eggs and steak. Lex indicated the former Motor Inn motel which she had nicknamed the Bates, the warmth, the light, the soft rugs. PEOPLE FEAR AND HATE US MORE THAN THEY DO ZOMBIES OR THE SOLDIERS.

EASY, Johnny told her. A couple of the other kids had picked up some of that. Johnny showed her quick images: empty towns, houses deserted, half dismantled, highways bare except for perpetual truck convoys rolling west to New York City, hauling away everything from crushed engine blocks to children. I MAY BE A TRAITOR, BUT I AM ALIVE. SO ARE YOU.

He looked at her across the table and asked aloud, "Isn't it time to do the exercises?" Brent and a couple of the others hissed, "Shiiiit," but Lex understood his point. Live traitors had certain duties. And since Lex herself was a most promising quisling, a Judas-to-be, it was up to her to form the image of the green Goblin face.

They were supposed to perform this exercise first thing in the morning and last thing at night. Lex projected an image of the only Goblin she had ever seen firsthand. It stood at a distance, yellow eyes surveying the assembled population of the district. Lex recalled the feel of its mind, flat and alien, the way it saw them as a collection of two-dimensional cutouts. Each time she remembered, Lex felt the same cold fear deep inside.

The others added the rest of the Great Goblin Chain as they had seen it assembled in an empty shopping mall parking lot. Johnny formed an image of the ranks of workers, neutered and lobotomized, sullen but still afraid. Sandy remembered the trembling crew of trustees and drivers who were one step above them. Someone else recalled the off-world soldiers in their black bucket helmets. Another mind put in the Zombies' servants, also from off-world, and one more visualized the Zombies, human telepaths like themselves.

It was the same chain Lex's sister Mandy had been memorizing months before. Except that this one was vividly firsthand and the apprentices added themselves somewhere between the trustees and the Zombies, eleven scared kids, telepaths in training, watching wide-eyed. They occupied a privileged position on the pyramid of fear the Goblins had erected.

Jets streaked over the Bates Motel and the image wavered as some of the apprentices lost their concentration. Lex steadied them and added her memory of the two Steeds at the assembly. They were a tall powerful-looking man and a handsome woman, both dressed in red velvet and scanning the crowd with dead eyes.

The Riders used their Steeds' minds to probe the crowd relentlessly, looking for signs of rebellion, of minds not paralyzed by fear. Lex showed the Steeds, commanded by their Riders to kneel in homage to the Goblins. Every human in the parking lot did the same. In all their minds appeared the first law of Time: ANY HUMAN WHO EVER SO MUCH AS TOUCHES A GOBLIN WILL BE EATEN ALIVE.

Brent always added the last image, the final symbol of their subjugation. His telepathy was shaky, making it look like a cheap gore movie. He pretended to love it, but they could tell it scared him more than any of them. He pretended to get off on the terrified teenage girl standing in front of the Goblin.

All of them remembered. The green head darted, the long teeth flashed. The girl screamed and they felt her rending fear in the moment the Goblin tore chunks out of her stomach and swallowed them. As she went into shock, the people prayed aloud, soldiers and servants, trustees and workers. Zombies and apprentices pleaded mentally, SPARE US FROM GOBLIN MARKET.

All eleven minds in the motel dining room held that image for a moment, understanding that except for the Goblins' mercy that woman could have been any one of them. Then they were aware of Vasa approaching the motel. GOOD, she told her apprentices. AS SERVANTS TO THE SERVANTS OF THE GOBLINS, YOU ARE ORDERED TO PACK AND PREPARE TO TRAVEL. TAKE NO MORE LUGGAGE THAN YOU CAN CARRY IN AN OVERNIGHT BAG. A couple of them tried to question her and were brushed aside. YOU WILL NEED CLOTHES FOR TWO DAYS. DRESS VERY WARMLY!

"Fuck you!" Brent said. But he shoveled the rest of his breakfast into his face and jumped up to do as he was told.

"I have to find a warm coat," Lex said and left the dining room. Crossing the lobby, she went down to the cellar. At the motel in the weeks just after her world had been invaded, the Zombies gathered those students from the high schools of Long Island able to respond telepathically. Younger telepaths were taken elsewhere to be trained. The fate of older ones was never discussed.

As truckloads of the less fortunate disappeared and a way of life ended for almost all the ones who remained, the storerooms of a motel were stocked with supplies. Record albums, videos, junk food, acne medication, beer, and designer wear.

The lucky few weren't allowed cars, but everything else necessary for the happiness of the American teenager was provided. Except for birth control devices, which were unobtainable. That left eleven kids with nowhere to go and a clear message: telepathy was genetic and Zombies, Riders, Goblins, and Gods wanted them to have children.

None of their servants were in the cellar as Alexis headed past cartons of unopened consumer goods to a back room near the furnace. Most of the kids didn't want to think about the origin of the clothes, Reebok sneakers and Calvin Klein jeans, jockey shorts and bras, prom dresses and school jackets stored there. Some were new but others were used, stripped off the backs of high school students or seized when their bedrooms were sacked. Like all gifts from the Goblins, these carried reminders of fear and shame.

At the start, Lex had looked for things she thought might belong to Mark. Sometimes memories of him were sweet: his laughter exploding, his arms around her. But if she thought about it long enough she'd recall the day she had first responded to the summons of a Zombie and walked away from him without looking back.

Just that previous spring everyone in the United States was in shock at seeing the President crying on television and telling them to worship the Goblins. No one wanted to know that people like Lex's father, who had disappeared, were never coming back. Only a few had felt telepathic minds directing theirs. None as yet understood that their world was just a moment in the infinite reaches of Time.

All anyone could focus on was the fact that radio and television were gone except for those moments when they blared out specific orders. In the first week, Lex's town received a notice that any kids who weren't in school the next day would be punished along with their families. Lots of students wanted to run but didn't know where to go.

Lex and Mark walked to school, since cars were forbidden and there were no buses to pick them up. She had been going with Mark for a year without her parents' approval. The only traffic on the road was a convoy of trucks driven by soldiers in strange gray uniforms.

Later she would understand they were from off her world, that they served the Zombies just as the Zombies served the Riders. At that moment the only thing she understood was fear. Her mother's, her own, the fear she knew Mark tried to keep hidden. They walked arm in arm; a lot of kids did. Some of them played taped music on sound boxes.

What she felt with Mark was pride at his looks and popularity, satisfaction that she had him as a boyfriend, and the knowledge that he loved her a lot. Her father had discussed it with her once. "Mark's a nice enough kid," he said and shrugged. As always with her father Lex understood the rest: she would be going on to college, Mark probably would not. If she wasn't careful, they could both get hurt.

When they got to school, none of the teachers were there. A few armed soldiers guarded the doors, a couple of gray-uniformed figures stood in the halls. "I bet there aren't more than two dozen of them altogether," Mark whispered to her. In their anger and fear two thousand American teenagers were getting rebellious.

Then for the first time all of them felt Zombies' minds inside their own. SENIOR BOYS TO THE GYM. SENIOR GIRLS TO THE AUDITORIUM. They saw images of themselves moving. Kids, stunned, began to do just that. JUNIOR BOYS . . .

She and Mark were inside the front door when a mind scanned the crowd, touched Lex, and seemed to break a lock inside her. WHO? she found herself asking. HOW?

The questing mind had caught that. It paused to give her a personal command. RAISE YOUR RIGHT HAND AND WALK TO THE PRINCIPAL'S OFFICE. DO NOT STOP OR TALK TO ANYONE.

"It's a commie plot!" one boy screamed as he turned to get out the door. Lex found herself raising her arm and moving down the hall. "Lex!" Mark yelled as he tried to grab her and flee. She saw him go rigid. The boy who screamed had fallen to the floor, silent and unmoving. The others, stunned at the lash of an alien mind, shuffled into lines. Lex found herself walking alone and not looking back.

She told herself later that the first encounter with another mind had overwhelmed her, that she was mesmerized. "This is Auschwitz," a girl had sobbed as Lex walked with her hand in the air.

A soldier standing at the principal's door holding a machine gun had stepped aside and opened it as she approached. Inside, Lex saw a tall gray woman—gray hair, gray eyes, gray jump suit—facing her. Sitting in the room were three scared kids. A quiet boy named Larry who later disappeared, Amy and Johnny whom she half knew. "Kind of like *The Breakfast Club*," he said in a shaky voice.

The gray woman looked through Lex's eyes and into every

corner of her mind and brain. Lex felt her heart and breath resting in the woman's power. PUT YOUR HAND DOWN. I AM VASA. YOU ANSWERED MY SUMMONS. UNDERSTAND THAT MEANS YOU HAVE TELEPATHY, THE ONLY HUMAN SKILL VALUED IN THE CORRIDORS OF TIME. BECAUSE OF IT, YOU ARE GIVEN A CHOICE BY THE GOBLINS. YOU CAN STAY IN THIS ROOM AND BECOME THEIR SERVANT. OR YOU CAN LEAVE AND BE THEIR SLAVE. Vasa indicated the panic and pain out in the halls. OTHERS HAVE NOT BEEN GIVEN THAT CHOICE.

On that awful day, the fright outside the door was like a flood. SHOES IN THE CARTON ON THE LEFT, PANTS ON THE RIGHT, a mind ordered again. Once Lex's mind had been opened by a trained telepath, her own latent ability came alive and couldn't be turned off. She felt thousands of kids shuffling to their doom but couldn't pick out individual minds. Then through an open window she heard a voice shout, "Lex!"

Standing up before Vasa could stop her, she saw the trucks, the naked kids shivering, heard their weeping, smelled their fear. A boy stood on the back of a truck and looked toward the school. Mark tried to cry her name again and choked as a mind seized his and throttled him. Lex could never forget that hopeless moment before Vasa made her sit back down. When she looked out the window again, the trucks were gone.

Six months later whole towns were razed, their populations gone. If asked, Vasa responded vaguely that the ones who disappeared were on work details. But Lex knew better. The ones hauled away were the ones without telepathic skills whom it would have been too much trouble to subdue. Stripped of any valuables, they had been taken somewhere and murdered.

As she stood in the motel cellar remembering that, Lex heard motors running outside. Then Vasa probed, slipped expertly through Lex's defenses, batted the other students' minds away. MOST PROMISING OF PUPILS AND MOST TROUBLING. She showed an image of the motel and its supply cellars twisted into the shape of a cornucopia. TO WHOM MUCH HAS BEEN GIVEN.

Lex formed the image of a herd of grazing cows with the faces of her fellow students. The teacher made her reply sting. APPRENTICE, YOU HAVE ACCEPTED THE BOUNTY OF THE GOBLINS. THEY HAVE LET YOU LIVE AND LIVE WELL. AS YET YOU HAVE DONE NOTHING FOR THEM. Breaking contact, Lex grabbed a sturdy down jacket and prepared to storm out of the cellar.

The door opened as she got to the foot of the stairs and Vasa, tall and gray, gave her a hard look. YOU WILL NOT BLOCK ME FROM YOUR MIND, she told the girl. YOU MUST EARN THE RIGHT TO DO THAT.

"So the Goblins want my firstborn," Lex said. In reply, the Zombie cut into her brain's automatic responses, held the girl's breath and heartbeat. For a moment Lex wondered if she could break the other's hold.

NOT QUITE. The woman relaxed her grip. BUT EVEN WHEN YOU CAN, REMEMBER THAT THE RIDERS OWN YOUR BODY AND MIND JUST AS THE GOBLINS OWN THE RIDERS' SOULS. WHAT THEY DO WITH US, THEY DO WITH THE BLESSING OF THE GODS. YOU AGREED TO SERVE ALL OF THEM WHEN WE MET. Lex saw an image of herself trembling, eyes rolling in terror on the day when students were sorted like produce. Remembering that made it impossible for Lex to look the other in the face. It seemed that one surrender had ended her innocence and integrity.

Once Vasa was sure the girl understood, her face softened. "Let us walk," she said aloud in Russian, nodding at how Lex picked up the meaning, the intent of the words. As they crossed the lobby and went out the front door, apprentices probed after them clumsily. VAS, WHERE ARE WE GOING? WE ARE COMING BACK, RIGHT? ARE WE TAKING THE SERVANTS?

HOW QUICKLY THEY BECAME USED TO THE SERVANTS. Vasa projected the thought, Lex caught it on the inhale, blocked the other students as she exhaled. The effort was somewhere between concentrating and imagining, and she knew she was getting better at it. On the highway outside the door, a convoy of trucks rolled toward New York, travel-

ing fast. The drivers were all women with young children held
hostage for their loyalty.

The air was still crisp but the sun was warm. Lex wondered
why they needed heavy clothes. YOU WILL GO TO NEW
YORK AND THEN BE TAKEN FROM THIS WORLD,
Vasa answered as they walked down the driveway, past servants loading two vans and the jitney.

Across the highway and through some trees lay the edge of
what had been a housing development. Lex looked over an
almost empty field. Most of the houses had been demolished
right down to their cellars; a few still stood for the workers.
WHERE WILL I GO? she asked, feeling cold seep into her
heart. A large crew of laborers of both sexes and all ages had
just stopped work and were lining up, ready to climb onto
trucks. They were supervised by a couple of off-world soldiers armed with machine guns.

YOU WILL BE TRAINED FURTHER. Vasa ignored her
question. PERHAPS JOHNNY WILL ALSO. A flight of jets
streaked through the clear September sky. In their wake a
small prop scout plane flew low over the highway. A Zombie on
board scanned and Lex saw an image flash between him and
Vasa: kids in black, springing out of the ground to the west.

Probing in that direction, Lex detected nothing. WHAT
WILL HAPPEN TO THE OTHERS? she asked Vasa. As
awful as someone like Brent could be, he was part of what
little was left of the world she had known. WHAT ABOUT
THE BABIES YOU WANT THEM TO HAVE?

Vasa riffled images as if they were a deck of cards: bucket-
helmeted storm troop commanders, blank-eyed Steeds, gray
Zombie administrators, drugged slaves on the block, disem-
bodied minds sweeping through the air, kids eaten alive by
Goblins. Some of it Lex didn't understand, but she knew that
those were possible fates for the apprentices at the Bates
Motel and their offspring.

Lex caught a tremor of fear in the woman's mind when she
formed the image of the Goblin feast. YOU HAVE A KID
SOMEWHERE? It had never occurred to her that the cold,
dour woman could have been a mother. WHAT ABOUT MY
NOT GETTING PREGNANT?

YOU HAVE NOT BEEN THE MOST COMPLIANT OF

PUPILS. NONETHELESS I RECOMMEND YOU TO THE RIDERS.

Lex remembered the Steeds she had seen in the parking lot. THEY HAVE BIG PLANS FOR ME?

PERHAPS. WHERE CAN YOU TURN BUT TO THEM? Vasa showed her the dulled minds of the workers across the way, the servants loading supplies in the vans. Under their layers of numbness and fear was a spark of hate for Goblins and Riders, Zombies and soldiers. It was a hopeless, ridiculous hate which any telepath could detect and for which a slave could be struck down dead. But Lex saw that as much as they hated those others, they hated the traitors, the kids of the Bates Motel, more. YOU HAVE TAKEN THE GOBLINS' BOUNTY, Vasa reminded her.

In school Lex had been bright in all subjects without having to study. Her specialty had been languages. Her father's skill as a translator had bordered on the uncanny. Lately she had understood how that ability was a fraud, how she had pulled words, ideas, test answers out of other people's minds. She was a parasite who had become a traitor.

I WAS BORN IN THE CAUCASUS IN A WORLD WHERE IT WAS THE MID NINETEENTH CENTURY, Vasa told her. IT WAS A COMMON ENOUGH SORT OF WORLD, BUT IT WAS ENJOYING A PERIOD OF PEACE. Lex smelled the mountain summer as the woman remembered it. THE CZAR IN MOSCOW RULED WHEN HE THOUGHT OF IT. Lex saw a tall serious girl with blond pigtails. I WAS NOT CONTENT WITH MY LOT AS A DOCTOR'S DAUGHTER.

From Vasa's memory came a series of images: soldiers with guns more powerful than anyone in her Russia had ever seen, gray-clad holy people with vague eyes whose minds broke into others' thoughts and dreams. They were led by a moon-faced Oriental boy, a strong telepath who was controlled by another mind inside his own. Lex recognized him as a Steed with a Rider.

The process by which the mountain villages were looted and their people sorted was familiar. Those who were strong and submissive marched as slaves, carrying any valuables. The weak, old, or rebellious were shot and kicked into ditches. Those who had something to offer, a rare talent, unusual beauty, telepathic potential, rode horseback in the train of the Rider. Vasa had been about Lex's age when she had followed that Rider into the service of the Goblins.

IN THEIR HEARTS THEY CALLED ME WHORE AND JUDAS, BETRAYER OF MY PEOPLE. BY THE TIME WE HAD MARCHED DOWN THE MOUNTAIN, MY FRIENDS AND RELATIVES WERE MY ENEMIES. Vasa showed memories of corpses lying on the line of march. MY PARENTS DIED BUT I LIVED. I HAD THE GIFT. ALSO THE STEED DESIRED ME AND IT AMUSED HIS RIDER TO LET HIM HAVE ME. Alexis saw the moon-faced boy reach out, felt his mind inside Vasa's, felt the ice-cold Rider controlling the Steed as the boy controlled Vasa, moved her body, played with her fright.

I LEFT MY WORLD AND HAVE NOT SEEN IT SINCE. Lex shared Vasa's memory of Time pulsing endless and empty as she passed along the trade routes. In the plaza of a blue marble city, at an outdoor slave auction, Vasa first saw people sold and sent on their way to Goblin Market. There too Vasa first saw Goblins, felt their stark alien minds, saw them eat live flesh, first knelt on the ground and begged to serve them.

I COULD SIMPLY ORDER YOU TO GO WHERE YOU ARE TOLD, AS WAS DONE TO ME. I WISHED INSTEAD FOR YOU TO UNDERSTAND HOW LITTLE CHOICE YOU HAVE. Lex detected something like envy in the Zombie's mind. YOUR SKILLS ARE GREATER THAN MINE, LEX. YOU COULD BECOME STEED TO A GREAT RIDER. Vasa reached out to touch her shoulders.

As she did, both heard gunfire in the distance and felt the telepath on board the scout plane that had passed earlier. Lex caught the word COMPANIONS, saw an image of figures moving on the ground, firing up at the plane.

Then Vasa blocked her. GO INSIDE. PACK WHAT YOU NEED FOR THE NEXT TWO DAYS. When she hesitated, Vasa turned away, telling her, GO. YOUR LIFE BELONGS TO THE GOBLINS.

She gestured up the driveway to where the apprentice Zombies' personal jitney stood. Until the summer before last it had met the Fire Island ferry. On its sides yellow lettering in a red field said *Island Girl*. Ordinary enough then, now it was a flash of color in a gray world and one more thing to make the apprentices stand out and be hated. Dee, the former paralegal, sat at the wheel with the motor running.

Their other servants stood beside the two loaded vans. Along with Lex they saw the flash of light, heard the explosion, and realized that the sound of the plane's engine had ceased. Then from somewhere to the east, Lex caught an image of the boy she had seen that morning. He stood on a hill as a V of wild geese flew over him. The image was third- or fourthhand, but the ones sending it did so with all their strength and souls. RISE UP. RISE UP! SLAVES OF THE RIDERS, GARVIN WARCHILD TELLS YOU TO RISE UP AGAINST GOBLINS AND GODS.

Vasa saw that also and paused at the bottom of the driveway. For an instant, Lex caught the older woman's memory of childhood: an early autumn day with farm geese doomed to slaughter flapping their wings and watching as wild geese flew above.

The girl glimpsed Vasa's tired disgust with herself and the bargain she had made. She was disgusted by her apprentices in the school, the little Zombies-to-be. Most of all she was disgusted by Lex, lovely, young, and self-involved. Lex saw herself standing, mouth open, swaying from one foot to the other, as if deciding which way to jump.

Minds projected a chilling image of Goblins dead and hanging from a tree as the jets shrieked back, flying east. Exploding bombs shook the ground and Vasa caught herself. THE TIME FOR PACKING IS DONE, she told Lex and indicated the jitney. GET ABOARD. Grabbing the mind of Brent, who was at the motel door, loaded down with bags, Vasa ordered, DROP THOSE AND GET THE OTHERS OUT HERE. Brent tried to summon the apprentices telepathically and couldn't. He ran inside as Vasa broadcast, ALL WHO ARE NOT IN THE JITNEY IN ONE MINUTE WILL BE LEFT TO THE MERCY OF THE GOBLINS' ENEMIES.

WHO IS HE? Lex asked and showed her the Warchild. Until then it hadn't seemed that the Riders and Goblins had anyone that they feared. She tried to probe Vasa's thoughts. A MATTER FOR GODS AND GOBLINS, NOT YOU.

The Keeper smacked aside Lex's defenses, entered her brain, and sent the girl staggering through the open door of the jitney. YOU WILL OBEY OR YOU WILL DIE.

Just then Lex felt a worker in the field across from the motel bring his shovel down on the neck of one of the soldiers. She heard the burst of gunfire as the other guard fired off a clip of bullets, taking half a dozen workers with him before he too was clubbed to the ground. Then Vasa's mind was among the workers, choking and tearing at them.

Lex in the jitney remembered two things: a spring day when she had come home and found her whole family on the sun deck, beautiful and alive, and Mark that last time she saw him, standing on a truck, screaming her name.

Images hung in the air of kids in Mohawks and black uniforms. THE IMMORTALS' COMPANIONS OFFER YOU FREEDOM. WE HOLD THIS PORTAL IN THE NAME OF GARVIN WARCHILD. Vasa stood at the bottom of the driveway, crushing the breath out of the workers.

In the jitney behind Dee, Lex felt the woman's fear and rage and the first hope she had known in months. Dee's hand was on the clutch, her foot poised above the gas. Dee's body was like a tool, a weapon waiting to be used. GO, ordered Lex. The clutch popped, the gas pedal hit the floor. The jitney rolled down the curving driveway.

Vasa saw it coming. She grabbed Dee's brain. BRAKE, she ordered. At that moment Lex threw back at her teacher Vasa's own memories of being raped by the Steed, of seeing her mother dead in a ditch. YOU WANT TO DIE, Lex told her as the jitney rolled. The bus hit the woman and Lex heard a scream, felt crushing pain. Then Vasa was still.

WHAT HAPPENED? Lex felt the apprentices on the front steps of the Bates Motel. VASA IS DEAD. Brent formed that thought and started to cry. LEX KILLED HER. She could feel his fear and that of the others. Dee, the driver, was sobbing as Lex made her stop the jitney.

WHAT ARE YOU DOING? Johnny asked, angry and scared.

It amazed Lex how cool she was. Holding Dee in check, Lex told the apprentices, the servants, the wrecking crew across the highway, YOU HAVE ONE LONG BREATH TO

DECIDE. STAY OR GO. DEATH OR HOPE. YOUR CHOICE.

A couple of the servants ran down the driveway and jumped aboard. None of the apprentices joined them. They stood paralyzed by fear.

GIVE MY REGRETS TO THE GOBLINS. Lex brushed aside one or two minds that tried to grab at her. Workers from the wrecking crew got onto the jitney. FLOOR IT. Dee rolled onto the highway and headed east.

Lex stood beside her driver, scanning ahead. Workers ran west over the open fields. A truck on its side half blocked the road. As Dee swerved, soldiers fired and cobwebbed a window at the back of the jitney. The jets roared back for another strike but stayed high in the air. A bomb exploded over a hill to their left. Lex felt minds call, GARVIN WARCHILD SUMMONS YOU.

Then her mind was caught by a Companion relay, saw the red and yellow jitney as they saw it. DO NOT SHOOT, she told them. WE ARE FRIENDS.

PROCEED. PROCEED. Minds scanned hers. Lex felt them flinch at her firsthand experience of the Goblin Chain. ZOMBIE TRAINING, one of them told the others. THE WARCHILD HIMSELF HAS A RIDER. That made it all right. Buildings still stood to the left of the highway. Lex saw Mohawked figures in black setting up a mobile missile battery. SLOW DOWN. YOU'RE SAFE, someone told her. Lex eased Dee's foot off the gas. PARK THE BUS ON THE LEFT. GET OUT.

Lex felt minds touch hers gingerly, eyes watch as she stumbled out of the jitney. ZOMBIE, HAVE YOU JOINED THE REBELLION? someone asked. The other people getting out of the bus were crying. YOU PROMISE TO SERVE THE WARCHILD TILL THE GODS AND GOBLINS FALL? Lex nodded and realized she was crying too. WELL? the mind asked again.

YES. I PROMISE TO SERVE THE WARCHILD. Then hands and minds reached out. Through her tears, Lex saw ragged uniforms, overgrown haircuts, scars, earrings.

What Lex thought was a skinny boy staring at her turned out to be a tough girl with an eye patch. It was she who scanned Lex briefly and ordered, GET THIS ONE TO DIVISION HEADQUARTERS.

So it was that Lex, within minutes of joining the rebellion, was taken to a portal and carried into infinity. Chilled by the heartbeat of Time, she tumbled toward Garvin Warchild.

CHAPTER

Two

The God and a few of his mortal advisors sat in leather chairs in a comfortable chamber beneath the Hall of Glass. It was a place of dark wood and deep carpets. Scramblers in the walls and ceiling emitted electronic patterns which kept outside minds from intruding. Drinks and sandwiches were laid out on a table before a window. Outside, bright birds flashed against green leaves, deer walked among the trees of a park.

"The problem, most gracious one, is lack of confidence," the Chancellor Coli said in a soft voice. He showed them images of Goblin Market, the empty slave pits, the dimmed ceiling lights. "That has emptied more stalls than your son's actual rebellion." He looked across the room to where his master, in the form of the Granter of Gifts, a florid man in a rumpled suit, a derby over one eye, sat with his feet up on a desk.

"You mean," said the God, "that unless they are sure there's no trace of hope, they won't be happily led like pigs to the knife?" Here, surrounded by his administrators, people who owed their lives and livelihoods totally to him, the God of the City appeared in less formal personas. As the Granter of Gifts he looked and sounded like an early twentieth century American city boss. Scanning the half dozen faces, he asked, "How bad has it become?"

"The Riders are still able to operate in parts of the four quadrants of Time," the Comptroller Zachberg, a thin man in black who looked like an assistant undertaker, told him. "But they are able to harvest less and less. As rumors of the Warchild rebellion spread, mutinies spring up. Most are crushed, but they take their toll. The supply of telepaths especially dwindles. The Winds . . ."

"The Winds and their upkeep are the responsibility of the Goblins." The God shrugged like a city mayor placing the blame on a state governor. "How is business?" he asked Oublie, the human manager of the City Out Of Time.

"At this moment, divine patron, the stalls at Goblin Market are fifty percent full," the handsome young woman answered. "But they remain full because business is slow. The Goblins, of course, still buy most of the telepaths for their Winds. And some nontelepaths too, of course." The knowledge that those last were to feed the Goblins floated in the air without being expressed. "But human customers are far fewer."

"People don't want to buy slaves if they think my son is going to free them? Night Town has always been the steadiest buyer of nontelepaths." He looked toward an older woman with a placid Oriental face. "Madame Ling?"

"Fewer visitors to the City with less money, fewer mercenaries. Echbattan's world lies only a few days in Time from the City. As he advances . . ."

She started. Behind the slightly soft facade of the politician flickered a hard young face with gunman's eyes. The God within the God spoke to each one of them. I SAVED YOU FROM GOBLIN MARKET OR NIGHT TOWN OR WORSE. BOUGHT YOU FROM THE ONES WHO OWNED YOU. Every advisor saw the particular moment of his or her rescue. AND I TELL YOU THAT EVERYONE IN THIS CITY, SLAVE AND FREE, TELEPATH AND NOT, MORTAL AND GOD, IS CAPTIVE TO GOBLIN MARKET. OUR SALVATION LIES OUT BEYOND ECHBATTAN'S WORLD.

"You mean the . . ."—Coli didn't know how to put it gracefully—"the defeat of your son?"

NO. I MEAN HIS VICTORY. WITHOUT THAT, I GUARANTEE ALL OF YOU WILL BE IN THE SLAVE PENS BEFORE SUMMER TURNS TO FALL ON ECHBATTAN'S WORLD.

Then the killer's face was gone and the Granter of Gifts returned. "None of this, of course, leaves this room," he said, and they all nodded, understanding that, if nothing else.

The God of the City smiled and asked, "Anybody need a drink?" Somewhere in his shaping Time, forming worlds, and populating them, the God had lost track of his own true shape. Personas came and went with each emotion that he felt. He had lived for so long he was no longer sure of which of his identities was real. But the one who had just put in a brief appearance reminded him very much of a young man named Brian Garvin who he had once been.

Out in the Echbattan Empire, where it was summer in the north, Garvin strode Time. Companions moved faster among the worlds than Riders or Zombies. Their trick was to visualize a certain elaborate Edwardian drawing room full of knick-knacks like peacock screens and ivory elephants and a table set for tea. None was better at it than Garvin. Feeling as if the mirrored room was imprinted on his chromosomes, he shuffled Time like a deck of cards.

Worlds appeared one by one in the glass of the huge mirror over the drawing room's fireplace. Garvin automatically passed by worlds which had never supported human life, worlds pillaged and empty. He had reports about the place he sought. After letting it lie fallow for years, the Riders had recently moved in and started exploiting it brutally.

A world swam into view on the mirror. The Warchild caught the feel of it through portals, the brutal grinding horror, the cringing slaves and systematic Zombie looters, the horrors of his father's universe. Garvin found himself wishing for someplace else, a place of generosity and hope, of music and human feeling.

Instead he was confronted with yet another slave world. Garvin spun the antique globe in the drawing room. As he

did, the world revolved under him until he found a certain
portal in Mexico that he knew he wanted. Behind him, in the
infinite emptiness of Time, he towed hundreds of members of
Warchild Cluster. In Time, where there was no physical sensation, no telepathy, they weren't even a faint murmur to Garvin.

Until recently, he had loved Time, had swum in it like a
fish, spun worlds like toys. Suddenly the gold-framed mirror
burned Garvin's tongue, the blue oceans on the globe smelled
like mildew. 'the oracle,' his Rider told him.

Garvin saw its prophecy again. There was too much detail
for him to catch it all, but he saw himself fight his way onto
Echbattan's world. There, in a confusion of dark passages,
telepaths fell dead, their minds stripped away by Winds.
Troopers were killed in explosions. Garvin's body was just
one of many that was dragged into the light and looted for
souvenirs and plunder.

He looked in vain for a familiar face among his fellow
victims. Various of them had the motto, GROW OLD, WHY?
tattooed on their foreheads. All were hauled across an open
plaza under a dying red sun and thrown onto a pile of corpses.
A fire was lighted and flames leaped up and a half-dead soldier writhed. Garvin, on top of the pile, remained absolutely
still.

Then the Oracle was gone and Garvin floated in space
again, alone with his thoughts and his Rider. BACK AT THE
BEGINNING OF THE REBELLION AND BEFORE, THE
ORACLE WAS AROUND ALL THE TIME. IT WAS GONE
FOR SO LONG I HAD FORGOTTEN ABOUT IT. NOW IT
COMES BACK TO SHOW ME THAT.

'they say,' the Rider told him, 'that the oracle is the con-
science of your father. didn't i detect winds in the under-
ground passages?'

MY FATHER TOLD ME THAT THERE WAS NO ORA-
CLE. YOU WERE THERE.

'perhaps we misunderstood. you must change your plans as
regards echbattan's world.'

SCREW THAT. YOU PLANNED THE CAMPAIGN SO
WE WOULD BE RIGHT IN MY OLD MAN'S FACE AT

THE END OF SUMMER. IS THERE ANOTHER WAY TO
GET AN ARMY TO THE CITY?

'no, the rebellion is focused entirely on this campaign. the
strategic problem is that the army is guided only by your
charisma. it will go where you lead, but only if you lead. it
will die if you do and the oracle tells us that you will die on
echbattan's world.'

The sight of himself on a pile of corpses chilled Garvin
more than he could admit. His Rider searched for a way
around the prophecy. 'there are contradictions in what the oracle shows. winds, except for the one your uncle has, have not
appeared outside the city for longer than even i can recall.
perhaps that is the oracle's warning.'

Unable to do anything about the prophecy, Garvin turned
toward the portal he had sought. It opened onto a slave empo-
rium, a crude, outdoor version of Goblin Market at the City
Out Of Time. Into it emptied human tribute to be sold and
transported down the Time Lanes to the City.

The market gave Garvin the opportunity to act. Followed
first by Darrel and Maji, then by half a dozen telepaths, then
by hundreds of other Companions and soldiers, the Warchild
tumbled out of Time and into the slave market, mind blazing.
DIE, SLAVEHOLDERS!

Telepathic minds tried to block him. They got torn open.
Fear and nightmare, fire and mutilation, all the horrors of the
subconscious, walked in the bright sun. Someone who pointed
a gun at Garvin screamed in agony, shoved it down his own
throat, and fired.

Resistance collapsed fast. Warchild Cluster was disap-
pointed that there were no Goblins. Half a dozen Zombies lay
dead; some slave traders and guards prostrated themselves on
the ground. Several thousand freed captives stood dazed. Garvin's anger had been like a seizure. When it was over, he
found himself standing in a liberated slave market, trembling.

At that moment, he was touched for the first time by the
City of Guitars. From somewhere came a musical riff, one of
the old simple ones that lie at the base of everything. With it
was an image of gas lights winking on in a stone city on a
blue mountain evening. And in the memory of the one who
showed that, the air itself pulsed with chords, and the river

that swept through the town maintained a fine loose beat.
Garvin heard what sounded like a mandolin and a soft voice
singing:

> *THEY SAY THAT OLD GUITARS WILL DIE*
> *BUT NOT BEFORE IT RIDES THE WIND.*

The Warchild paused for a moment, listening, soaking up
images of Guitars. He looked at the musician, a young, very
black man, and said aloud, "That was great! You've seen this
City?" The man smiled and nodded.

"Where is it?" The musician showed Garvin the dozen
worlds he had traveled. First he had been a minstrel who
knew nothing of Time and had stumbled through a portal. He
had just been taken captive and brought to market. "And this
world exists near here without Echbattan knowing about it?"
Garvin wanted to know. The man smiled, nodded and sang:

> *AIN'T NO ONE FINDS GUITARS*
> *UNLESS GUITARS WANTS THEM TO.*

The Rider interrupted. 'this is all very interesting. but you
have to arrange a meeting with the immortals. as useless as
they are, you have given them command of the armies of
winter and spring. they are making slow progress. your own
army of summer is scattered over dozens of worlds and you
have just wasted a day freeing slaves.'

WASTED! I WAS SOLD AS A SLAVE! TO YOU! Gar-
vin's anger flared. Aides, soldiers, freed slaves, captured
slave dealers felt it and winced.

'the talking suitcase and the rose and thorn assisted in that,'
his Rider replied, 'and you gave them command of armies.
herself and her rider, neither of whom i would trust, were
given command of the army of autumn. they were the ones
who bought you as a steed for me. your immediate situation is
that you are on a hostile world and out of contact with most of
your forces. what do you intend to do about that?'

WHO IS THE RULER OF THIS WORLD AND WHERE
IS HE RIGHT NOW?

'the ruler of the world is a steed whose rider owes allegiance to the house of echbattan. as nearly as we can tell, steed and rider are at Peking, gathering an army.'

I AM GOING THERE AND FREE THAT STEED.

'suicidal. it is what they expect. wait until more of the army of summer comes up.'

THERE IS NO DANGER. Garvin recalled the image of himself on the pile of corpses and felt his Rider squirm. WE FIGURED IT OUT, REMEMBER? I AM GOING TO DIE LATER THIS SUMMER ON ECHBATTAN'S WORLD.

His Rider paused a long while before replying, 'very well. now what about the problems with your army commanders?' It showed Garvin a map of Time with the Armies of Summer, Spring, and Winter going forward in a disorganized mass. 'herself and the army of autumn is too far away. still, you must meet with the talking suitcase and the rose. there are several worlds where that meeting can take place.'

Garvin wanted someone to tell his troubles to. He thought of the Talking Suitcase, a mental presence in a leather satchel carried by an old mute called Roger. He thought of the Rose, a child's head and mind on the body of an immortal woman. They and their Companions, whom he had inherited, had fought Goblins and Riders for millennia before Garvin Warchild appeared. Increasingly now, they seemed to have grown weak and erratic. In any case, Garvin couldn't imagine confiding in either of them.

The Army of Autumn was under the command of Herself, a Steed who, like Garvin, fought a Rider for control of mind and body. The thought of the tall woman in her late twenties dressed in green, of her pale skin and red hair, excited him. His Rider didn't trust Herself or her Rider, while the Warchild had a passion for her that was famous throughout the army. She loved Garvin as a sister would. To keep them away from each other, Herself had been sent off to form the new Army of Autumn and bring it to Echbattan's world.

Garvin remembered the Guvnor, traveling in Time with a pet Wind, like a figure out of an adventure story. But the Guvnor was his uncle and Garvin's Rider didn't trust him nor, in truth, did Garvin. The Guvnor had sold him to Herself's Rider.

He recalled his best teacher, Scarecrow, tall, gawky, and

compassionate. But Scarecrow was gone, dead back in the
Republic as the Warchild had dawdled on the way to rescue
him. Garvin remembered the first Companion he had known,
Nick, who had recruited him on Garvin's home world. He
remembered the kid only a little older than he was now who
had shown a scared recruit the rudiments of telepathy. Nick
was someone he could trust in a tight place. But Nick had
taken a bullet, guarding Garvin. More than anything, he
wanted Nick back.

'there seems to be a pattern,' his Rider told him. 'either
they cannot be trusted or they are dead. now where and when
shall we hold the meeting?'

I WILL MEET WITH THE IMMORTALS AT GUITARS.
Garvin felt the entity inside him begin to assemble its plans.
RIGHT AFTER I MEET THE RULER OF THIS WORLD IN
SINGLE COMBAT, he added, just to feel his Rider's fear.

The musician standing nearby showed morning light over a
mountain, hitting a city just going to sleep:

> *COULD BE A YOUNG DADDY FOR THAT OLD TOWN
> AND JUST A DAY BEFORE THE RENT FALLS DUE.*

Lex stood on a hill in Wales in a late summer dawn, receiving instruction with the twenty-three other members of her
recruit platoon. All were in their teens and wore sneakers,
khaki T-shirts, and shorts. The hair on each head was shaved
except for the start of a crest running front to back.

Doria, their instructor, a young Jamaican woman with a tall
Mohawk and a long bushy ponytail, stood behind them holding a four-foot green stick. Behind her, in something its
builders had called the Park of Human Progress, the Immortals' Companions had set up a training camp. In front of the
platoon, at the foot of the hill, a valley of shining human
bones testified that the Riders and their armies had reached
that world first.

THE NUMBER WHO DIED IN THE VALLEY HAS
BEEN ESTIMATED AT OVER TWO MILLION. Elgatto, a
crippled Companion overcommander, showed them the fate of
the builders of the Park of Human Progress. METHOD OF
EXECUTION VARIED. MANY WERE THROWN OFF

THE CLIFFS, A FEW WERE SHOT, SOME POISONED.
THOSE WHO SHOW NO SIGNS OF PHYSICAL VIO-
LENCE WE ASSUME WERE KILLED BY TELEPATHY.

Lex heard a sob, felt tears forced through clenched eyes,
saw an image of lines of prisoners setting off on a death
march. Sight of the valley had torn out of Sung, at thirteen the
youngest of the Green Stick training platoon, a memory of his
own world.

Some of the others stirred uneasily. HEY, one of them told
him. KEEP THAT INSIDE YOUR HEAD.

Doria, Green Stick instructor, on training duty while recov-
ering from an ankle wound, leaned on her cane and looked
with disgust at the one who told him that. I WILL TELL
YOU WHAT TO KEEP INSIDE YOUR HEADS. All felt her
mind like a slap.

EYES FRONT. MINDS FRONT, Doria snapped and Green
Stick platoon stared at Elgatto, who was nothing but a head
and torso resting on a tree stump. He had stopped projecting
the story of the Valley of Bones and patiently let Sung cry
himself out before continuing.

Green Sticks understood the crying to be part of their training. They already understood the overcommander himself to
be another part. His long ponytail, secured by a silver ring,
hung down past the small of his back. Some guessed Elgatto's
age to be as much as twenty-four. It was known that he had
followed the Immortals and been injured even before the appearance of the Warchild.

Elgatto had stood too close to a car bomb in one of the
twentieth century Rios two years before. Now he lived in
what had been a park custodian's cabin at the edge of the
Valley of Bones and delivered this lecture to each training
platoon that came through. For Lex, just the fact that he
stayed in the same place, wasn't moving constantly from
world to world in Time, made the damaged overcommander
seem like stability itself. The night before, she had tried to
remember all the worlds she had seen in her brief career in
Time and fell asleep somewhere around eighty.

When Sung stopped sobbing, the lecture began again. BY
ITS OWN ACCOUNTING THIS SOCIETY WAS IN THE
THIRTY-SECOND YEAR OF SOMETHING CALLED THE

NEW ORDER OF THE PEOPLE. A MORE COMMON WAY OF FIGURING IT IS 1912. Images came to them of pictures, films of this world which Elgatto had seen. The people wore unfamiliar clothes and stood in places Lex couldn't identify. But their eyes, happy, serious, startled, fierce, looked out of the black-and-white photos directly into the camera and the eye of the viewer.

THEY HAD A KIND OF WORLD GOVERNMENT, AT LEAST IN EUROPE AND NORTH AMERICA, AND THEY HAD EARLY TECHNOLOGY. WORLD POPULATION WAS ABOUT A BILLION AND A HALF TEN YEARS AGO. TELEPATHY WAS NOT EVEN A MYTH. A PICNIC FOR THE GOBLINS. LESS THAN FOUR HUNDRED MILLION PEOPLE ARE STILL ALIVE HERE. Lex felt Elgatto's anger. He had traveled a long way from his own world and thought of this place as home. He could only avenge its rape by telling its story again and again.

He paused, and Reban, a seventeen-year-old with blond hair and dark skin, took the opportunity to ask, DID THE IMMORTALS KNOW ABOUT THIS PLACE?

The Companion overcommander nodded slowly at the question. YOU WONDER WHY WE COULD NOT INTERVENE. I UNDERSTAND THAT YOU WHO FOLLOW THE WARCHILD CANNOT BELIEVE HOW FEW IN NUMBERS WE WERE. THERE ARE FOUR HUNDRED INSTRUCTORS AND RECRUITS IN THIS TRAINING CAMP. They felt him lift his mind down the hill toward the park, shared his surprise at the number of telepaths he found. THAT IS MORE COMPANIONS THAN I SAW IN TOTAL BETWEEN JOINING THE IMMORTALS AND GETTING MY ARMS AND LEGS BLOWN OFF.

Then Elgatto showed them his memory of the old-fashioned mirrored drawing room. Green Stick platoon knew their session with him was almost ended. They felt the twenty-four Blue Sticks and their commander climbing the hill for instruction. NEVER BEFORE HAVE WE RETAKEN WORLDS AS WE DO NOW. NEVER BEFORE HAVE WE HAD A HERO LIKE THE WARCHILD.

Lex opened her mind along with the others to the paradox of the reflection of the empty room. Whoever had seen that room and remembered it must have been standing looking into the mirror and yet was not reflected in it. Elgatto finished with another magic image, Garvin telling them, RISE UP. He had it at fifth or sixth hand, a talisman passed from mind to mind along the Time routes.

All images of Garvin Warchild were at fifth and tenth and twentieth hand. At first Lex kept noticing elusive things partly forgotten in the chain of memory. When he commanded, RISE UP, there was a burned-forest smell around him. The kids hanging on his presence looked battle hardened. There was an old man holding a leather case and a stocky adult with a child's head standing in places of honor. She learned that the satchel and the child were the Immortals, the Talking Suitcase and the Rose.

That image of Garvin had drawn Lex in that moving target of a bus to where the Companions held a bridgehead. Bits and pieces of his story had sustained her as she had been dragged terrified through dozens of portals along the Time Lane from her world to this one. Lex had felt the eternal pulse of Time and had her soul twisted by the black emptiness, always sustained by the cry, RISE UP!

But when Elgatto bade them farewell and broke contact, Lex was left feeling that the image of Garvin was as worn as an old coin. As Doria led the twenty-four Green Sticks past the twenty-four Blues coming up the hill with their instructor, Lex wanted something more. She turned to see the overcommander, or what was left of him, perched on the stump and wondered what kept him going.

YOU, GIRL, DO NOT BE LOOKING BACK. Doria suddenly was inside Lex's defenses, twisting her head to make her face front. IF I WERE A ZOMBIE . . . IF I WERE RIDER SCUM I COULD HAVE CHOKED YOU WHILE YOU DREAMED ABOUT THE WARCHILD.

Lex knew that the young instructor of Green Stick platoon had come out of a West Indies conquered by the Riders and tasting slavery for the second time. Doria had joined the Companions determined that no human being would know oppression again. When she had hesitated on the term Zombie, Lex understood that it was because she had found a trace of it in her. Despite herself, Doria gagged at the hint of Goblin in the mind of this recruit.

At the bottom of the hill, Doria was brisk. Twirling the four-foot green baton, she ordered, ATTENTION, and the platoon snapped to. LINK. Twenty-four minds came together in a relay, a couple fumbling and a little uncertain, but all calling up the image of a room full of old-fashioned furniture.

The platoon recalled the details as they had been shown them: half-drawn drapes, an elaborate screen with a peacock, a globe. But it was impossible to focus on any one of them. Like Garvin telling them, RISE UP, the image of the room had passed through so many minds that it had lost all clarity and was as tantalizing as a dream. Suddenly Doria made a building appear in the mirror. HERE IS YOUR ASSIGNMENT FOR THIS MORNING, she told them. BREAK CONTACT.

The mirrored room faded from the Green Sticks' minds and they found themselves staring at the building Doria had shown them. It lay straight ahead, massive and marble, across a quarter mile of walks and lawns. It had been called the Museum of Industrial Progress by the ones whose bones lay bleaching in the valley.

DO NOT PROBE THERE, Doria ordered. SILVER STICK PLATOON IS INSIDE. AWHILE AGO RED STICK PLATOON WENT IN AGAINST THEM. As they watched, tiny figures poured out from between the columned entrance and ran down the stairs. THAT IS RED STICK NOW, Doria told them. YOU ARE THE NEXT PLATOON WHICH WILL TRY TO THROW THE SILVER STICKS OUT OF THAT BUILDING.

SILVER STICKS! Various Green Sticks protested. NOT FAIR. THEY HAVE MORE EXPERIENCE. The Silver Sticks had already gone through training. Everyone knew they had seen actual combat and that one of them had been badly wounded.

NOT FAIR. WE ARE NOT READY. The image shown was of Silver Sticks as adults and soldiers, Green Sticks as kids.

Lex ignored this. If the orders were to go in, they would go in. She hoped the exercise would be interesting, because much of the training bored her. A lot of the exercises in mental concentration she had already learned in different form from the enemy. A lot of the Green Sticks worried about what they would do in combat. Lex knew she could kill.

Doria told them, IF THE OVERCOMMANDERS SAY YOU ARE READY, YOU ARE READY. IT IS NOW 09:50. AT 10:00 YOU WILL ENTER THE FRONT DOOR OF THE MUSEUM. YOU WILL HAVE UNTIL 10:20 TO TAKE THE SILVER STICKS' PLATOON BATON AND CLEAR THEM FROM THE PREMISES. AFTER THAT YOU WILL HAVE TEN MORE MINUTES TO SET UP YOUR DEFENSES AGAINST THE BLUE STICKS WHO WILL BE ATTACKING YOU. Lex appreciated the fact that Doria never seemed to consider the possibility that they might lose.

YOU WILL NOT LINK MINDS UNTIL YOU ARE INSIDE THE BUILDING, AND NONE OF YOU WILL PROBE AHEAD. OVERCOMMANDER JUDGES WILL BE CHECKING CAREFULLY. She waved the baton. ANYONE WHO DOES THOSE THINGS WILL HAVE THIS STICK BROKEN OVER THEIR ARSE BY ME, UNDERSTAND?

Some members of Green Stick groaned audibly and mentally. Doria's mind stung them like a whip. YOU WILL NOT DO THAT NOW OR EVER IN THE PRESENCE OF YOUR ENEMY. TWO THINGS I CAN DO FOR YOU. FIRST IS TO TELL YOU THAT SILVER STICK HAS FOUGHT THREE RECRUIT PLATOONS THIS MORNING. ALMOST CERTAINLY THEY ARE GETTING TIRED AND PERHAPS CARELESS. AND ONE OF THEIR MEMBERS IS ABSENT. YOU ARE TWENTY-FOUR STRONG.

SECOND, I WILL APPOINT A RECRUIT COMMANDER FOR THIS FIGHT. LEX IS OUR BEST-TRAINED TELEPATH. She nodded without touching the girl's mind. THIS IS NOT A TEST OF HER ABILITY TO COMMAND BUT OF ALL OF YOUR ABILITY TO OBEY. Doria held the green stick out, indicating to Lex that she should come forward and take it. YOU CAN USE TELEPATHY TO FORM THEM UP AND MOVE THEM OUT.

Lex stepped out of line, grasped the baton as Doria hobbled past her, and faced the twenty-three recruits. OPEN ORDER, she told them, and they were too surprised and too thoroughly drilled to do anything but obey. Turning, she faced the museum. She wanted to get there fast while Red Stick was still around the doorway. DOUBLE TIME, she ordered, and they set off at a trot. All of them were careful to stay within themselves and not probe ahead.

Lex too kept her mind away from Red Stick, who stood panting in front of the building, clearly in disgrace. Their instructor, a tiny kid who had lost most of both lungs in a gas attack, screamed aloud in French. Four who must have bolted first were the objects of his special wrath. *"Quatre cochons!"* the instructor sputtered and tried to kick them. He began coughing uncontrollably.

One boy, in tears and with a growing lump over one eye, said, "They used that machinery. . ." then choked as his instructor throttled him to keep him quiet.

Lex felt the minds of Doria and other veteran Companions flicking through the air, making sure none of the Green Sticks had linked with each other or were probing. As they approached the front of the Museum of Industrial Progress, she saw engraved in the marble over the door the words "Erected by the United Peoples of the World for Greater Harmony and Understanding."

Doria looked up at the sky. Hesitating almost imperceptibly, she touched Lex's mind. IT IS 09:59. WHEN YOU ARE UP THE STAIRS, YOU MAY ORDER THEM TO LINK MINDS. I WILL STAY HERE. Leaning against a tree, she sighed and took the weight off the ankle that had been shattered by the bullet. GOOD LUCK.

Lex ran up the stairs and reached for the twenty-three minds. Several hesitated and she forced herself not to wonder which of them faltered out of weakness and which because of the taint of her Zombie training. FORMATION, she ordered, and they fell into their drill pattern of three squads of eight each. Lex was in the middle with the second squad. GREEN STICKS FORWARD. She held up her four-foot baton. FIRST AND SECOND THROUGH THE DOOR, THIRD BRING UP THE REAR.

As the first kid of the first squad's rubber sneaker sole hit the threshold, they all felt Doria tell them, NOW YOU MAY

PROBE. YOU HAVE NINETEEN MINUTES, THIRTY-EIGHT SECONDS.

Inside the door, Lex formed the image of a circle. They fell into that formation and stared around the huge, silent rotunda. The attack could have come right then as their eyes adjusted to the twilight. Sun filtering through dirty skylights revealed looming forms. Around the circular rotunda was machinery: everything from simple hand tools to dark, majestic steam locomotives gathering dust on marble platforms. Fragile flying machines bobbed near the ceiling. Nothing else moved.

On the floor were broken batons, a red, a black, and a purple. From the neatness of the arrangement, Lex guessed that they had been broken elsewhere and thrown here to intimidate them. She showed that to the others and told them, THE ATTACK WILL NOT COME HERE.

Three galleries opened off the rotunda. Lex saw shafts of sun from windows and skylights, felt the enemy somewhere inside waiting. She wanted the first contact to be on her own terms. PROBE TO THE RIGHT, she ordered, knowing that the longest that they had held a mental relay was a little under five minutes, wanting to scan fast without exhausting their concentration.

Lex wished she had paid more attention during the tour of the museum all recruits took when they first came to training camp. Green Stick formed an image of the mirrored room and let their minds sift forward like gas, seep slowly down galleries and halls. All of them jumped; a couple gave little cries when they felt hurtling sparks of fear: mice. STEADY, Lex said as her own heart turned over.

Suddenly black-and-white radar images exploded in their relay: floor, ceiling, and walls swept through their minds. Lex saw stars and the dark outline of South America. She remembered a gallery with a map of the world on the floor and a chart of the heavens on the ceiling. Lex saw the Green Sticks from far above as a clutch of staring eyes. HERE THEY COME! was etched in panic on a lot of minds. Something flew so close that all Lex wanted to do was fall flat. Then someone told them, AN OWL. WE WOKE UP AN OWL. Lex said, "Shit," breathing the word out like a long sigh.

They felt the bird fly back into the huge room to their right and come to rest again. Probing delicately, Lex looked through the owl's eyes. The room it was in was very dark and nothing moved there. If the owl had been at rest, it meant that in the few minutes they'd had after beating Red Stick, none of the enemy had passed that way. SEVENTEEN MINUTES, EIGHT SECONDS, a judge told her.

PROBE THE CENTER GALLERY, Lex ordered, starting to recall the layout of the building. The Green Sticks' minds followed hers in a lurching chain. The relay brushed against Silver platoon. Its minds were linked in a tight defensive pattern, projecting an image of the gallery itself, long and high-ceilinged.

Windows near the roof cast shafts of light on dioramas of man's triumphs. Full-size mannequins, men in knee breeches and wigs, held pieces of paper in their wax hands. Brown half-naked farmers marveled at a new plow. A woman in white robes strode down a railway track into an oncoming engine. No one looking like a Silver Stick was in sight.

WITHDRAW, Lex ordered as the mirror-room image started to lose cohesion. It was hard to tell exactly, but it seemed to Lex that there weren't enough of the enemy.

MAYBE TWELVE BUT NOT TWENTY-THREE, Reban with the first squad thought, and that seemed right.

Lex felt her platoon's eagerness to attack, to get it over with as soon as possible. She let them relax into a defensive perimeter which was easier to maintain than the probe. FIFTEEN MINUTES, a mind told her as Lex made plans. It seemed unlikely Silver Stick would have had the time or the need to vary their attack. What they had done to Red Stick they would try to do to Green. Half of them were in the central gallery, disguised among the mannequins.

The left-hand gallery, she remembered, had a gentle slope leading down to the cellar. On the walls of the gallery were pictures of towns, factories, and farms. The cellar was set up like a mine. A track ran from down there to the door of the gallery. In the cellar was an electric mine car. When the museum had electric power it would have been used to carry visitors from the gallery down into the depths and back again.

Detaching her mind from the platoon, Lex probed downstairs cautiously, knowing what she would find. The Silvers formed the image of the mirrored room when they felt her. In the glass was the reflection of a terrified recruit platoon shitting in their shorts and their leader throwing down his baton. FOURTEEN MINUTES, a judge told her. Lex called up her memory of the Goblin and concentrated on the mirror room.

The Goblin face was an old shock device, one that quickly wore out its power to frighten. Usually the ones projecting it had the image at twentieth hand from someone who had seen it from far away. Those who saw Goblins usually either submitted or died.

Lex had seen one quite close. She showed its teeth and its flat yellow eyes. She let Silver Stick see its mind, the cartoon figures it imagined when it thought of men. YIELD YOUR MINDS, HUMANS, it ordered, and a parking lot full of people knelt.

For a moment, Lex broke the concentration of the Silver Sticks downstairs. In that instant she isolated one of their minds, saw the dark cellar with his eyes, heard the humming of a transformer with his ears. Aware of her, he began to block. The rest of the Silvers reformed around him.

But not before Lex learned the plan. THIRTEEN MINUTES. She caught the Green Stick relay in her mind. She felt comfortable using it as a weapon. FORWARD, she ordered and led them to the door of the central gallery. As though they smelled Goblin on her, the platoon bridled just a bit. As she led them through the door, she showed them what was going to happen.

Even knowing, they jumped when the power went on and the mannequins all started to move. The history of a dead world came alive. Wax laborers along the wall began hammering railway ties, men in wigs signed pieces of paper, women in long dresses spun wool, brown-skinned farmers threw up their hands in amazement at a plow, and a tall lady in white threw herself in front of a train.

Silver Stick had reactivated part of the crude electric system and found the mannequins' wardrobe room. Amid the welter of moving figures in the animated dioramas were members of the enemy platoon. Drowned out by the whirring of machinery, the mine train was rolling out of the cellar.

As others had all that morning, the recruit platoon should be struck with terror and confusion. Half the Silvers would leap from the dioramas; the rest would jump out of the mine car, dash out of the left-hand gallery and into the center. The Green Sticks, trapped, would drop their baton and run.

This time was different. Green Stick came in the door running right at the dioramas. BREAK THEM UP! Lex ordered and swung her stick at the face of a man in a high silk hat. She sent hat, wig, glasses, and wax head smashing on the floor.

Dim lights sputtered, dioramas began to move jerkily; the veteran Silver Sticks tried to form an image of frightened kids backing out of the room. They let the Greens smell the panic their predecessors had felt as they were caught in the twilight waxworks. Green Stick platoon hesitated. Lex heard the rumble of the mine train in the next gallery and knew this was the decisive moment of the battle. Instead of trying to block the image of frightened kids backing toward the door and into the trap, she just added her memory of the Goblin, imagining him at the door of the room.

The Goblin strode toward the leader of the Silvers. Its mouth tore into his belly as Lex had seen one do in the shopping center parking lot. She put all her own fear and trembling into it. Both Silver and Green platoons hesitated, shocked. The train reached the end of the left-hand gallery. The dioramas continued to move but the Silver Sticks stood out because they remained frozen. Little Sung broke the spell, rushing up and kicking a figure in a long robe in the shins.

That figure yelled. A couple of the others took a step backward. Without breakfast, they had been up since dawn getting the electric systems to work and fighting an unending parade of recruits. Now they faced a genuine Zombie.

SON OF MAN, Lex imitated what she remembered of a Goblin mind. YOUR PLAN IS PATHETIC. USELESS. DROP YOUR BATON AND DEPART. The Silvers in the gallery stumbled off the dioramas and began backing away, panic starting as Green Stick minds began poking them. One of the Silvers tripped on a moving platform and fell. Another one got knocked down. EIGHT MINUTES, a judge told Lex.

SQUAD ONE AND TWO PURSUE, she ordered. SQUAD

THREE BLOCK THE DOOR. Gingerly, only a little less afraid of her than the enemy, Green Sticks obeyed. The enemy was divided. The ones in the gallery were beaten, but the ones in the rotunda were led by Allyn, the Silvers' recruit commander.

Desperately, he formed an image of the only real battle his platoon had seen, the skirmish in which a stray piece of shrapnel had wounded one of their number. He put into it all the heat and confusion of veteran Companions urging their troopers on, an injured Zombie letting his pain gush over the battlefield like blood from an artery wound.

For a moment the Greens buckled. Then Lex let the enemy feel the thump of the jitney on Vasa's body, let them look into her mind as she was down. They had seen death; she had killed. Lex ran at Allyn, holding the Green baton like a stave.

He stood in the rotunda alone as his half of the platoon broke. Lex whacked him on the hands, knocking the baton on the floor. She picked it up and broke it. WITH FIVE MINUTES LEFT, GREEN STICK IS THE VICTOR, a Companion overcommander announced. Allyn was a tall kid who reminded Lex a little of Mark. He backed toward the door, staring at her. ZOMBIE! was the word on his mind.

YOU HAVE THOSE FIVE MINUTES AND A TEN-MINUTE BREAK BEFORE THE BLUE STICKS ARE ON YOU, Doria told Lex from outside the building. GET READY, GIRL. YOU HAVE A LONG AFTERNOON AHEAD OF YOU. As Lex headed for the cellar to check on the electrical systems, she felt a mixture of fear and respect from her platoon.

When the Greens finally left the Museum of Industrial-Progress, it was getting dark and they had broken the batons of eight other training platoons. Lex was nursing a twisted knee, a bruised shoulder, and a mind so numb she didn't feel she could have penetrated the defenses of a caged rabbit. As Green Stick straggled across the park toward their dorms, Lex felt someone fall in and limp beside her. "You enjoy leading," Doria said as a simple fact.

Lex shrugged but remembered the platoon feeling like an instrument. "You trained us . . ." she began to say.

Doria nodded, knowing that was so. "You want to lead, there is always a chance with the Companions as they now are. But what will you do against an enemy that doesn't let you go home for supper, one that has seen Goblins too?"

Lex, tired, showed her commander the twilight galleries, the wax mannequins grotesquely mauled by the time the day was over, wax mouths smiling on smashed-in faces, wax hands and glass eyes crushed on the floor. She caught the feel of panic she had gotten from the enemy, and hefted it like a club. Her instructor stared at her for a moment, then told the platoon at large, TEN-MINUTE WASH-UP, THEN FALL IN FOR DINNER.

Lights were on in the windows and Lex smelled food and bad coffee from the mess hall down the way. Green Stick was quartered in a building with "Dormitory of the Children of the People" engraved over the door. From what the Companions had been able to find out, it had housed wards of the state, orphans who worked in the Park of Human Progress. Under the inscription, some recruit in a platoon recently in training there had etched a motto, GROW OLD, WHY?

Lex's room was a six-by-six cubicle. All she possessed were a few changes of T-shirts and shorts, two pairs of sneakers, and a small personal hygiene kit. She sat for a moment on the bunk and changed shoes and put on a fresh T-shirt. Dressing for dinner. In the communal bathroom at the end of the hall, her fellow Greens didn't make way for her at the toilets or sinks. But she caught them watching her, felt their minds glance against hers.

As she washed up, Lex remembered being led off her own world and tumbling in Time. She had passed rapidly through worlds where Long Island was a desert, to ones where it was a frozen waste or a place of ruined stone cities. Once she had been led through a field filled with wrecked pens and burned platforms and was told, A SLAVE MARKET. THEY FLOURISH ALONG EVERY TIME LANE.

Lex was made to understand that people were the commodity most easily moved from world to world. Markets great and small existed on thousands of worlds, and those people who had beauty or talents were the currency traded there. And the talent most valued was telepathy. Lex remembered the prayer of the Zombies: SPARE US FROM GOBLIN MARKET.

As she had traveled, the seasons ran backward and fall turned to summer. She learned to identify the distant muffled beat of the City in the dead night of Time. And while she learned, Lex collected images of Garvin Warchild.

She was shown an angry-looking Warchild striding through marble streets in a soft, artificial light. THERE IS THE WARCHILD IN THE CITY OUT OF TIME, the one who showed it had told her. He was a young mercenary with a certain ability at World Spinning who had attached himself to the rebellion. The image was fleeting but vivid. The mercenary had it at third or fourth hand from one who had seen Garvin in the City. He had been interested in Lex, but she was gone from his station before he could try to get friendly.

From someone else she had caught an unofficial image of Garvin standing on a low hill beside a scrawny tree on which hung the bodies of three Goblins. She thought of that when green faces haunted her sleep. When her hair was cut and her clothes replaced with trainees' khaki, she thought of the razor Garvin wore around his throat, symbol of his readiness to kill himself rather than submit to the Rider planted inside him.

The evening after their triumph in the museum, Green Stick Platoon fell in outside their dorm before marching to the dining hall. In the last rays of the sun, Lex could see Elgatto being taken down from his tree stump and carried to the cabin.

Doria clumped out to stand in front of them and announce, REMEMBER THAT HERE YOU GET TO FEED YOUR-SELVES NOW THAT IT IS OVER. IN BATTLE, WIN OR LOSE, HOT MEALS WILL BE FEW AND FAR BE-TWEEN. She let them see corpses being eaten by insects under a blazing sun. The game in the museum was trivial.

SO WHAT WE DID WAS NO GOOD? they asked, tired and hungry.

IT WAS WELL ENOUGH. NEXT TIME MORE WILL BE EXPECTED. Then Doria started. The Greens saw as she did a rough crew passing by. Half a dozen Companions with tattered uniforms and overgrown haircuts led a recon unit that was actually a Sioux war party. The recruits recognized combat troops. At their center, with them but not of them, was a Companion at whom Doria stared.

Lex heard some intakes of breath as the others noticed him. In profile, seen in the light from the dorm doorway, the guy looked like a Companion recruiting image: black leathers and uniform correct but worn just casually enough, hair tall and black and shiny, skin smooth and tanned, face tough but with something almost innocent about the eye.

NICK! Lex felt Doria reach out.

The Companion turned to face her and Lex felt recruits' stomachs turn. The other side of Nick's head looked as if it had been smashed by a huge metal fist. Cheek, ear, and temple had been crushed; the eye was a sealed slit.

When he saw their instructor, the good side of Nick's face started to smile. "Doria." The word came out long and drawn, as if he were remembering how to talk.

YOU KNOW HIM? the recon commander, a guy around twenty who wore war paint, asked Doria.

HE WAS WITH THE COMPANION UNIT THAT RE-CRUITED ME. HE CARRIED ME THROUGH MY FIRST PORTAL. Doria reached for Nick's mind. Lex probed also and found nothing. It wasn't that she was blocked. Nick's mind was as hard to grasp as smoke.

The Companion commander told them, CAREFUL. SOMETHING GOT SCREWED UP WITH HIS TELEPA-THY. HE WALKED OUT OF NOWHERE AND SAVED OUR ASSES, THOUGH.

"What did they do to you, Nick?" Doria asked with a surprising softness in her voice.

Nick shook his head. "I don't know what happened. This is the last thing I remember." The Companions and Indians who had found him indicated that everyone should watch. Nick showed them figures in recruit khaki headed toward a brick cupola standing in the morning sun. The park they hurried through seemed almost familiar to Lex. Suddenly sirens sounded, enemy minds probed. One of the recruits turned and Lex looked, as Nick must have, into the very young and uncertain eyes of Garvin Warchild just before he passed through his first portal into Time.

CHAPTER

Three

Behind a sliding wall in the comfortable room where the Gods held their informal meetings, a few steps led to a bronze door. Only the Gods could unlock that from outside. Beyond it, along a carpeted corridor, lay their private quarters. On one side of this hall were doors to the divine study and the master bedroom and bath. At its far end were the kitchens and, behind them, rooms for the servants, Thomas and Mary. Across the hall from the bedroom, double doors led to the drawing room.

Inside the quarters, by the will of the Gods there was morning, noon, and night and the orderly progression of the seasons. So it was that early on what felt like a fine May day Thomas in the kitchen heard the drawing room doors open and turned to help his Mary load a breakfast tray. It was the foremost rule of the place that neither of them was ever to go into, or so much as look into, the drawing room while the Gods were inside. And they, at once devoutly superstitious and totally unimaginative, would not have dreamed of disobeying.

Outside the Palace, half the City was constantly day, the other half night, and there were no seasons in the artificial atmosphere. From inside the Gods' chambers, windows looked out on a park where the nights and days, the feel of the light and air, followed the pattern of the latitude and longitude of Dublin.

Thomas and Mary never left those rooms to walk through the City. But if they had and happened to look back at the Palace, they wouldn't have been able to find the park they saw from the windows. Not that Tom and Mary would ever question one who had walked through the flames of their burning cottage in Meath and taken them to safety. Since serving the Gods, both had seen miracles that would have made the magic park a small wonder indeed.

That morning, passing the open drawing room door, Thomas heard soft laughter. He looked inside since he knew the Gods weren't there and saw two Swift Ones, long-legged little children with pointed ears, tumbling over each other on the Turkish carpet. Three or four years old, naked, mute, just barely housebroken, there were always at least a couple of them around the place. They would appear, stay for a while, then be gone, always with others to take their place.

Calling back to the kitchen, "Company, Mary," he listened at the study only long enough to make sure the water wasn't running in the bathroom and that he could be heard. Thomas knocked once, waited, and knocked again.

"Enter," answered a voice with a brogue. Thomas knew the sound, deep and a bit raspy from graveside eulogies in bad weather, firm and just. As so often in the mornings, he would be talking to the Gods in their persona of the Reverend Father. He pushed the door open and put breakfast down as usual on the small table between the desk and the fireplace. The slightly ruddy face under the gray curly hair nodded and smiled. The Reverend Father, in black with just the trace of a white collar, leaned back in his leather chair and asked, "How's Mary this morning?" which meant that he wished to talk.

"Well as always, your divinity," the servant replied, glancing for signs of dust around the room, with its pictures and bookshelves, the computer terminal discreetly in the corner, the tall windows beyond which a magnificent willow bloomed.

"Do you know what they are saying about me in the town?" asked the God, buttering his toast and spreading it with jam. Thomas smiled and shook his head. It was a game they played that this was a country house and the City Out Of Time a sleepy village full of idle gossip.

Like Thomas bringing breakfast and never being surprised at the identity of the God who appeared to eat it, this was a ritual. Sometimes the face and costume in which the God appeared was well-known to them. Sometimes they were new or ones they hadn't seen so long as to have half forgotten.

"Because power was cut back in the City this morning, they say I'm losing my hold," the Reverend Father answered his own question. "That I am being ground between the Goblins and the Warchild." Thomas turned away and straightened a chair. From the kitchen came the sound of children's laughter as his Mary spoiled the Swift Ones.

"I shall show myself to them," said the God. The voice of the Reverend Father was gone. This one was soothing as a cello. Thomas saw the flickering halo of red-blond hair and short beard framing the face of the Golden Singer. "I shall sing a tale of fathers and sons and the quarrels they have."

It had been a long while since that face of the God of the City had appeared. As the Singer in his cloak of lights strode toward the door, Thomas hoped that Mary and the Swift Ones would be at the kitchen door to catch the magnificent sight.

For Brian Garvin the appearance of the Golden Singer was almost as much of a surprise as it was to Thomas. He knew he was going to have a confrontation with his Goblin partners. He wanted to reassure the people of the City before he did. That part of him which was the Golden Singer had emerged the way an ordinary man's expression might change. Thomas had been made to turn away without realizing it. Brian Garvin, the man inside the Gods, wanted no one ever to be sure that his changes were not some cheap theatrical trick.

Lex stood with the rest of Green Stick platoon, facing Doria in the gray of a drizzly dawn. Five other recruit platoons and their instructors were in line along with them: six Companions with one hundred forty recruits dressed for the first time in Companion-apprentice black. They were minus the Silver

Stick wounded in battle, two other kids who were sick, one who had gotten pregnant, a fourteen-year-old who had flipped out and tried to kill himself when he discovered his girl-friend's platoon wasn't coming with them. They were plus one. Nick stood with his good side to Lex.

AS YOU KNOW, Doria told them, ELGATTO HAS NAMED ME TO LEAD STICK APPRENTICE COMPANY. YOU ALSO KNOW THAT IMMORTALS' COMPANION NICK WILL ACCOMPANY US. HE WILL MARCH WITH GREEN STICK. WHILE I AM LEADING THIS COM-PANY, LEX WILL BE ACTING HEAD OF MY PLATOON. That too was expected and not particularly welcome to some of the recruits or even, Lex could tell, a couple of the instruc-tors. But the tense exhilaration of the company's departure from training camp made this a good moment for the an-nouncement.

NOW MOVE OUT. ELGATTO WILL SEE US OFF. Nick and Lex marched at the front of Green Stick. The few days since Nick had appeared had been busy and thick with rumors. Some said the Goblins were coming; some said the Warchild. Everyone had seen Nick and been shown his mem-ories of Garvin as a brave, scared recruit. They all wondered where Nick had been for the last few years. His mind was as hard to catch as smoke, his presence like a ghost's.

Lex hadn't had much contact with Nick. She knew that he was blind on his bad right side but that the vision on the left was better than good. And she had seen the memories of the Companion war party he had saved. They were beaten, ready to die, pinned down by an armored unit controlled by a Rider. Half the Companion officers were dead. Then Nick had seemed to rise out of the ground and break the Steed's neck with his bare hands.

When the company reached the top of the hill, Elgatto was out on his tree stump. YOU GO TO JOIN THE ARMY OF AUTUMN UNDER THE COMMAND OF HERSELF. THOSE OF YOU WHO SURVIVE WILL COMMAND TROOPS. SOME OF YOU WILL EVENTUALLY TRAIN RECRUITS. THIS IS TRUE OF ALL APPRENTICE COM-PANIES. IN YOUR CASE, HOWEVER, THERE IS A SPE-CIAL MISSION. He indicated Nick. YOU WILL SEE TO IT

THAT THIS COMPANION IS BROUGHT TO THE WAR-
CHILD. As they gasped at their mission, he added, DO NOT
FORGET US OR THIS VALLEY OF BONES.

Easing his foot off the gas, Garvin let the roadster coast
down the dirt road. Across the river, the gas street lamps and
colored marquees of the Free City of Guitars turned streets
and bridges into jeweled ornaments in the night. Feeling the
breeze on his face, Garvin formed an Umbra, an outer mind
buffer, and reached for the music. Over the rush of the river
he felt the telepathy of a thousand musicians make the air hum
in an elongated chord.

At the head of a tiny escort from Warchild Cluster, Garvin
had reached this world and Guitars only a few hours before. It
had taken longer than he had thought. Worlds loyal to the
house of Echbattan had to be cleared. The Warchild's own
Army of Summer and both the Immortals' armies moved
more slowly as resistance increased.

The delay made Garvin savor this place all the more. The
song of Guitars across the river soaked into him:

CROSSROADS—ONE WAY'S SLAVE, ONE WAY'S FREE,
YOUR CHOICE HERE IS TO WALK OR CRAWL.

The air hummed with music. Guitars even seemed to have
changed the Oracle. It had appeared to Garvin just before he
found the portal. Once again the pyre began to burn, the
bodies writhed. But the vision was dim, flickering. Just before it disappeared, Garvin saw figures in Companion black
running across the plaza. They were far away, but one of them
seemed familiar.

From outside Guitars, Garvin caught images of the ones
called Sojourners who had traveled a long way. Many were
black but others were white or brown. A lot of them were
plain people, loyal followers, but some had a power of music
so strong it wouldn't stay inside them. It started when the
wars of the French Revolution had spread all over the globe
and brought chaos and the dream of freedom to the New
World. The Sojourners had found a spot where a river cut a

gorge in a mountain, made a fair treaty with the Indians, laid foundations, and called it the Free City of Guitars.

The Sojourners went about unarmed because it was music they relied on for protection. That had stood them well against all their enemies. Garvin, rolling downhill, was falling into a place he knew part of him had always wanted to find.

> *OUR FREE CITY IS AN OPEN TOWN,*
> *OPEN TO YOU AS YOU OPEN TO HER.*

He caught the invitation of Guitars, formed a mental Curtain layer, and used it to touch the consciousnesses of those in the cars following his.

They were some of his first and most loyal followers. The telepaths and soldiers were all from the Republic, members of Warchild Cluster who had fought in his name and left their homes when Garvin asked them to. Maji and Darrel, his oldest friends, rode in the back seat. Garvin opened his mind and let them react as he did to the music and images as they fell into the lights of Guitars.

They reminded him of the Republic and of Scarecrow, his teacher. Scarecrow had taught Garvin how to harness his telepathy, had shown him how to perform three mental functions at once: Umbra, Curtain, and Keep. The Warchild caught the notes of a guitar being tuned on a roadside porch they sped by and formed his Umbra. From the feel of his foot on the gas, he formed the Curtain. On the smell of pine trees and exhaust, he molded his Keep.

In that Keep, the innermost chamber of his mind, Garvin kept his secrets and dealt with his Rider. As they approached Guitars, traffic grew heavier. A truck driver turning out of a side road heard horns, caught a mental warning, and pulled over to let them pass. 'please watch out for traffic.' The Rider was like a nagging ache.

SAW IT IN PLENTY OF TIME, Garvin lied. The Warchild's mind was stronger than any Steed any Rider had ever known. It was a prisoner. 'you drive like a maniac, warchild,' it told him quietly. Having become an enemy of the Goblins, the Rider could only hope that the Warchild

would live forever and it would live forever inside him. 'may
i remind you that we have formulated no strategy for dealing
with oracle's prophecy. aside from our death, i detected winds
when it showed . . .'

NOT TONIGHT. The Warchild's party kept their hands on
the horns. People turned to look. Some sensed that the minds of
these visitors were different from any the Free City had known,
but they shouted, "Welcome pilgrims!" raised their arms in
greeting. A young musician walking into town was touched by
the minds in the cars blaring past. He felt something that made
him strum his strings and add a line to the evening song:

PILGRIMS GET BLOWN HERE FROM THE STARS
SEEKING REFUGE BEFORE THE WINDS.

The references to the Wind caught at the back of Garvin's
memory like déjà vu. 'this world lies within echbattan territory, has plenty of portals, and yet has never been exploited or
even discovered, as far as we know.' He felt his Rider chewing over that paradox and was content not to have to think
about it.

'we have less than a foothold on this world. please do not
allow yourself to compromise security here tonight,' his Rider
advised. 'the strategic session is arranged for tomorrow.' It
showed him images of the Immortals. 'the commanders of the
armies of winter and spring will be here.'

Garvin thought of a tall woman with long red hair. THE
ONE I REALLY WANT TO SEE IS HERSELF.

'we have been through that. the army of autumn is coming
in on the flank of the enemy, and is not yet linked up with the
other armies. this world is in a very exposed position. it
would be better to wait until more troops have come up before . . .'

Garvin took his hands off the wheel, they hit a bump, the
car swerved, and his Rider died a little. NO MORE RIGHT
NOW, UNDERSTAND. YOU HAVE NOTHING TO
WORRY ABOUT UNTIL WE GET TO ECHBATTAN'S
WORLD. Both Steed and Rider thought of the image of his
funeral pyre.

Reaching out with the Curtain of his mind, Garvin touched

his escort and told them, TRY TO KEEP OUR PRESENCE HERE QUIET, OKAY? The horns stopped blaring, the telepaths allowed their minds to float on the blue notes drifting from across the river. Even so, the town was aware of them before they entered it. Garvin saw himself and his party as they were seen by the citizens of Guitars. They were wild outlanders, but the Free City had known and tamed worse.

As they drove up to one of the bridges, a constable of Guitars, a tall old black man in a high hat and tails, directed them to a parking lot.

OUR RULES ARE THESE: NO WEAPONS, NO MOON-SHINE,
NO SLAVES, NO MASTERS IN OUR FREE TOWN.

He gave his orders to the beat of the music, but he was used to being obeyed. Garvin, staring toward Guitars, said quietly, "Leave your guns here. This guy will watch them."

He started toward the bridge and the constable was about to point to the gold razor around his neck. Originally he had worn it to remind his Rider that he had the power to kill them both. Garvin deflected his mind gently. In the Oracle's vision they took the razor off him. To Garvin that more than anything meant he was going to be dead.

Thrusting that to the back of his mind, Garvin concentrated on the music, caught the rhythm on his Umbra, let gaslight and sound meld together. EVERYONE GET BACK HERE BY DAWN, he told his escort and they nodded. Darrel and Maji stuck with him, the rest fell back. The telepaths kept in loose contact with each other, confident the Warchild would be able to protect himself and them as well. Their troops, disarmed and at liberty, felt the sweet release of the Free City.

Telepathy in Guitars was tied to music. The brick of the streets, the stones of the buildings throbbed with it. Music was the magic that kept them free and their enemies at bay. Telepathy was what made their music famous over that entire world, brought travelers, students, young runaway adepts. By local reckoning it was 1923. North America was a mosaic of small- to medium-size states. In the world at large the European powers were still exhausted from long wars. Guitars didn't have a gun within the City or a nation in the world that wasn't in awe of it.

The Free City had grown up the mountain by the rushing river. Hundred-year-old buildings of wood and stone on narrow dockside streets gave way to iron and brick as Garvin climbed uphill. Gas lamps flickered, doors and windows of inns, taverns, cabarets were open on that warm night, drug emporiums shone soft lights on side streets, figures at second-floor windows beckoned. And the music flowed over everything.

Darrel took Maji's arm as they followed Garvin. The War-child walked as if he were being pulled on a string. A couple of times they asked him to stop at bars for beer. Once they bought and shared a couple of joints with him. The rhythm of Guitars was in them and they would have been happy to sit anywhere and soak it up. Garvin paused with them but always silently, distracted. Once or twice he brushed them with his Umbra and they saw a young black woman, heard her singing.

Garvin had caught that coffee face, the dark eyes wide, surprised, looking through the eyes of the ones who sat listening to her. Bethel Truth was her name and he heard her words, followed them in the meld of sound, the music and minds of a thousand musicians playing that night.

WRONG LOVE IS LONG AND HARD AS PRISON WALLS

Music danced in the gaslight, seemed to make the buildings sway. The telepathy of Guitars was creed and magic, meal ticket and safeguard for the City. Everyone who passed through got touched by it and yielded some of his or her self. The young guitarist the Warchild's party had passed on their way into town arrived and showed the other musicians what he had seen and felt: young rebels who saw their world as one among many.

As Bethel played and sang, she listened too with that inner ear which grace had given her, picking up the mood of Guitars, at the same time adding to it. The beat of the Free City was fast and supple early in the evening, raunchy and a little wild. Salesmen and traders looking for entertainment, work crews passing through town on the roads and railway were in the meld, being soothed by it even as they gave it energy.

People around the town noticed the visitors, tough-looking kids with funny hair who paid in gold coins. Guitars was polite in that it never pointed but always noticed. Bethel picked up a fragment of the young guitarist's excitement: PILGRIMS FROM THE STARS, so she wasn't taken altogether unaware when she saw three of them at the back of the crowd.

Garvin moved with Darrel and Maji toward a table set up on the sidewalk outside a tavern on a square. The stage was in front of the doorway. Most of the band was black, but a white girl played bass. Bethel Truth was out front on guitar, playing the fast riffs on "Sojourner." Garvin never took his eyes off her. Darrel and Maji looked at Garvin and were amused. The Warchild had been known to get caught like this.

"Found someone?" Maji asked and snapped bubble gum. They had all tried on their way there to inhale a joint, then blow a green bubble full of the smoke. A few years before, when they were kids in the forests of the Republic, Garvin had a rivalry with Darrel for Maji. But that was before war and his destiny had changed everything. As they sat down, Maji took the joint out of Garvin's hand without his seeming to notice, drew and held her breath, gave the wad of gum in her mouth a couple of chews, exhaled, and blew a bubble as big as her face.

Washed in the rhythm of music halfway between jazz and blues came images of Sojourners, the saints who had founded the town, the pilgrims who had come afterward. Bethel threw out fragments of her own memories: a delta summer, hot and endless in the way only a childhood summer can be, an old man playing fiddle and tapping his foot on a front porch. Bethel, watching her grandfather, had thought of falling up into the sky and finding it was a huge cool lake. "Sojourner," was that kind of music, gently driving and yearning:

SOJOURNER DRAWS YOU NEARER,
DRAWS ME FARTHER FROM HOME.

Bethel remembered something that she had almost forgotten. It was right after they discovered she had the gift and first got Guitars stuck in her mind and her family knew that they were going to lose her. She had gone outside in the hot night. The screen door had opened again when she was down in the yard and her mother came out on the porch, stepped out of the light from the kitchen, and threw a pan of dishwater into the dark. It floated in the dark, catching bits of moonlight.

As she showed them that, Bethel saw eternity in the water and saw the bits of moon as lighted worlds, thousands of them, separated from each other by the dark. The word TIME echoed in her brain, its emptiness fascinating and terrifying. Her fingers slid on the strings, making them cry out. The bass sounded like a heartbeat. A pan of stars stood suspended in the night and her sidemen yelped and the audience drew its breath at the glory and terror they suddenly felt.

Bethel looked at the kid with the blond horse mane who stared back at her. He was younger and a lot lighter than she usually got interested in. But after the night was over, after the musicians all over the City had wound down the crowd and put the pilgrims gently to rest, she and Garvin still looked at each other over empty tables. He had the gift more strongly than any person she had felt. At first she had wanted to think he was just a drunk and crazy boy with the vision and no music. She knew he was more. "You're Garvin from the stars?" she asked.

He nodded slowly. When Bethel Truth thought of her gift, she thought of it as part of her world, arising out of the earth, air and water. She knew that what she felt in him was something outside that. "What brought you to Guitars?"

I WANTED TO HEAR YOU. Garvin smiled at the way her eyes widened.

"They heard about me out there in Time?"

He showed her an image of the minstrel in the slave market. ONCE HE SHOWED ME, I HAD TO HEAR YOU. Bethel felt cold looking at Garvin's memory of the slave market and the minstrel who knew about Guitars. She knew that a secret was out and Guitars's peace was about to end.

Garvin stood up and held out his hand. WALK YOU HOME? he asked and showed Bethel how striding in infinity felt. He showed her how he had imagined the lighted worlds

as reflections in her eyes, heard her voice over the pulse of
Time. Someone a few streets over strummed and sang quietly,

> *YOUNG MAN GOT HIM SOME MOVES,*
> *INDIAN HAIR AND DEVIL GROOVES.*

She showed Garvin the grin on his own face, the little
dance he did in the light from a street lamp. Her place was on
the third floor across the empty square from the tavern. Bethel
experienced Garvin in layers. The first was like a fun park.
When Garvin got turned on, the air exploded between them.
She felt his pleasure in her curling around the pleasure she
felt. He was young but not dumb. Bethel didn't believe all
that came out of Garvin. But he had definitely been somewhere and learned some things.

The second layer was graver. He leaned on one elbow,
touching the gold blade on his neck, and asked very seriously,
WHAT WAS THAT YOU SANG ABOUT A WIND?

Half awake, she showed him an old Guitars legend about a
big Wind coming and taking the Free City off to the stars.
"Kind of like where you come from," she said and ran her
foot along his leg.

Thinking back on that night after she understood more,
Bethel remembered being chilled when, on the edge of a moment's doze, she caught a presence like a knife inside Garvin's mind. 'escort assemble,' something cold and sharp was
telling other minds. Bethel felt then that everything, her
music, her world, human warmth and understanding, were
nothing. On that night, it occurred to her Guitars had been
created for a specific reason and that reason would shortly
become known.

She shivered in the mild mountain night, reached for Garvin, and didn't find him. She opened her eyes to see him
against the gaslight outside the windows, buttoning his pants.
I WILL BE BACK, he told her and she wondered how many
others he had said that to.

Then Bethel saw Time as he saw it, the thousands of worlds
circling a City that thudded like a metal heart. She saw em-
pires and icebergs, farms and deserts and people in their
hundreds of billions. Crowds cheered heroes, and children

cried on the slave block. Behind it all was the sound of her guitar tearing into "Sojourner." Bethel always remembered that when she thought of Garvin in the wonder and horror that followed.

Car engines coughed to life in the parking lot the moment Garvin appeared on the bridge from Guitars. His leather jacket hooked over his shoulder on one finger, he seemed pensive. Troopers woke up in the first touch of dawn, telepaths roused themselves and waited for orders. From inside his brain, Garvin's Rider asked, 'is it permitted to mention our situation?'

Without replying, the Warchild walked to his car. Darrel and Maji stirred in the back seat. Long and low, the car was a red roadster convertible built for speed. LET ME TEST IT OUT, Garvin told them and slid behind the wheel. Doors slammed as the motorcade got ready to follow him. A Companion showed a stretch of winding open road. JUST OUTSIDE OF TOWN, WARCHILD. The ones around Garvin knew his moods.

The Rider told him, 'you have had your pleasures, warchild. now there are strategic problems . . ." Gears ground as the car pulled away from the curb, bumped over cobblestones. 'we are perched in a relatively undeveloped north america with a tiny force.'

An image floated in his escort's minds, of Garvin's roadster looking like a big red roller skate. They climbed a hill opposite Guitars. Lights were on in a few windows as the sun came up on a summer morning. Tires squealed and Maji and Darrel leaned right as Garvin hung a left. Just around the corner he swerved to avoid a parked milk truck. The three cars and two open trucks following him did the same. MAKE WAY FOR THE WARCHILD! minds told the milkman, who stood shaking his head.

'this is not protecting the people of the worlds of time from the goblins,' the Rider told Garvin.

WHICH IS SOMETHING YOU REALLY CARE ABOUT. He was getting the feel of the shift stick.

'i care about having at least this area firmly in your grip.'

TIME FOR THAT WHEN THE ARMY SHOWS UP.

'you must immediately overawe the local leaders.'

Gravel rattled on the underbody. Garvin concentrated on his driving. Ahead, through trees, he spotted the stretch of highway. He came out of the side road with his foot on the gas. The sunlight shone over distant mountains behind Guitars. The rumble of a long freight came out of the dying night. I AM NOT INTERESTED IN SCARING THESE PEOPLE. I WANT TO LEAVE GUITARS LIKE I FOUND IT. Some things about this world were so familiar they scared him.

'because you have me, you don't have to dwell on the un-pleasant.'

NO, ALL I HAVE TO DO IS WITNESS IT. Garvin saw a white railway crossing sign way up ahead and went into first. The morning world looked blue and beautiful. The crossing bell started to ring. Garvin saw the headlight on the front of the engine. The dark outline of a fast freight rolled downhill toward a railway bridge and the Free City. Garvin was sure that he could beat it to the crossing gate.

His escort slowed down. WARCHILD? a Companion in a car behind asked respectfully as he saw Garvin pull away from the motorcade. A white crossing gate began to fall. Piercing horn blasts came from the pounding engine. Garvin saw its headlight as a single mad eye. The danger made him concentrate. Every part of him disappeared but the hand and foot drawing every bit of speed out of the convertible.

The crossing gate fell like a white guillotine. It just missed the top of the front window. Garvin felt Maji and Darrel in the back throw themselves flat as it scraped the top of their seat. Tires bumped on rails, the wheel bucked in his hands, the motor whined and coughed. Garvin felt the heat of the engine on the right side of his head and face. The whistle shriek deafened him and his Rider screamed inside his brain. Garvin held on to the memory of Bethel Truth singing:

CROSSROADS SAYS ONE WAY SLAVE AND ONE WAY FREE.

Then the little car bobbed over the rails, wobbled for a moment in the hot suction of the train, and sped along the highway again. Garvin lifted his foot off the gas. WAR-CHILD? the escort probed from the other side of the train.

The Rider was quiet inside him, which was what Garvin had wanted. "That was close," Darrel said evenly and Garvin realized that he had risked Darrel and Maji without even considering them. He slowed down and let the motorcade catch up.

"The Rider was giving you trouble?" Maji asked. These two had known him as a barefoot apprentice without memory or control over his telepathy, had seen the land of their birth destroyed, had left their world and followed him. Their loyalty was absolute and they didn't deserve to die as they almost had.

"The day the Companions recruited me," he found himself explaining, "I stood down Red Eddy, the neighborhood bully." He showed them the Manhattan street, the big man with face contorted in fear as Garvin forced his way into his mind and twisted it. "I didn't think about it. I just did it."

'and you have neither looked back nor thought since,' his Rider told him from the corner of his brain where it had hidden.

"I wasn't thinking. I'm sorry," he told the two of them but not his Rider. Darrel and Maji nodded. Their understanding made him ashamed. In their minds Garvin could see that dying with the Warchild was a glorious way to go.

The train was a dying shriek. The motorcade tagged behind Garvin as he drove at a moderate speed toward camp. Drained of adrenaline, subdued, sleepy, he turned the car onto a road that led up the mountain toward his headquarters. As he did, Garvin was struck by the way the roads, the trees, the dust he could see rising behind his car brought back another world, one he had found when he was first on his own in Time.

A lot of things didn't match up: that North America was French, and still largely wilderness, this one was English speaking and more heavily developed. But the rich, idle kids he had known there had lived for radio broadcasts of black music from the South. It was true that they had lived in Canada and the music came from the Gulf, but as the sun rose and hit the trees, the smell of warming pine caught Garvin and his memory seemed real enough for him to bite into and chew.

As Garvin approached camp, minds reached out for him.

WARCHILD. WE HAVE QUARTERS FOR YOU IN A FARMHOUSE. An aide showed him the building. White wood and gray stone nestled on a rise of land. Again Garvin's memory was hooked. The place evoked the Republic, the first place besides his own New York that he had really known. It reminded him of Scarecrow and his mate Amre, who had been his best teachers.

He drove up country past white-and-gray country stores, slate-roofed barns, filling stations with red signs advertising Land of Abundance Gas. Garvin touched Darrel and Maji and knew they felt it too. Amid the differences were images—a stone-and-white-wood farmhouse, a cart full of kindling pulled by an old horse ridden by a little kid—that evoked the homes they had left to follow the Warchild.

On the dirt road leading to his headquarters, Garvin passed gawkers from that world. Mostly kids, they stared as the mercenary officer commanding the sentries, a boy with spike-cut hair dyed crimson, saluted Garvin. HEADQUARTERS OF THE ARMY OF SUMMER IS SET UP JUST BACK OF HERE.

THANKS. Garvin parked the roadster in the front of a farmhouse they had rented the evening before. He nodded to a couple of the sentries, twin riflemen, one with an eye patch with an eye painted on it, the other sporting a long vivid scar next to his Mohawk.

WARCHILD, a fifteen-year-old aide told him. AS WAS ORDERED WE CONTACTED THE PRESIDENT OF THE PRAIRIE CONFEDERATION AND THE PRIME MINISTER OF THE LAND OF ABUNDANCE. DO YOU HAVE A MESSAGE FOR THEM?

GARVIN, someone else inquired respectfully, SHOULD WE SEND PEOPLE TO EUROPE?

Garvin batted their minds away easily. IT WILL BE TAKEN CARE OF, he told them. I NEED SOME SLEEP RIGHT NOW.

"Your bedroom is upstairs, if that's all right," an orderly, who had followed the Warchild all the way from the City Out Of Time, told him. "Your bodyguards can sleep in the next room."

Garvin nodded and climbed the stairs. He felt exhaustion

coming on, remembered Bethel and the night in Guitars, tried not to think about the train. Again he felt the faint tingle of recognition, as did Maji and Darrel, who followed him. It was as if they had all climbed these stairs back in the Republic.

Garvin recognized his room by the three small black boxes on the floor. He flicked on the Scramblers and turned the constant telepathic communication of his army into mental white noise. As he did, he noticed one of them wasn't working. Along with Warchild Cluster he had brought the Scramblers from the Republic. The only other place he had ever seen them was in his father's palace. REMIND ME ABOUT THAT, he told his Rider, kicked himself out of his clothes, and fell asleep.

After a while the entity in the Warchild's mind stirred and summoned the staff. The bedroom door opened cautiously and two Companion commanders, that day's duty officers, stood in the room. Careful not to disturb Garvin, the Rider used a part of his brain to communicate with them. 'tell the rulers of the prairie confederation and the land of abundance to send delegations here this afternoon.'

IS THIS IN THE WARCHILD'S NAME? asked one Companion who had recently joined the staff. He had been told about the Rider that had tried to tame the Warchild and been broken by him. A Sikh, he had stood up under machine gun fire and dueled with the minds of Zombies. But feeling that presence in the dark room, imagining it in his own mind, made his blood cold.

The Rider caught that repugnance and felt something like amusement. 'have you known him to countermand any of my orders?'

NO. The other commander was Blaze. YOU CAN ASK THE WARCHILD LATER, the girl with the silver mane told the Sikh. BUT . . . She flashed an image of Goblins in a brightly lighted operating room implanting the Rider in Garvin, then flashed an image of a worm in an apple. The Warchild always approved the orders issued while he slept.

That morning, the constables of Guitars set up informal roadblocks on the roads leading toward the farm and the woods around it. Telepathic linking in that city was usually reserved for music. But in times of danger, a kind of relay could be set up. It was as open as a party line, but until then it had been the most powerful mind display experienced on that world.

Bethel awoke to catch flashes of what the constables on the road saw. Farmers showed the gold they had been paid for use of their land, their houses, their cars. The wooded hills across the river from Guitars were full of people. Bethel caught sight of whole battalions of kids, all shapes and colors, all dressed like Garvin. EVERY TIME I LOOK THERE ARE MORE OF THEM, one of the observers told Guitars. AND I KEEP SEEING THIS. He showed an image of a mirrored room.

YOU GOT THE BALLOON SURVEYING THE WOODS? the Archdeacon asked.

YES'M. BUT AS FAR AS I CAN TELL, THEY ARE JUST GROWING OUT OF THE GROUND. AND I AM YET TO SEE ANYONE WHO LOOKS LIKE AN ADULT.

Bethel started to get interested when she felt the entire relay focus on her. BETHEL TRUTH, WOULD YOU BE KIND ENOUGH TO PAY US A CALL? The ancient Archdeacon of Guitars was a woman old enough to have known people present at the founding of the City. WE HAVE BEEN GIVEN TO BELIEVE YOU MAY HAVE SOME SPECIAL UNDERSTANDING OF OUR LATEST VISITORS.

As Garvin slept, observation blimps drifted above the hill in the dry heat of a mountain summer, biplanes buzzed into the airport on the flat lands downhill from the Free City. Companion minds probed, felt the alert constables, the gawking kids curious to see travelers no older than them. "They touch you like a singer, but there's no music," someone whispered as a telepathic mind sifted through the crowd.

Radio was forbidden in Guitars, newspapers unnecessary, but young musicians moved up to the roadblock and put questions to the sentries. WHERE ARE YOU FROM? The answer to that appeared in their minds: worlds like rooms, an endless rambling house all lighted up. And between the lighted rooms were corridors empty of light where the only sound was the beating of a heart.

"What government do you represent?" The answer to that

appeared in their minds like an image in a song: the kid who was in town the night before told them, RISE UP!

BIG COMMOTION, a constable told the Deacons. All of Guitars felt him concentrate, trying to understand what he was seeing. THEY CALL HER THE ROSE. The image he picked up from the kids in the woods was of a little girl, eyes wide, head perched beside a bandaged lump on the shoulders of an adult body. YOU HEAR THEM SHOUT? THERE ARE SO MANY NOW THEY HARDLY FIT IN THE WOODS.

The Immortal Rose moved through cheering troops, her child face trying to smile, her adult body dragging. On her wide neck was the lump which had been the woman's head called the Thorn. For longer than anyone could tell, Roses had reached maturity and become Thorns. When that happened the old Thorn died and later grew into the head of a child. If things worked properly, wisdom and innocence, maturity and impetuosity would be combined in the Immortal called the Thorn and Rose. With only the Rose currently alive, the Immortals' Companions who followed Garvin looked on her as something between magic and mascot.

The Rose's maturity was in a future the army didn't expect to live to see. All of them firmly believed that the war would be won and they would be dead by the time they were twenty. Meanwhile, having a seven-year-old mind in control of the Warchild's Army of Spring seemed right to them. The Rose stopped suddenly and looked out toward the blue smoke rising over the Free City of Guitars.

SOMETHING ELSE IS HAPPENING, the constables reported and showed Guitars a tall, gaunt old man with a bald head who carried a leather satchel in one hand. THAT OLD GUY IS ROGER. As the constables and the army watched, Roger seemed to stagger.

Several Companion officers jumped forward and caught him. When they did, memories and images emerged from the satchel, woven like a song. The song was about Roger, the servant, mute, mindless and untiring, who had carried the satchel for over fifty years. FROM WHAT I UNDERSTAND, THEY CALL THAT LEATHER BAG THE TALKING SUITCASE.

If the Rose was a mascot, the Suitcase, the commander of

the Army of Winter, was a talisman. The Immortals had existed for almost as long as Time itself, recruiting Companions, raiding slave markets, slowing down the Goblin advance. Now as a Companion medic bent over Roger, the Immortal sang a song of Roger dying on this quiet hillside as Time passed from the control of the Gods and Goblins.

The medic shook her head and called for a blanket to cover the old man who had borne the Suitcase for so long.

As that happened, the Rose stood in the front yard of the farmhouse and continued to look out at Guitars. I WANT GARVIN. WHERE IS THE WARCHILD? she asked like a frightened child.

ASLEEP.

MAKE HIM WAKE UP.

The Warchild had been in the middle of a sweaty jumble of a dream in which musicians played in a smoky place that started as a club. It turned into the familiar mirrored room when Garvin looked in the glass over the bar. In the mirrored room was a young man smiling and holding up an infant boy, telling him, SOMEDAY IF ALL GOES WELL, YOUR MAGIC WILL REPLACE MINE.

Garvin recognized the man as his father, groaned, and half sat up. "Everything leads to him."

'are we ready to begin the day?' his Rider asked as Garvin lay down again, wondering if what he felt in his stomach was hunger. A knock came at the door. "Yeah?"

An orderly said, "The Rose and the Talking Suitcase are due, Warchild."

"What time is it?"

"After noon. Would you like breakfast?"

"Yuuch! Maybe. Coffee." He tried to spit the dust out of his mouth.

'while you slept, i negotiated with delegations from the city of guitars and several neighboring states.'

WHY?

'because a whole army cannot survive eating in all-night roadhouses and paying for everything with off-world gold. eventually they will die of malnutrition and the local economy will be wrecked. you must show these yokels who you are and demand supplies.'

Garvin rolled off the bed and headed for the bathroom. He was glad to find it had a shower. HOW MANY TROOPS ARE HERE?

'seventeen thousand five hundred and nine at last count. nine hundred and thirty of those are telepathic. within the next two days the number of your followers on this and adjacent worlds will be over half a million. supply. . .'

The entity inside his brain got lost amid the hot water and steam. Out of the shower, Garvin carefully dried the gold blade that hung around his neck and reached for the lather, intending to shave his temples. Then he realized that though he hadn't tended it for days his hair still looked perfect. 'proof if nothing else that you are the son of the gods.'

As he slipped a thick gold band around his ponytail, Garvin remembered the Oracle had shown him a soldier with a machete chop off the tail and wrap it around the ring. Garvin screwed a diamond stud into his ear and put on some rings he always wore. Each was the gift of a grateful world. Echbattan soldiers would steal them all before they threw him on the pyre.

He felt frustration and anger, as if he were still inside his dream. WHY AM I MEETING WITH THE IMMORTALS?

His Rider showed him the Armies of the Four Seasons as glowing dots of bright red. Each army was made up of three corps named after the months of that season. Each corps was composed of four divisions. A blue, irregular diamond shape was the Echbattan domains. Three of the armies were in a jagged arrowhead formation jutting into the blue field.

Garvin saw that the point of the arrow was detached from the rest of his forces. That was the advance guard of his own Army of Summer here at Guitars. It was supposed to be flanked by the Armies of Winter, commanded by the Suitcase, and Spring under the Rose. 'lately the immortals have been flagging and their deployment of the flanking armies is very ragged. to prevent a successful echbattan counterattack, we must make them move their troops more rapidly.'

Approaching Echbattan's world from the other end of summer was the Army of Autumn under Herself. 'as far as we can tell, the echbattan forces are concentrated entirely against us. the plan is that as the defenders block our advance, they leave the way clear for autumn army to smash their flank. if that works, there will be no need for you to lead assaults on ech-battan's world.' Both thought of the Oracle and wondered why the plan wasn't going to work. 'the problems are that our armies are lagging and that i don't trust herself's leadership.'

The Warchild found clean black jeans and shirt on the dresser. There were even new socks. Garvin kicked off the Scramblers with the toe of his boot. Immediately the presence of his army hit him, the thousands of minds, telepathic officers, curious soldiers.

THE WARCHILD WAS IN TOWN LAST NIGHT TO MAKE SURE IT WAS SAFE, one Companion told a recent arrival. This was accompanied by an image of a gray train streaking out of the dark, shown casually just as the escort had shown it that morning.

The newcomer was admiring, amused. GUITARS HAS SEEN THE WORST WE CAN DO. Then their attention was caught by the approach of the Rose and the Talking Suitcase.

Maji and Darrel were still asleep. Garvin went past their room and down the stairs. There he was met by Blaze. She handed him a mug of black coffee and gave him a look of concern which he ignored. There was another Companion with her, a big guy with his head almost shaved like he had seen some hard action. WARCHILD, THIS IS WILHELM OF JULY CORPS. She continued on upstairs.

The tough-looking Companion bowed. I HAVE A MESSAGE TO BE DELIVERED ONLY TO THE WARCHILD. Garvin blocked other minds and indicated Wilhelm should proceed. CAPTAIN TAGENT SENDS YOU HIS GREETINGS AND WANTS TO TALK TO YOU ABOUT HIS FAMILY, was the message. Along with that was an image of the one who sent it, a tall, amused-looking Englishman, and the location of the world where he could be found. Garvin recognized his uncle, the Guvnor.

A sudden confusion outside interrupted his thoughts. ROGER IS DEAD! Floating above that, Garvin felt the song of the Talking Suitcase and something like panic from the Rose. GET GARVIN, she was telling the army. TELL HIM I CANNOT MOVE.

He ran out of the porch and saw people bent over the still

form of Roger. The Rose was stationary, looking away toward the City of Guitars. Garvin went to her first. WE CAME FROM WORLDS AND WORLDS AWAY, she sang. BUT HERE WE STAY, HERE WE STAY.

Garvin went to the Rose and put his arms around her. She felt stiff and hard inside her clothes. Her child eyes stared at Guitars. I CANNOT MOVE ANYMORE, she told him. I AM LIKE A TREE. Her mind felt as if it were in a kind of shock.

The Warchild thought of how the Thorn had died fighting for him. He remembered the dream he'd just had, his father telling him, SOMEDAY IF ALL GOES WELL, YOUR MAGIC WILL REPLACE MINE. It made him sad and scared and he wondered what kind of therapy could help a six-year-old child who had died and reblossomed for thousands of years.

"I'll be back," he whispered to her. Then he went over to where the Talking Suitcase lay on the grass beside Roger's body. Someone had closed the old man's eyes. The army watched silently as Garvin picked up the satchel and took it inside the farmhouse.

Blaze had set up the Scramblers in the dining room. He went in there, closed the door, and put the leather bag on the table. WHAT HAPPENED TO ROGER? he asked, sitting on a chair in front of which Blaze had placed his coffee mug.

The answer came to his mind very faintly as if from a radio station fading out of range. A presence inside the satchel sang of old age and duty done and a faithful servant gone to a well-deserved rest.

WHAT HAS HAPPENED TO THE ROSE? WHAT IS HAPPENING TO YOU?

The answer was one word, GUITARS, and one image, the city over the river wreathed in blue smoke.

HOW DID GUITARS DO THIS TO YOU?

Very faintly, he felt the answer. I AM THE OLD CRE-ATION. THIS IS A NEW CREATION.

Though he listened hard, Garvin got nothing more from the satchel than what felt like late night static at the end of a radio dial. He got up and walked around the table. WHAT DID MY FATHER INTEND WHEN HE CREATED YOU AND THE

THORN AND ROSE? he asked, not expecting an answer. Until he had the satchel in his hands, he didn't know what he intended to do.

The anger that shook Garvin took him by surprise. It arose from fear. In the middle of his army he felt very alone. His Rider froze as the Warchild flung the contents of the bag at the wall. They stuck there and on the floor, countless pieces of light sparkling like specks of glass in sand, like dishwater tossed in moonlight, like the worlds of Time, twenty thousand pieces of light joined by invisible threads.

'this complicates things. one of your army commanders has turned out to be a bag of glass fragments. the other is turning into a plant on the front lawn,' his Rider told him. It tried to conceal it, but Garvin recognized that his Rider was afraid also. It was afraid of him. Garvin didn't quite understand yet what he was afraid of.

He didn't want to be in the room with the Immortal a moment longer. He went outside quickly and found his silent army looking at the Rose. As they watched, she turned into a bush with a single flower. Garvin ordered, BURY ROGER NEAR THE ROSE AND THORN. NO ONE IS TO DISTURB HER NOR THE TALKING SUITCASE INSIDE. From the Free City over the river came a song:

> *HE IS TO BE OUR DESTINY,*
> *OUR FATE TO RIDE THE WINDS.*

Garvin saw an image he recognized as being from Bethel. It was him pale in the night showing her Time. He shuddered but gave an order to his staff officers. I WANT AS MUCH OF MY ARMY AS POSSIBLE TO GET LEAVE IN TOWN. He wanted all of them to see what he could create.

'it is always well to let them off the leash,' his Rider told him. 'what are the rest of your plans for them?'

THE ARMIES OF SUMMER, SPRING, AND WINTER WILL ATTACK AS HARD AND AS FAST AS THEY CAN. I WILL JOIN THEM LATER. Garvin headed for the portal on the mountainside.

'where are we going? much has to be organized.'

TO VISIT MY UNCLE. I HAVE FAMILY QUESTIONS.
Garvin didn't want to think of what he did as running away,
but he couldn't remain on that world. Guitars was something
he had invented himself and that responsibility scared him.

CHAPTER

Four

God and Goblins met privately on a world adjacent to the City Out Of Time. Three Goblins stood on a grassy lawn in a vast overgrown park. The God had chosen to appear as the Seeker of Worlds. He stood a short distance from the Goblins on a small hillock, wearing safari clothes, his thick beard tinged with gray. As he watched the green-skinned aliens, his eyes crinkled like those of a man who had seen too much sun.

No humans had ever been on this world except for a few park keepers and their families scattered over the surface of the planet and unable to leave. None of them were anywhere near this meeting. But behind the Seeker of Worlds, sometimes approaching close enough to stick their hands in his pockets for sugar, sometimes looking at the Goblins but never coming close to them, were several dozen naked brown figures.

Tom and Mary would have recognized some of them as children they had cared for who now were fully grown. Adult Swift Ones were tall with copper manes on their heads, not telepathic nor even human in intelligence. Smart as dogs, beautiful as horses, they frisked and seemed to pick up nothing of the exchange.

One of the Goblins narrowed its yellow eyes to slits and began the meeting. Forming a crude image of the angry kid with the yellow comb of hair, it told the God, YOUR SON.

IF YOU BRING ME HIS HEAD, I WILL ASSUME HE IS NO SON OF MINE.

An image followed of the stick figure Garvin in the Market, in the Palace, walking free in the City Out Of Time. WHY? was the question.

FOR REASONS OF MY OWN. WE HAVE BEEN THROUGH THIS BEFORE. I UNDERSTAND THAT HE VEXES YOU. BUT HE IS NOT INVULNERABLE.

The Goblins stood absolutely still, except for one whose tiny green ears twitched as it formed what looked like pencil cartoons of the Talking Suitcase, the Rose and Thorn and their Companions. ALSO YOURS. FORMED LONG AGO.

YES, I CREATED THEM IN A MOMENTARY LAPSE. BUT IN ALL THE GENERATIONS IN WHICH THEY HAVE EXISTED, HOW MUCH HAVE THEY EVER SLOWED DOWN YOUR HARVESTING? AND HAVE THEY EVER HARMED A GOBLIN?

The Goblins seemed to consider that for a moment, then one showed the God an image from its mind: a Companion, partly vivisected but still alive, his eyes mad with pain, his mind begging for death. Again as seen by the aliens, the human was no more than a two-dimensional sketch. The God watched carefully, though, as the Goblin showed what had been extracted from the twenty-year-old's memory.

That Companion, before his capture, had commanded a raiding party operating independently deep in Rider territory. Again and again while tumbling between portals in Time, that Companion had felt himself seized, his senses scrambled. Repeatedly, the Companion had been shown Herself's Rider's chateau and his own raiding party going there. The Companion saw them rescue a new Steed before he could be broken by his Rider and saw them cast him into Time. The God saw the leader of the raiding party follow these instructions. He recognized the Steed they rescued as his son, Garvin.

The God understood that the Goblins were complaining to

him that the Companion had seen the entity called the Oracle. They were angry at the God for having created it. He wanted to believe the Oracle didn't exist, but there was something powerfully familiar about it, something he had almost been made to forget. Even trying to think about that made him shift his stance uncomfortably. The Swift Ones stirred; more of them appeared.

Not wishing to deal with denying that he had created the Oracle, the Seeker of Worlds chose to misunderstand the problem. WE HAVE BEEN THROUGH ALL THIS BEFORE. MY SON WAS RESCUED AFTER YOU PLANTED THAT PARASITE IN HIM. THE BASIC CONTRACT SAID YOU WOULD NOT HARM ME OR MINE AS LONG AS OUR PARTNERSHIP LASTED. IF MY SON HAS BROKEN THE CONTRACT, THEN SO HAVE YOU.

The three Goblins stared at him. BASIC CONTRACT, the first one told him. BASIC CONTRACT SAID NOTHING ABOUT IMMORTALS, OR ORACLE, OR WARCHILD. The God saw a caricatured figure. Despite ordinary 1920s clothes and haircut, this looked not unlike the image of Garvin. But instead of anger this one showed wariness that was almost fear, cunning a step short of desperation.

That young man standing like a trapped beast, the God knew, was him, Brian Garvin, in his first meeting with the Goblins. It had occurred right about where they now stood, at a time before there wasn't much more of Time beyond that one world and a mirror image of Lady Tagent's Crawing room.

I REMEMBER THE TERMS OF THE BASIC CONTRACT, the God told them.

BASIC CONTRACT, the Goblin repeated and showed the infinite worlds, each with children able to read minds. As many as the God created, it was never enough. YOUNG TELEPATHS FIT FOR HARVESTING. YOUNG TELEPATHS FIT FOR RIDING. NOTHING ABOUT IMMORTALS, NOTHING ABOUT ORACLES.

MY CREATING WORLDS FULL OF TELEPATHS WAS ONLY ONE OF THE TERMS. Brian Garvin remembered himself so infinitely long ago that it could as easily have been only days before. He had been a young man who thought he was going to find new wonders in a universe beyond his own. Instead the first world he created had drawn the Goblins to him. He was never sure how they had sensed his presence, around the void where universes joined. But they were drawn like flies to cow flop.

The ones he called the Goblins had been on an expedition that was somewhere between fuel exploration and piracy. Brian Garvin had never been entirely sure what had happened to them, but they were marooned and fairly desperate themselves. They had wanted an entrance to his own world. Judging from him, they thought it would be a good place to harvest minds to fuel their Winds.

It was the Winds that powered their ships through hyperspace. The Winds absorbed the kinetic energy of minds. The more of what was called telepathy that those minds contained the better. The God looked up to where even in the noonday sun he could see a satellite shining like a star. Up there was the Cave of Winds. With well-fed Winds, the Goblins were able to power their ships and carry on exploration and trade to the stars.

YOU CREATING WORLDS WAS THE TERM, a Goblin told him. In all the generations he had dealt with these green pirates, the God of the City could only just tell them apart. This one was a little taller, perhaps older than the others, and wore a black instead of yellow garment. Privately he called that one Black Robe. It had been present at those original negotiations.

THAT TERM ALLOWED YOU TO SURVIVE, Black Robe told him. It showed a cartoon image of young Brian Garvin before he had become all the Gods of the City Out Of Time, promising to create worlds rich in telepathic human life. On the grass near that original meeting lay the bloody corpses of half a dozen of the original Swift Ones, their stomachs devoured by the Goblins. There were other ways for the Goblins to get their food. But by observing young Brian Garvin's reaction to their casual brutality, they had discovered a double function, getting fed and spreading terror all at once.

YOU AGREED TO CREATE WORLDS OF TIME. WE ALLOWED PRIVILEGES FOR YOU AND YOUR FAMILY, the second Goblin, the one the God thought of as the Aggrieved Goblin, told him. The second point of the treaty had been freedom from harm for the God and any children he might have. In return no human was ever to so much as touch a Goblin. People were, in fact, to be created with an inborn fear of Goblins. The one he thought of as the Aggrieved Goblin had been manhandled by the Warchild on his visit to the City. It was still angry at not having been allowed to eat the living heart of the boy while his father watched.

PRIVILEGE FOR YOUR WORLD, the Goblin with the flicking ears told him. The God thought of that one as Twitch. It showed him the Goblins building the City Out Of Time. It was a duplicate of the space station that circled above them, but hanging in Time halfway between the Swift Ones' world and the one from which Brian Garvin had come. That too was part of the agreement: none of them got to his home world.

The first thing young Brian Garvin had created when he had left his own world was a mirror image of Lady Tagent's drawing room. He hadn't even intended to do it, but there it sat, a fire going, late afternoon light at the French windows, and nothing outside them but cold and infinite emptiness. For a long while he had sat hardly daring to think about it, much less step into Time. At last he had decided that, if the drawing room was nothing more than a reflection of his own mind, he could create something more.

He had a couple of false starts, dead worlds with unbreathable air, grotesque planets populated by monsters. Those he had destroyed. Something else happened there which he couldn't remember. What he did recall was that at the moment he created this Eden with its Swift Ones halfway between Sidhe and centaurs, the Goblins had appeared. It had made Brian Garvin, that angry young man, weep to see them tear the flesh off his children. Even their Winds when they touched him were not as horrifying. In fact, they seemed not to want to do him harm.

Though he had thought when he left it that his world could go to hell, he could not, when it came down to it, let the Goblins in. Besides, what would they do with him when they had looted it? So to safeguard that and distract the Goblins he had created all the thousands of worlds of Time.

The agreement had lasted until the third year of his son's

rebellion. As the Seeker of Worlds saw the image of the three Goblins hanged by the Warchild floating in the air, he knew it was all but over. YOUR SON AND YOUR ORACLE HAVE TAKEN GOBLIN LIVES, the Aggrieved Goblin told him. THE SUPPLY OF TELEPATHS TO MARKET HAS DRIED UP. THE TREATY HAS BEEN BROKEN. WE HAVE THE RIGHT TO SEE YOUR WORLD.

The God formed the image of brown long-legged people. The Swift Ones stood in single file off to the side. At the command, they moved slowly at first, stamping down in unison with each step, moving more quickly as the Goblins started climbing the hill. It was a dance that they did, prancing faster as they passed between God and Goblins. The original Swift Ones had included many with a certain telepathy. The Winds had stripped their minds away and left their corpses rotting in the sun. Over the centuries, the God had bred new talents and abilities in his first and favorite creatures.

Having passed to the other side of the God, they turned and faced the yellow-eyed Goblins. All leaped in the air and came down on their heels at the same moment. The ground shifted; the earth tore itself open at the foot of the hill. A long chasm ten feet wide and hundreds of feet deep stretched between them and the Goblins.

The God looked up at the sky and the Goblin satellite. IF YOU CAN JUST BE PATIENT, he told the green creatures, I PROMISE A FEAST FOR YOUR WINDS SUCH AS YOU HAVE NEVER KNOWN. THE WARCHILD GATHERS FODDER FROM ALL OVER TIME AND BRINGS IT TO ECHBATTAN'S WORLD. I WILL TELL YOU WHEN THE MOMENT IS RIGHT TO GO AND HARVEST HIS ARMY LIKE WHEAT.

The Goblins halted, staring into the pit. NOT POSSIBLE, Black Robe told him, WE WILL NOT TAKE THE WINDS INTO TIME.

"Think it over before giving me your answer," a voice said. The Goblins looked up, but the Seeker of Worlds was gone. All that was to be seen was the herd of Swift Ones disappearing into the parkland. The three Goblins made no attempt to follow. High above, satellite cameras tracked the Swift Ones, but even they could not tell which one was Brian Garvin. Nor could they tell the exact point at which he picked up two tiny children and carried them through a secret portal to the drawing room in his private quarters.

Out in late summer, Doria's company marched from one portal to another, then tumbled in Time from one world to the next. Along the route they would pick up the image of the Warchild and feel the question, WHO GOES? of lone Companion sentries posted to point the way to Echbattan's world.

STICKS APPRENTICE COMPANY, OCTOBER CORPS, ARMY OF AUTUMN, would come Doria's answer. In her place at the head of Green Stick platoon Lex still felt a thrill at their name. Commander Doria usually had her old platoon up front where she could keep watch on it. Always Nick was at Lex's side like a shadow as they moved through chill drizzle, slogged over mud fields, were attacked by mosquitoes large as dimes, fought blisters, dysentery, frostbite, and heatstroke.

On one world they marched down the deserted street of a medieval village and passed the foundations of a squat castle burned out by napalm. OPEN ORDER, SCAN THE SKIES, a Companion mind somewhere on a hill nearby warned. THE ZOMBIES HERE GOT AIR POWER.

Beyond the village, past places where the grass was burned black, the air shimmered between two rocks. PORTAL. ROPES OUT, was Doria's order. In the packs of Lex and the other platoon commanders were sixty-foot lengths of nylon cord. They pulled these out, unraveled and tossed them toward their units without looking. Hands caught the cords and minds steeled themselves against the emptiness of Time with an image of Garvin Warchild. Huge, he strode across worlds like they were pebbles on a beach.

GREEN STICK FIRST, THEN SILVER, Doria commanded and stepped aside to let them past. "Easy jump," Lex heard Nick, the constant mentor, murmur in her ear. "Otherwise she wouldn't let us go first."

Through every portal was the same dead emptiness, the dull thudding beat of Time. Tumbling between worlds, Lex reached into her image of the mirrored room like someone drowning and felt heat. She grabbed for that and found sunlight and another portal. It opened onto a flat, hot plain a quarter of an hour earlier into summer than the world they had left. TROPICAL GEAR, Doria ordered and Stick Company stuffed jackets, pants, and boots into their backpacks, got on shorts and sneakers, broke out fatigue hats to ward off sunstroke, and filled canteens from a muddy trickle in a streambed.

A sign scratched on a wooden board read "6 Kill-ometers" and pointed away from the afternoon sun. As they marched, Lex could see something dark moving against the sun-brown prairie grass. Small herds of buffalo, bunches of wild sheep had fled as they approached. She couldn't judge distance, but this looked like something much more deliberate.

She never felt Nick use his telepathy. But when she pointed to the dark shape, he whispered, "Marching column." Lex saw Doria quicken her stride, move out in front. HALT. PREPARE TO FORM A DEFENSIVE RELAY, she ordered. Other Companions saw what she and Lex had seen; their minds reached across the plain. KEEP WITHIN YOURSELF, Doria ordered. Hobbling still on her bad ankle, crouching low, she went forward alone and stopped absolutely still.

Lex watched, holding her breath, aware of the rest of the Companions, tense, expectant, wondering if this was the enemy. Then Doria was up and waving them forward. FRIENDS, she told them. Maybe it was the heat or Doria's own relief, but she fell in with Nick and Lex as they walked by. The image in Doria's mind was of little rivulets of rainwater coming together to form a mountain stream. OCTOBER CORPS ASSEMBLES, she told them and thought of streams running into a river.

Company D heard the other column singing before they could make out individuals in the glare of the sun. Lex recognized the song. It was the old "Stand By Me," shouted in a dozen accents. Probing, she found that most of the other column were nontelepaths, thousands of kids from a world of Kennedy and Khrushchev and missile crises and freedom fighters. Guided by a dozen Companions, they were frying in the sun, singing their hearts out as they marched toward Garvin Warchild.

Most of them still had their hair and civilian clothes. They felt themselves touched by the minds of Stick Company and stared at the figures approaching in the glare of the sun. Lex saw the tanned, Mohawked figures they saw, caught the recruit troopers' idealism and anxiety. Some of them were older than she, but Lex suddenly felt immensely protective of those kids. At the next portal were tons of yellow slickers and rubber boots piled on the brown grass. YOU ARE GOING TO FIND BAD WEATHER AND OCEAN TRAVEL ON THE NEXT WORLD, the twelve-year-old Companion in charge of the outpost told them.

In a London in 1899 on an early summer evening, Garvin searched the mosaic of minds for a Wind, certain it was there. He found a girl daydreaming about her boyfriend gone to the widening African wars, an old man who saw a regiment march past and thought himself back in '56 and the Crimea. Garvin skimmed minds filled with buying and selling, trading and promising everything from ostrich feathers to a bit of fun.

As he sifted, Garvin found a mind stealing a Latin sentence from another mind. It was someone named Christopher Beame, a scholarship boy at St. Paul's, a poor kid who had impressed all his teachers with his brilliance. Garvin recognized a natural telepath just entering his full abilities and having only a vague idea of what they were. 'like a goat laid out for a tiger. if we could wait, the wind would find him.'

Garvin, sitting in a carriage, touched the razor and prepared to finish his search. Then he felt Master Beame sense something familiar. The boy thought of it as a kind of invisible crown, one that settled on his head without anyone being able to see it. He thought of the crown as being covered with jewels and of each jewel as being a person. Some were from his London, others from places far away and strange. He had felt the crown before when he was only half awake and remembered it as a dream. Now it returned and began calling him away.

AWAY FROM SCHOOL AND ITCHING FLANNELS AND THE HURT OF BEING POOR AND THE BAD MOMENTS WHEN ANSWERS CANNOT BE TAKEN FROM OTHERS AND THE STRANGE DREAMS AND THE

GUILT OF AWAKENING SEX AND THE REST OF THIS WORLD THAT HOLDS YOU, it called.

As the Wind detached the boy's mind from his body, as young Master Beame's eyes turned back in his head and he slumped at his seat, Garvin reached out to the Wind and coaxed, COME TO ME.

The Wind hesitated like a dog that hears an almost familiar whistle. As it did, Garvin reached beyond the mind of Master Beame, past the dozen other Londoners taken in the Guvnor's stay on this world. He passed the minds the Wind had absorbed on other worlds, in Victorian Londons and Inca Perus and Mongol Chinas, amid prehistoric tribes and the Japanese provinces of Australia.

As he went through the Wind, Garvin could trace the Guvnor's own wanderings through Time. He found a burning busload of children all calling, GARVIN, and Zombies who died calling out for the Goblins to save them. The Wind blew around Garvin's carriage, lifted men's hats and women's skirts. The Rider was like ice inside him. 'no wind has ever absorbed a rider,' it tried to reassure itself.

HEAD IN THE LION'S MOUTH, OLD MAN? Garvin felt his uncle ask. RETURN, the Guvnor ordered, and the Wind streamed away from the carriage.

YOU WANTED TO SEE ME, UNCLE.

I WAS JUST ON MY WAY OUT. The Guvnor showed his nephew a young woman in costume posed coquettishly on a lighted stage. OFF FOR A TASTE OF CIVILIZATION AFTER THE RIGORS OF UPHOLDING THE EMPIRE. He showed an image of the same woman in the same pose but in a bedroom wearing a chemise. MARY BRIGHT. TO ME, THE VERY EMBLEM OF CIVILIZATION. I WONDERED HOW YOU WERE DOING, NEPHEW.

I HAVE FAMILY QUESTIONS.

MISSING THE FIRST ACT IS NO GREAT LOSS. THEY EXPLAIN THE PLOT. I AWAIT YOU. The tall man with dark hair and mustache broke contact with Garvin. He nodded with satisfaction as the Wind settled outside the open windows of his river rooms at the Savoy.

"James, I won't be going out just yet," he told his man, who waited at the door with his hat, stick, and gloves. "I just remembered an appointment with my nephew. He'll be here in a few moments. Let him in. You may notice his hair and clothes are somewhat out of the ordinary. He has just been traveling among the Indians in America. A very delicate mission for Queen and country."

"Yes, Captain Tagent." As always in these late Victorian worlds, the Guvnor fitted himself in as Captain Anthony Tagent.

The Guvnor recalled having sold his nephew in a slave market. It was an undertaking for which he'd been well paid, though he had no need for money. The Talking Suitcase had outlined the plan, the kidnapping, the journey across Time, the sale, told him it had been revealed by the Oracle.

The Guvnor thought little of the Immortals and the Oracle. He saw them as pawns, pieces moved without understanding why. In London society Captain Anthony Tagent was often compared to adventurers of the past like Drake and Raleigh. The mission that began with Garvin kidnapped and saddled with a Rider had ended with the Warchild raising a revolt against the Gods. It had been undertaken by the Guvnor in the interest of a higher power. An enigmatic goddess whom he tried to serve as a faithful knight.

The Guvnor put a smile on his face, shielded his mind as he sensed Garvin at the door. One way or another his long adventure in Time was drawing to a close.

Taking Garvin's cloak and high hat, Captain Tagent's servant looked right through the Mohawk and leather jacket. "Nephew!" The Guvnor stepped forward and shook hands. "That will be all for tonight, James. What can I get you after your long journey?"

"Family history, uncle," said Garvin.

'do not ask. reach into his mind and take it from him,' the Rider urged. The Guvnor picked that up, catching the fear and urgency the Rider felt.

"A long tale. We may miss the second act. Just as well. That's when the comics try to amuse the audience." Walking to the side bar, the Guvnor observed the changes in Garvin over the last two years. The Warchild had come into his growth; his face had gotten a bit banged up, which made him look less like a boy. Also his bearing was different. He had gotten used to command.

"Whiskey?" Garvin nodded. He'd gotten used to other things as well. "Soda?" Garvin shook his head. His uncle caught a trace of something like concern, a fascination that was close to being fear. "Have you enjoyed your travels in the infinite worlds of Time, dear boy?"

'stop his jabbering. get what you want out of him and let us be gone. we must solve the problem of the echbattan campaign.'

Garvin swallowed half of his drink and showed the Guvnor an image of his father facing him in the mirrored room at the Palace of the Gods. Behind Brian Garvin the glass showed neither of them. "Who is my father?" He asked that quietly, intensely.

The Guvnor sipped his whiskey and nodded. "A good question. We all wonder about the one who came before us, so to speak. To tell you about your father, I will have to tell you something of my own. There's much I don't understand about old pater, and I was born within the sheets as far as I know."

In his uncle's memory, Garvin saw from a small boy's perspective a tall, dark man who seemed to smile down. The man's face reminded Garvin of the Guvnor, not his father. Except for his eyes, which were a familiar light blue and not smiling at all. The Guvnor told him, "Lord John Howard, 'Black Jack,' as they called him, is what your father and I hold in common. My father was the rogue prince of late Victorian society. The Howards were said to descend from an indiscreet son of old George Three, although they seemed a bit too alive for that."

Watching Garvin carefully, the Guvnor continued, "I saw him rarely myself and only when I was very young. After that, he disappeared and my grandmother would never tell me anything about him. In school, though, I found boys more than willing to let me in on rumors of his delinquency and death. Madness, fornication, and bankruptcy were the main scandals of that age and Black Jack provided plenty of all three when he fell.

"Very dramatic it must have been. I found out much later that he had turned up filthy, bloody, half naked, and ranting in the streets of a small Irish town. From there he went abroad and within a week had killed a streetwalker in Marseilles. It turned out he had been a member of something called the Rings of Hell Club, a cult that dabbled in diabolism and de- flowerings."

Garvin finished his drink. 'what concern of ours are these stale scandals?' his Rider wanted to know. The Warchild stirred impatiently.

"Understand," the Guvnor told him, "that all of this took place on the first, the original, perhaps even the real world. The one from which your father and I came." Garvin nodded and quieted his Rider.

His uncle continued, "My birth killed my mother, and Black Jack's scandal killed her father, old Lord Tagent. It's in his memory and my grandmother's that I call myself Captain Tagent on these worlds. Most of the affair was kept out of the papers. But at school the boys knew with that instinct they have, and my father got me into quite a few fights.

"At first I lost the fights and got caned afterwards. Not the sort of thing I enjoy. I learned to win the fights and stopped finding out things about my father, which was what I wanted. Can I get you another, old boy?"

Garvin handed over the glass. 'if you must spy on the doings of the gods, at least open this one's mind to see if he is telling the truth.' The Rider's unease was intense. As his uncle refilled his glass, Garvin asked him, WHAT ABOUT MY FATHER? It wasn't entirely a polite request.

The Guvnor saw the flickering behind Garvin's eyes and understood the impatience of Rider and Steed. He smiled. "I'm coming to that. I only saw Brian Garvin twice, and on the first occasion I hardly noticed him."

Projecting his memories carefully, the Guvnor showed Garvin the morning of a fox hunt, the welter of dogs, the scarlet coats, the purple faces, the dogcarts and carriages. He recalled the yapping, whickering, shouting, horn-blowing, hoof-pound- ing din, the smell of horses and leather soap and mist and stirrup cups on people's breath, the feel of a saddle under him and the taste of excitement in his mouth. "It was 1913 on the Tagent estates in Ireland and I was born with the century.

"The term before was when I had blackened both the eyes

of a future bishop of Ely and become a young man to be reckoned with. I'd begun to discover the pleasures available to someone with a touch of telepathy in a world where no one believed in it."

Garvin saw crude, vivid memories of the hunt moving out, past the grooms and servants and ones too old, too young, too wise, or too badly injured in prior hunts to ride that morning. Then he felt, as his uncle had, the unmistakable sensation of being observed. "I had what I thought rather a sixth sense about those things." The Guvnor turned in the saddle and got caught in the gaze of a boy his own age.

This kid was barefoot, sandy-haired, and staring intently with Black Jack Howard's blue eyes. As the Guvnor's hunter carried him by, something hummed in the air between them. Garvin inhaled with a soft whistle as he saw his father, poor and gawky, young and intense.

"Those eyes should have told me something, but my father was a puzzle I didn't much want to solve. Looking back, I can see that my half brother had marked me out at that moment. But Ireland was full of mystery and resentment in those days. I'd taken a precocious interest in one of the housemaids and convinced myself the boy was a rival suitor.

"I completely forgot about him until a few years later at my grandmother's house." The Guvnor showed Garvin his memories of the place: polished wood banisters and carpeted corridors, an aged butler hurrying downstairs in front of the Guvnor, who strode through the house like its master. "And he demands to see Lady Tagent and will not leave," the long-ago man said. "I thought it best that you decide whether to summon the police."

"My grandmother had spent much of her time in her drawing room and garden since the family debacle. I was twenty and at loose ends because the Great War had stopped just before it could claim me. The family money had dried up and it seemed that I had become a great disappointment to my grandmother. I thought she had gone quite gaga. Showing a tradesman the door struck me as possibly being fun."

The Warchild saw his father just as his uncle had. Brian Garvin stood just inside the door, a little more than Garvin's age, dressed in a good suit and looking around expectantly.

"Can I help you?" Garvin heard the Guvnor ask, then felt him remember where he had seen those eyes before.

"I have something to show Lady Tagent." Hearing that reply, Garvin stirred in recognition of his father's voice.

"Merchandise? You have something to sell?" He felt his uncle recover, come all the way down the stairs, and stand next to a half-opened door. Through it, Garvin saw a corner of Lady Tagent's drawing room, the edge of an oriental rug, the glow of firelight, and in the ornate golden mirror the reflection of a woman beyond the French windows. "There's a tradesman's entrance . . ."

"What I have is not for sale. But I thought it might be of interest to this family," Brian Garvin said. Then he looked at the open door of the drawing room, seemed about to walk through it. Garvin felt his uncle move to stop the intruder and suddenly stop. The other looked him right in the eye and planted in his mind an image of an ivory elephant with a flag in his trunk. On the flag was an ivory elephant holding aloft a flag on which was a star and quarter moon and an ivory elephant holding up a flag with a moon and stars and ivory elephant.

"That was the statue I called Tantor when I was a boy," the Guvnor told Garvin. "Supposed to be something my grandmother had brought back from the East. It always stood on a table in the drawing room and I had never seen it holding the flag." Pausing, he indicated the decanter and Garvin realized that he had been holding his breath.

The Guvnor knew he had his audience, nephew and Rider. He poured slowly, tantalizing them, before continuing. "That was the first time I had consciously experienced another's telepathy. I don't know whether it surprised me most that your father could put a thought into my mind or that Tantor held a flag in his trunk. I had looked at that elephant a thousand times as a child and wondered why his trunk was curved to hold something but was empty."

Garvin remembered the hypnotic effect of that flag with an image of a flag with a sickle moon and stars held aloft in the trunk of a caparisoned ivory elephant. That elephant also held a flag with an elephant on it. And as they got smaller and smaller, the viewer strained to see them and was drawn into a void. For the Guvnor standing in Lady Tagent's front hall, it had been like plunging down a well into his own image on the water below. He had closed his eyes and staggered as the flags spun before him. As he fell, he heard the intruder speaking not aloud but mentally.

I GREET YOU DIANA, LADY TAGENT, NÉE DE VEREY, BY BIRTH AND DEED HIGH WITCH OF ENGLAND. The drawing room door was shut. Brian Garvin had gone inside.

"You have the advantage of me, young man," a firm, clear voice had answered from the garden beyond the drawing room. Garvin saw her grandson's memory of a handsome woman with a face like ivory and dark, deep eyes. "And with manners like yours, you doubtless need every advantage you can seize."

The Guvnor said, "And that was my grandmother. Once when Lord Tagent governed in Malaya, a gardener at the palace ran amok and beheaded his whole family. She confronted him and made him lay down his bloody knife. Her only child had died giving birth to me.

"Ever since I could remember, I had lived in my grandmother's house, played in that drawing room with Tantor, spun that ancient globe, hidden behind the peacock screen, set up lead soldiers on the carpet. I don't know how often she had held me up to that mirror and let me touch the glass with my fingers. I didn't understand that it was all in the nature of an experiment. All I knew was that my grandmother had been better to me than anyone in the world. And I was useless at the moment she went to her doom."

His uncle showed Garvin how he had struggled to his feet and pulled on the drawing room doors. They were locked. Garvin felt him try to reach out for the intruder. "I had no real control over my telepathy."

Garvin saw how the Guvnor had suddenly found himself looking through the other young man's eyes. Lady Tagent stood at the French windows, her garden hat off, static electricity making her white hair float around her face. She rested one hand on the frame of the windows. With the other she held before her a black stick ringed with thorns. She closed her eyes with the effort, and the command, GO FROM THIS PLACE, crackled in the air.

As she did that, her grandson was caught by her mind. Through her eyes he saw the intruder smile and reach into his pocket, felt him tell her, DON'T TROUBLE YOURSELF. I HAVE SEEN ONE WHO MAKES YOUR POWER NOTHING. He brought out a small piece of what looked like cloth embossed with glass. AND SHE HAS GIVEN ME A FRAGMENT OF THE WELL OF STARS. Smiling, he found the elephant on the small table and put the flag into his trunk.

Lady Tagent was absolutely still for a long moment. Her grandson caught for the first time a glimpse of an intricate maze that was the old woman's mind. Not wanting to tire herself with telepathy, she asked the intruder aloud, "Who are you? What have you done with my grandson?"

"Ah, my name if you knew it would do you little good and do me some harm. Let me just say I was sent by She who watched you all your life and knows all of what you sought. As for your grandson, I think I could call him half brother. You didn't think Black Jack would have rested content with the experiments of you and your little coven, did you? No, he had business in Ireland as well, the business England has always had there: rape and robbery."

Then he turned toward the mirror and said, "As for the rest, you have prepared this room well. This glass ground from the sands of Time. The peacock screen woven of Time's threads. The globe with a fragment of another world buried inside it. You spent your life gathering the pieces of another universe that found their way to this. And it amused you to place them out where any might see them and none would know what they saw."

He nodded at the tiny flag. WITH THIS FRAGMENT FROM THE WELL OF STARS, I COMPLETE THE PORTAL YOU HAVE BEEN SO LONG IN BUILDING. With that he bowed triumphantly and, laughing, ran toward the fireplace.

HALT! she ordered, raising her stick. Her grandson in the hall felt as if his head were going to split with the force of the old woman's command. But through his pain, he saw her image of Brian Garvin barely slow down before jumping headfirst at the mirror.

Instead of shattering, it seemed to fold around him and he seemed to fold into it. For one moment Brian Garvin was inside the mirror looking out, the triumph in his face replaced by uncertainty. Lady Tagent backed into the garden. For a long moment the glass shimmered in the empty room. Then there was a whining in the air and a huge explosion.

"And that was the last I saw of your father," his uncle told Garvin, refilling their glasses. The Guvnor saw disappointment and a hint of desperation in his nephew's eyes.

"That's all you remember about my father?"

"Except for what I've been able to deduce from what I've seen here in Time." The boy still wasn't asking the right questions. The Guvnor tried to steer him. "Have you sought out your mother and her people?"

"I haven't seen her since you kidnapped me," Garvin answered brusquely, obviously bothered.

"That might be something of interest to you."

"Listen, I feel like I walked out on her. If she's okay, I'm ashamed to face her. If she isn't I couldn't face myself." Garvin poured himself more whiskey, touched the minds of London outside: a party of Zulu chiefs in London to pay homage to the Empress Victoria, shopkeepers and soldiers, streetwalkers and pleasure seekers, playgoers and actors. Then he asked, "What about your grandmother? Who was she? How did she know how to build a portal?"

The Guvnor said, "She was something between a witch and a scientist. The memory is rather a sore point with me, just as your mother is with you."

GUVNOR. SHOW ME OR I WILL TAKE IT FROM YOU.

"Very well, old man." His uncle touched the Wind casually as he showed Garvin how he had bent over his grandmother in her garden as bells clanged and the house burned. "They came upon me in my time of weakness and old age," she said, her eyes bloody and blind from splintered glass, her body shattered. "Your birthright was to be a Tunnel to the Stars, the world beyond this one for you to conquer. I married your grandfather because his wealth and privilege would allow me to travel wherever I needed to in order to gather pieces of that other realm. And now this one has stolen it all while you gaped."

She traced a mystic pattern with her blackthorn stick. "Where there was knowledge, in coven and cult, buried in the minds of priests or professors, I took it. And it was all to be for the child of my only daughter and the man I forced her to marry. And that child turned out to be you."

With that, old Lady Tagent opened her mind and showed her grandson her life. She had discovered what she called the Great Sight within herself when she was very young. It was faint at first and always sporadic: an ability to see into other minds and bend those minds to her will. He saw his grandmother wed Lord Tagent for his wealth and willingness to travel. From all over the world she gathered the fragments that eventually found their way to the drawing room in Mayfair.

Her only childbirth had nearly killed her. The child inherited her father's dull and compliant nature and had only a trace of the Great Sight, a mild disappointment to Lady Tagent. Then she found young Lord Howard, a younger son of an old family, a rogue and a devil. Not an intelligent man, not even a sane one, but a man who possessed the Great Sight almost as strongly as she did. It seemed to her this gift was connected to the hints she had of that other world, that place of magic just beyond this one.

Garvin shared his uncle's memories of the old woman dying in her garden. She had showed him how she had raised him in the hope that he would inherit the stars. INSTEAD I FIND YOU ARE AS MUCH A WASTREL AS YOUR FATHER AND AS MUCH AN IDIOT AS YOUR MOTHER. The old woman tried to sit up. WITH THE BURNING OF THIS HOUSE THERE IS NOTHING LEFT FOR YOU TO INHERIT. YOU MUST FIND YOUR OWN PASSAGE TO THE STARS.

"And having shown me that I was a failed breeding experiment," said the Guvnor, "she died. The explosion that destroyed the house was attributed to a faulty gas line." Looking at his nephew, he understood some of his grandmother's disappointment. Was this boy really going to be able to rescue Time from Gods and Goblins? It seemed doubtful. "What is it that's driving you, Garvin?"

Out of his drunkenness, over the protests of his Rider, Garvin let it slip. He showed the Guvnor the pyre in the open plaza at Echbattan. He showed him the Immortals inert outside the City of Guitars and his horror at the grinding, endless death of the war he had begun.

His uncle looked very grave for a moment, then asked, "What happened to you in the Republic after I left?"

That triggered Garvin's anger. "They wanted me to report to the Retreat; you know what that is?"

"An island near the capital."

"A place they send brain-damaged telepaths! The patients there sent me this image and told me to come and join them." The Guvnor saw Garvin, tattered, haunted, hanging on to a piece of rock, looking up into a black night sky with an expression of awe. THEY THOUGHT I WAS SOME KIND OF APPRENTICE WHO HAD GONE BAD. I SAVED THEIR FUCKING ASSES AND THEY WANTED ME TO GO INTO A HOSPITAL.

"Perhaps you misunderstood, old boy." The Guvnor remained calm. His Wind swirled through the windows.

YOU THINK I SHOULD HAVE GONE THERE? WHO ASKED YOU?

"The one I serve," replied the Guvnor and went to the windows. "I have business out of town, as it happens."

STAY WHERE YOU ARE. I AM GOING TO FIND OUT EVERYTHING YOU KNOW.

"I'm not sure you're ready for that, Garvin."

The Rider told the Guvnor, 'there are many unanswered questions.'

"Always."

'i remember the boys' adventure story you told, but how did you really tame that wind?'

"In truth, by showing it this." The Guvnor touched the Rider with a distorted image of a landscape where sound was thick as fog, and pinkish pyramids that smelled of curiosity and were ringed with electricity.

'and i am to understand that led it to follow you?'

"Let's see what effect something similar can have on you."

And the Guvnor let the Rider see a huge creature with a

mouth full of teeth bounding high in the air, pulling its legs and head into its body in order to roll down a rocky slope.

The Rider gasped and went silent. "Time is passing," the Guvnor said and pointed to Garvin, who stared at him. "Perhaps new Gods arise, perhaps not. See me again when you return from Echbattan's world."

"Who do you serve?" Garvin felt the whiskey and the anger drain out of him.

The Wind was around the Guvnor. He stood at a window and said, "One older than the Gods, wiser than the Goblins. I will be waiting for you at the house of your mother's people. And if you have no idea where that is, you may as well roast on the pyre." With that, he leaped aboard his Wind and was gone.

CHAPTER
Five

The Goddess of Plenty stood before a fountain in a square that lay along the route from Goblin Market to the Gate of Onyx. News had spread that the Goblins and their Winds were about to pass through the City Out Of Time on their way to Echbattan's world. Huge crowds had gathered and all the population was linked by telepathic relay. Household troops loyal to the Gods lined the route out of the City.

Power in the City had recently been cut by ten percent, and the square, which was well outside Night Town and usually brightly lighted, was now in twilight. The Goddess caught concern about that and the fate of the City on the minds of the people who clustered behind her.

Worry for these people and for the Warchild had brought forth the persona of a dark-skinned Madonna with black hair flowing out from the shawl she wore over her head. Shawl and robe at first glance seemed a simple dark blue cloth with yellow flecks. A closer look revealed the flecks as tiny stars that twinkled and moons that went from full to half to silver to nothing and back again. The Goddess's nose and lips were large. Her calm, deep eyes held an eternal compassion. Be-

hind the mask Brian Garvin held in a private corner of his
mind the awful details of his most recent agreement with the
Goblins.

"Fountain of Plenty," asked a keeper of a hotel for nontelepathic mercenaries. "Why do you allow your son to strangle
the City?" The Goddess touched his mind, saw that the business he had inherited from his father was dying. Mercenaries
who had once flocked to the City to sell their services headed
now for the rebel camp or Echbattan's world. This was a family man, with a son and daughter in training for service with
the Gods of the City, as solid a citizen as a place whose main
activity was the trade in human flesh would allow. "Is he not
your son, Madonna?" he asked.

The Goddess spoke aloud; her voice fell like a haunting
whisper in every ear. "Assuming he is my son, are all of your
children subject to your will?" He shook his head. There was
an eldest son who had run off with a mercenary band and
never been heard from again. "Do not think that I am not
tested," she said.

"My grandfather told me," said an old woman whose hydroponic farm was not receiving enough water or artificial
sunlight, "that his grandfather told him of a man called the
Wind Tamer who called himself your son."

The Goddess of Plenty's smile evoked a peace beyond sadness and happiness. "So he claimed," she whispered to each
one crowded into the square. "And he claimed that Goblins
would bow down to him and the Winds come to his call." An
image appeared in all their minds, the face of a young man
with long black hair. He was upside down and his eyes stared
blank and drugged, hung like a side of beef by a meat hook
through his feet. They recognized the plaza in front of Goblin
Market, looking much the same all those generations ago.
Goblins lined up so that each one could step forward and tear
a chunk out of the living body with its teeth.

"If he was your son, would you have allowed that?" asked a
pretty Oriental girl from Night Town, a slave prostitute whose
master could neither sell nor feed her.

"If he were my son, could he have ended so?" In the Goddess's eyes were the tears of tranquility which she cried for all
of these refugees who thought they had found a safe harbor in

the City Out Of Time. The tears were also for those others before and after the Tamer of Winds who had sought to prove themselves to be children of the Gods.

Then the mind that had called thousands of worlds into existence became alert to activity in Goblin Market. Just hours before, God and Goblins had stood in the world of the Swift Ones and completed the plans that would send the Winds against the Warchild.

It was the Master of Battle who showed his Goblin partners an image of the Echbattan defenses, of the ragged inroads the rebel armies had made. He showed them how Warchild and his armies would be goaded into more and more furious assaults. Then, in total disorder, the rebel army would be a banquet for the Winds.

The Goblins, as Brian Garvin had long ago discovered, were merchants, not strategists. The equations under which they operated were that Winds could move quickly in Time, but the journey to Echbattan's world would use up energy. On the other hand, few telepaths were being brought to Market and Garvin Warchild had gathered tens of thousands of them, enough to feed all the Winds. The God didn't doubt that the Goblins had commitments to fulfill, interstellar ships which they had agreed to power.

That part of the decision involved some accounting procedures. The rest of it, the God knew, was more subtle. No Wind had been allowed out beyond Goblin Market since the very early days of Time. It had been awhile before the God learned that was because one Wind had gone out and never returned. It had upset the Goblins no end. When he saw the identity of the one who had taken it, Brian Garvin was bothered also. His half brother's presence in Time, his ability to tame a Wind, nudged a deep, sleeping memory.

On this occasion, just as the Master of Battle had thought, greed won out over Goblin reluctance. After a long pause in which his partners communicated with each other, Twitch's ears flickered and it asked, IF THIS FAILS?

IT WILL BE MY LOSS AS WELL AS YOURS. I WILL BE YOUR SERVANT, YOUR SLAVE, YOUR LUNCH IF YOU LIKE, answered the God. MY CITY, MY MIND, AND MY WORLD WILL BE OPEN TO YOU. After another long pause, the Goblins had nodded agreement. Shortly after that, the Swift Ones sniffed at the air as the Winds began coming down from their cave, that satellite, large as the City which sailed under the alien stars.

Shortly afterward, as the Goddess of Plenty stood with her people in the square, the fast, terrifying parade of the Goblins took place. Zombies and their servants went first, most of the ones in the City, marching past ranks of the Gods' troops which lined the way. The population was used to Zombies and barely reacted. Then, dozens of Riders rode past on their Steeds and the sight and feel of so many of those made some flesh crawl.

Then flags on the fronts of buildings stirred. The City which knew no weather favored fantastic architecture, slender spires and flying staircases, ornamental pools and colorful banners. Flags hung from every building, celebrating businesses, identifying individuals, honoring the Gods. Suddenly, all of them moved and there were Goblins, hundreds of them, each on the back of a Wind, floating over the avenue that led from the Market to the Gate of Onyx.

The half million inhabitants of the City drew their breaths as one. Telepaths felt the Winds like the hot breath of lions. They tried to lie low and to shield themselves. Ordinary people gaped in awe and prayed to the Gods for safety as the floating Goblins stared through slitted eyes and sailed above them on invisible dragons. Brian Garvin's mind brushed the Winds and again a sleeping memory stirred. At the same time, the Winds seemed almost to recognize something in the God. As the mighty procession sailed forth to destroy the Warchild, his father thought, "It's all up to Garvin now."

In the sudden quiet after the Goblins passed through the gate and out of the City, a voice asked, "Giver of light?" An elderly man wearing the blue and gray colors of the Gods, a pensioner of the City Out Of Time, raised his hand. "It was not so long ago that the lights of the roof were stronger. This square was always brightly lighted." He was a simple man asking a question, but his tone broke the mood.

The God of the City stood in a khaki shirt and pants, the blue robes of the Goddess of Plenty at his feet. Now the God had a beefy red face and wore a tin hat with the words AIR

RAID WARDEN printed in red. "Hey, buddy," he replied.
"Dontcha know that there's a war on?"

Out beyond Echbattan's world, death touched Garvin while
he was deep in Time. Not the Oracle with prophecies of death
on the plaza. That hadn't visited him since Guitars. This was
the death of others and came to him in a flash of pain like
white light. The Warchild felt a sudden vacuum where there
had been millions of lives. He screamed inwardly and lost the
image of the mirrored room with which he was Time Striding.
'a nuclear explosion,' his Rider told him quietly. 'taking out a
major population center.'

WHERE? Garvin groped for the nearest portal, seeing a
million burned-out eyes staring, hearing a million cries.

In reply the Rider showed him its mental map of the Echbattan campaign. The worlds still in enemy hands were dark
blue. The blue was cut by jagged red wedges where the
Armies of Winter, Spring, and Summer had driven in the defenders. Time Lanes, the passages from world to world and
on the worlds from portal to portal, were dark black.

The rebel advance tended to follow the lanes. Some of the
worlds along those routes glittered sharp as diamonds. Those
were the places where it was known the enemy had atomic
defenses. Several worlds were represented as glowing dully.
Those were places where atomic explosions had already taken
place. The Rider showed one of the bright diamonds flash and
begin to glow dully.

"i believe the blast occurred right there. on a world just in
front of us.' Another flash, another wave of burning death
washed over Garvin, who screamed inside himself. 'yes. that
is the world,' his Rider told him. 'they are scorching the earth
in front of us.' A third wave followed, a million more human
lives snuffed out in flames. 'the defense has begun in earnest.
our attack is coming apart as we advance. also, it is one of
your weaknesses as a leader that human death disorients you.
the army of autumn has to make itself felt.'

Garvin summoned the image of the mirrored room and
began looking for a safe portal. Again death crackled. Garvin
visualized it as being like flames, fire raging through Lady

Tagent's drawing room. The room burned up as Garvin tried to hold the image in his mind. Even with the Oracle gone, Time was no refuge. Garvin thought of the questions he should have asked the Guvnor. HE SAID HE WAS GOING TO BE WAITING AT MY MOTHER'S PLACE.

'the house of your mother's people.'

CRAZY. SHE HAD NO FAMILY. SHE GOT RAISED BY AN AUNT WHO DIED.

'i only repeat what he said. i am convinced that he knows much . . .' Another blast interrupted the Rider.

Hastily, Garvin summoned the image of the mirrored room again. It looked huge, vivid, seen by an infant who had seen little else. He remembered his father telling him, YOU WILL REMEMBER THIS AND RETURN HERE, and knew that was from deep in his memories.

As Garvin recalled that, he caught something from his Rider, a radarlike image of a huge animal leaping, spinning in low gravity. WHAT WAS THAT THE GUVNOR SHOWED YOU?

'i am not sure. it is necessary for me to consult with herself's rider. let us make arrangements to link up with the army of autumn.'

Out in late summer, amid the snow of an ice age world, the streams Doria imagined had become racing rapids as they drew closer to the Army of Autumn and Echbattan's world. Lex had turned Green Stick platoon over to Reban in order to take over Stick Company. Stick and three other companies now made up a four-company formation called the First Cadre Battalion of the Army of Autumn led by Overcommander Doria. That formation of young telepaths was only a small part of the thousands of kids climbing an icy cliff.

By remembering to make a mark on her knapsack each night before falling asleep, Lex knew she had slept on two dozen occasions since leaving Elgatto and the Valley of Bones. But she had lost any other sense of how many days had passed.

A supply dump at the last portal had yielded some winter equipment, but not enough for everybody. Lex felt lucky to have grabbed a pair of gloves. She wore every bit of clothing in her knapsack. Most of it was dirty, and all of it had gotten bug infested during a campaign on a jungle world. The vermin clung to her for dear life. Her hair, growing out in a spiky crew cut around the Mohawk ridge, itched unbearably.

Beside Lex, Nick, silent as smoke, carried Sung on his shoulders. Several other Companions, unable to keep up, were being hauled by nontelepathic recruits. They had requested and gotten the help automatically without false pride, knowing better than to fall behind. Everyone was extra careful on the slope. Even the rawest kid carrying an unloaded rifle which he had yet to learn to fire or the most scared Companion recruit yanked out of her bedroom by the image of Garvin knew better than to get left in a place like this.

A few scouts on snowshoes had been assigned to guide the column when it had tumbled out of the portal onto that world. Lex saw them up ahead, signaling the column on. As lead company commander, she linked with Doria, who traveled in front of the Cadre Battalion. Doria had caught the minds of the scouts, seen what they saw: an ice fort. Ramparts and towers, guarded approaches, glittered and seemed to waver in the cold sunlight.

Patches of black stood out on white surfaces. Around those patches, the ice walls were sunken; one of the turrets looked like a half-melted candle. "You see what I see?" she asked Nick. He nodded his head and pointed down. At their feet as they approached the crest of the ridge were dark rust stains, some drop size, some as big as a human body: blood. Both understood immediately that a Zombie attack on the fort had gotten at least as far as this ridge, and not all that long ago.

"Those black patches are where some kind of petroleum-based explosive burned on the snow," Lex said and Nick smiled with the good side of his face. It was impossible to probe him. It wasn't that Nick blocked, just that his mind didn't seem to be there. A lot of the other Select shied away from him, awed and scared. Sometimes Lex felt as if he were a kind of secret sharer, an imaginary friend like the one she'd had in childhood. But he could carry a kid with a twisted ankle on his back and still keep up with the column. And everything he knew or noticed he shared with her.

"Different kind of fighting than the jungle," he said. That

was where Sticks had been blooded as a unit. It had been back on a world where followers of the Riders still held out and contested the Companions' right-of-way. She remembered the rain forest, tried to recall the stifling heat now that frost was eating into her.

The Riders had kept that place sewed up for generations, Lex knew. The Army of Autumn had done no more than drive them out of the major population centers, to close down the slave markets and destroy all images of the Goblins. They had no time to do anything more. No one wanted to get stuck on garrison duty in the rear. "The Riders got out as soon as the going got rough," she said, as if working out a formula.

"But they left most of their Zombies," said Nick, shifting the weight of Sung, who had fallen asleep. "I guess you could dress them up but couldn't take them anywhere nice." That world lay along a Time route and had done quite well by the Riders' presence. The Warchild revolution was seen as nothing but a great hindrance to trade and an excuse for some of the wilder kids to run away from home.

Out in the hinterlands, Zombie-led guerrillas persisted. In the Amazon basin they were strong enough to contest control of a large chunk of South America. It had been decided that every Companion recruit who passed through that world had to go south and take a crack at them.

Stick Company had arrived in a fairly prosperous England and were immediately put in the hands of a World Spinner. This was a chain-smoking Companion in her twenties with a shaggy mane gone prematurely gray. The possessor of an exotic expertise, she had told them to grab their ropes, looked once to make sure they all had hold, and jumped through the portal with them holding on.

In Time, Lex thought of the antique globe in the mirrored room, tried to imagine herself crawling over the surface of the world like a fly on a melon. That was what she knew the World Spinner was doing. Somewhere in the bulge of Latin America, the Spinner found the right portal and pulled them out of Time. There, wilting in the sudden tropical heat, they discovered the other companies of what would become the Cadre Battalion, all as dazed and inexperienced as they were. They also found a Companion, obviously an Indian, wearing nothing but his Mohawk and loincloth, accompanied by a few local kids carrying guns. He stared at them long and hard, then spat and pointed at an altar. The life-size carving of a Goblin above it was green, not the pale green Lex remembered their skin being, but a dark mossy color. The details were right, though, the slit eyes, the long teeth. On a stone slab placed before the idol, stinking in the steaming warmth, was an offering of meat.

AN APPRENTICE, the Companion told them, indicating the flesh. SHE WAS FROM A VILLAGE UP THE RIVER. He showed them what she had looked like, her smile. He had obviously been in love with her. Doria and the other company commanders showed nothing, waited to find out more. But over five hundred newly minted Companions' hearts leaped in anger. The Indian pointed into the jungle and showed them the image of a village surrounded by a barricade of skulls. THE ZOMBIES CLAIM THAT IT CAN NEVER FALL. THAT THE GOBLINS WILL ALWAYS RETURN TO SAVE IT, he told them, and they were ready to run there and tear it apart barehanded.

"How long did the campaign last?" Lex wondered aloud. With the blinding white fortress in front of her, the jungle campaign seemed even more like a hallucination than it had while it was going on. The strategy decided on had been short and simple. The four companies, the twenty-four platoons, would sweep the area and break the Zombies. Guided by the Indians, they marched through the jungle, grabbing every human mind they could find and planting in it an image of Garvin Warchild standing on a rainy tundra beside a tree hung with dead Goblins.

"I think we were there maybe three days," said Nick. Already that campaign was nothing but images of green leaves and flashing birds, sounds of monkeys screeching, of a kid who had fallen into a trap and started screaming because her leg was broken. Lex remembered frightened natives, men, women, and children filing out of the jungle, eyes wide in the presence of gods more powerful than any they had worshipped. Lex recalled her hunger turning to nausea at the smell of food, the snake that slithered out of the brush as she watched, too startled to grab its mind, the burial of Allyn.

Silver Stick platoon, as the most combat experienced unit, had the point position in their company. The plan was to herd the Goblin worshippers into the village and once there, to break them with a concerted mental assault. Allyn, up front with the first squad of Silver Stick, walking out front in plain sight, having, Lex thought, something to prove after his defeat in the museum, took a poison arrow in the stomach within sight of their objective. In his pain and anger he lashed out at the villagers with an image of himself tearing the head off a Goblin and drinking its blood. Lex recognized the Goblin as the one she herself had sprung on him.

At that point the hundreds of Companions in the jungle seized minds, turned the people on the Zombies. The village chief was ripped apart in the bare hands of his followers as Companions paralyzed his mind. In the grip of their enemy, the villagers tore down their own defenses, screaming aloud the name of Garvin Warchild. The Companions urged them on.

Lex, standing at the edge of the fighting, caught the mind of a woman who had lived with a Zombie. She saw her fright, corruption, selfishness, and fallibility. In short, she saw a human being, one she could have been. Through that woman's eyes Lex saw another villager about to club her head in. Lex grabbed control of his mind and made him drop the weapon. As she did, Doria stepped in to prevent Silver Stick from starting a massacre. LET THEM GO. THEY MUST TELL OTHERS WHAT THEY HAVE SEEN.

The village was dismantled that evening, the skulls buried, the houses burned. Allyn died as his whole platoon tried to ease his passing. Again and again he broke away from their hold. Supervising a burial party for the villagers who had died, Lex saw in Allyn's delirium the porch of a tiny house on a wide pampas. The sunlight fell like molten gold, the grass baked in the heat. She felt, as they all did, Allyn try to get up and talk to his father. Unable to, each time, he remembered his telepathy and tried to reach out as Silver Stick caught him.

HE WAS THE STRONGEST OF US, his second in command told the others just after the pain ceased, the questing mind went still. Three night birds flew over the red jungle moon. HE WOULD HAVE COMMANDED US ALL, HAD

HE LIVED, he told them. Lex heard Nick beside her mutter, "He was dumb as rat shit, but you got to say stuff like that when someone snuffs."

Remembering that, Lex passed through the ramparts of the ice fort at the head of Stick Company, Cadre Battalion. The snow fort was no more than the outer defenses. Behind them were caves, miles of them. They were the real fortress.

From the minds of their escort, Lex learned that the garrison was a mixed lot, two cohorts of Roman legionnaires taken from a Dalmatia several worlds distant and retrained as riflemen. They were commanded by a telepathic mercenary, the sixteen-year-old daughter of a Hong Kong opium merchant. Her boyfriend, a year or two older, was from that icy world and had recruited the local ski and snowshoe patrols. Half a dozen shot-up Companions commanding a skeleton battalion were there also.

One of the Companions, a skinny kid with a wiseass sneer and no arms below the shoulders, stood at the mouth of a cave and shook his head at the sight of them. SLY IS THE NAME. LEFT BACK HERE BECAUSE OF POOR PENMANSHIP. THE ORDERS I RECEIVED FROM DIVISIONAL HEADQUARTERS ARE THAT EVERYONE ELSE IS TO HALT FOR THE NIGHT. EXCEPT FOR CADRE BATTALION, WHICH WILL BE TIME STRIDING IMMEDIATELY. Cadre Battalion groaned mentally and Sly looked at them with contempt. FUCK YOU. ANY ONE OF YOU ASSHOLES WANTS TO STAY HERE AND LET ME GO TO ECHBATTAN'S WORLD JUST SAY SO.

ECHBATTAN'S WORLD? Lex felt Doria ask.

WHERE THE ACTION IS, OVERCOMMANDER. He stood aside as they filed across mats laid on an ice ledge and into the damp, smoky stench of the cave. After the glare of the sun, Lex found herself hardly able to see. The Cadre Battalion blundered forward as Sly told them, ANYONE WHO IS ANYONE IS GOING TO ECH WORLD, THE WARCHILD, HERSELF. BE THERE OR BE SQUARE.

THE WARCHILD IS WITH HERSELF? Doria asked.

YEAH, EVERYONE SAYS HE IS SUPPOSED TO BE COMING UP TO LIGHT A FIRE UNDER ARMY OF AUTUMN. They filed into a vaulted cavern dimly lit by tiny oil lamps and full of the smell of wet boots, unwashed bodies, stale smoke, and something not unlike coffee.

Their guide showed them a red-haired woman on a big gray horse. HERSELF, COMMANDER OF THE ARMY OF AUTUMN. MAYBE SHE GOT THE APPOINTMENT BECAUSE SHE IS A STEED WHO REBELLED AGAINST HER RIDER. MAYBE BECAUSE BEFORE SHE WAS A STEED SHE WAS SUPPOSED TO BE A COMPANION. MAYBE BECAUSE SHE JOINED THE WARCHILD WAY BACK. MAYBE BECAUSE HE HAS THE HOTS FOR HER. SORRY WE HAVE NO TIME TO STAND AROUND AND CHAT. BUT I GOT TO LET YOUR PILOT INTRODUCE HIMSELF.

Sly stood aside and all of them felt the tingle of a nearby portal. It lay somewhere at the dark end of the cave. As Lex looked that way, she probed automatically and caught an image of a mirror full of stars. Seeing it filled her with such emptiness that she broke contact. Focusing in the dark, Lex caught sight of a small Companion with his face and eyes covered by bandages. I AM JOSS, GIVEN THE GIFT OF TIME STRIDING BY OUR WARCHILD. HOW MANY ARE YOU?

FIVE HUNDRED AND SEVENTEEN, Doria answered. Down from almost six hundred, Lex realized and wondered where the others had gone. On the cave wall she made out a scrawled graffito, "Grow old, why?"

THEN I MUST TAKE YOU IN TWO RELAYS. ALLOW ME TO TOUCH EACH OF YOUR MINDS. I WILL DO IT QUICKLY. Lex felt him flipping through them like a deck of cards. She remembered Nick standing beside her and started to warn him, WE HAVE ONE HERE YOU WILL NOT BE ABLE TO PROBE.

But Nick stepped forward and said, "Joss!" The Time Strider reached out and started to run his hand over Nick's face. As he did, out of Nick came an image of a white room with a dozen recruits, their faces scrunched up as they practiced telepathy.

YOU HAVE KEPT HALF YOUR FACE, OLD FRIEND, Joss told him. I LOST ALL OF MINE AT THE SIEGE OF THE FIRE GATES. I ONCE SAW GARVIN ASK THE

TALKING SUITCASE ABOUT YOU. IT WAS IN A PLACE CALLED THE ROMAN FIELDS. Suddenly, clearly, the blind Time Strider showed them Garvin at firsthand, standing in the morning sun, his arm bandaged, his nose still unbroken, probing minds for news of Nick, sad and angry when told he was lost. I WILL SET YOU ON THE WAY TO HIM AS QUICKLY AS POSSIBLE, Joss promised.

HOW MANY OF YOU HAVE BEEN TOWED BY A TIME STRIDER? Doria and the other company commanders had. After a moment's thought, Nick remembered he had too. BRING OUT YOUR ROPES. The platoon commanders produced them. COMMANDERS OF THE FIRST TWO COMPANIES, GATHER THOSE ROPES IN ONE HAND. Joss reached out both his hands. EACH OF YOU GRASP ONE OF MY HANDS. FOR THOSE WHO HAVE NEVER FELT THIS, LET ME SHOW YOU WHAT THE WARCHILD SHOWED ME.

They watched and Joss showed them what it was like to wake up without sight in a ward full of wounded telepaths, to see through the eyes of a girl without legs in the bed next to his. He showed them the hospital ward at a fort called the Fire Gates, caught the excitement, the stir as Garvin walked among the wounded. The Warchild had a banged-up nose and a black eye and moved as if he hurt pretty badly. YOU LOST WHAT YOU DID BECAUSE I TOOK MY TIME GETTING BACK HERE, he told them. IF MY APOLOGIES GDID ANY GOOD, YOU COULD HAVE ALL YOU EVER WANTED. INSTEAD, LET ME TRY TO GIVE YOU SOMETHING.

The image he showed them was the eternal mirror, but this time it was dark and lights rushed past, each flickering for a moment, then disappearing. It reminded Lex of the view from the window of an express subway car plunging through a tunnel. The rows of lights were distant worlds; the stations flashing past were portals.

Joss showed them how he had played with this image as he lay in his hospital bed, concentrated on it. Lex caught his feeling of Time, terrifying at first but a place where his blindness was no greater than anyone else's. NOW IF YOU WILL

COME WITH ME, he told them and towed two companies through the portal.

Marching could be hard, but the brute terror of the Time Striding was worse. Time made every mortal feel like nothing and amplified the knowledge that any or all the worlds passed by might contain your absolute double, no less real than you.

Any world, even one with the ground shifting under you from earthquakes, Zombies assaulting you with nightmares, was better than Time. There, all sense of self disappeared. The mind was gone, eyes didn't see, ears didn't hear. All that remained was a sense of infinity, of worlds like endless variations. And always there was the measured thud of the City, not heard but reverberating in each skull as if it had originated there.

Then it was over and Joss set them down in a pleasant spot in a pine woods near a lake hundreds of worlds away from the ice fort. Lines of tents stretched under the trees. Doria's stream was growing into a river. TRAINING DIVISION, OCTOBER CORPS, ARMY OF AUTUMN, he announced and disappeared back through the portal.

Before they could enter the camp, their clothes were burned, and they were deloused. Standing in line next to Nick, waiting for new clothes, Lex noticed that what she had thought were birthmarks on his left shoulder and his right buttock were tattooed letters and numbers. "Laundry marks," he said, feeling her question. "The first guy who owned me called them that." He pointed to his shoulder. "B-eighty-seven. I think the B stood for boy."

Over any Companion camp, wherever it was, desert outpost, under the stars on the great plains, before exhausted bodies fell out, the air writhed with teenage lust, bodies tumbled, sharp rebuffs got delivered, sparks of loneliness and longing filled the night. One of the two sex rules of the Companions was that telepathic Companions did not make it with the nontelepath soldiers. That was because coercion would always present itself. Any Companion found violating that rule was out.

That the pregnant wouldn't see combat was the other rule. The rules worked pretty much: everyone carried birth control and Companions and troopers stayed away from each other.

Mostly they worked because no one remained still long enough to worry about them. Ages like twenty-five and twenty-six were a mythic land. Everyone knew they were going to be dead by then. And all of them had given up too much, family, native country, world, to believe in a future anyway.

In the midst of all that, Lex found that the only one she thought about was Garvin. It wasn't uncommon: the Warchild was an icon, a mental pinup, the object of a lot of long distance crushes. But usually someone close by would do as a substitute. No one in camp interested Lex. Her only close friend was Nick. She didn't even know if he still qualified as a telepath, and from what she could see, Nick would be interested in boys if he were interested at all. He scared everyone else: a handsome face ruined, a telepathic mind damaged were things that made everyone ask themselves, "What if that happened to me?"

Sometimes Nick and she talked at night. On the second night at Training Division headquarters, Lex drew first watch and Nick came out and sat with her. He had traces of a street kid in his speech and attitude. But other things had happened to him. Once he told her what it had been like as a slave before the Companions recruited him. "The Riders infiltrated my world when I was about twelve. Without them, I would have ended up dead or in jail. Because of them, I ended up sold off-world. First a merchant kept me as a kind of toy. That division, you know, between humans and animals? It isn't there when some of the humans are owned." Lex thought of the kids at the Bates Motel.

"The Talking Suitcase explained that to me," Nick said softly. "I was a piece of meat up for sale in a local Goblin Market. The problem was I had some telepathy so I couldn't just be a slave. But I wasn't really good, which meant I couldn't be a Steed and I was too rebellious to be a Zombie. I changed hands a few times because I was pretty. If the Companions hadn't rescued me I was about to be sold either to someone who'd kill me for kicks or to the Goblins for Wind fodder."

Suddenly, Lex caught Nick's memory of standing drugged and bound on a platform, waiting to be sold for the last time,

of black-clad kids breaking up the Market. Then she saw a
vivid image of the Talking Suitcase, felt the leather bag as
Nick had hugged it. Doria, Elgatto, and other Companions
had shown her the leather bag carried by the tall old man,
shown how they had been touched by the presence inside. But
Nick had spent whole nights huddled close to it. "The Suitcase sang me to sleep a lot of times; that's how crazy and
wired I was."

Lex felt a touch of the Talking Suitcase's tapestry of young
minds saved and lost, of the short, heroic lives of the Companions. "It taught me to harness my telepathy." She felt his
pain rise, his breath start to come in sharp pants. Lex touched
him on the arm. "Watch it," she whispered.

"I never had it all the way under control. I pretended everything was okay. But I almost killed Garvin once," he told her.
"He got into the memories I had of the real bad times, when
they beat me, used me. It was stuff so humiliating, I couldn't
stand for any kid recruit to know. I had my hands on his
windpipe."

Lex could feel the explosion begin to rise, his body get
rigid. "Leave it there. Let it go," she whispered, rubbing his
shoulders.

"The thing was, after he broke my grip, he apologized for
not having adventures like mine," Nick gasped. Lex saw a
flash of Garvin very young and apologetic, saying, "If I had
anything like that to share with you, I'd let you have it."

For a moment Nick held his breath, then slowly released it.
He nodded his head. "I'm okay," he said quietly. "I wasn't a
real good commander. You're already a lot better. I got the
rest of my recruits killed that last day. I guess I died too. But
then Garvin brought me back. It's like I got another chance."

He fell silent and Lex scanned the perimeter until her relief
came up. She felt it was true that Nick had been summoned.
The camp was silent as they walked back from the sentry line.
Before they said good night, he told Lex, "You're summoned
too. You've got a part in this."

The next day was the first time the enlisted people of Lex's
rifle battalion saw her. All their hearts turned over and every
one of them in his own way fell in love with her. There were
five hundred military cadets from an 1850s Virginia. Shocked

out of their snobbery and racism when their world was invaded, they were savage, idealistic teenage boys, a lot of them still wearing their tall gray shako hats and bits of their cadet uniforms. Under other circumstances they would have died following Lee into the wilderness or on the hills at Gettysburg. As it was, they had volunteered en masse when Companions had shown them an image of the Warchild.

I AM LEX, YOUR COMPANION COMMANDER, she told them and felt their desperate homesickness. She saw herself in each mind, proud, beautiful, magic. For such base stuff as satisfying their own desires, girls from the towns, whores from the cities, or in a pinch their own hands would do. But when they thought of the higher virtues, honor, bravery, freedom, the sovereignty of the state of Virginia, each saw an image of Lex with her tall ridge of hair and black uniform.

Lex managed to keep her reaction to a smile. As she stood with them that first time, a veteran battalion formation marched by: Ibo youth, male and female, black skins and black uniforms, automatic weapons slung, boots hitting the ground in rhythm, two dozen of their own Companion telepaths leading them. Each mind held an image of the Warchild, his features changed to something like their own. A black Garvin stood in front of the mirror, worlds gleaming like stars behind him.

Lex saw her unit's attention on the other unit, felt their shame at themselves, ragged, untrained, armed with brown Bess muskets. Reaching out, she ordered, EYES FRONT, broke the spell. She spoke aloud then for the first time. "You will be as good. We're going to call ourselves Sticks Battalion," she told them. She showed them Nick's memory of Garvin, shorn and bare-assed, shivering as he was handed his first apprentice uniform. "That was the Warchild himself a few years ago."

In the days of their training and the weeks that she led them in battle, Lex cared for them, turned their thoughts from loneliness at night and fear before combat. She cut the searing pain when their bodies were smashed. Once they were out of camp and on the march, they got filthy and most of them smelled. Most couldn't shave and those who could didn't. There wasn't one Lex hadn't felt like choking at one time or another, and there wasn't one she didn't try to soothe when they died as die they did.

Training was brief, no more days than it took for the Companions to grasp the reins of the commands, for their troops to learn not to shoot each other. The Cadre Battalion Doria had led into camp marched out of camp and into Time as the officer corps of a reinforced division fifteen thousand strong.

Doria, commanding the brigade to which Lex's battalion was assigned, understood what things had come down to. "I have thirty-five hundred people under me, one hundred fifty of them Companion officers who have never led nontelepaths in battle," she told Lex. "I have three line battalions, not one soldier of which has seen combat. There's an artillery unit from Brazil, an electronics unit formed from a French resistance to a twentieth century Chinese invasion. If you survive our first combat, girl, you will be a brigade commander. If you march all the way to army headquarters, you will do it leading a division." She showed Lex images of a mighty river. But it was a river of blood.

On the morning of her unit's first combat, the troops were singing, "Going to Echt-banny," to the tune of "Oh, Susanna" and spitting on the *echt* syllable. The sight of the first dead shut them up. The Ibo battalion was the point unit of the division. The corpses of a couple of dozen of their soldiers were hung up around a ruined Esso station, each of them stripped and mutilated. "That's the Zombies," Nick told her. "In the Time Lanes, slaves and the dead are left naked in the sun."

Lex's battalion marched right behind Doria's headquarters. She felt her commander's mind returning to the dead Ibo. THERE ARE NO BATTLE WOUNDS ON THOSE TROOPS. THEY SURRENDERED AND WERE MASSACRED, Doria told Lex. THAT MEANS THAT SOMEHOW THEIR COMPANION COMMANDERS GOT OVERMATCHED. STAY ALERT. Beside her, Nick muttered, "Sounds like Winds? But they stay in the City."

It was later that afternoon that Doria's brigade came up against a section of a First SS Panzer division operating in the ruins of a twentieth century Wilmington. On Doria's flank, the remains of the Ibos and the rest of their brigade still held

on, but only barely. WHOLE UNITS GOT OVERRUN BE-
FORE THEY COULD EVEN GET IN CONTACT WITH
ME, Lex felt the commander tell Doria. However, the tank
command had taken heavy losses also. Their telepaths stayed
out of mind contact; the remaining armor fell back before the
fresh brigade.

Leaving the wreckage of the other Companion brigade behind, Doria pressed on into a hole in the enemy lines. Lex's
battalion was between brigade headquarters and the mobile
artillery unit. As they crossed an open railroad right-of-way,
Lex scanned ahead. As she did, she detected the portal and at
the same moment caught the minds emerging from it.

The images on those minds were gray and crude. She saw
Doria's unit as they saw them. The brigade stood up in rows
like corn. Some of them had heads that pulsed. Those were
the Companions. The pulsing heads swayed as a swath cut
through them; they fell dead. GOBLINS! Lex broadcast.

As she did, Lex felt Nick leave her side, head for an automatic-weapons section. She saw distant green on a hill: the
Goblins around the portal from which they had just emerged.
There was more movement on another hill behind the portal
and soldiers with Zombies leading them. The enemy was as
much surprised as she was.

The Brigade stopped for a moment, stunned. Lex felt Doria
think, FOR GOBLINS TO BE THAT CLOSE TO COMBAT
WITHOUT TELEPATHIC SUPPORT, EITHER THEY OR
THIS BRIGADE HAS MADE A BIG MISTAKE. She gave
her orders. ARTILLERY OPEN UP ON THAT HILL. FIRST
AND SECOND BATTALIONS FORWARD ON THE DOU-
BLE. THIRD BATTALION IN RESERVE.

It was then that Doria picked up the image of her troops
harvested like grain and saw some trees bow down. WINDS!
Lex felt her warning pass down the line like a ripple. Nick
broke past her at a dead run, heading for the hill. As he did,
he punched her arm. "Break mind contact with the relay," he
warned her. "Try to hide your mind in your unit so they don't
identify you. Get everyone firing at that hill. Make those
Goblins move their asses."

FIRE! Lex felt Doria telling the telepaths. ALL TROOPS
FIRE! COMPANIONS BREAK THE RELAY. DO NOT LET

THE WINDS FIND YOU. EVERYONE FIRE! Lex closed
her mind to the telepaths around her. Her own troops were out
of range of the enemy. She seized the mind of a pair of soldiers on a rocket battery. Through their eyes she saw their
commander, Reban, one of the old Green Stick training platoon, stand up with an empty look in his eyes. He was in the
mouth of the Wind, dead, slipping away from the world. The
soldiers were screaming, "Winds! They've got Commander
Reban!"

Lex shoved her way into their minds, directed their attention to their weapons, forced their hands to load, their eyes to
aim. FIRE! The rockets went off. Erratic shooting went on all
along the line. RELOAD, Lex ordered. Kids from the battery
were lying on the ground, crying. Lex heard a low moan go
up along the line. The rockets exploded along the side of the
hill. RELOAD, DAMN IT! Lex hauled gunners onto their
feet.

Then Lex felt Doria too grab the minds of the soldiers from
the battery and stand them up like toy figures. With her in-
fantry out of effective range, she fought back with what she
had. A moment later Lex felt another Wind, was aware of all
the other minds it had taken, four Ibo Companions absorbed
that morning, a score or two of prisoners consumed along the
Time Lane, hundreds of thousands of slaves devoured at Goblin Market over the years, a mass of lives consumed. She felt
them pull her out of her body like waves drawing her out to
sea. She heard the rocket battery fire again.

As in drowning, Lex knew it was death to panic. She
formed an image of the Goblin she had seen, thought of the
Goblin chain of command. Then Lex was aware of Doria's
mind scanning the battery. RELOAD, Doria ordered and the
Wind let go of Lex and took her commander.

Lex slumped to the ground. She saw an image of an immense hollow metal shell, the Cave of Winds. From across
the field, Goblins were frantically calling the Winds back to
the portal. Lex felt Doria's mind sail through the air, as her
body fell lifeless. Doria joined with the other Companions the
Wind had taken that day. Lex cast her mind after it. DORIA!
As she did, she saw a single figure in black run toward the
slope, firing. Goblins reached out in vain to stop Nick. One of

them went down, shot in the face. The others picked up the fallen one and scrambled through the portal ahead of the Winds.

The enemy troops, seeing the Goblins flee, broke and ran. The Companion brigade was dazed, leaderless. Doria and one of the battalion commanders were dead, the other in shock. Lex ordered her battalion and the rocket battery forward and joined Nick on the hill.

Thirty Select had died in a matter of minutes and Lex had her brigade command. She cried as they buried the bodies of Doria and the others on the ridge near the portal. In her commander's sparse luggage, Lex found a four-foot green baton. She stuck it upright in the dirt over Doria's body and thought of rain turning into a thousand trickles, under trees, in ditches, on suburban streets, forming streams, running into rivers on its way to the sea.

CHAPTER

Six

Somewhere outside and blocks away, a single voice, hoarse, demented, was screaming, "Die, Daley pigs," again and again. Farther off, sirens, lots of them, screamed away toward a distant emergency. A taint of smoke and tear gas drifted through open windows on the breeze of a summer night. The girl turned from where she had been staring out at the exhausted city of Chicago. "And you're with the IRA?" she asked, with her headband and long hair, her soft eyes and the curve of her cheek caught in the flicker of a single candle.

From where he lay on a mattress on the floor, her partner felt her as the calm center in a dark town where the only light came from burning trash cans and police cars. For him, the sight of her and the quiet of her voice kept back the dead emptiness of Time and its endless throbbing beat. "Oh, yes," Brian Garvin answered her and saw himself in her eyes as young as she was, wearing hair and a headband much like hers, the shadow of a beard on his face, a silver ornament hanging on a chain against his bare chest.

"Was it like this in Ireland?" she wanted to know. "I mean the shooting, the dying?" He knew she asked that to make him talk, to dispel an uneasiness she sensed in him. Already she had absorbed the horror of the riots, the bombing at the convention center, the police firing volleys into the crowd in Lincoln Park. Something in her filtered them away without her even being aware of it. That reminded him of something which he couldn't quite place, a dream that was always half forgotten.

"That depends on when and where," he told her. For a moment the God of the City saw another city, older, grayer, more scarred, khaki-clad troops charging down the decaying Georgian streets of Dublin. The God of the City had created thousands of Dublins, but that was the one he had first known. From those memories he had woven whole worlds. At that thought, his face and form flickered for a moment, his body thickened, his hair and beard turned long and white, and dark prophet eyes shone on either side of a powerful nose.

Brian Garvin caught himself, made her think that what she had seen was no more than a nightmare twitch after the long day of exhilaration and despair. "Don't let us think of that now," he told her, his voice low and musical, and gestured her toward him. The power unleashed when he leaped through the veil in Lady Tagent's drawing room allowed him to weave and reweave the world he had known.

But just as everything he had seen or read was implanted somewhere in Time, so everyone he had ever seen or imagined surfaced on his face and body. Lately Brian Garvin had felt himself begin to stabilize. The young man he was tonight was not so far from the young man he had been before he went from his own universe to this one. It was always easier to be himself when he was around one of what he thought of as the calm sisters.

The young woman stepped out of her sandals and jeans, slipped her shirt off, all in one motion that the candlelight turned into a ritual dance. Her name was Cindy. As young Brian Garvin touched her soft skin, felt her hands on his shoulders, he dipped deep into her mind. Somewhere in back of her perceptions of him and of this moment, beneath the details of her pleasant family in the Michigan suburbs, her college in Ann Arbor, the God caught a taste of strings being plucked, heard thousands of stars like diamonds on black velvet. Those things hooked the edges of something, evoked again a memory he couldn't quite grasp. He took these calm sisters to be entirely of his own creation. Without knowing how he had done it, he was happy that he had.

The God kissed her breasts, and that room and Cindy became all that existed. This was how it had been on dozens of nights, in bed with Garvin's mother Claire, with the mothers of the pretenders who arose and were crushed in Time and the mothers of all the poor by-blows who never made it out of childhood or off the world where he had conceived them. Cindy's arm brushed his chest and he felt her shiver. She raised her hand to touch him, but he kissed her fingers and rose on an elbow to blow out the light.

He had the mirrored room and loaded factor, with its telepathic message, already in place in Chicago. Brian Garvin would leave this world and return in a year and show the child what he showed all his potential heirs. Even as he remembered that, he knew that the child Cindy bore would be too late or unnecessary. If the Warchild fell into the trap the Goblins and Riders would spring, then he didn't deserve to win. If that was the case, Garvin and his father and Time and the original world would all be doomed. If, on the other hand, Garvin won through, then his father would have no need for any further heirs. So he was doing this for the pleasure and the company and nothing more. "What are you thinking?" she asked.

"I was thinking about you," he told her in the dark to hold the mood and keep Time at bay.

Garvin tumbled out of a portal and into a clinging early August night on the world where Herself was headquartered. He was near a highway access ramp of a huge airport not far from the Great Lakes. Tractors towed smashed planes away from the main runway. A line of corpses hung by the neck from the chain-link fence that ringed the field. All of them were human and stinking in the humid heat. All had signs in what looked like Arabic; one wore a crude Goblin mask on his face. Garvin wanted to spit in disgust but had no moisture in his mouth. He felt himself sweat and shiver.

WELCOME, WARCHILD! the Companion commander of

the airfield told him in greeting. WE HAD BEEN IN-
FORMED THAT YOU WOULD APPEAR. I HAVE A BUL-
LETPROOF CAR READY FOR YOU. THE ROUTE TO
ARMY HEADQUARTERS IS SECURED.

The commander had served the rebellion almost since its
beginning, had fought under the Warchild two years before.
Garvin hardly recognized the bright kid he had been in the
driven, harassed veteran who had spent the morning killing
traitors. GOOD TO SEE YOU, he replied and headed for the
limousine.

Just behind their leader, his escort, the ever-dwindling
number of warriors that went under the name of Warchild
Cluster, started piling out of Time. Most kept their distance;
the Warchild was known to be in a strange mood, most with-
drawn lately. Waving off the offer of a driver and an armed
escort, Garvin slid behind the wheel and asked, WHICH
WAY? Darrel and Maji got in beside him and he sped off in
the direction they indicated.

IS SOMETHING WRONG WITH THE WARCHILD? the
airport commandant asked.

EVER SINCE GUITARS, HE HAS BEEN POSSESSED,
Blaze replied.

'the last image of the oracle was a warning, not an invitation to suicide,' the Rider told Garvin as it had many times
before.

SHUT UP! Garvin started to mash down on the gas of the
huge car he drove, then remembered Maji and Darrel sitting
beside him, hanging on to the dashboard, and slowed up.
WHAT DO YOU SUGGEST? END THE REBELLION,
TELL DAD AND THE GOBLINS IT WAS ALL A BIG
MISTAKE?

'the guvnor...'

YOU DON'T TRUST THE GUVNOR, REMEMBER?

'herself and her rider...'

YOU DON'T TRUST THEM EITHER.

'the answer lies in your memories. and perhaps in mine.'

YOU HAVE NO MEMORIES, EXCEPT ONES FROM
ALL THE MINDS YOU INFESTED. He had begun to drive
faster. The road they were on was empty of traffic.

The towers of a silver city reflected pink evening sun. Dar-

rel had turned on the radio. The music was pipes of some kind
and percussion that sounded like steel drums. What they
played seemed to be a dance. Garvin imagined figures in
robes moving in a circle under the moon. Maji reached over
the back seat, twisted and banged around until she had the
fridge open, began pulling out bottles of cold beer. Somewhere back there, she found cigars and stuck one in Darrel's
mouth.

Minds touched Garvin's at regular intervals, then withdrew
respectfully. A security relay was in force along the first part
of the Warchild's route. The road they were on took them
away from the silver towers and curved through an area of
landscaped estates. "They were rich here once," Maji said as
they passed a lakefront mansion half burned out. On a lawn,
around what had been an avenue of oaks, wrecked tanks and
half-tracks lay under the black skeletons of trees. Garvin
knew he should care more about how this world had come to
these circumstances.

The pipes and drums on the radio stopped abruptly and
were replaced by a soul horn fanfare and a voice speaking a
language of which all Garvin recognized was his own name
repeated again and again. 'intense propaganda,' the Rider told
him. 'this world is not yet yours.' It showed him a nuclear
blast. 'there is an atomic capacity here,' the Rider stated
flatly.

NO SHIT, Garvin replied and tried to place the moment the
Rider had changed. He could still make it jumpy, but in the
days since they had seen the Guvnor it seemed quieter, more
contemplative. YOU AND HERSELF'S RIDER ARE
GOING TO TALK OVER OLD TIMES.

'something like that.'

Darrel belched. Maji blew a smoke ring. On the radio was
the voice of Bethel Truth:

> *Haunted boy stumbles out of Time*
> *With no news but bad news to tell,*
> *Saying Halloween'll be here soon*
> *Trouble in the dark outside town.*

Then, as if that had been a commercial jingle, a voice came on, loud, almost shouting in English spoken with a southern accent. "The Warchild orders us all to rise up! Throw off our oppressors! Let our minds touch yours! Let us show you the death of Goblins at the hand of the mighty Warchild."

"Jesus," Garvin murmured. Suddenly he heard two shots, felt two sharp cracks on the window next to his head. Against the light at the edge of an evening thunderstorm, through the ornamental willows next to a lake, three figures moved fast. The car wobbled for a second until Garvin recovered and probed after them.

"Snipers!" Maji somehow had a machine pistol in her hand. From before and behind them, Companion minds along their route reached out for the intruders. LET ME, Garvin ordered, brushing them away. He touched the mind of the sniper leader, withdrew as if it burned.

"You get them?" Darrel wanted to know.

Garvin shook his head. "It doesn't matter. They won't make it far." After a moment's silence he said, "Those were their parents hanging on the fence back at the airport."

Then, just when he wasn't thinking about her, Garvin felt the touch of a familiar mind. THEY SAY YOU CAME OUT OF TIME LIKE A WILD MAN. Looking up at a hill beside the road, he saw a lone figure. With distant lightning behind her, a breeze making the trees dip, her long red hair flow, Herself walked toward him in the evening.

Garvin braked and pulled over, remembering the moment he had called on her to rise up against her Rider. That had been back almost at the start of his rebellion. Herself had reminded him of a prisoner in a tower, locked into a corner of her own mind, allowed only to provide telepathy for her Rider and a living body to contain it. When she had felt his touch, recognized a Steed who had tamed his Rider, she was just able to throw herself off her horse. She broke her own shoulder and part of her Rider's hold.

He was aware of her Rider, the icy point inside her mind. 'greetings, divine master,' it told him. 'she thinks of you often.' Garvin ignored the Rider.

Some of that feel of her being a prisoner was still there as he encountered Herself now. But seeing her again, Garvin felt as he had a couple of years before when he wanted, with a fifteen-year-old's desperation, to have an affair with her. HOW IS THE SHOULDER? he asked, getting out.

'how goes it?' Garvin felt his Rider ask hers.

SO WELL I NEVER THINK ABOUT IT. HOW ARE YOU? She touched Garvin's Umbra and frowned. He touched her mind and was aware of it as a vast castle in which she had managed to open some of the locked rooms. They embraced on the lawn. "Shall we walk back?" she asked aloud. "I find the weather suits me. We can just beat the storm."

'things go well enough,' her Rider answered his. Both Riders used a part of their Steeds' telepathy and could communicate as their hosts did. 'i find i am an outcast among my own kind. i know that my steed is mortal and if this rebellion succeeds, there will be no more goblins to transfer me to another steed. i also know that if the rebellion fails the goblins will not give me another steed when they eat this one's flesh. but aside from those considerations, all is perfection.'

Garvin signaled Maji to drive the car to Herself's headquarters. Then he took his fellow Steed's arm and went over the lawn toward some trees. The very first time they had seen each other, when her Rider had bought Garvin as a gift for the Rider Garvin now had inside him, she had been taller than he. Now at six feet he was taller than Herself but not by much. Turning to look at her, he found she was still frowning at him, felt her wonder what was chasing him.

Two things Garvin recalled about his unsuccessful suit. The first was that she thought of him as a kid, loved him like a younger brother. He had thought that now might have changed. The other was the attitude of the Riders. His had been very opposed even to having her around. 'the combination,' it had told Garvin, 'is too unstable. neither steed nor rider is firmly in control.'

His own Rider's opinion made Garvin want Herself more than ever. Her Rider, though, had thought an affair was a wonderful idea. 'i will use all my influence, o master of time and space,' it had told him. That plus her unwillingness had been enough to make Garvin back off. But it hadn't made him stop wanting Herself. There was never a day he didn't think of her. As they walked, the Warchild let her see that. The red

head shook, the pale face gave a wry smile, but the green eyes
were serious.

'how goes things with you?' Garvin felt her Rider asked
his. 'the echbattan campaign seems to proceed apace.' He
knew that among Riders, these two were despised and feared.
All Time understood the implications of a Rider controlled by
its Steed.

'i have been thinking about our origins. our lives before we
were placed inside human minds.'

'we were created for that purpose by the goblins.'

'so we were taught.'

Garvin tuned out their conversation. "Are you learning to
get your Rider more under your control?"

She nodded. "A little more." She showed him passage-
ways, halls lined with closed doors with a single door open at
the end of one and letting in some light. "Ah, I'm not like
you, Garvin. The Goblins captured me when I was a Companion recruit. Then I was a Steed for years and years before
you showed me how to tame a Rider. It's only now I'm un-
locking my memories of the time before I was saddled."

They heard thunder rolling in and quickened their pace. At
the top of a hill they came out of the trees and looked down
the slope at the headquarters of the Army of Autumn. It was a
white Victorian wedding cake of a house that seemed to rise
out of a lake. Lightning shot through the last dusk and thunder
rolled. Garvin saw his limo pass saluting guards and pull into
the driveway, felt the minds of Herself's staff. Then he felt
something beyond the horizon rip and millions of minds burn
open. He staggered as they screamed like scraping metal in
his brain.

"What is it, Garvin?" he heard her ask very quietly in her
soft brogue. "What is it that's hurting you like this?" Then he
realized she was helping him off his knees, leading him to a
summer house. It was a miniature version of the mansion and
stood at the top of the hill, white and silent, with long silk
curtains blowing through its open windows.

"There's been a nuclear blast somewhere on this world."

The dying was still going on as she led him into the summer house. He felt her contact her situation room as he sat
down on a couch. She had brought Scramblers from the Re-

public also. She turned one of them on. Lightning split the dark and the rain came down. She sat beside him. WHAT IS IT THAT BRINGS YOU HERE IN THIS STATE?

And suddenly, as if he couldn't keep a shameful secret any longer, he showed her the Oracle's image of Echbattan's soldiers looting corpses of their weapons and jewelry, cutting scalps from bodies covered with blood and pieces of brain tissue. He allowed her to watch as the gold blade on his own neck caught a looter's eye. The soldier pulled it off along with its gold chain, tore the diamond stud out of the Warchild's ear. Garvin watched as the soldier settled down on his body like a raven. He wondered if he was already dead when that happened or if that came later. The man pulled the rings off Garvin's hands and stole his leather jacket. Someone around Garvin's size ripped off his Companion uniform and boots.

What Garvin caught in her mind was a caring so great that she would give him any comfort. She placed her hand on his chest, said, "Your heart beats like a bird's blown before a storm," and kissed him. Then for Garvin, armies and Time, Riders and Steeds, the lives of whole worlds burning, his own corpse roasting in the sun, disappeared.

While he was with this beautiful woman nothing could touch him. Garvin was glad she had made him wait. He had never needed her more than just then. She was right, he had been running scared. Now he just wanted to touch all of her, to make her kindness turn to pleasure. In a flash of lightning when they were both undressed, Garvin saw her body as pure white and her hair as black. She laughed and showed him that she saw the same.

Each heard the thunder move out, saw lightning flashing in the direction of the airport, smelled the damp on the screens, heard water drip in the trees outside in the other's mind. Their bodies linked; everywhere they touched brought pleasure. Then they were still for a few moments, except for their breathing almost in unison.

AH, Herself said aloud and in his mind. She paused and Garvin knew she was thinking it over. "The Oracle has never spoken to me," she told Garvin softly, soothingly and let him feel her doubt. "Do you trust it?"

"I have a feeling that was its last prophecy. It was never

wrong before. It showed the Talking Suitcase where to find me, the Guvnor selling me to your Rider. It showed that whole deal before it happened."

"Or was responsible for its happening."

At that moment, they both felt their Riders. His was asking hers, 'why else would it have this evocative power?' The two of them reminded Garvin of snakes stretched against sleeping bodies for warmth. He caught great agitation on the part of her Rider. And from his, he saw an image. Like a radar blip, a creature of light swam in a thick atmosphere, came down with outstretched talons on its prey. Garvin felt his own Rider's excitement and dread. 'it is us, i tell you. what we were.'

'no!' Herself's Rider denied it desperately, but Garvin could feel the outline of a memory start to form inside it.

Then his attention was diverted from that. Her Rider's distress seemed to release an image from Herself's subconscious. She and Garvin saw a long dim hall lined with locked doors. It looked much the same as the one Herself had showed when she thought of how much of her own mind was still hidden from her by her Rider. This was an early recollection, a hallway she had seen as a child as she was being carried along it. As that child, she had looked at the worried face of a beautiful woman with long red hair and green eyes. "My mother," whispered Herself. "Long, I have tried to recall her."

Her mother stopped before a door which opened as soon as she got there. A man stood in the dim light, tall, bearded and sandy-haired. He reached out for the child who clung to her mother. The man laughed, but his blue eyes never wavered. "Is Herself afraid?" Garvin held his breath as she remembered a mind touching hers, removing her fear. HERSELF MUST NEVER BE AFRAID, he told her and tickled her to make her giggle.

THAT WAS MY FATHER! MY MOTHER MUST HAVE BROUGHT ME IN SECRET TO SEE HIM. Garvin lay absolutely still as she shared her memory of that man. MY MOTHER WAS LADY-IN-WAITING AT THE COURT OF THE LORD OF THE AIR. She showed him a few blurred memories, recollections others had shared with her later: castle walls and computers, flying pennons and helicopters. All

the Warchild was interested in was her father's eyes. ALL OF
THAT WAS DESTROYED WITH THE COMING OF THE
GOBLINS, she told him.

AND WHAT IS THIS? Herself was so amazed by what she
remembered that she didn't notice that Garvin was up and
getting dressed. He did it fast, like someone anxious to cover
his nakedness. She recalled her father holding her aloft to look
into a mirror. The room, of course, was a duplicate of Lady
Tagent's. In the mirror the little girl saw her own image floating like a cherub in a painting. She turned and grabbed at her
father's nose. HERSELF WILL BE YOUR NAME, he said
aloud.

NAMING ME! she said and was aware of people outside.
"Warchild! Army Commander!" they called. "Baghdad has
been destroyed."

Garvin turned away from her to stick his shirt in his pants,
almost happy at the interruption. He kicked the Scrambler off.
ATOMIC BLAST? he asked as Herself threw on her clothes,
still stunned by what she had just remembered.

YES, WARCHILD. The staff officer outside showed him
images of the largest city in that world. Glass towers and
minarets, twelve million people. MULTIPLE EXPLOSIONS
IN THE HUNDRED-MEGATON RANGE.

Garvin was out the door. Lights were on everywhere in and
around Herself's headquarters. Behind the elaborate baronial
facade, he could sense computer terminals and technicians.
For a moment, Garvin thought of Herself as being the same, a
lovely facade behind which was cold and deadly truth. The
rational part of his brain knew it was nonsense. But that was
not the part which functioned after he saw her father's eyes
and recognized Brian Garvin's. He wondered how many other
children his father had lost track of in time.

'was it a missile strike?' the Rider wanted to know.

Garvin formed an image of silos and rockets. NUCLEAR
WARHEADS? he asked.

"Not so far as we know, Warchild."

'atomic weapons buried onsite?' Instinctively the Rider
tried to assess what had happened. 'activated by radio?' As it
did, Garvin again felt the searing pain of lives burning out. He
put his hands to his head and screamed as Herself's staff

looked on in horror. Darrel and Maji pushed their way forward and stood on either side of him.

'they are killing those people to confuse you.' The image his Rider showed was of Mongol horsemen using rockets to stampede the chargers of Western knights. 'they understand your vulnerability.'

From downhill came the message, WE THINK RIO HAS GONE. At the same moment they heard gunfire from the direction of the airport.

'perhaps there is an atomic device somewhere nearby,' the Rider suggested.

"Get me back to Warchild Cluster," Garvin told Maji and headed for his car. THIS WORLD IS BOOBY-TRAPPED, he told Herself, refusing to let her beyond the fringe of his Umbra. GET YOUR COMMAND OFF THIS WORLD AND ON TO THE ATTACK, he ordered. I WILL MEET YOU ON ECHBATTAN'S WORLD.

'this one is out of control,' his Rider told hers. 'if anything should happen to us, do not forget what i showed you.'

'how could i?' was the reply.

Herself looked stunned. "Garvin, stop a moment," she said. "We have much to show and talk about."

'listen to her,' His Rider told him. 'wait. i have things to discuss with her rider.' As Darrel got into the front seat beside Maji and Garvin slumped down in back, it asked, 'won't you even explain to her what you just realized?'

NO! YOU JUST WANT TO HOLD ME HERE. Garvin sat in the back seat of the limo. SHE CAN FIGURE IT OUT. MY FATHER IS EVERYWHERE. Feeling as if he were going to smother, he rolled down a window.

"Snipers?" asked Maji.

"Don't worry about it. I'm not going to die here."

They nodded, accepting absolutely that he would know. All the same they remained alert, scanned the sculpted treelines, the blank windows they drove past.

'you wish to die because you committed incest? i rode once on a steed bred through a line of mated brothers and sisters. it was faster than any i had until you.'

YOU THINK THAT MAKES ME FEEL GOOD? I AM TIRED OF BEING A PAWN IN DAD'S GAMES. THE OR-

ACLE SHOWED ME PREVIEWS. NOW I WANT TO
CATCH THE WHOLE SHOW!

Garvin remembered in the Oracle's vision how one looter
grabbed his long ponytail and used a knife to cut it and most
of his Mohawk off as a trophy. He remembered hearing a
soldier bleeding from a severed leg plead "Cold, leave me my
clothes!" in her death spasm. An Echbattani clubbed her forehead right on the crude "Grow Old, Why?" tattoo. A looter
cut off one of her breasts and another cut off a boy's scrotum
as souvenirs. Garvin covered his face with his hands. LOOKS
REAL GREAT, he told his Rider shakily. THE ONLY THING
THEY DON'T STEAL IS YOU.

'are you going to let warchild cluster die?' the Rider asked
and Garvin understood it was looking for an escape.

I GUESS NOT. NONE OF THEM ARE WITH ME ON
THE PYRE.

'we are on the verge of great discoveries. the guvnor
showed me a piece of my past.' Garvin saw that as another
Rider attempt to stop him. 'and i believe that you have the
power to shape time, to reshape yourself as your father does.'

SHUT UP! The image of his father changing faces as he
spoke burned in Garvin's mind. I WANTED TO STOP HIM,
NOT BECOME HIM.

'i have found my memories. herself has uncovered hers.
what about yours?' it asked. Then something Garvin began
being aware of back at the summer house struggled to the
surface. Elusive, primitive, it dragged itself up from the
depths beneath speech and rationality.

A pattern of moving dark shapes bobbed into the upper
layers of Garvin's consciousness, as evocative as a dream, as
cold as fear. He knew that he had once seen those shapes
move through a gray light in a world too large and new to be
understandable. Garvin remembered the noises he had heard,
long animal growls from giant presences. Then a voice he
knew was his mother's cried out and the wet, terrified little
animal Garvin had been raised his voice in answer.

'the primal scene,' his Rider said. 'all mortals fear the
knowledge that they are the product of no more than a tumble
of flesh. but you must be different. more depends on you.' As
it tried to calm Garvin, they reached the airport and the War-

child burst from the car. A Zombie attack on the far side of the airfield had just been beaten back. His exhausted bodyguard leaped to its feet. FOLLOW ME, he ordered. EVERYONE WHO CAN WALK IS GOING TO ECHBATTAN'S WORLD.

Out in Time, Garvin remembered the plaza. He seemed to float above the scene as a crew of slaves stacked the corpses in a bloody pile. When they were through, the Warchild was an anonymous form, covered with others' blood and his own. Throwing down bundles of oil-soaked kindling, the slaves lighted fires, then moved away to the next site. Someone nine-tenths dead writhed as if he were having a bad dream while his legs burned, and Garvin raced to work out that prophecy.

Lex came out of Time at the airport at dawn the day after the Warchild departed. She felt the tension of the troops, an excitement that bordered on frenzy. A hot wind whipped up dust. One crashed helicopter had brought down a length of the fence. Several other copters were wrecked out beyond the perimeter. A line of body bags lay on the field; dead Companions and regulars, mercenaries and camp followers intermixed. Several hangars were full of wounded, not waiting for planes, Lex understood, but to be taken off-world. That meant this place was a very temporary position.

"Let's everybody split! The Warchild has been here and gone!" a kid driving a truck shouted. The truck was full of more dead heaped in a bloody tangle.

Lex had inherited the divisional command just as Doria had predicted. She had gone ahead with Sticks Battalion as an advance guard. As she got them lined up on the tarmac, Lex caught someone's image of Garvin, his eyes wild, leaping into Time just before a Zombie attack ripped the airfield where she now stood. "We just missed him," she told Nick.

IS IT TRUE HE SPENT THE NIGHT WITH OUR COMMANDER? a junior Companion on perimeter patrol asked a more senior friend.

MAYBE TWENTY MINUTES, TOPS. Lex saw a summer house with lightning flashing over it and felt a pang in her heart when she understood what had happened inside. THEN

CITIES STARTED TO GO AND HE HEADED FOR ECH
WORLD WITHOUT EVEN SAYING GOOD-BYE. THIS
PLACE IS CURSED.

AND LOYAL TO THE HOUSE OF ECHBATTAN, someone added. EVERYONE'S WORRIED WE COULD BE SIT-
TING ON A BOMB.

The Companion commander of the airport, head covered
with stubble, uniform dusty, strode out from behind a hangar,
trailed by three or four equally bedraggled aides and asked,
WHO?

OVERCOMMANDER LEX, LEADER OF TRAINING
DIVISION, OCTOBER CORPS. I WAS ORDERED TO AU-
TUMN ARMY HEADQUARTERS TO REPORT TO HER-
SELF. She indicated Nick. HE HAS TO SEE THE
WARCHILD.

The airport commander, red-eyed, returned Lex's salute,
did an exhausted double take at Nick's bad side, asked an aide
in Dutch, "Don't those shitheads in October know this portal
is a one-way street out of here?" Then he told Lex, THIS IS
AN EXPOSED POSITION. I DO NOT THINK ARMY
COMMAND IS GOING TO BE INTERESTED IN YOU OR
THIS ONE. "God knows," he said to an aide, "Army Commander doesn't seem interested in much today." Then looking
into the distance, he told Lex, HERE SHE COMES. YOU
CAN TELL HER STAFF ABOUT IT.

A line of vehicles, jeeps, a convertible with a machine gun
mounted on the back, half-tracks, rolled onto the field through
a gaping hole in the fence. A couple of them looked as if they
had been shot up fairly badly. Lex noticed bodies hanging
along every section of fence that remained. Guards around the
perimeter saluted; Companions formed a relay and reached
toward their commander.

The convoy drew up in a semicircle in front of the portal.
The runway swarmed with black-clad figures and a few
brightly dressed mercenaries. A car door opened; a tall red-
haired figure in a green jump suit emerged and was immediately surrounded by staff. TRAINING DIVISION
VANGUARD, OCTOBER CORPS. The airport commander
indicated Lex's troops drawn up on the runway to a fairly
senior aide. One or two Mohawked heads turned in her direc-

tion; a couple of minds grazed Lex's. PUT THEM ON PE-RIMETER DUTY UNTIL THE EVACUATION IS COM-PLETE, a staff officer ordered.

The green-clad figure didn't turn toward her. But for a moment Lex was touched by Herself as the Army Commander reviewed the airport defense. Lex felt the impersonal competence of someone who had done this sort of thing often. Then Lex was grabbed by something else: the feel of a Rider's mind, a cold ageless reptile. She remembered standing in the parking lot on Long Island, holding the Goblin Chain in her mind. She remembered those Steeds, beaten and tamed, telepaths at least as powerful as Lex, reduced to living as slaves in corners of their own minds.

Herself caught that memory too. Lex felt the commander's attention stumble and return to her. Herself opened the outermost layer of her consciousness and Lex caught a whiff of sadness, a touch of curiosity around a hard, gleaming ruthlessness. The Rider in Herself's mind was like a knife in a velvet case. Then the two women's eyes met and Lex was inside the mind of the Army of Autumn's commander. YOU WERE GOBLIN TRAINED? Herself asked and Lex felt the other's sympathy.

'once turned, never trusted, as we know,' the Rider suggested and was shunted briskly aside.

I HAVE A MESSAGE FOR THE ARMY COMMANDER, Lex announced. I ALSO HAVE ORDERS TO PRESENT THIS COMPANION TO THE WARCHILD. She indicated Nick, who stood next to her.

THIS COMPANION? Herself fumbled as she tried to probe Nick. WHERE IS HIS TELEPATHY?

As if in reply, Nick showed her and the headquarters relay what he remembered: figures in recruit khaki moved across a park. One of them turned to Nick and looked very familiar. It took a moment, but when they recognized the Warchild, everyone gasped.

All of them fell into the memory of that cold fall morning, felt Nick glance around, aware of people jumping out of cars, of a dozen minds reaching for his. All felt the Zombie minds, heard the shot that smashed Nick's face and threw him into the long dark.

As Herself stood at the portal staring at Nick, something fiery stirred the hot morning air. A CITY SOMEWHERE IS BLOWN, someone announced. AND NEARBY.

'perhaps this one can catch the warchild,' the Rider told Herself. Lex felt its concern, realized even it was worried. The Army Commander nodded and ordered her, FOLLOW ME.

On the airport runway in front of the portal, two years into Warchild's rebellion, Lex heard distant gunfire and felt one mind tell another one, DETROIT WENT THIS MORNING.

"The radon count in this place is going to go through the sky," someone said. As Autumn Army headquarters staff disappeared through the portal, Lex waited beside Nick and scanned the contracting perimeter. Somewhere beyond it, she felt telepathic minds: Zombies, frenzied, willing to burn to ash on their world rather than lose it. From Nick emerged one vivid image, like the last one printed on a dying man's eyes: Garvin standing in front of a portal, scared and angry.

It was later that morning on the central steppes two worlds away from the airfield, minutes closer to Echbattan's world, that Lex and Nick stood in the outer room of a huge tent. Its floor was covered with rugs. A generator supplied a soft electric light. A soldier in Companion black typed on a telex in a corner, several aides stood at ease, motioned for Lex and Nick to have a seat. Protocol forbade probing a Companion superior, but Lex couldn't help reaching out to brush the inner room. Her mind wasn't blocked so much as shunted aside. A pattern of electrical signals caught her thoughts and turned them away. That was her first encounter with a Scrambler.

The walls of the room were hung with mirrors and silks. Art books, illuminated maps of the nations of some world, possibly this one, lay on pillows in front of a low divan. Nick crouched down and Lex sat next to him.

"This was the summer home of a Mongol Zombie who liked his comforts," a voice with a brogue told them. Herself stood in the doorway. An image in her mind of Lex and Nick getting up and walking with her was the invitation which drew them to the inner room. Seen this close, Herself was beautiful, cheekbones forming perfect arches, hair like a halo. Even dark shadows under her green eyes served to make them softer and warmer than they might have been. But something about those eyes was troubled, as if the commander of the Army of Autumn was struggling with inner questions.

A curtain fell as they passed into the room. The Scramblers cut them off from the minds outside. This room was small, containing a bed, a desk, some chairs and a table on which food and drink, chicken and fruit, wine and Canada Dry ginger ale were set out. Herself smiled at Lex and touched her mind. Lex inhaled sharply, expecting the reptile touch of the Rider. It was there, but very faintly, as Herself brushed Lex's outer defenses and asked, YOU HAD GOBLIN TRAINING?

Lex showed her the Bates Motel, forming the images carefully against the background distortion of the Scrambler. She remembered Vasa and her Zombies-to-be, recalled the image of Garvin on that frosty morning, her escape, the worlds she had crossed, the battles she had seen. IT FEELS LIKE YEARS AGO.

In return Lex received an image of a girl Companion recruit being hurried through what looked like a hospital. Doors swung open and revealed a gleaming laboratory. In it stood half a dozen green figures in yellow robes. Lex realized she was seeing Herself delivered to the Goblins. TIME CHANGES EVERYTHING, Herself told them. Turning to Nick but not probing him, she reached out and touched the scarred side of his face, saying softly, "You received that guarding Garvin."

"I led him into a trap. The bloodsuckers got him, stuck him with a parasite . . ." Nick remembered who he was talking to and trailed off . . .

'more important questions,' the Rider interjected, 'would be where this one has spent the last few years, and why he reappears now.'

IT IS THAT WHICH MAKES ME BELIEVE THAT GARVIN HAS SUMMONED HIM, Herself replied. I WILL NOT QUESTION THE TOOL THAT COMES TO HAND.

'his injury would seem to make him almost useless. her goblin training is an interesting asset.'

SHE IS SUMMONED ALSO, Herself told her Rider. DRAWN BY LOVE.

'it is his strength. all children love him. they are willing to die for him. he, in fact, is quite willing to die too. you saw his reaction to his rider's memories and to yours.'

Speaking to Lex and Nick, Herself said, "You are on a mission from the Warchild. You may not know it, but I do." She looked at them and for a moment her great eyes clouded before she said, "The Warchild is heading an all-out assault on Echbattan's world. I am sending you to find him. He will want to see his old friend," she smiled at Nick. "And you, Alexis, are the living spirit of his army. I believe his resources are greater than even he knows and that you are meant to save his life even against his will."

Then Herself stood up and looked at them with wide, fierce eyes. WHAT I WILL SHOW YOU NOW MUST GO NO FARTHER THAN THE TWO OF YOU. IT IS SOMETHING THE WARCHILD FOUND IN THE ORACLE. Lex saw the plaza on Echbattan's world, the bodies on the pyre. After what she had seen in war, it didn't move her much. Then she recognized Garvin's face.

"I would go after him," Herself told them. "But now I am one of the things he flees. When you find him, tell Garvin that I understand what happened and do not regret for a moment the comfort given and the memories shared with my brother."

Nick and Lex were on their feet and ready to go. 'excellent,' her Rider told Herself. 'more loyal to garvin than garvin is.'

CHAPTER
Seven

The lights had dimmed further in the City Out Of Time. Its air tasted stale; fresh produce was scarce. Those who had to go inside Goblin Market reported that the slave pits were nearly empty. Rumors raced from mind to mind about the decisive engagement of the Warchild rebellion. Simultaneous tenth-hand accounts arriving in the City showed Echbattan's world cut off from the rest of Time, showed the rebel armies in full retreat, Echbattan itself destroyed, the Warchild dead. It was known that a vital meeting of the Gods' Council was to take place. The population watched the advisors assemble at the Crystal Chamber.

Bystanders around the Palace showed greatest interest in the arrival of two members of the Clan Echbattan, brought to the City from their world by their Goblin masters. Dark-skinned, unobtrusively good-looking, of medium height and frame, the Echbattans had been bred over the centuries for physical durability, telepathic capacity and complete obedience. The older of the two was already saddled with a Rider; the younger was not as yet. As a car surrounded by an escort of Zombies drove them through the streets, both endured the probes and stares of the crowd as unquestioningly as they had being towed through the abyss of Time.

It was because of the first of their clan that all Time knew it as Echbattan's world. He had come out of a Persia from which a Russian empire was sweeping aside a Chinese at the beginning of a world war in 1892. "Short and dark as a cheap teapot, his face placid as a cat on a warm stove's" was how a British journalist described him. "But the man's a magician. Once under his wand you are bound to do his will." Russia fell to him and China, Britain, and the rest of his world went under too.

That was many centuries before, when Goblins first carved their way down the Time Lanes to harvest the worlds Brian Garvin had called into being. The original Echbattan was long dead, but the Rider who had guided him lived on in the body of one of his direct descendants. Echbattan's world was a gateway, a major transship point between Time and the City. Its inhabitants and those of the worlds around it had done well on trade. They were uninfected by the Warchild rebellion and showed little inclination to rise against their masters.

In the Crystal Chamber, the Gods had not yet manifested themselves. The Echbattans sat quietly in front of their Goblin lords, while Steeds less well trained than they fidgeted, twisted their necks. The Gods' mortal advisors, never entirely comfortable in the presence of Goblins, looked toward the doors which led downstairs to the Gods' private quarters. Everyone tried not to dwell on the fact that through the glass walls they could see darkness over three-quarters of the City. Once or twice Coli, the Chancellor, politely probed the attendants in the reception room. HAVE THE GODS BEEN INFORMED THAT WE AWAIT THEM?

Whenever that was asked, the attendants would go to the bronze doors of the Gods' private quarters and knock politely. Behind those doors, shielded from intrusion by batteries of Scramblers, Tom heard them. On each occasion, he stood in the hall outside the drawing room and called softly, "Your worship?"

All morning he and Mary had heard voices from inside, sometimes speaking solo, sometimes overlapping, men's voices, women's voices, young and old, laughing, whispering, screaming with anger, shouting enthusiastically. All of the voices were distant and distorted, as though traveling over troubled waters.

Several times Tom's and Mary's minds were filled with an image of a woman's face, huge and serene. Once they heard an agonized voice from the drawing room asking almost in a whine, "The lights fail, my magic dies. Why did you send me here and when will you send any other to take my place?"

Once a little later, there was an image of lights flowing like water over a falls and a hedge of roses with the faces of children. WHY, the God asked, DO YOU TEMPT ME WITH THESE HALF MEMORIES? Shortly afterward they heard a thump as if something, a body or a piece of furniture, had fallen to the floor. Tom and Mary knew that they were never to look or go into the drawing room when the Gods were inside.

Finally, after a stretch of silence broken only by one more faint rap on the bronze doors at the end of the hall, Tom looked at Mary, who nodded. The doors of the drawing room were slightly ajar. Standing a careful distance down the hall so that he would see nothing inside, Tom called once, then called again, "Your divinity?"

For a long moment there was no reply. Then the servant noticed that the crack of light where the doors were not quite shut had disappeared. He lowered his eyes and heard the door open. "Good morning, or, as I am afraid I should say, good afternoon," said a dry voice. Looking up, Tom saw the thin, gray figure of the Comptroller of Worlds.

The God's suit, the fringe of hair around his bald crown, his eyes, even somehow his skin, were gray. His frame, his voice, the gold-rimmed spectacles, the portfolio he carried under one arm, were thin. "Would you be wanting breakfast, Your Godship?" Tom asked.

"Thank you, I ate earlier. I would like a light lunch after this business meeting, though." Images of a salad and a piece of broiled sole entered Mary's mind. "The drawing room is quite disorderly," the God told Tom and headed for the bronze doors, which swung open as he approached. Looking inside, the servant saw discarded maps and books, empty glasses, an ashtray full of cigar butts spilled onto the rug. The peacock screen leaned askew against a wall. The little ivory elephant holding the flag had been knocked over.

All mortals and Steeds stood as the Comptroller entered. The Goblins stayed put at their end of the Crystal Chamber. "Be seated," the God said, planting himself precisely in a large armchair at the head of the table. "There is much business to discuss, as you know. All of it depends, however, on the report from Echbattan's world."

With that the Comptroller touched the mind of the Echbattan Steed. I BRING YOU WORD THAT YOUR PLAN IS IN PLACE, COUNTER OF WORLDS, TELLER OF LIVES, the Steed responded, rising. Then at its Rider's prompting, it showed the chart of the worlds around Echbattan. They saw in blood red the Armies of the Four Seasons spilling over the blue that represented Echbattan's Empire.

At a signal from a Goblin, the younger Echbattan kinsman showed them images from the tactical campaign. Spear-armed hordes led by Zombies had fought and lost along the worlds that formed the outer defenses. But each victory cost the War-child's armies lives and disrupted the pattern of the advance. In the middle defenses, on a ring of satrap worlds, technologically more sophisticated forces under Rider command fought and fell back where they had to, hung on where they could, went forward again when the opportunity presented itself. The rebels' advance had been funneled into several long, precarious salients stretching like bloody arms toward Echbattan's world itself.

Then the Rider ordered its Steed to show the map again and directed their attention to white lights on the blue worlds. Some of these still shone amid the blue, some had been overrun by red. As they watched, several of the white lights in red territory flared to a brilliant yellow, then flickered out.

O COMPILER OF OUR FATES, ATOMIC WEAPON SYSTEMS IN PLACE ALONG THE APPROACHES TO ECHBATTAN WERE DETONATED, DESTROYING LARGE NUMBERS OF NONTELEPATHIC LIVES. A few of his mortal advisors noticed a flicker in the God's eyes. IT HAS COST THE HOUSE OF ECHBATTAN DEARLY IN TERMS OF WEALTH. BUT AS YOU, ALL-WISE ONE, HAD PREDICTED, THIS ACTION FORCED THE WAR-

CHILD TO A PRECIPITATE ADVANCE. THIS IS THE CURRENT SITUATION:

Skimming the Steed's memory, the God confirmed that the rebels had broken through all the outermost defenses, the lightly held primitive worlds. In places they had smashed through the satrap worlds that lay inside those. From some of those, they had reached the core worlds right around Echbattan itself. In one or two places, the Warchild's Army of Autumn was only a few portals away from the central world. But the pattern of its advance was jagged, disjointed, the gains rapidly made and shakily held. A counterattack could break the rebels and roll them up.

The Steed paused and its kinsman showed images of troops, brutal-looking small units lightly clad and heavily armed. They stood in a city of rock and steel in sunlight tinged red by polluted air. AN ARMY HAS BEEN PREPARED AS YOU SUGGESTED, COMPILER OF LIVES. RECRUITED AMONG NONTELEPATHIC GLADIATORS AND CRIMINALS, IT IS READY TO FOLLOW THE WINDS. THEY HAVE PROMISE OF LOOT AND OF FREEDOM FOR THOSE WHO BRING BACK REBEL SCALPS.

All eyes, all minds turned toward the God. He chose to speak aloud, shielding them from his mind. "That will do for the rebel soldiers. But for the telepaths among them, one more element remains." The God of the City looked to the Goblins standing at the back of the hall. "Is it in place?"

The one he thought of as Black Robe stepped forward and showed the God and his advisors what looked like an ancient cartoon on an old black-and-white television set. The humans in the Goblin's mind were spindly stick figures standing in battle formation. Toward them over an open plain several dozen Goblins walked slowly. The grass bent first one way then another before them. Trees that looked like twigs swayed wildly and dust devils arose and were torn apart.

The human army was black-clad and some of the human heads pulsed slightly: rebel troops led by Companion telepaths, the viewers understood. Just as the first snipers in front of the rebel position were about to fire on the attackers, the grass and trees bowed in their direction, dust blinded them.

Their telepathic Companion officers realized what was happening and tried to give the order to retreat.

Everyone watched as the Goblin showed the pulsing heads being extinguished, snuffing one after another like small candles as the Winds feasted on the Companions. The nontelepathic troops broke and ran. From behind the Goblins, Zombie-led cavalry and armor moved out to cut them off. The God watched as the Goblins reached out and recalled the Winds before they started to consume Zombies.

THE GREAT HERD OF WINDS HAS FED ON THE WAY TO MY FAMILY'S WORLD, the Echbattan Steed told them proudly. THREE HUNDRED YOUNG TELEPATHS OF THE ARMY OF WINTER WERE HARVESTED ON THAT FIELD, THEIR TROOPS SLAUGHTERED OR ENSLAVED. NOW THE WINDS AWAIT THE WARCHILD. ECHBATTAN'S WORLD WILL BE THEIR GRAZING GROUND. AS YOU FORETOLD, YOUR SON HAS GATHERED YOUNG TELEPATHS BETTER THAN THE SLAVE DEALERS EVER COULD.

Many of the mortals sat silently terrified by what they had seen. Another Goblin stood forward, clashed its teeth, and showed them a human youth with hair like a cock's comb and an angry face. The boy's anger turned to terror as a Goblin tore his stomach open with its teeth. When the human was dead, the Goblin chewed through his neck and held the head up by its ponytail. TO YOU, GOD OF THE CITY, WE PROMISE TO BRING THE WARCHILD'S HEAD, the Goblin told the Comptroller.

The God of the City recognized the Aggrieved Goblin that his son once had held at knife point. HIS HEAD ON THIS TABLE MEANS HE IS NO SON OF MINE, the Comptroller told the crowd. As he did, the thin gray visage flickered for a moment and a wild hairy-faced creature looked out at them with mad red eyes. Then the Comptroller of Worlds reasserted himself. Gesturing very precisely at the darkened streets outside, he said, "And I estimate that when that occurs, rebel minds will light and power my City for several years."

YOUR WARCHILD LEADS YOU TO THE SLAUGHTERHOUSE. A Rider mounted on a powerful and docile

Echbattan Steed broadcast an image of kids with Mohawks hung up like meat in a refrigerator. The Warchild stood in the basement of a wrecked apartment house amid twisted bars of steel, broken chunks of concrete. He heard in the distance fighting going on for other portals. But the one held by the Rider was the key. If that fell, the defensive line would collapse.

The air was full of the acid reek of electrical fires and the all-pervasive stench of too many filthy, scared, and desperate human beings. The Warchild/Mao brigade of Red Guards had put in an assault down the street outside half an hour before Garvin had arrived. A few dozen corpses out in the no-man's-land at the end of the block marked the Red Guards' courage and devotion. Garvin saw himself in the minds around him, teeth clenched, eyes wild, pale with tension. The ones who looked at him, the survivors of his mad dash, saw Garvin through a red haze of exhaustion.

WHERE IS YOUR WARCHILD NOW THAT YOU ARE DYING? a Zombie mind asked. It threw an image of a Companion prisoner, lobotomized, hung on hooks, flesh flayed off while he was alive and screaming. That had happened the evening before out in the no-man's-land when another Companion attack had failed.

RIGHT HERE! The proper tactic would have been to winkle them out of the portal with telepathic terror and artillery fire. But the blood ran hot in Garvin's brain and he scrambled up the side of the ruined cellar, reaching out for Warchild Cluster.

RELAY! RELAY! the aides around him ordered and grabbed for the minds of Companions commanding skeleton brigades. They in turn linked up with their battalion leaders, who grasped the minds of their company commanders, who joined with any remaining who still led platoons. They touched the minds of the nontelepathic troopers and all of them saw the Warchild's image of a *V* of geese burning its way through the Echbattan position like a flaming arrow, felt him screaming at their enemy's minds, SLAVES, RISE NOW OR DIE NOW! The flaming spear tore through an image of the stomach of an old and bloated Zombie.

From behind the Warchild's position, a work crew of apprentice shipbuilders and sailors from a seventeenth century Holland, half trained as a field artillery unit, opened up with everything they had. Garvin felt the battle fatigue of the troops who leaped up from cover to follow him.

Besides the fragments that remained of Warchild Cluster, and Warchild/Mao, he led a mercenary brigade of Vietnamese river pirates, a contingent of medical volunteers from an Edinburgh, and a twentieth century California formation trained to operate captured aircraft which had been hastily converted into a reconnaissance battalion. Guarding the assault's flank were a few hundred Companions and soldiers of an Army of Autumn division which had once numbered ten thousand. Garvin caught his Rider thinking grimly of parts of a smashed ship washed up onshore after a hurricane.

Darrel and Maji ran right behind Garvin. Beside him, a shell took off the front of the head of a Companion, sixteen years old and worlds away from home. His blood sprayed like a fountain as Garvin ran toward the open ground at the end of the street. The linchpin of the enemy defense was the remains of a public building set in the wreckage of a fountained park. Garvin imagined himself tearing the defenses apart with his hands and kicking the crawling defenders until they were puddles of bloody mucus.

The Companion relay caught that and smashed it into the minds of the enemy gun crews. Enemy fire faltered as Garvin's mind cut through them and found the Steed whose Rider commanded the defenders. He was a minor member of the Echbattan clan who had borne a Rider for sixteen of his thirty years. Garvin ripped through the generations of inbred loyalty, the terror and conditioning that bound him to his master.

'let me touch them,' the mind inside Garvin's begged. Once Garvin would have tried to turn Steed and Rider. But that would have taken time and compassion. At that moment the Warchild was running low on both and didn't want to know what message his Rider would send the other.

TURN, DAMN YOU, Garvin told the Steed.

ECHBATTAN! the other Steed proclaimed. And Garvin tore into his mind, ripped away memory and motor control, made him stand and spin, bite his tongue and scream insanely, spitting blood.

Garvin, first out of cover, was out in front of the attack. His boots hit the pavement in no-man's-land when the last scattered round of enemy fire came in. As he focused on the Echbattan commander, twisting the life out of Steed and Rider, one of the last shots exploded just behind Garvin. He was aware of something warm hitting the back of his neck. Reaching for Darrel's and Maji's eyes to see what it was, he felt their minds slip through his grasp.

Turning, he caught blood in his eyes as Maji's headless corpse fell forward. Darrel, down on the ground with his stomach blown open, stared awestruck at the Warchild as he died. The enemy Rider tried to wriggle its Echbattan Steed out of Garvin's grasp, but he strangled them both at the portal while screaming aloud, "No prisoners! No fucking prisoners!"

It was bad, and when it was over, Garvin stood next to the portal and looked at the remains of Warchild Cluster. Of all the thousands with whom he had left the Republic, only a few hundred still followed him. A lot of them were vacant-eyed, shell-shocked, more zombie than the Zombies. Beyond his oldest unit, he caught an image of the remains of the Army of Autumn division that guarded their flank and recognized the troops he was fated to lead.

Turning to the Warchild Cluster, he ordered, GO BACK. TELL HERSELF TO WITHDRAW HER TROOPS AND THE OTHER ARMIES TO GUITARS. ALL OF YOU SPREAD THAT MESSAGE. He turned to the portal. I WILL CONTINUE THE ATTACK AND COVER THE WITHDRAWAL. There was no response from his Rider. Garvin wondered if it had died of fright.

"Warchild! Don't leave us." All of the Cluster—telepathic Select and Citizen soldiers from the Republic, Companions and their troopers, mercenaries and their followers, ones who had followed him across Time—tried to stand up, groggy and sick but terrified of losing him. He smashed them back. GARVIN! they cried as he turned toward the unit he recognized. When he was gone, they stood stunned and abandoned.

FOLLOW ME! he ordered the Army of Autumn division. The command echoed in the minds of kids who had been summoned from a world the Goblins had ordered burned. Their Companion commanders had trained under Elgatto in front of the Valley of Bones, had played the same game Lex was to play a few weeks later in the Museum of Industrial Progress. The troops had taken a blood oath to die fighting.

The unit's private nickname was Home Is Yesterday. Most of them had crude tattoos on their heads that read, "Grow Old, Why?" Every one of them lived day and night with the single idea that he or she wouldn't outlive the revolution. All who could still stand leaped through the portal after their leader.

Out in Time, Garvin spun worlds under him and felt the populations of mighty cities die in atomic blasts. Echbattan's world lay right before him. The heartbeat of the City seemed like his own blood pounding.

Hanging there, Garvin could feel the place beyond the portal, hot, crowded, polluted. Everything he recognized that reminded him of the Oracle's vision brought Garvin something almost like relief. Very shortly he would either find peace or discover what lay beyond death.

The Echbattani guards on the other side of the portal were nontelepathic, lightly armed, more bounty hunters than trained troops. Home Is Yesterday tumbled onto the world and disposed of them in seconds. Immediately, their Warchild led them into the mouth of a barely lighted tunnel. It seemed to be a place he knew well.

Dozens of hungry Winds caught them just as they entered the dark and carried away the minds of most of the telepaths with "Grow Old, Why?" on their foreheads. The same Winds sniffed at Garvin but felt his Rider and avoided him. He was barely aware of that as he plunged forward. Enemy stood at the other end of the tunnel. FIRE! he ordered and his troops emptied their guns. Behind him, Echbattan forces cut down the rear guard left at the tunnel entrance.

Garvin led fewer than a hundred kids at that point. For a moment he wanted to warn them. But he recognized some of their faces from the Oracle's vision and wanted to fulfill that prophecy. I AM COMING TO YOU, FATHER, he broadcast down the long dark tunnel.

The Winds caught them again there in the dark. They took the rest of the Companions but only nuzzled around Garvin like stray dogs. He reached out for enemy telepaths but found none. He realized that his throat was raw from screaming, but he didn't know what words he had used. When the exploding percussion grenade took him out, it was just as the Oracle had shown.

The enemy approached, carefully. They dragged the bodies out into the light, where they shot most of the wounded, then settled down to plunder. Garvin felt paralyzed, unable to probe them mentally or even to move. It reminded him of how the Steed who had previously borne his Rider felt as it died in a Goblin operating room.

As if from somewhere far above, he saw himself picked clean, anonymous. As he looked down, one of the gladiator soldiers grabbed his ponytail, intending to cut off his head. Subtly, concealing its presence, Garvin's Rider deflected the man's mind, led him to cut off the Warchild's ponytail and crest as a souvenir.

When the slaves dragged him out into the red afternoon sun of the plaza, it was more familiar than almost anyplace in Time. From a balcony, Goblins looked down, scanning the corpses casually. Behind them, their Winds made banners flutter. Then there was an outburst of gunfire in the distance. Another rebel unit had broken into Echbattan's world, more Wind fodder. All but two of the Goblins departed the plaza; a single Wind danced behind them. Then slaves kindled the fire. A bloody soldier, not quite dead, writhed as flames burned his legs, and Garvin's assault was over.

Lex led her command in the wake of the Warchild's advance and thought of Doria's image of October Corps's formation being like a river. If that was true, what had accumulated on the way to Echbattan's world was like the aftermath of a flood. The worlds she passed through stank of death. The Army of Autumn's advance had seemingly fallen apart. Except that each unit she passed held memories of the Warchild storming forward with everyone able and willing to follow.

The shell-shocked garrisons left behind clung to those images of their leader's passing through. HE TOOK OUR MOBILE UNIT WITH HIM, ORDERED US TO GET ALL THE WOUNDED TO THE REAR, she was told in a field hospital on a muggy summer morning. They were evacuating the patients, and the pain of radiation-burned kids was like a fire at the back of her mind. Lex saw Garvin in the chief medic's memory, his eyes like flames in the dusk before he had turned and stalked away. WHEN? she asked.

YESTERDAY NIGHT. She nodded and turned as Garvin had done. On a cliff wall over the hospital, painted in red, was, "Home Is Yesterday". Under that in larger, jagged letters was "Grow Old, Why?" and Lex felt as if she had followed those words all the way across Time and that her quest was almost over.

After seeing that, she could neither rest nor sleep. Lex would not have been able to say if days or hours had passed as she plunged with Sticks Battalion down the narrow passage which Garvin had cleared. Once the path led between portals in an Echbattani forest preserve. It was on that world without indigenous human life, near an abandoned rebel position, that her advance guard encountered a broken unit trailing back to the rear. Its commander was a silver-haired Companion. IDENTIFY YOURSELF, Lex told them, prepared to order the stragglers off the path and out of her way.

WARCHILD CLUSTER, Blaze replied. WITH ORDERS TO REPORT TO HERSELF.

Lex looked again at the thin trickle, weighted down with its wounded, and Nick at her side whispered, "Almost there."

WHEN DID YOU LAST SEE THE COMMANDER? Lex asked.

THIS MORNING, was the answer and it was barely afternoon. On the minds of Warchild Cluster was the image of the tattoos that said, "Grow Old, Why?"

Leaving in their wake anyone who couldn't keep up, Lex and Nick jogged to the next portal and followed the trail of dead to the final portal before Echbattan's world.

The portal was guarded by a Zombie-led unit. Sticks Battalion went forward and smashed it in a bloody assault. In the distance Lex heard gunfire. On the far fringes of her telepathy she felt Winds feeding on the minds of rebel telepaths. "Leave the battalion," Nick said in her ear. "They're only going to attract fire and Winds."

HOLD ON HERE, Lex ordered her depleted, exhausted

command. WE'RE GOING ON RECONNAISSANCE. Before they could react, she grabbed Nick's arm and jumped into Time. The portal on the other side was unguarded. On the ground around it, beside a tunnel mouth, Companion corpses lay scattered. On each forehead was tattooed, "Grow Old, Why?" Lex thought of the Winds at the same moment that she felt them not too far away. One bloody arm seemed to point at the tunnel down which Nick immediately plunged. Summoning a mental image of the Goblin Chain, Lex followed him.

She slipped on the blood that slicked the floor of the tunnel, felt something sticky splattered on the walls. Far in front of her, Lex saw a dime-size light. WHO? a mind ahead of them asked and Lex recognized a Zombie. Instinctively, she let him see the Goblin Chain.

That stopped him from sending an alarm, but he was suspicious. WHAT DO YOU WANT? The Zombie couldn't detect Nick, who was running toward him fast, but he tried to probe Lex. She had to distract him. Showing him the pile of corpses on the plaza just as Herself had showed it to her, Lex ordered, DOUSE THE FIRE. WE HAVE JUST LEARNED THERE MAY BE SOMETHING IMPORTANT IN THERE.

Again that held the Zombie and he didn't immediately sound the alarm. Over Nick's shoulder, Lex saw the tunnel light as half-dollar size and getting bigger as they ran forward. STOP THERE, was the order. I WILL ALERT THE GOBLINS.

I OBEY, Lex responded and kept on coming. As she did, she probed beyond the Zombie, caught sight of the plaza in the eyes of a guard. Lex saw the huge mound of corpses, the red sunlight, the slaves around the lighted pyre, the Zombie bowing toward two green figures. Then she saw it again, this time in black and white.

She recognized the Goblin mind. It viewed the conflagration as nothing more than fire eating garbage. A second Goblin reached out for Lex. It brushed aside the chain, found an image of the Warchild in her mind. INTRUDER! it told the Zombie. Lex felt the other Goblin reach above them, form an image of a cloud enveloping a stick figure with a slightly pulsating head. TAKE, the Goblin ordered the Wind.

The tunnel mouth was twice the size of a basketball. Lex no

longer saw Nick in front of it. Neither the Goblins nor the Zombie had detected him. At the moment the Goblin hied the Wind on Lex, Nick came out of the tunnel at a crouch and put three rifle shots into the Zombie's stomach. As he did, Nick felt the Wind pass by and go down the tunnel. The only people in the plaza were slaves who stood in shock as Nick ran at the Goblins, screaming, "Die, scum."

The Wind began to envelop Lex. She felt the two Companions it had just absorbed, kids who had tattooed "Grow Old, Why?" on themselves and now were caught halfway between life and death. She understood that. As she stood in the tunnel, feeling as if she were inhaling an endless breath, the Wind lifted her mind from her body.

In that instant both the Goblins pulled the Wind off her, ordering it, TAKE THIS ONE! They showed a puppet figure flying at them. Nick had crossed the plaza and leaped onto the platform on which they stood.

Lex stumbled and almost fell as the Wind let go of her. At that moment she felt something ancient and desperate touch her mind. Garvin's Rider told her, 'i order you to rescue the warchild.'

Lex ran to the tunnel opening. Glancing across the plaza, she saw Nick kick a green head in with his feet, stamp on a face as the Wind circled around him, unable to find his telepathy. He was invisible to it.

In the other direction, flames had started to climb the pyre. Lex grabbed the minds of the attendants. DOUSE THE FIRE. Grabbing a leather apron from one of them, she threw it on top of flames and leaped over it onto the pile of dead. Smoke choked her and she gagged on the stink of burning flesh. Trying to avoid stepping on empty eyes that stared up at her, she slipped on a bloody chest. The corpses all looked alike. The Rider directed her, 'we are on the top. no. yes, there! that is his arm. pull us out. do not let us burn.'

The shoulders Lex held seemed lifeless, the face was covered with blood, the head hung limp. 'we are still alive.' She felt the pile of human flesh collapsing under her as she staggered back down it. Nick reached out and took Garvin from her and she leaped free of the pyre.

'no one else must know who this is,' the Rider insisted as

Lex and Nick got the unconscious Warchild back through the tunnel. Echbattan troops were closing in as they emerged from the other end. Nick, with Garvin over his shoulder, never broke stride. Lex flashed the Goblin Chain at every mind that tried to probe her. She also fired a rifle clip at a couple of Echts who got too close. Grabbing Nick's arm, she leaped through the portal just before two Winds came down on them.

The Winds didn't pursue onto the next world. Nick put Garvin onto a stretcher. Lex got the troops formed up and fell back the same way they had advanced.

One of the stretcher-bearers said, "This is one Companion who really showed the enemy his ass," and the other one laughed. Lex was about to crush the life out of both of them.

Nick shook his head and the Rider told her, 'ignore them. it is inconceivable to them that this could be the warchild. leave it that way. it would panic the army to find he had come this close to death.'

"He got every soldier under him killed, I bet," one of her troopers said.

WHO IS HE? a Companion company commander wanted to know, and reached out for the stranger's mind.

'even the rumor of the warchild's injury will tear apart an army created only by his charisma. get your troops away from us.' Lex noticed that whenever his Rider made itself felt, Garvin's hand automatically twitched. 'he should recover shortly. but get him away from the troops.'

Lex blocked the minds of any Companions who tried to probe the unconscious mind. HE IS AN INJURED INTELLI-GENCE OFFICER. HIS KNOWLEDGE IS TO BE SHARED ONLY WITH THE WARCHILD.

They fell back fast. On the empty world where they had passed Warchild Cluster, they caught up with other retreating rebels. Lex ordered her unit to form a relay and gave her orders. WE HAVE MISSED THE WARCHILD. RETURN TO HERSELF AS QUICKLY AS POSSIBLE. TELL HER I SEND HER THIS. She showed an image of a body being pulled off a pile of corpses.

She wanted to speak aloud but found she couldn't. FOR THE WARCHILD, she told them. Sung and the other Com-

panions started to protest. She smacked them away. IT IS OF
THE GREATEST IMPORTANCE THAT YOU RETURN TO
HERSELF. NICK AND I WILL GO TO THE WARCHILD.
She used all the strength she had to command them. GO. Her
troops, exhausted, confused, had no strength to stop her as
Lex and Nick hauled Garvin into Time.

On their advance through the Echbattani forest preserve,
Lex had learned of some hunting lodges that the Warchild's
army had used as a campground. She floated in Time and
came back through another portal on that same world. The
Warchild's mind brushed hers and he mumbled aloud. Lex
saw the mirrored room with a figure standing in it. As they
got to the hunting camp, he touched her again and she saw a
dark bedroom. Both of them felt immense and frightening.

They got Garvin into one of the lodges. Lex sat down sud-
denly on the bed where he lay. Nick looked around and said,
"I think we outran the Echts. This place got abandoned fast.
Let me see if they left any food before I fall out."

He left and Lex was alone with the Warchild. Everything
had happened so fast that fact hadn't fully sunk in. Before she
could dwell on it, Garvin turned over on his pallet and started
to probe. DARREL? MAJI? he asked as his Rider tried to
control him.

Lex touched the fringes of Garvin's mind. I AM HERE,
WARCHILD.

THAT SHELL TORE HER HEAD OFF! Lex saw a head-
less figure with a neck spouting blood. Garvin sat up with his
eyes closed.

IT WAS A DREAM. Hesitantly, she held him. Garvin ran
his hands along her arms, grabbed hold of her shoulders.

I GOT EVERYONE WITH ME KILLED. THEY
PLUCKED US LIKE CHICKENS. He reached up, traced the
outline of her Mohawk. The cabin was dark and his eyes were
pressed shut. Lex saw from above and far away, as if viewed
through a long dark tube, the slaves tossing corpses onto a
pyre.

"You are fine," she whispered, holding him. "Everything
will be fine." Garvin's hands pulled at her blouse, tugged
open the buttons of her pants. His eyes still closed, he wrig-
gled from under the blankets and pressed himself against her,

crushed his mouth on hers. Images tumbled from his mind so fast that she could barely keep them from drowning her.

A girl with an elaborate hairdo and large breasts under a bright sweater sat in a high school classroom. By candlelight a dark girl slipped off her tunic and reached out for Garvin. A young black woman crooned in a room lighted by gas lamps outside on the street. But none of the desire Garvin had felt those other times was as great as his need right then.

Lex got out of her shirt as Garvin held on to her with his hands, his mouth. He wrapped his legs around hers when she had slipped her pants off. Insistent images from his mind swamped hers. She felt him swimming toward her as if she were an island of safety, comfort, peace. Mouths joined, they breathed into each other on the narrow pallet. Lex saw her path through Time lead like an arrow to this night. His hands and legs were cold, as if all the heat in his body were being used in his headlong flight into her.

Later he opened his eyes and looked right at her. "The others all died," he said. It wasn't a question, but she let him feel what she had felt, the pile of corpses with the small clear entity amid it, like a sentinel. The Warchild shivered and stood up.

"Get under the blankets," Lex ordered him as if he were a sick recruit. Many times she had imagined meeting the Warchild. Never had she thought of anything like this.

He took a great gulp of mountain air. "You're the one who saved me," he said.

WE WERE SENT TO FIND YOU. Lex touched his Umbra with the image of Herself in the tent, saying, "I understand what happened and do not regret for a moment the comfort given and the memories shared with my brother."

Without letting her finish, Garvin pushed that away and looked out the window. At that moment Nick knocked and said, "I got coffee and food and some pants for our friend." Lex opened the door, and the Warchild, turning, saw the Companion who smiled with half his face. Garvin paused for a long moment. It seemed to Lex that he recognized Nick immediately but understood something else as well. Then he stepped forward to hug Nick and mumble again and again, "Oh, man, I'm so glad it's you."

Garvin got dressed, grinning at the battered leather jacket and high tops that Nick had found for him. Then he sat cross-legged on the floor of the hut in the outpost halfway up a mountain and ate tinned meat and biscuits. "What happened to you?" he asked Nick. "I thought you were dead. Where have you been?"

Nick just smiled at him and shrugged. "Gone."

Sitting there, Lex realized she had picked up Nick's attitude to the Warchild. On some level, to him Garvin was just a kid, a recruit he was fond of. Without most of his Mohawk, sitting on the floor drinking coffee, Garvin could have been any fairly junior seventeen-year-old Companion, veteran of a couple of skirmishes, visitor to a hundred worlds, who had been injured up in a minor battle.

"You look like there's nothing much wrong with you except for some bruises and cuts," Nick told him. "The hair will grow back."

Garvin nodded. "The Rider says I'm okay." He spoke quietly, but images flashed in the air as he did. The Rider, when the Warchild mentioned it, was a black lizard perched just inside the back of his skull. Whenever he said the word, his hand automatically touched his throat where the gold razor had hung.

Noticing that, Lex reached into her pack and found a piece of string and a razor blade. She pulled the string through a hole in the blade and held it up for Garvin. He bowed his head and let her put it around his neck.

"Thank you, commander," he smiled at her. "You both need rest. Get it and I'll keep watch. Tonight, I want you to go with me."

"Where?" Nick wanted to know.

HOME. I KNOW THE GENERAL DIRECTION. He paused and Lex saw his eyes cloud, knew he was communicating with his Rider. YOU KNOW THE SURROUNDING AREA? Nick nodded as if it were the most normal thing to lead the conqueror of a thousand worlds back to the old neighborhood.

Then the drive that had brought Lex over worlds to rescue Garvin broke. They got her to eat a little before she collapsed.

Nick's eyes began to close also, and he went next door to fall out.

'you could travel faster by yourself,' his Rider told him.

I NEED THEM. In all of Time, only they thought of him as human. If he let go of them, he would be absolutely alone.

'you abandoned an army that needs you more.'

Garvin squirmed. THEY SAVED MY LIFE.

'which is why you created them. you must know that.'

Garvin jumped up at that suggestion, disturbing Lex, who stirred. He fingered the razor at his neck and his Rider withdrew discreetly.

Seeing him again, Garvin realized that Nick was the image he always imagined when he thought the word Companion. Fascinated and horrified by the way his first teacher now looked, he tried to imagine where Nick's lost years had gone. A voice inside that could have been the Rider told him what he already knew. 'nowhere. he was dead. you summoned him back to rescue you.'

AND LEX? Burlap-bag curtains had been nailed over the windows. Garvin pulled one aside and let a slice of sunlight fall on the figure on the bed. She put her bare arm over her eyes and squirmed. Seeing Lex there, Garvin wanted to crawl into bed next to her, to hold her for his own comfort. 'you created her also,' something inside told him. It was cold as his Rider could be, but Garvin wasn't sure whether it was the Rider's thought or his own knowledge.

He turned away from her, wondering where he had seen Lex first. As a face glimpsed in a car window? As one of a crowd of suburban kids in the city on a Friday night?

Standing in the hunting lodge, Garvin remembered his father's face in that mirrored room long ago. It had seemed immense because Garvin had been so very small. He remembered the way the face flickered, other faces appearing almost subliminally. It frightened him just as the primal scene in the bedroom had. His father had taken him to the mirrored room to tell him something, but had managed to scare him so much as to insure that he would forget it.

Garvin wondered if that was the same kind of urge that had made his father create worlds for the Goblins to plunder while also forming Immortals and Oracles, maybe Garvin himself, to stop them. He remembered how when he had seen his father in the Palace, the God's voice, form, sex had changed. Then he had thought that he was witnessing a stage trick. Now he wondered if in shaping worlds his father had lost control over his own physical being.

A piece of glass hung on the wall of the lodge bathroom. Garvin took it down, went to a window, and held it in front of his face. Concentrating, he started to change himself. First he fixed the ear damaged when the stud was torn out. He cleaned up the bruises on his body. Then, remembering something, for just one moment he straightened his bent nose and made his hair long enough to stick out over his ears. "Garvin Reilly," he whispered, recognizing the dumb, awkward kid he would have been had Time and telepathy never touched him. "How many millions have you slaughtered?"

Carefully, Garvin reconstructed the face and hair he and everyone else was used to, kept his nose a little flat, his clothes the way Nick had given them to him. As he did, he caught his Rider observing him with uncertainty, as though it had never seen him before. OKAY, he told it, NOW EXPLAIN TO ME VERY SLOWLY WHAT MY UNCLE SHOWED YOU THAT WAS SO EXCITING.

CHAPTER
Eight

Outside the Palace of the Gods in the darkened streets of the City Out Of Time, the people waited for news from Echbattan's world. They started at every shout in the street, tore images out of the minds of all who came out of summer through the Gate of Gold.

Inside the Palace servants walked quietly and spoke in whispers. They looked toward the locked doors, ran their minds along the Scrambler shield of the Gods' private chambers. Once Tom came to the door to receive a delivery of food. To the respectful telepathic inquiry HOW REST THEIR DIVINITIES? he only shook his head.

If any telepaths had dared violate the privacy of the servant's mind, they would have found images of closed doors and the sound of a single hoarse voice shouting far into the night. In the private chambers, Tom carried the delivery down the hall, past the locked drawing room. Even he, without a trace of curiosity into what did not concern him, heard the words spoken in the quavering voice of a crone: "The past is on my tail like a pack of hounds!"

Hurrying toward the kitchen, Tom caught images as worn

and haunting as old dreams, a bush with human faces instead
of flowers, a castle wall of shiny ebony stone that reflected
like a mirror. That black stone flickered for an instant with
infinite points of white, like a spatter of milk drops on a slate,
or a swatch of stars reflected on dark waters. Then the effect
was gone before it could fully register.

In the kitchen Tom shut the door behind him. He and Mary,
staring at each other, heard a voice full of despair crying,
"Once I stood at this mirror and worlds ran out of my eyes and
through my fingers like tears that turned to jewels. Thousands
on thousands of them I fashioned out of my poor knowledge
of geography, my scanty grasp of history and philosophy and
politics and men's minds. Some worlds were born dead, some
came to grief all on their own."

The voice cried on, "But the rest, where people lived and
hoped and where some had the gifts of telepathy, were looted
and raped by the Goblins. They used my poor people for
food, for fuel, for stepping-stones to the stars. And all of it
was done with my collaboration. I spun those worlds the way
a worm does silk so that they could be used.

"Now it's lost, that gift. The jewels slowed to a trickle and
those there were had flaws. The atom was split, the nations
were at each other's throats, the air was fouled, the oceans
died. Then it stopped altogether. Not a world appeared to me
in this mirror, no matter how long I stood. Not laughter nor
tears could raise a single one. The Goblins have long suspected that Time was not growing. But recently they have it
calculated pretty clearly that the Well of Stars has run dry."

Amazed, the Irish couple saw an image, elusive as a long-
ago dream, of a woman whose cloak was the night, whose
hair was the leaves of trees, and who wore the quarter-moon
as a crown. "I am being torn in two by the Goblins in their
star ships and Cathleen ni Houlihan. The Goblins do no more
than use me as I try to use them. But long ago she touched
me, offered me a new universe, and gave me the keys to
unlock it." The voice broke, almost sobbed. "Then in her
infinite mercy and contempt she abandoned me."

There followed a low sound, a crooning, and afterward a
feel of the empty calm after hysteria. Mary moved to the stove

and put on the kettle. Fetching down a skillet, she said, "He'll be wanting some breakfast."

Neither of them moved to look when they heard the drawing room door open and the padding of feet, quick and bare on the hall carpet. The study door opened and closed at the same moment that someone scratched outside the kitchen. Pausing to cross herself, Mary opened it and had her apron grabbed by two tiny Swift Ones, their dirty faces streaked with tears.

Moments later she and Tom heard water running in the Gods' bath. On the bronze door at the end of the hall, the chamberlain rapped three times with his mace. As Tom went to answer it, a familiar voice with a North Dublin accent called over the noise of the bath, "Would you just be telling them I'm busy and could you take a message?"

Tom did and a few minutes later, carrying a tray, he knocked on the study door. "Come in, come in. It's unlocked," answered the God in the same voice as before. Tom shook his head and entered to find the one he knew would be sitting in what he always thought of as the Reverend Father's chair. This one had his bare feet up on the desk and a stubby, unfiltered cigarette in his mouth. He had a towel around his waist and his wet hair dripping onto another on his neck.

Mary always said she found this aspect of the God handsome. But Tom, seeing the young man with his body too hard for a seminarian and not thick enough for a laborer, the blue eyes quick and quick to be bored, saw an infinity of spoiled priests and hedge poets and layabouts and wild boys enlisting for foreign adventures. Privately he thought of this one as the Young Lout.

"What did they want?" the young God asked, looking with some revulsion at a plate of eggs and bacon.

"The news has come from Echbattan's world, carried by an Echbattan Rider. It is this: 'The Winds have feasted and the Rebels are in retreat.'"

"What meaning do you make from this?" asked the God while opening a cabinet.

"Myself?" Tom hesitated, not having considered the meaning. "That the lad's thought better of making war on his father?"

"In a pig's ass he has. We're too much alike for me to believe that of him," said the Young Lout, giving a smirk and pouring whiskey into his tea. "I think it means he's gotten just a bit smarter and he'll be trying tactics other than direct frontal assault. I wonder if the Goblins have thought to be putting a watch on his mother's house?" He took a swallow and then another. "That's where desperate boyos go when they find the world's turned hard around them."

His Rider estimated that the place of Garvin's birth was out in early autumn. Garvin himself guessed that it was somewhere very near the place that the Companion patrol had met Nick. That would mean the same thing. So the Warchild went there, Time Striding, doing it in fairly easy steps because of the two who were with him. He learned a lot about Lex, saw the world where she had been born in her memories.

Then on a Friday evening out in late summer, just about where he had imagined one might be, they found a world so much like her own that Lex wanted to explore it. Nick looked doubtful, but curiosity led Garvin to agree.

Their visit ended out on Long Island with Lex watching from behind the garage across the street as her family packed the car. The neighborhood had the deserted feel it got when half the families in it were on vacation. "Labor Day," Lex whispered to herself. "It's the Labor Day weekend and we're . . . they're going upstate. There was a place we used to stay." Her mother came out looking a little harried but still beautiful, not the gray, beaten slave Lex had seen her become.

Her sister Mandy carried a picnic basket down the walk to the car, hopping conscientiously every other step. "I used to love it up there when I was little. Later, vacations with my family got to be a bore." Lex shook her head as her brother Bobby carried a couple of pieces of luggage to the back of the station wagon, strutting to the beat of the music in his earphones. Their father came out of the garage and helped him stow them in the back of the station wagon. "They all look so . . . whole," she murmured.

Her father turned toward the house and called, "Lex." It wasn't loud, probably not loud enough to be heard by anyone indoors. Lex found herself reaching automatically toward him, as she now understood she had always done. He expected a response, braced for it without knowing that was what he did. After the minds she had felt in Time, his telepathy was negligible, untrained. But the remembered familiarity, the comfort of it made Lex gasp. She felt a hand on her shoulder, Garvin whispering, "Maybe we should go."

Her father, aware of something, half turned toward the garage across the street. At that moment Lex felt her double. She was bored, planning to call Mark as soon as she could get to a phone, more than a little sulky, wanting to be away from adults and their stupid plans. After a long delay and a few more summonses, the front door of the house opened one last time and Lex saw herself standing on the stairs, sixteen, a little pudgy, her hair twisted into a new and original shape, showing her disdain for the trip by the languor with which she moved.

The Lex in shadows stared frozen, unable to probe or speak or even, it seemed, to breathe until her family was in the car and driving down the street. Then she reached out and caught the fringes of all of their minds except that of the other Lex. She exhaled and said to Garvin, "That was me."

SOMEONE SIMILAR. Garvin glanced once at a tree where, weathered and overgrown, was carved, "Garvin Reilly, '82." It was just where he imagined it would be when he had used what he had seen of Lex's memories to consciously create a world for the first time.

"That was me," Lex said to him and Nick. "This is my world. Everything is the same except that the Goblins never found this place. She's my exact double. Maybe there are a thousand others in Time." She realized that she was breathing heavily, coming close to sobbing. Garvin had hold of her. THEY SAY EVERYONE WANTS TO KILL THEIR DOUBLE. I UNDERSTAND THAT NOW, she told him.

SHE IS NOT YOU. WHAT HAPPENED TO YOU MAKES YOU DIFFERENT, he told her, wishing he hadn't let her see this, wondering what he had proved by creating it. Lex fought back tears. "Maybe we can make it so these people get to live their own lives," he said.

At the same moment his Rider asked him, 'now that you

are satisfied that you can create worlds, what does it mean to
you, master?'

"Let's find another place to stay," Garvin told Lex and
Nick.

Worlds away from there, beyond the ragged end of summer, Lex stood next to Garvin and watched as Nick's near
double walked through the morning rush on Delancey Street.
An ancient elevated train rattled overhead. This Nick was
lean, wore a mustache, and had a hat pulled down over his
eyes. He was a petty hood in a hard and desperate city, but
one with both sides of his face.

"The first time I saw him," Nick said, "I thought he was a
kid who wasn't doing so bad, you know. I mean the world he
was in wasn't Goblin infested. He had enough control over his
telepathy to do okay in his life. Not great, maybe, but the
place I came from was like a radioactive slum and I'd gotten
screwed every way possible. I half wanted to kill him and take
his place."

Lex didn't want to look at the fear-driven young guy stick-
ing to the shadows of the El as he crossed the street against
traffic. But she understood that Nick had brought them here
for her sake. "Does it hurt still, seeing him like that?" she
asked.

"Not much," Nick told her. "Anytime you get this kind of
world, this kind of New York, there's a good chance of finding some guy like me. Unless he's already gotten shot or
jugged or sold as meat."

Lex felt the emptiness of Time. Somewhere hundreds of
worlds behind them, someone just like her was about to start
her senior year. Somewhere up ahead near winter, the world
of her birth lay dead. She touched Garvin's shoulder and he
put his arm around her. But his attention was on Nick, who
indicated the double standing between two parked cars outside
a coffee shop and said, "Something's coming down."

They skimmed the information from Nick's alter ego that a
medium-sized hood named Sid the Face and two of his asso-
ciates were eating breakfast in the coffee shop. Sid had ob-
jected to Nick's operating in the Lower East Side and
announced that he was gunning for him. As the three

watched, the other Nick bent forward, stared intently. They felt him summon the telepathy that came to him erratically, caught the fear underlying his toughness. The door of the coffee shop opened. Three men emerged, one a big guy with an overcoat over his shoulders.

That Nick stepped forward, probed for Sid, who saw him before either of his bodyguards did. Sid's hand went inside his coat. He pulled out an automatic. Then his mind was seized and twisted. Sid went purple; his eyes bulged. One of his guards spotted Nick and drew his piece. Sid swung around and fired three quick shots into the other man's chest.

The man fell at the same moment that Sid turned his automatic back and blew his own brains out. The third man stared for a long, terrified second before running away. Then Nick turned and walked fast, mixing with the crowd.

"The Suitcase showed me him, then told me what I had." Lex caught Nick's image of an old man holding a leather satchel, felt the ancient being inside it touch the fledgling Companion and invest him with a mission. Nick saw himself holding young minds, handling bright, screwed-up telepaths like himself as if they were precious jewels. The tough, abused kid had understood that he was to be a shepherd and teacher.

"That's what I did. I was in a Companion recruiting team in the worlds around here. We went into places before the Riders could wreck them. I got a lot of kids out before the Zombies did them in. The Suitcase had told us to be on the lookout for someone like Garvin. It happened I was lucky.

"Whatever happened, Lex," Nick said, "I didn't end up like my double on this world." Then he turned to Garvin. "And I was the one who found you . . . twice. That's enough for me." Garvin looked at him, slowly raised his hand, and touched the scar. Lex thought that the Warchild flinched for an instant as he did it, but she couldn't read his face or mind.

Garvin put his hands on both their shoulders and led them toward a portal. As he did, Lex was filled with an end-of-summer it's-all-over feeling. "Both of you are more than close to me," Garvin told them as they walked through a battered city park. "Not just by saving my life." He hesitated, seeming to have trouble with words. "But by letting me understand things." He could have shown them what he meant, but instead kept his mind closed.

Garvin could stride Time and spin worlds like nobody Lex had ever seen, but he let Nick lead them the rest of the way. Nick brought them through a portal into an early autumn woods where they felt themselves close to their destination. "No humans native to this world," Nick said. A ruined shack caught his attention. "The Companions had a station there. It's where I reported that I found you."

Garvin's eyes looked inward. Lex watched his hand touch the razor. 'are you still so unwilling to believe in your own divinity,' his Rider asked deferentially, 'that you need the help of these two?' When Garvin didn't respond, it told him, 'while they delayed you, lives elsewhere have been snuffed out.'

Then the Warchild answered, THE ARMY IS A TRICK, A TRAP. IT WAS ME BEHAVING LIKE MY FATHER. MAYBE I CAN BEAT HIM AND THE GOBLINS THAT WAY, MAYBE NOT. BUT IF I DO, ALL THAT HAPPENS IS THAT I BECOME HIM. THERE HAS TO BE ANOTHER WAY. THAT WAS WHAT THE ORACLE MEANT BY SHOWING ME ON THAT PILE OF BODIES. THAT WAS WHAT THE GUVNOR TRIED TO TELL ME. BUT KNOWING IT MEANS I KNOW I WASTED A LOT OF LIVES.

'and the answer lies on your home world?'

THE HOUSE OF MY MOTHER'S FAMILY. CLAIRE HAD NO FAMILY. I MEAN, SHE WAS RAISED BY AN AUNT WHO DIED WHEN I WAS FIRST BORN. BUT MY MOTHER MUST REMEMBER SOMETHING. AND I WANT TO SEE HER.

'there may also be a message from your father.'

SOMETHING THAT HE WANTED TO SHOW ME. BUT IT GOT BURIED UNDER ANGER.

'and trauma. part of your father wanted you to follow him back to the city and part of him wanted you to forget, to take another path.'

THE WAY THE GUVNOR TALKED, MY MOTHER IS THE KEY. I JUST WALKED OUT ON HER. I HAVE

TROUBLE THINKING ABOUT CERTAIN THINGS, ESPE-
CIALLY MY MOTHER AND FATHER.

'you were willing to die rather than think about them. i
understand that also. my own past came back painfully. but
you can remember just as i can.'

Gingerly, as if touching a wound, Garvin recalled over-
whelming color and noise and smells on a bouncing journey
through city streets. Signs and buildings were incomprehensi-
ble bulks; brightness he had never seen before pressed itself
on his wide eyes. Like a small beast, the child was aware of
the aftershave and tobacco, the male scents of his father. Raging wails, grinding motors, smeared shrieks of reds terrified
Garvin as one, two, three fire trucks roared past. He turned
crying to the one who carried him. His father smiled and
soothed Garvin's mind.

'you believe that is a true memory?' the Rider asked. But
they both knew it was.

I WAS A FEW MONTHS OLD. HE WAS CARRYING
ME TO SHOW ME THAT ROOM. I GUESS MY APPEAR-
ANCE AT THE CITY YEARS LATER WAS NOT WHAT
HE EXPECTED. HE NEVER RECOGNIZED ME PUB-
LICLY AS HIS SON. BUT HE DID LET ME GO TO SEE
WHAT I WOULD DO.

'even the gods have a subconscious. we know where you
came from. but where did i come from?' the Rider wondered.

They were interrupted by Nick saying, "There's the portal
that will take you home." Garvin, distracted, tumbled into
Time. He barely scanned the world before he was on it and
standing in an empty Tompkins Square Park.

He reached out for the cacophony of minds that was New
York and felt nothing. "Where is everyone?" he asked aloud
to break the silence. Nick and Lex both crouched in the park,
guns ready, watching Garvin, who stood wide-eyed, looking
as if he were sniffing the breeze.

Garvin scanned and showed them what he found: a pack of
dogs over near the East River, the quick, small lives of birds
and squirrels in the park trees, the minds of rats in sewers.
The few people who woke up as the September morning wore
down were elusive and frightened, ready to run or fall dead at

the hint of another's mind. Then he touched someone familiar and pulled back as if it burned.

As he did, Nick whispered, "Evacuation," and pointed to tattered notices hung on lamp posts, on trees, on the sides of buildings. MARTIAL LAW! NUCLEAR THREAT! EVACUATION OF NEW YORK! YOU MUST COMPLY.

Garvin gestured north and the three set out. Automatically Nick kept watch behind them while Lex scanned to the flanks and Garvin probed ahead.

Fading signs on the sides of buildings declared in large red lettering, ANY PERSON OR PERSONS REMAINING IN THIS CITY AFTER JULY 20TH 1987 WILL BE TREATED AS LOOTERS AND EX-TERMINATED. They were signed by a Companion overcommander acting in the name of the Warchild. "Stupid," Lex muttered. "If there were any Companions in the city they wouldn't have to post notices."

"This lets everyone know our forces pulled out." Nick spoke under his breath. The only other sound was water running in the sewers, leaves and rubbish crunching under their feet.

As they spoke, Garvin, scanning, caught two rats feeding on a kitten they had just killed and a woman, a lonely brain-damaged lunatic who thought Garvin was the devil, and tried to fill her mind with the Lord's Prayer. Avoiding her, Garvin touched again the mind he recognized and caught a memory of his mother.

Nick looked east toward Avenue B and the building where he had first met Garvin. It was the moment that had meant his whole life made sense. Nick recalled the white-painted cellar where he had trained recruits. Suddenly Garvin was distracted from his probe by an image of himself in Nick's memory, young and scared and trying not to show it, forming the mirrored room in his mind. "No one ever caught on as quickly," Nick told them.

'but that was not the first time you had seen it,' the Rider remarked. 'your father had showed it to you before.'

Garvin thought of the shifting personae of the God when he had visited him in the City Out Of Time and felt his own face quiver. THEN HE WALKED OUT ON MY MOTHER AND EXPECTED ME TO FOLLOW HIM.

'which you did. with the help of the immortals and the oracle.'

They walked up Avenue A toward Fourteenth Street, passing an overturned delivery truck, a fire engine without wheels, a pile of smashed bicycles. As the other two guarded the flanks and rear, Garvin reached north to the familiar mind he had found, caught it lightly, saw the ruins of a classroom through its eyes, liquor bottles, pharmacy jars, and Syrettes on the floor.

The one Garvin found wasn't telepathic but had learned a few tricks for avoiding telepaths: staying drugged, cultivating madness. NAME? he asked, putting the question carefully, making sure Nick and Lex weren't paying attention.

"Joe." That name popped into the other mind, along with a feeling of dark, chill sickness coming on, the beginning of a junk hunger. Garvin cut right through that. YOU USED TO BE CALLED CAL, he told the other.

The man was defenseless. Garvin could see as much of Cal's mind as he wanted to. Before he was known as Cal, the man had been called Etienne. He had changed it by the time he became one of the assholes who went out with Garvin's mother.

WHERE ARE YOU? he asked and found that Joe/Cal/Etienne was on the top floor of Stuyvesant, the high school Garvin had once attended. He stopped Lex and Nick at the corner of Fourteenth and Avenue A. Across the street from them, Ike Town, the Eisenhower apartment houses, had been reduced to empty, blackened shells. I HAVE TO DO SOMETHING, he told them. He showed Lex an image of the morphine Syrettes in her medical kit.

She handed them over as he told her, "You and Nick stay here and wait for me. Don't try to probe unless you yourselves are in danger, understand?" They nodded as he turned and headed for the high school. When he was gone, both looked around uneasily at the dead quiet of the city.

Garvin kept a grip on the mind on the top floor of the old school. To the extent that Cal wasn't drugged, he was scared, held like a rat by a light. All he knew was that he had been grabbed by a powerful consciousness. "Companion?" he whined aloud. "I got left behind in the evacuation." Garvin made no sign. "Zombies?" Cal asked. "The Goblins coming back? You going to deactivate that A-bomb?"

Garvin held Cal's life in his hands. YOU REMEMBER CLAIRE REILLY, he told the man. It took a moment before that registered, and when it did, Garvin started at Cal's memory of his mother. She was caught from behind in soft light, pretty, laughing, an older woman who never made Cal feel like the fool he knew himself to be. It was a memory from the world before the Goblins, the sweet times before things went to hell.

Garvin tried not to flinch at the images of Cal and his mother's sweet times. As a kid, intermittently telepathic, he had accidentally intruded in his mother's mind and had always jumped away, burned and frozen. Now he remembered the woman who had supported him, kept him fed and dressed and living in this neighborhood. Something about her had been so comforting he had never had to think about it.

The power of Cal's memories had made Garvin cautious about probing. WHAT HAPPENED TO HER? he asked.

"It was her boy, master." Garvin saw himself as Cal remembered him, a skinny kid with problems. He saw his mother, the life drained out of her eyes. "He left just as things went sour, and it was as though her world ended before everyone else's did." Garvin felt drug hunger twist Cal's spine.

I HAVE MORPHINE, Garvin told him as he stood at the locked front door of Stuyvesant High. Across the avenue, hollow windows stared blindly from the wrecked buildings of Ike Town, built for radiation victims of the Second World War. The silence and emptiness of streets that Garvin had never seen this still got to him.

Then he saw a pale face through the wire-reinforced glass. Hands worked a set of locks. "Companion!" he heard Cal say. "I was being worked to death on a labor gang before the Companions showed up and overthrew the Goblin Zombies." The door opened just a crack and a white hand reached out.

WHERE DID CLAIRE GO? Garvin held one of the Syrettes just out of range of the hand. If the Goblins had gotten his mother, it was his fault, his stupid negligence.

"Someplace special. The guy who took her was someone. And it was just her alone. A little later the Zombies hauled everyone else away. It was just before the time they showed the president getting eaten on television . . ."

Garvin felt the other mind start to swirl with images of prison and pain. He probed hard, asking, CLAIRE? and saw and felt as Cal had: the chill apartment, a draft stirring his mother's hair as she sat up in the deep of the night as though she were hearing voices. She put on her slippers and red robe. Cal tried to stop her as she went to the door. A draft blew her robe. Down the stairs from the roof came fast footsteps.

Garvin held his breath as Cal remembered his mother slipping the locks. A figure stood in a trenchcoat and wide-brimmed Borsalino. "Claire Reilly," said a familiar voice. "The taste of the Gods is as impeccable as ever." The Guvnor swept off his hat. "May I have the honor of escorting you home?"

As Garvin stood absorbing that, Cal's pale hand grabbed the Syrette and pulled it into the dark. Garvin felt him tear open a seal and go unhesitatingly for a vein. In the light coming in the door, Garvin saw a tangled beard and hair. The smell from Cal was foul. "Good stuff," the man said, sinking to his knees. Garvin stood waiting for him to look up.

When Cal did, opiates had cut his fear. He stared into the Warchild's face while taking the plastic cap off another Syrette. "Garvin," he said slowly. Then, "I couldn't protect her. Besides, I think it was because of you they got her." Garvin saw the Guvnor bow Claire out the door. The Wind slammed it shut behind them. "I guess he must have been a Zombie. All I know is a couple of days later they got me and I never saw your mother again."

Cal stared at Garvin's uniform. His voice was slow and stoned. "I don't blame you for wanting to join the Companions. You did okay. You're some kind of officer. But your mother's long gone and the Companions evacuated the city."

"They missed you, though." Garvin couldn't look at the man as he handed him the second Syrette.

"They weren't real careful because they figured no one wanted to stay. New York's a danger zone and this is ground zero. Before they got chased out, the Zombies left an A-bomb stuck up on the Empire State Building. Because they couldn't disarm it, the Companions evacuated. They say there are a

million New Yorks but I didn't want to find out. Kid, I'm real
sorry about Claire. Got any more of these joysticks?"

"Sorry. Nice seeing you, though, Cal." Garvin turned and
headed east toward Stuyvesant Park.

"Yeah, keep in touch, man. You know where to find me."

Garvin walked away from the school, past a building that
had collapsed onto the sidewalk. 'that bomb, if it exists, is a
danger,' the Rider told him. Garvin, ignoring that, stepped out
into the street. The Rider showed him the Guvnor saying, "I
await you outside the house of your mother's family."

IT LOOKS LIKE HE SAVED HER LIFE. I DON'T SEE
HIM HANGING AROUND, THOUGH.

'she had no family.'

HE MEANT SOMEPLACE ELSE. I THINK I KNOW
WHERE.

'yes.'

Garvin walked through a gap in the iron fence, around the
park. A rusted personnel carrier lay on its side where the
fountain had been. Something drew him to this spot. BE-
FORE WE GO LOOKING FOR HER, I WANT TO FIND
WHAT MY FATHER SHOWED ME. I REMEMBER THE
MIRROR ROOM. I REMEMBER BEING CARRIED. I
DON'T REMEMBER WHERE.

'it is hard to get beyond the primal moment. look up at the
sky. try to concentrate on that blue sky.' Garvin stood looking
up. Then he gasped as something inside snapped and he remembered his father's mind touching his, remembered looking into his father's face.

Garvin felt himself being dressed and saw the enormous
shape which was the front door fall away. The hall and stairs
were a pattern of light and dark. Then he was outdoors. Sunlight made Garvin blink; noises rushed at him. Shop signs and
flashing cars, a blaring radio, the smell of garbage and the
touch of chilly air on his face: all of those were strange,
frightening, new.

His father had never taken him out before. Red shapes,
huge and screaming, frightened Garvin. JUST FIRE EN-
GINES, his father soothed him, shifted the burden in his
arms, carried Garvin past a black iron fence, the bright shapes
of flowers, the sound of a water fountain. And Garvin recog-

nized, undamaged, the park in the wreckage of which he stood.

As if sleepwalking, Garvin followed the route his father had used: up Second Avenue, west on Twentieth. He didn't notice the figure slipping through shadows behind him. The empty blocks were much the same as they had been. Some buildings were down, but a Lone Wolf cigarette sign still stood where it had been. A banner strung between buildings proclaimed, BY ORDER OF THE WARCHILD, EVACUATION. . . . But the Warchild himself walking under it saw only the street of seventeen years before.

Garvin knew where his father had been taking him before he reached it. But he continued on the same route at exactly the same pace as Brian Garvin had used. At Irving Place, his father had turned right and stopped at the gate of a townhouse with boarded windows. Later, as a little kid, Garvin came to know it as a haunted house. Older kids in the neighborhood told him it was the scene of a murder. Their parents insisted it was just tied up in litigation.

Garvin remembered boys daring each other to break a window and go inside. Something had always made them turn away. The house stood on a corner, brick cornices and cement gargoyles, small plots on its front and sides full of overgrown trees and bushes, starting to turn brown now, but trim and green when his father had paused in front of the building and held him up.

I WILL SHOW YOU THIS ONCE, he had told his infant son. AND IF ALL GOES WELL, YOU WILL FIND YOUR WAY BACK HERE WHEN YOU ARE READY. WHEN YOU DO, REMEMBER THIS. He looked right into Garvin's eyes and showed him an image of a young man reflected in a gold-framed mirror. The young man wore a silver watch fob. He took it off and held it up so that Garvin could see that it spun in his hand, could feel that it pulsed like a heart. Garvin recognized a tiny model of the City Out Of Time.

Holding that image in his son's mind, Brian Garvin had walked up to the front door which swung open before him. Seventeen years later, Garvin walked to the same door and found it rusting, peeling and closed against him. The unnatural quiet of the city bothered him. Hurriedly he formed the image of the room, of the young man and the pulsing silver ornament. Nothing.

He thought of getting a gun and blowing the lock off. 'unlikely to work,' his Rider told him. 'slowly,' it prompted, 'walk back to the street and try it again.' So he did and held in his mind the memory of his father bearing him up the stairs, pausing at the door. His father had shown the model of the city, the door had swung open, and he had walked down a hall.

Garvin called that back and the door flew open before him. He remembered being carried down the hall he found inside. He walked down it, paused as his father had done, turned to his left, and walked into the mirrored room. As he did, a light came on and he was aware of a high-pitched sound that could have been air escaping or a warning signal.

Garvin saw himself in the glass, tense and wild-eyed. In the mirror of the drawing room at the Palace of the Gods both he and his father had been invisible. He noticed that the peacock screen was cardboard, Tantor the Elephant plaster, the globe a mockup. The room was designed to look like the one through which his father had entered Time, but only at a glance.

Then Garvin was aware of a factor snapping on, of electronic impulses forming a message in his mind. WELCOME, SON. TO HAVE GOTTEN THIS FAR, YOU MUST HAVE COME INTO CONTROL OF YOUR TELEPATHY. EVEN IF YOU HAVE MET OTHER TELEPATHS, YOU MUST REALIZE THAT YOUR OWN POWERS ARE UNIQUE. UNDERSTAND, SON, THAT MY OWN POWERS ARE FAR BEYOND YOURS, THAT I CREATED EVERYTHING THAT YOU HAVE SEEN OR HEARD.

NOW YOU MUST LEAVE THE WORLD YOU KNOW. THERE ARE TWO THINGS IN THIS BUILDING TO MAKE THIS EASIER FOR YOU. THE FIRST IS WHAT THEY CALL A PORTAL, A GATEWAY TO OTHER WORLDS. IT IS LOCATED IN THE CELLAR. YOU WILL WALK THROUGH IT AND INTO THE INFINITE WORLDS OF TIME. THE SECOND THING TO AID YOU IN YOUR DEPARTURE IS AN EXPLOSIVE DEVICE SET TO GO OFF TEN MINUTES FROM THE MOMENT YOU

BROKE THE SEAL OF THE DOOR. IT WILL DESTROY THE BUILDING AND SEAL THE PORTAL.

The message from his father went on, but it was intended for another Garvin Reilly. That Garvin would have been a naive kid just discovering telepathy, drawn to this place by a memory so buried it amounted to instinct. 'the oracle and the immortals diverted you from that. was that one part of the god operating against another? or something else entirely?'

Just the feel of his father's presence made Garvin's blood rise. "What about my mother, you bastard?" he shouted at the factor, the mirror, the phony room. "What was supposed to happen to her? What was supposed to happen to me if the Goblins got here before I figured this out?" He only half heard a shot echo on empty streets blocks away, ignored something that stirred in the cellar.

On the factor his father said, COME TO ME AS MY SON AND LEARN, OR AS MY FOE AND TRY TO TAKE MY CITY AND ALL OF TIME FROM ME. THIS ROOM IT- SELF IS YOUR KEY TO OTHER WORLDS. SEVEN MIN- UTES REMAIN IN WHICH TO MEMORIZE ITS CONTENTS AND USE THEM TO TRAVEL IN TIME. I WILL NOW SHOW YOU HOW. As Brian Garvin explained how to tumble from portal to portal, his son saw a green face in the mirror.

The Goblin came at him, its head moving in a circular rhythm, its teeth snapping, its yellow eyes fastened on his. Garvin saw himself in the Goblin's mind, a gray stick figure with a big angry face. Behind it in the doorway appeared two Zombies with their guns aimed at him. Garvin saw himself in the alien mind, saw himself with a razor at the Goblin's throat, felt the other's indignation and hate. He knew that this was the one which he had manhandled on the way to visit his father.

He understood that his stomach was to be torn open, his neck chewed through, and his head delivered to the Gods of the City. If he resisted, the Zombies would shoot him before the Goblin feasted. 'six minutes, forty-two seconds until the building blows up,' the Rider told him.

The yellow eyes held Garvin. The Goblin was halfway across the room when a black form appeared at the door behind the Zombies. In seconds Nick snapped one's neck and kicked the other's gun aside. As he did, Garvin spun around and fell away from the clashing teeth. They tore through the sleeve of his jacket.

Garvin probed the Goblin mind, felt its contempt for him. That disdain turned Garvin's anger to hate. He grabbed the poker from beside the fireplace. SHOOT HIS LEGS, the Goblin ordered the Zombies and showed an image of Garvin hamstrung on the floor. It turned in time to see Nick kill the second one. Garvin brought the poker down across its head.

The Goblin broadcast pain and also something that felt to Garvin like indignation. As it fell to the floor, he tried to catch its mind again. But it was elusive, slipping away from him and into a kind of suspended animation. Garvin probed but knew there was only one way to kill it.

He looked at Nick, who stood, barely winded, over the bodies of the two Zombies. Garvin formed the image of them hanging the Goblin with their belts. Nick shook his head and pointed at the cellar. From down there, Garvin caught the minds of other Zombies and Goblins. 'five minutes, thirty-eight seconds,' his Rider told him.

Minds reached out from the cellar, grabbed at Garvin's mind. Probing them, he found an image of a bulge near the top of the Empire State Building. The Goblins' atomic bomb was keyed into the bomb in the townhouse. When that went up, the whole city would go a moment later. The Goblin and Zombies would jump into Time just before that happened. They weren't going to let the Warchild through the portal.

The Zombies couldn't catch Nick's mind. He turned and dashed into the hall. Garvin lurched after him, batting away the Zombies. Two more dead Zombies lay inside the front door. Outside and to the east Garvin heard gunfire, felt Lex probe, saw her image of enemy between her and the park and between her and Garvin.

Nick was at the cellar door, a pistol in one hand and a knife in the other. "I'll take care of them. You get Lex off this world." It was an order, not a suggestion, Companion to recruit. "four minutes, thirty-five seconds,' the Rider chimed in.

Garvin shook his head. "Warchild, let me go!" Nick whispered. "You brought me back and let me do great things. They'll remember me in Time as long as they remember you. But my Time has run out. You've taken me far enough, man. Save yourself, save Lex. She deserves that from you at least. But let me do this one last thing and rest." His live eye pleaded. Garvin hesitated and Nick was through the cellar door and down the stairs, screaming, "Wake up and die!"

Garvin hesitated at the door. 'four minutes, twelve seconds. please, master, leave him. all of Time depends on you.'

As Garvin went through the door, he heard gunshots, felt Nick put a knife through someone's chest. Outside, Lex signaled, GARVIN, NICK, COME ON, as Nick downstairs kicked the legs out from under one Goblin, smashed another's face with an elbow.

Then Garvin leaped the distance from porch to sidewalk in two bounds. It seemed to him that his legs got longer as he ran down Irving Place to Fourteenth. He probed east as he did. 'three minutes and fifty-two seconds.' From behind he heard a human scream from the cellar, then silence. He knew Nick was gone again. But the Goblin and Zombies weren't interested in probing anymore.

Garvin felt the roadblock across Fourteenth Street at First Avenue before he rounded the corner and saw it. A dozen Zombies were lined up across the street. COMING IN ON A NUCLEAR WIND, Garvin yelled and ran right at them. 'three minutes and thirty seconds,' his Rider announced

THREE AND A HALF MINUTES UNTIL *DOOMSDAY*. A couple of them reached for his mind and got an image of a bomb and a blinding flash. TRY TO STOP ME, AND WE ALL GO. Some of them hesitated, others leveled guns. The moment they did, Lex popped around the corner behind them, carrying an automatic rifle.

'get out of her line of fire,' his Rider ordered. Garvin swerved into a storefront. Lex let off a clip. Half of the Zombies went down. She spewed images of dead Zombies and dying Goblins she had seen. The rest broke, running for portals.

Then there was no one between Garvin and Lex, and they were running toward each other. Garvin motioned her to go back toward Tompkins Park. Lex halted. NICK?

'two minutes and twenty-five seconds.'

Garvin tried to explain, "He came as far as he wanted . . ."

She stood uncertainly, staring off to where Nick had gone. "Me too," Lex said. Garvin grabbed her and started running again. 'two minutes, ten seconds.' His sneakers hit the pavement as if they were driven by pistons. His lungs were bellows gulping air and spitting fire. Lex was pulled along by him.

Rounding the corner toward the park, Garvin turned his attention to the ornamental gazebo which contained the portal. Zombies stood waiting. DOOMSDAY, SHITHEADS. STAND, AND YOU ARE GOING TO DIE. He saw himself in their eyes. He was huge. Sparks flew from his hair. His eyes glowed like fire. 'one minute, thirty-six seconds.'

The Zombies broke and ran away from the portal. They raced to their deaths as Garvin roared across Tompkins Square Park. He reached the portal with his legs burning, his mouth full of smoke. He hauled Lex into Time as the Rider told him, 'thirty-one seconds.'

In the emptiness Garvin felt the atomic flash and wanted to scream, BURN, SUCKERS!

Only then did he remember Cal and the other poor souls like him. Those few dozen lives being snuffed out were nothing to the great cities he had felt die. A couple of Goblins got caught and their dying didn't bother him. It almost seemed for a second that he had caught a trace of something that might have been fear. Even the death of their Zombies he could accept. But the innocent humans were few enough that he felt each pair of eyes burned open, each body outlined for a millisecond on a disintegrating wall.

Garvin and Lex got through the portal on the neighboring forest world and leaned against a tree, held on to each other for comfort. "I wouldn't even let him rest. I had to bring him back to save me a couple more times," Garvin gasped when he recovered enough breath to talk. Lex looked at him and for an instant saw Nick's face, young and undamaged, instead of Garvin's. She felt a chill like a knife. Then Nick's face was gone and the Warchild was kissing her hard.

CHAPTER
Nine

Goblins again faced the God in the overgrown park world next to the City. A chilling mist hung over the trees. On this occasion, the God wore a trenchcoat and had a cap pulled down over his eyes. This was an incarnation Brian Garvin thought of as the Gunman, but which Tom would have recognized as the Young Lout. He counted several dozen Goblins out where he could see them. Others were still inside the shuttle craft in which they had flown down from the orbiting Cave of Winds. By his estimate, the satellite would be overhead again in less than twenty minutes.

The God had summoned the Swift Ones and they had responded in their thousands. Long-legged, seeming equally impervious to the weather and the meeting taking place, they gamboled around him, appeared in packs on the wooded hills behind the Goblins. "To what do I owe the pleasure of the sight of all your bright faces?" he asked, knowing the partnership was going to end right there.

That Goblin the God thought of as Black Robe stood in front of the others, indignation tinged with something not unlike fear, as it revealed a tale of woe. It seemed that the one

the God called the Aggrieved Goblin and several companions
had lain in wait for the Warchild on his old home world. They
had found the mirrored room the God had left and had set up
an active nuclear device with its detonation tied to the explosion which would follow Garvin's entering the house. Their
idea had been either to eat Garvin's heart out and bring his
head to his father or, failing that, to trap the Warchild in New
York and let him die in the atomic blast.

The Gunman smiled. "Ah, the bomb in the townhouse was
a little trick of my own. It sped potential heirs on their way to
seek their fortune and eliminated the stupid and the soft-
hearted before they could do any harm. You went me one
better there as you so often have in rigging up the infernal
device," he told the Goblins, who stared blankly.

WAITING AT HIS MOTHER'S HOUSE, Black Robe told
the God, and showed him the story gleaned from a surviving
Goblin. Black Robe appeared sure Garvin's father would understand how wrong the Warchild was to resist simple justice.
The Gunman grinned as he saw the stick figure that was his
son lay the Aggrieved Goblin out with a poker. Another Goblin had been injured in the cellar by the Warchild's bodyguard
and only dragged to safety in the last seconds before the bomb
went off.

Black Robe pointed to the survivor. That Goblin's skin was
darker green in several spots where its injuries had been
patched up. The God recognized another miracle of the alien
metabolism and laboratories. Black Robe indicated a full
Wind. That meant it had taken the equivalent of the energy of
a newly fed Wind to repair those Goblins who were injured
and carry them to the God. For the Aggrieved Goblin there
had been no rescue. Even Goblin science could not bring back
one who lay at ground zero of an atomic blast.

Brian Garvin knew that if the Goblins believed there was
the slightest chance of his son being dead they would have
told him he was. He also hoped the boy hit on a better strategy
soon. Aloud he asked, "Now which is it that bothers you
most, the injury and death or the expense it took to bring this
one back to life?"

They understood that and several bared their teeth. "Ah,
none of that," said the Gunman. "When first we met, you

made a sorry crew. Lost in the void between stars and running low on fuel. Our partnership has made you rich and given you such honor as applies among you." As he told them that, the Gunman looked into alien eyes and knew they were about to move. He reached out for the Swift Ones.

YOUR SON HAS KILLED ANOTHER GOBLIN. OUR AGREEMENT IS BROKEN, Black Robe told him.

"I'll admit that the lad is a bit headstrong." The Gunman jammed his right hand deep in his pocket. "And his head on my Council table would be only the justest of penalties."

HIS MOTHER. A Goblin showed something that a Zombie interrogator had gotten from the memory of Cal: Claire Reilly taken away by the Guvnor. The Goblins had planned to use her to bait the trap for Garvin. THAT ONE CONTINUES TO PLAGUE US. HE AIDS YOUR SON. HE SAVED THAT WOMAN AT YOUR ORDERS.

"At my orders?" And here the God himself wondered at what they showed him. "Haven't I put a reward out for that rascal?" He watched the Swift Ones fill up the slopes behind the landing craft.

HE HAS STOLEN A WIND. THAT WAS ALSO WITH YOUR HELP.

"That happened long ago. It angers me as much as you." The Gunman looked up in the sky, then at the surrounding hills, dark with Swift Ones. The time was almost right. To distract the aliens he shouted out, "Now what about the other side of the agreement? The Winds have fed. Where are the ones that will light and power my city? My people are in near darkness. And they are cold. That I will not tolerate."

THE AGREEMENT IS OVER. The Goblins started forward, their heads moving with an hypnotic circular motion. The guns in the landing craft bore in on Brian Garvin. As that happened, on the hills all around them, Swift Ones danced in unison, stamped their feet and lifted their eyes and hands toward the sky. The ground under the landing craft trembled and cracked. A laser bolt fired harmlessly overhead.

"It touches me in the heart, the lad fighting his way out of the house." The God produced a pistol and fired twice. A Goblin fell, but the others kept coming. The sky darkened and thunder rolled. Sheets of rain slashed along the abandoned park and the God falling back step by step emptied his gun into the advancing Goblins. "It should cost you dearly in repairs," the God told them.

The ground under a landing craft gave way. Lightning struck Black Robe, twisted him and threw him to the ground. Only then, with grass burning around them and their machinery wrecked, did the Goblins stop and stand watching as the Gunman turned and strode rapidly into the gathering darkness with his Swift Ones about him.

As always, a couple of the smallest of his favorite creation came right up to him, reaching into the God's pockets for candy. He had none with him but he gathered them in his arms. As the God passed a ruined walk and a stone wall overgrown with brambles, the rest of the Swift Ones stopped and faced in the direction of the Goblins.

But the God, continuing on, carried the young ones through a portal and over the garden that lay on its other side. The three entered the mirrored drawing room where a fire danced on the hearth. The table was set for tea. In the mirror two young ones floated and the God wasn't there at all. He put them down and they ran for the cream cakes and bread and honey, giggling.

"Thomas," the God called out in a voice familiar to the servant.

"Reverend Father?" came the response from down the hall.

"Summon my Council, human and Rider, to meet immediately. Tell the guard commander I said to lock the gates of the City and to seal off Goblin Market. No one is to enter or leave. And tell Mary there are two here to supper."

Garvin and Lex came to rest on a fine fall night at a small inn run by Moors on the coast of Normandy. Their hosts knew enough about Time and telepathy to be very discreet. They showed the oddly dressed young people to their best room. Inside, Garvin took off the jacket Nick had given him, examined where the Goblin's teeth had ripped it, and said, "I'll keep it this way as a reminder."

Lex felt a great distance separating them as the Warchild sat down beside her on the bed. It seemed that she was a reminder too. Garvin caught the thought and said, "Without you, I'd be dead. When things get too complicated for me, I always want to run away. You're what's holding me to my purpose."

"That's why you invented me." In this quiet place, after all she had done and seen, Lex felt empty. She remembered how when she was little, she would wonder if the whole world was just something she had made up, if it had existed at all before she thought of it. She felt the start of that same cold uncertainty when she tried out any of her memories from before that morning when the image of the Warchild had possessed her.

"I don't think I could have invented you." Garvin looked very thoughtful. "You're better than I am, smarter. I love you because of that. And because you know what a fuckup I am and it doesn't bother you."

Garvin took her in his arms, and it was much later that Lex told Garvin, "We have to go back to the army."

There was a long pause, during which Garvin communicated with his Rider. Then he shook his head and told her, "I want you to go back to a place called Guitars. I have someone who can take you there as fast as I could."

"Who?"

"My uncle." He showed her the Guvnor. "I'll send him to pick you up here."

"What about you?"

FAMILY BUSINESS. Garvin's face flickered for a moment and he looked very serious. Subtle changes occurred and he turned into an idealized image of the Warchild.

"With your uncle?"

NO. She sensed his uncertainty. WITH THE OTHER SIDE OF THE FAMILY. THERE ARE THINGS I HAVE TO FIND OUT. He touched the razor and added, MY RIDER DOES TOO.

"What am I going to do at Guitars?"

Standing before her, looking into her eyes, looking into her mind, was the Warchild, the one who had first summoned Lex. I ORDER YOU TO TAKE COMMAND OF THE ARMIES OF THE FOUR SEASONS IN THE DEFENSE OF GUITARS.

"I can't do that," Lex said. "A million people, the Immortals, Herself . . ."

YES, YOU CAN. I WILL SHOW YOU WHAT I WANT DONE. THE GUVNOR WILL HAVE MORE OF THE PLAN WHEN HE PICKS YOU UP HERE.

Garvin showed her a strategy worked out by the Rider. "And what you're doing isn't just running away?" she asked.

The idealized Warchild faded into a kid chewing his lip thoughtfully. Garvin sank down on the bed beside her. "If it is, then I think it will be better to let the war end right there at Guitars."

Garvin reached up to the Wind and touched several dozen minds taken since young Master Bream had gone into the belly of the beast. Bream had begun to blend into the thousands of other telepaths absorbed over the centuries.

Garvin and the Guvnor stood on a prairie in Canada. Beyond the world on which it existed was an appendix which stretched back to the Republic. Before them, a portal made the sun of an early spring morning shimmer as if it were passing through spiders' webs. "This was what you meant by waiting at my mother's house?" he asked.

"It's how I think of the place." Garvin saw Claire in his uncle's memory, stunned and scared by Time but smiling bravely as he escorted her home. "I'm sorry if that offended you."

"Thank you for saving her," Garvin said.

"No thanks necessary." The Guvnor smiled. "You may not regard me as the very type of the parfait knight. But I think of what I did for your mother as part of my chivalric duty toward She Whom I Serve." His uncle said that as if it were a title.

"I got angry before. Would you explain again what you know about my mother . . . and her house?"

'and how he found out what he knew about my origins,' the Rider urged him.

"Your mother is one of what I think of as the Soft Sisters. Acting for My Lady, I have managed to plant quite a number of them out in Time. Your father has found a goodly proportion of those. Thinks of them as his own invention. In part they are. But they come from the Republic, not from the worlds on which he finds them. Your father has one kind of breeding scheme: trying to raise an heir. The Lady has another one. They intersect. Damned cleverly."

"What about Herself's mother? Was she part of that?" Garvin asked very quietly and looked away.

The Guvnor nodded and didn't fail to notice. There were wheels within wheels, he knew. "She too. Couldn't get her back out. Can't always or your father would suspect."

"Tell me about that."

"It's easier, really, to tell you my own story. You'll find out the rest soon enough." Garvin nodded. The Guvnor leaned against a tree and offered him a cigar. Garvin shook his head and his uncle lighted up.

"Your father both opened and shut down Lady Tagent's private railway to the stars," he said. "After that, I was left sans house, sans funds, sans family, sans purpose. I had telepathy, but it frightened me. The only knowledge I had which was worth anything was what I had heard your father and my grandmother discuss. Perhaps the One I Serve was guiding me even then, but I became convinced that if Brian Garvin could find a new world, I could do the same.

"It was obvious that Black Jack Howard was the link between your father and the Tagent family. I returned to Ireland and to the Tagent estate, where I had first seen Brian Garvin. The place was tied up in debt. The lawyers had explained that there would be nothing left for me to come into. That didn't matter. I never wanted money, you know, just a sort of freedom. A throwback in a way.

"Those were hard years in Ireland, between the end of the war and the coming of the Free State. During the Troubles, they had tried to burn down Tagent Manor. Someone had stolen the lead off the roof." Garvin saw images of the ruined great house.

"The people remembered my father and the girl he had wronged. They remembered your father also, how his mother was a bit mad before her seduction and far more than that afterwards, how as a boy your father had read and thought more than was considered healthy and how he had gone off in the spring of 'sixteen to serve with the Sinn Fein. He had returned just a short while before to be with his mother at her death, then disappeared again.

"That was a few weeks before my half brother had appeared in London. The timing of those two events meant to me that Brian Garvin had found at his mother's death something about that one item that would complete Lady Tagent's drawing room."

Garvin saw his uncle's memory of the star on the flag held in the elephant's trunk, the one his father had said was snatched from the Well of Stars. "You thought that was where he had gotten the jewel?" he asked.

The Guvnor nodded and relighted the cigar while looking toward the sunlit portal. "Despite all that had gone on, the Irish were friendly enough to me. Residual interest in the Tagent family, perhaps, or the national love of a good disaster. Or it may have been Her doing. She had been worshipped on that spot as Virgin and saint, wood sprite and goddess as long as people had lived there.

"Margaret Garvin was your father's mother's name. It took very little mind reading to find that she had served the Goddess before she met my father. And served her afterwards as well.

"I had thought I was going to find out my father's secrets. But it may be that Black Jack himself did no more than serve Her in his own brutal way. It was after he seduced young Margaret Garvin that his life and mind came unraveled. Perhaps the Goddess had no more use for him. Just as Lady Tagent had her little schemes, the Goddess has her great ones. Your father may be part of one that went awry. Or his doings may be according to Her plan. All I know is that She had a place for me."

Garvin shared his uncle's memories of woods and moonlight, of two local women, one ancient, the other just at puberty, leading him. "Since I could open minds, I found out about the cult." Garvin caught his uncle's memory of trying to look like a hard and bored young man. Ahead of him, shining through the branches of a tree, was a quarter-moon. Just below it was a single bright star. "I hadn't even noticed my two guides' disappearance."

Then the moon and the star shifted in the sky and Garvin

saw, as his uncle, young Anthony Tagent, had, that the moon was the frontpiece of a crown and the star an eye. As they moved, he saw the other eye and a face smiling with the gentle restraint that came of absolute power. Wisps of night clouds passed before the face of the Goddess and the night breeze whispered, "Come walk with me."

On the Canadian prairie, Garvin shivered and the Guvnor pointed toward the portal, saying, "She treated me well. There were tests that I was allowed to pass. Not all were so lucky. I saw the place my father failed. The Goddess took me in and made her agent in my half brother's domain. I have followed her without looking back. She has summoned you. Go."

"My father's Time is ending."

"So it seems. He and his partners had a falling out. The Goblins are creatures of business and I never understood business. But your father's Time has been good to me: ten million fine cigars, a million bottles of cognac, women when I wanted them, brisk little scrapes when life grew boring. I'll be sorry to see it end."

"I need your help, Guvnor. I don't know what will happen to the worlds of Time after my father goes. So all I'm offering may be a reprieve."

"That's the most anyone has ever had."

"Not you and my father. You live forever."

"We have both dwelt long in Time. That's something different from immortality, old boy. Now, what are the terms of the reprieve?"

"My Rider's guess is that the Goblins are advancing on the City of Guitars with all their Winds. If they win there, Time itself won't be big enough to hide in from them. Or from me, if I come back."

The Guvnor relighted his cigar. "Just myself against the Goblins?"

Garvin showed him the Rider's plan for the defense of Guitars until the Warchild could return. He showed the rebel armies falling back, the Goblins organizing a slow and careful pursuit. When Garvin gave out orders, he turned into the idealized Warchild. Firsthand memory of him issuing them would be absolute authority in his armies. YOU, he told the

Guvnor, WILL HAVE A FIELD COMMAND, and showed his uncle exactly what he wanted done. Looking at him, the older man grew very thoughtful.

Then Garvin showed an image of Lex and her location. SHE IS MY CHOICE AS COMMANDER. YOU WILL BRING HER WITH YOU TO GUITARS ON THE WIND, the Warchild told him. AS FAST AS POSSIBLE.

"As you wish." The Guvnor smiled again and bowed slightly.

Garvin found that he wanted to ask more questions, but his Rider told him, 'you are wasting energy gossiping with the gatekeeper.'

His uncle laughed when he was shown that and told Garvin, "The secret sharer is right, old boy. All answers lie with Her. Go." Then the Guvnor leaped into the air and was grabbed by his Wind. Turning, he saluted Garvin and disappeared into the morning sun.

Past the portal lay a short appendix in Time. It was a string of six worlds, five of them created empty of human life and devoid of interest. The sixth, at its end, had been partially blighted by war. But in its North America was a society, the Republic, which as far as Garvin knew was unique in all of Time. Its world was unique too in that no portals were known to lead past it. Past the end of the appendix, Time itself seemed to come to an end.

Instead of Time Striding, Garvin tumbled from portal to portal and walked over ice and jungle and veld and tundra. He had passed these worlds with the Guvnor years before, a scared kid ignorant of Time and struggling with his Rider every step of the way. It was on that journey that he had first learned to spin worlds and stride in Time. Passing through them again, Garvin saw how the five worlds discouraged travel. That had worked to isolate the Republic until the Riders had found rumors of a place where telepaths were strong and thick on the ground.

The appendix contained a lot of memories for Garvin. Four worlds down, he found the place where the Guvnor had driven their jeep off a cliff and right through a midair portal. He had returned to that same world with the tiny beginnings of his rebel armies and linked up with the Guvnor. Together they had destroyed Rumack and saved the Republic.

On a wide veld, Garvin found the portal through which he had emerged to help Herself break her Rider's absolute power. Thinking about that, Garvin walked toward a tree on a low rise. Three black skeletons hung from the branches, arms and legs bowed and misshapen, crisscross patterns of bones covering the upper trunks, the skulls seeming too small to contain the rows of teeth jutting out of them. It was there that he had hanged the Goblins and begun his revolution back before he had any idea what that meant.

It was almost evening before Garvin tumbled from a portal and into a shallow cave in the world at the end of Time. He stood in the midst of a burned-out forest of the Republic's Border District Four and noticed green shoots sprouting among the black stumps. The Warchild composed himself and probed toward the minds in the gray stone and white wood of the town of Weatherhill.

He touched first the nontelepathic Citizens of the Republic. Some of them he recognized; many of them recognized him. He felt the name Warchild and remembered that this was where he had received it. AMRE? he asked.

Then the telepathic Select in the town linked together and reached toward him. WHO? they demanded. The Select were a captain of horse commanding the garrison, a forester trying to regrow the woods, and a couple of her young apprentices.

In the dusk Garvin could just see the captain's black uniform, the old forester's white robes. It seemed so innocent and homey that Garvin almost expected to sight Scarecrow, his best teacher's lanky frame and long blond hair. The captain formed up his soldiers, the telepaths linked against him, unsure what to do. This was the one who had first saved their land, then taken away thousands of their children. Garvin told them, I AM ON MY WAY TO THE RETREAT, BUT FIRST I WANT TO SEE AMRE.

That was when he was aware of a tall woman with gray in her dark hair walking toward him. He realized how much like his mother Amre was. Garvin thought again of Scarecrow, her mate. He remembered the spring morning when he had first awakened lost and battered in that town in the middle of the green woods. That evening years later as Amre put her arms out and he felt her welcome, Garvin remembered that his last tears had been shed here.

When he touched her mind, Garvin felt the question, "How are the others?" In her memory were images of Maji and Darrel and the other children from Weatherhill who had marched off that world with Warchild Cluster.

He had returned knowing he would have to answer the question. "A lot of them scattered on special assignments, or in hospitals," he heard himself say. "A good number of them are dead." Amre nodded and put her arms around Garvin and he felt he was among his own people. Great effort and many lives had been lost to bring him here the first time. It had been no accident. He had been crazy and stupid not to have recognized that.

He realized that Amre felt fragile in his arms. "I'm going to the Retreat," he whispered. "But I wanted to see you."

"We have missed you here," she said as she walked with Garvin toward Weatherhill. The war which had wasted the forest had spared most of the town. Citizens who had known Garvin as a scared refugee still remained. He saw the toll that war and its aftermath had taken. The woods which had been their lives were gone and wouldn't be restored in their lifetimes. "Warchild, how are our children?" He felt the thoughts in a hundred untrained minds. "Did the ones who fell die bravely?"

Garvin winced as his Rider ran through a list of those it knew had fallen. The telepathic Select had great respect for Amre. She was the widow of Scarecrow, Guardian of the district, the one in all the Republic who had offered the best resistance when Rumack and his Rider had invaded. To them, Garvin was almost as much a symbol of the horrors of Time as Rumack. But Scarecrow had become the nation's hero.

GARVIN, CALLED WARCHILD, HAS RETURNED. The captain sent that information to New Liberty, the capital, by factor. He had been little more than a cadet at New Liberty when Rumack had come out of Hotlands and the Republic's armies had been destroyed and its government had all but collapsed. I AWAIT ORDERS.

As the captain stood, remembering that, a child ran forward, cried, "Garvi," and put her arms around the Warchild's waist.

"Miche!" Garvin recognized the daughter of Scarecrow and Amre. He picked her up and a kind of spell was broken. People whose lives he had saved, whose children he had taken, stepped up to touch his arm, to speak his name.

Everyone remembered when the Warchild had slain the ogre called Rumack. They remembered him marching toward New Liberty with his army of kids, Citizens and Select from the Republic, mercenaries who had followed Garvin from the City Out Of Time, Companions and troopers led by the Talking Suitcase and the Rose, young Hotlanders brought from the south by Rumack but belonging now to the Warchild.

On his march to the capital he was greeted as a hero by Citizens and Select along the way. Any mind the Warchild touched was his. He was conquering the Republic more completely than Rumack ever could have. Then from the Retreat, the island prison hospital for mad Select, the place where the nation kept its damaged telepaths, came a message and an image. LET THE WARCHILD COME HERE AND LEARN WHO AND WHAT HE IS was the message. The image was of Garvin in rags, dirty and bleeding, standing in near darkness on a barren rock.

The decimated, discredited Council of Councils at New Liberty had shown that to the advancing Warchild. Angry and hurt at what he took to be a summons to imprisonment in a madhouse, their fifteen-year-old savior had returned to the burned-out forestland on the border of the Republic and Hotlands.

He let the army around him swell with Select and Citizen, Hotlander and mercenary, any who would follow him. Then Garvin asked them to choose between himself and that world, and all had stepped into Time with him. To those they left behind, it seemed that everyone young and alive was gone.

Standing in Scarecrow's town of Weatherhill, Garvin looked around him at the faces of the Citizens and remembered one last thing his uncle had told him. "The Republic is the place where Her domain and your father's mix. The people are mostly his, but they all have a trace of Her in them.

Some more than that." Then Garvin caught the smell of stewing meat and fresh bread and he realized how hungry he was.

After he ate in the dining hall, Amre and Miche sat with him in the dark schoolroom where he plugged into children's history tracks. He felt his Rider thinking, as it had years before on first seeing these tracks, 'unique, a technology unlike any other in time.'

Images from one track showed white-robed telepathic wizards appear on a devastated world and set up enclaves in the North American wilderness. Garvin saw how, early in its history, the Republic started taking infants from their parents when they were discovered to be telepathic and raising them to be Select. He knew that Scarecrow, a Select, and Amre, a Citizen, had two of their children taken from them.

Besides the overt telepathy, there was a high degree of passive empathy among the Citizens of the Republic. Amre had that and Garvin realized that his mother Claire had it too. Otherwise she could hardly have put up with raising him. Along with the Selected infants, he guessed, a certain number of nontelepathic girls had also been taken from their parents. Those the Guvnor had stolen and planted out in Time. "A little bit of Her to go with a large dose of your father," he had told Garvin.

Looking at Amre, Garvin wondered if she might be his mother's sister. Thinking of that, he reached toward her and Miche and caught their loneliness. Seeing him again, they were reminded of Scarecrow and were twisted inside by their grief.

Despite their love for Garvin, neither of them could help wondering how it would have been if he had returned a day, or even a few hours, earlier. Then their husband and father would still be alive. Garvin, chilled by that, thought for a moment of how he had brought back Nick, his first instructor. He turned away toward the shadows before either of them could see his face shimmer and begin to form the features of Scarecrow, his greatest teacher. That was when he knew that the greatest kindness he could do for them and all others in Time was to go to the Retreat.

*　　*　　*

Garvin held a memory of Amre and Miche tightly as he stood on the shore and watched a ferry float out of the mist. As he stepped onto the deck, he felt the mental pulse from the city of New Liberty a few miles to the south. But almost as soon as the ferry was under way, he lost touch with everything but the minds on the Retreat. A tired-looking middle-aged Select in a black military coverall turned and told Garvin, I AM CHIEF MEDICAL OFFICER OF THE ISLAND. MY NAME IS SANGAM. THE RESIDENTS OF THE RETREAT CALL ME THE SANDMAN.

Minds ahead of them in the fog threw images of sheets blowing on a clothesline. As Garvin watched, the sheets turned first into Select in white robes dancing wildly, then turned into Select in white robes hanged by the necks and jumping in the breeze. One mind somewhere on the Retreat heard waves as bells, heard the bells play the tune to which the sheets danced. A dozen other minds took up the bell sounds, making them louder and louder. Then a damaged Select saw the sheets as licking flames in a white room and the fog as smoke, felt the fog seeping into his lungs and began to gag and broadcast an alarm, FIRE, FIRE. I AM CHOKING.

LIAR, LIAR, other minds echoed.

THERE ARE THREE HUNDRED FORTY-TWO RESIDENTS HERE RIGHT NOW, Sangam told him. YOU UNDERSTAND THAT IN A SOCIETY WHERE TELEPATHS RULE, ANY MENTAL DISORDER IS A THREAT TO CITIZEN AND SELECT ALIKE.

Garvin nodded and kept his thoughts within his innermost Keep. He considered his father farming him out, one of dozens, maybe hundreds, maybe thousands of bastards. 'he desired an heir,' the Rider remarked, 'but had all eternity to find the right one. if the guvnor is to be believed, you are the first whom the goddess has summoned.'

GARVIN WARCHILD, YOU WERE SUMMONED BY THE RESIDENTS. THE REPUBLIC NOW CONSIDERS YOU ALSO A RESIDENT, the Sandman told him. As trees and rocks onshore loomed out of the fog, Garvin remembered the time when he was too proud to come here. He had left the Republic and gone to war. 'i could not face that either. i did not advise you correctly, warchild,' his Rider told him. Garvin felt its own excitement and terror at what they were about to learn.

Looking around as they docked, Garvin saw a massive gray building, caught sight of white forms dancing in a sea breeze. He thought they were sheets on a line. Only when they probed him did he realized that they were Select, two men and a woman with long hair, their robes ragged. They caught the edges of his mind, dancing toward him. GARVIN HAS COME. GARVIN THE APPRENTICE.

Minds, hundreds of them, batted at his defenses. He stepped onto the dock, felt the salt air on his face. They found his Rider, who cringed away from them. GARVIN HAS BROUGHT US HIS LITTLE FRIEND! He blocked some but others got through. GARVIN WARCHILD, LOST IN TIME.

CONTAIN YOURSELVES! Sangam and the other doctors started to disentangle the mare's nest of minds, to break up impromptu relays. EACH MIND, STAY TO ITSELF. "They will calm down shortly," he told Garvin.

But Garvin stood staring off. A mind had swooped down like a gull, then disappeared. In its memory, he had seen a swath of lights, the Well of Stars.

After seeing to the residents, medicating some, soothing others, the Sandman and his assistants withdrew behind banks of Scramblers for the night. With a blanket wrapped around him, Garvin sat in the doorway of a stone house, shivered from the chill, and watched white figures approach in the dark. He winced at the touch of minds imprisoned in bodies, of minds scraping again and again on frustration like nails on a blackboard. He caught the aching suspicion of the damaged minds that something lay just beyond their grasp.

Then Garvin saw a patient twirl under the misty light of the moon. She broadcast as hard as she could an image of Select, dozens of them, clad in robes. They whirled in a field in bright sunshine, slapped at their skin, tore their clothes as if they were assaulted by gnats. Instead of insects, Garvin saw that the air was full of tiny worlds revolving, stinging like fire, impervious to the hands that hit them. Select clawed their own skin and screamed with pain. In the vision of the damaged mind, Citizens, nontelepathic, not understanding, stood around the edges of the field and looked on, bewildered, as their masters ripped themselves to shreds.

'a society which lived securely on a world which it thought the only world is shocked to the point of madness at finding it isn't,' the Rider suggested. 'many of these newer patients came here when the invasion from out of time occurred.'

Garvin added, GENERATIONS AGO THE WORLD MY FATHER CREATED WAS COMING APART THE WAY THEY ALWAYS DO IF THEY GET TOO ADVANCED. ALL OF A SUDDEN MAGICIANS IN WHITE ROBES AP-PEARED OUT OF NOWHERE AND FOUNDED THIS SO-CIETY. THE REPUBLIC IS AFRAID TO ASK WHERE THEY CAME FROM, WHO THEY WERE. JUST THE SAME WAY I WAS AFRAID TO LOOK.

He sat quietly. The telepathic Select of the Republic were powerful and there were enough of them on the island to wear down Garvin's defenses. As awful as was the anxiety and pain on every mind, the humiliation of being a mental patient, Garvin knew that part of him didn't want to go farther. He too feared the unknown, the knowledge that might make all he had done in Time seem as worthless to him as Time had made the Republic seem to these Select.

Cautiously reaching out, he found a woman, old and doz-ing, a longtime resident. She had been a middle-level admin-istrator in a northern town who one day had been unable to get out of bed, who refused to join her mind to other Select. The image that blocked her was of a wall of opaque black glass. On it were reflected stars, thousands of them. Again and again she bumped into that wall.

Garvin put into her mind an image from the children's in-structional track he had looked at that evening at Weatherhill. It showed a ship bearing a powerful telepath calling himself Rip Van Winkle who set up a fiefdom on this very island. A STORY, A STORY. I DO NOT WANT A STORY. The woman tried to shut her mind against Garvin. STORIES MAKE MY MIND DIE. He tried again gently. She blocked ferociously. The image she used to sweep his mind away was of an orchard. Instead of fruit, the trees bore human heads and the heads reached out to bite. GO THERE AND DIE, GAR-VIN WARCHILD, she told him.

GARVIN WARCHILD! GARVIN DEATH CHILD! Minds swirled around his. "Not a Select. Not a Citizen. Marooned on the Retreat." They screamed in unison and Garvin smelled the rhythm of their chant. A young man howled and bit the ground and Garvin heard the pain that tore through his teeth. The Warchild stood and started walking, forming Umbra, Curtain, and Keep. As he did he asked, WHY DID YOU CALL ME?

There was a moment's pause and Garvin felt what minds on the Retreat often felt in the moments before dawn, in the cracks of their shattered minds, something sighing, crying out, GARVIN, SON OF GARVIN, COME TO US.

Up on a hill, away from the buildings, past ruins, behind a disused latrine, in a hole where a tree and its roots had been ripped out by a long-gone landslide, was what felt like a portal, a tear in Time. Once recognized it was impossible to ignore. But it was unrecognizable to those ignorant of Time.

Until Time found it, the Republic knew nothing of portals. Since first Rumack and then Garvin had invaded the Republic, the Retreat was flooded with Select who didn't want to think about Time. The secret was still safe with them.

As Garvin went toward it, someone formed an image of two figures, a man and a woman. The man bowed and kissed the woman's hand, guided her to the hole. "Not a likely entrance to paradise," the Guvnor told Claire. As Garvin watched, something reached out for his mother, bore her gently down. When Garvin reached that place, nothing reached for him. Down the hole, far away, like the reflection on water at the bottom of a well, was a splash of stars.

Once portals had drawn Garvin in. They were freedom and escape. This one, as he tried to tumble into it, resisted him as if it were covered with ice. He thought of the mirrored room but nothing happened.

He thought of it again as he had seen it in his father's Palace. His father and he had both been invisible in the mirror, and only the child his father carried, the little Swift One, was visible and seemed to float in midair.

With that, the shield over the portal seemed to crack and Garvin started to tumble toward the distant stars. 'we are leaving your father's realm,' his Rider cried in his mind. Then it was quiet and Garvin found himself on a ledge of gray rock.

Cold air blew through his jacket. All the light came from the stars, which seemed no closer than they had been outside the portal. Garvin moved toward them and started to probe. His telepathy was like a weak flashlight beam shining down a well. He reached for his Rider and found a small ball of ice. He wanted to turn and run back to the portal. That's when he became aware of a row of shapes in front of him. They shifted slightly and he moved toward them.

As he did, he realized that what he saw was a long row, almost a hedge, of bushes. Suddenly hundreds of green eyes opened and caught the faint light. Garvin tried to reach for the minds that controlled those eyes and found himself blocked.

Garvin tried again, rubbed his fingers on his pants leg and tried to form an Umbra with the feel of that, hummed softly and listened to his own humming to make a Curtain and Keep. Nothing.

"Garvin born Reilly," came the slurred whisper of hundreds of tiny voices. Garvin looked toward the hedge. Each bush was about the same size as the body of the Thorn and Rose, but each of them was covered with blossoms, small heads with angry eyes.

"Garvin born Reilly, called Warchild." Garvin reached inside again for his Rider's advice and felt nothing but an echo of his own numb shock. The heads nodded and he knew they understood.

"Garvin born Reilly, called Warchild, destroyer of worlds, despoiler of innocence." Garvin shivered and thought of Amre and Weatherhill. Already that was a distant memory. His stomach ground on empty and he shivered again uncontrollably. He didn't know where he was, or all of who he was.

The hedge understood that too. "Garvin born Reilly, called Warchild, destroyer of worlds, despoiler of innocence, turn back while mind and manhood are left to you." Garvin's whole body shook. Then he remembered the cord and blade Lex had made for him and touched it.

There was no need to frighten his Rider, but it comforted Garvin somehow. All he knew was that he was lost and

hungry and freezing, with nothing but the clothes on his back
and the blade in his hand. "Rose and Thorn," he said, moving
forward, amazed at how thin and piping his voice sounded.
"Did my old man pass this way?"

"You know us!" came the rush of angry, tiny voices. "He
came this far once and no farther. He feared us."

"Yeah?"

"He stood for a long time looking past us. Then turned and
went back. You are welcome to do the same." By then, Garvin
was so close that he could see their eyes, hard and cold as jewels.
The fact that his father had turned back was enough to make him
press on. He spotted a space between two bushes that looked
large enough to squeeze through. A dozen mouths snapped at
him. One of them bit into his right thigh. He jumped back.

"Garvin Reilly, layabout," they whispered. "Garvin Warchild, how many have you slaughtered?" Since he wouldn't
turn back and he couldn't listen to that anymore, Garvin
wrapped his belt around his left hand, took off his jacket, and
held it over his head. In his right hand was the razor.

"How dry have you kept your own wick?" tiny voices
hissed as he plunged forward. "How many bastards have you
left behind you?" the ones farther off asked as he slashed and
punched his way past the biting mouths. They chewed at his
jacket. One of them bit through his pants at the knee and drew
blood. Another he kicked in the face as it tore his ankle. His
belt was eaten through. He lost his razor. For a moment he
felt as if he were going to trip. Then he wrenched himself past
the teeth that clung to him, staggered, and was free.

A long thin wail rose up behind him, but Garvin never
looked back. When he could no longer hear it, he sat on a
rock and tied up his wounds with strips torn from his shirt.

It was a long way and a hard one as he walked toward the
Well of Stars. Whatever else Garvin forgot later on, whatever
parts of his journey beyond the Retreat slipped back to the
place where dreams go, he always remembered the unvarying
gray light, the cold wind on his back, the hunger that made
him feel paper thin. Once he stopped to piss and felt that the
last warmth in his body had drained away.

In this place he had no way of telling the time. The wound

on his hands and legs ached and grew stiff. His sneakers blistered his feet. The light he moved toward got no brighter and he kept moving forward only because he was so cold and hungry that to lie down again would be to die.

Gradually, it seemed to him that death at least was warm and that he had no reason for not dying, that he had betrayed any companions and lovers he'd ever had, that all he had done was to substitute a more spectacular holocaust that he called a revolt for the slow ruthless slaughter of the Goblins.

In the instant that he lost any idea whether or not it mattered if he survived, he found himself, ragged and dirty, bloody and desperate, looking directly up at the Well of Stars. The well was far above him, its lights splashed in the same pattern as had spilled out of the Talking Suitcase. It was then that they shimmered and Garvin realized that they were a reflection. Turning, he saw the worlds of Time, tiny and distant below him.

All sense of up and down deserted him and his head began to swim. 'sit down, master,' his Rider told him quietly.

The Well shimmered like black water. Something touched his mind too quickly for Garvin to catch it. At the same moment a woman's voice called as though from the top of a high wall, "Garvin Warchild, why are you here?"

Garvin tried to answer telepathically but couldn't find the mind of the one who was talking to him. He called out as if he were still seven years old and yelling from the street at a window stories above. His mouth was dry; at first no sound came. Then he heard himself saying, "I'm looking for my mother." His own voice sounded weak, thin in the cold air.

"She has done well without you. Go back."

'he can't,' the Rider answered. 'he will die and i will die with him.'

"Why should that interest me?" asked the voice, and Garvin realized his mind was being read without his knowledge.

Still he said aloud, "Because you can show me some way not to be my father all over again."

'and you can show me who i am and what we riders were.'

Then the stars shimmered again and Garvin realized that they were a design on a long black robe. And he saw that above them rode the still, pale face of a woman of great beauty. It felt to Garvin that he was falling toward her as she said, "You are a well-matched pair," and Garvin almost thought he detected amusement.

CHAPTER
Ten

As the Warchild asked for word of his mother, the Goblins placed the City Out Of Time under siege. As his question was answered, Brian Garvin inspected the defenses of the Amber Gate in an identity his people had never seen before.

During the siege, the population of the City came to notice that it was the pleasure of the God to appear in that same form. Minutes, hours, whole days would go by in which there would scarcely be a flicker on the face of the tall Irishman in his thirties. It was known that he was to be called the Commandant and that at any moment in the day or the night he might appear at one of the defensive positions dressed in a belted trenchcoat, always clean-shaven, his eyes tired but alive with anticipation.

That face fascinated Brian Garvin whenever he saw it in a mirror or reflected in another's mind. It was a little older, perhaps a little wiser than the one he had worn when he first stepped through the portal in Lady Tagent's drawing room. If the grandeur of his godhood didn't show, neither did the crimes he had committed. "A likely enough face to take back to the world," he told himself and linked his mind to Coli, the

Chancellor, who commanded the defenders at the Amber Gate.

YOU HAVE ALL KNOWN FOR A LONG WHILE THAT THINGS WERE NOT WELL, THAT THE CITY LIVED OFF THE GOBLINS AND THEIR MARKET, he told the shopkeepers and prostitutes, soldiers and lodging house landladies, technicians and chamberlains thrown together as a defensive force. YOU HAVE BEEN LIGHTED AND WARMED BY THE WINDS AND YOU HAVE ALWAYS KNOWN THAT WHAT YOU WERE DOING WAS WRONG. They all nodded agreement, especially those who had never seen anything wrong with the arrangement.

FOR UNTOLD AGES I HAVE KNOWN THAT MY DEALINGS WITH THEM WOULD HAVE TO END. BUT TO DO THAT HASTILY WOULD HAVE MEANT THE END OF THE WORLDS OF TIME AND THIS CITY WITH ITS POPULATION, AND THAT I COULD NOT ENDURE. Everyone in the City had been or was descended from captives destined to be sold at Goblin Market. And all of them owed their freedom to the mercy of the Gods. That was the common thread that linked the entire population. NOW I AM CALLING IN MY DEBTS, their God told them.

A sensation between anticipation and a chill ran through the defenders. They had first felt that excitement a short while before when the unthinkable happened and Gods broke with Goblins. All the people of the City had seen the memories of the God's advisors, who had been present at that special session in the Crystal Chamber at the Palace. Summoned in haste, the advisors had arrived along with most of the Riders and Zombies in the City.

Neither the Goblins nor, at first, the God was present. No one at the meeting knew that a few minutes before the meeting was announced open conflict between God and Goblins had broken out on the world of the Swift Ones. No one, in fact, even knew of the world of the Swift Ones.

Chancellor Coli, standing with the God at the City gate, recalled for his forces how he had been sitting in a chair below the empty throne as the Council meeting had begun. The light in the City outside the Crystal Chamber had dimmed to gray. Several mortals were huddled in coats although the Gods' Palace itself was still warm.

ON ECHBATTAN'S WORLD THEY CALL THE WARCHILD THE SUMMER KING, a Steed just back from the front told the meeting. THEY SAY HE IS SLAIN AND THAT HIS REBELLION WITHERS AT THE APPROACH OF FALL. Images followed of worlds where the Warchild's forces had pulled back, of the slaughter of those who had declared for Garvin too soon. A note of the Rider's triumph crept into the report. Then it remembered and forced its Steed to bow low toward the empty throne. AS THE GODS FORETOLD.

"With all respect, mighty Rider," Oublie, the manager of the City, remarked, bowing her blue hair toward the throne. "We meet in the absence of my master. And yours," she said, jerking her thumb to indicate the Goblins' empty places. "Thus nothing said or done here will have any official weight. So let me ask unofficially why Winds have not been released to power the City Out Of Time?"

THEY ARE NEEDED FOR OUR COUNTERATTACK, answered another Rider, his Steed from the house of Echbattan smiling arrogantly. An image followed of flags flapping wildly, trees bowing down, figures dressed as Companions falling dead. IT IS THE WINDS WHICH BROUGHT US OUR VICTORIES. WE NEED THEM STILL TO BREAK THE RESISTANCE. THE REBELS HAVE FOUND A STRONGHOLD IN A PLACE THEY CALL GUITARS.

"But where is my son's head?" a voice asked quietly. No one had seen the figure in the jester's costume enter the room. But the God, in the person of the Holy Fool, hunchbacked, sharp faced, sat now on the steps of the throne. "I was promised his head when he reached your world. Now where is it?"

The Echbattan Steed gulped in discomfort, looked behind him anxiously at where the Goblins should have been. YOUR DIVINE MIRTH MAKER, WE HAVE FOUND ONLY THIS. Images followed, taken from captives as their bodies were broken, their minds torn open in a search for the last sighting of the Warchild. One dying prisoner had showed Garvin, blood spattered, leading a battalion near Echbattan's world, but nothing further.

"The Warchild's body has not been found, yet he is presumed dead while an army formed only by his name goes on fighting without him? A rare joke indeed!" The Holy Fool almost choked with laughter. Some of the Riders made their Steeds join in. "What do we know of Guitars?" the God asked suddenly, and they stopped laughing.

NOT MUCH, HEALER WITH WIT. IT IS A WORLD WE HAD OVERLOOKED WHICH IS WITHIN A HUNDRED WORLDS OF ECHBATTAN'S AND CONTAINS A TELEPATHIC CULTURE THAT . . .

"Overlooked a telepathic culture that close to you? Overlooked a chance to loot the place for slaves? Ah, Echbattan Rider, you make far better jokes than I do."

Embarrassed, the Riders had started to probe the City for a Goblin presence. As they did, everyone in the room heard a volley of automatic-weapons fire from the Market. DO NOT SEARCH FOR YOUR MASTERS, the God had told them. NO GOBLIN REMAINS IN THIS CITY. As the Council sat stunned at that news, the small hunched figure of the Holy Fool grew into the figure who would become known as the Commandant. IN FACT, NO GOBLIN WILL BE FREE TO ENTER THIS PLACE AGAIN AS LONG AS I RULE.

The gunfire outside grew closer and all in the Crystal Chamber felt minds broadcasting, THE ZOMBIES WILL FEED THE WINDS. The Steeds rose to their feet, their minds searching for their supporters. Guards in the blue and gray of the Gods appeared behind them in the door. Coli remembered that they wore green ribbons on their coats.

TO THE SLAVE PITS WITH THE ZOMBIES AND THEIR RIDERS, the Commandant ordered. THE ZOMBIES WILL SERVE A USEFUL PURPOSE FOR THE FIRST TIME. THE RIDERS WILL LEARN ABOUT SLAVERY. Turning to the Councilors, he asked, WILL YOU STAND WITH ME NOW AGAINST THE GOBLINS? Surprised and exhilarated by the drama of the moment, the Council stood cheering.

WE HAVE THE CHANCE TO MAKE RIGHT ALL OF THE THINGS WE KNOW WERE WRONG, the Commandant had told them. The Scramblers inside the Palace were turned off and the telepaths of the City linked minds and showed the populace their God telling them, STAND WITH ME UNTIL MY SON ARRIVES, AND I PROMISE YOU A BETTER LIFE THAN YOU HAVE HAD. LET US TRY TO MAKE THIS CITY INTO A PLACE WHICH HE WOULD WANT TO RULE.

A moment of stunned quiet had followed and then hundreds of thousands of voices shouted, "The Gods forever! The Eternal City will stand!" The God formed an image of Garvin Warchild, softened from what Goblin propaganda had shown them, looking in fact like a Mohawked version of the Commandant. THE GOD AND HIS SON VICTORIOUS OVER ALL TIME.

Then the Zombies were dragged through the streets and fed to the Wind, still hooked up beneath Goblin Market. All the slaves still waiting in the pits were freed and the Riders imprisoned. With that done, the Commandant walked the streets while the telepaths of the City linked every mortal man, woman, and child for the Gods' blessing. And as he touched them, all felt a weight lift which they hadn't known they carried and understood that a kind of justice was about to come down.

As the Commandant raised his hands, smiling at the populace, Brian Garvin thought, deep inside himself where none could know, "Either eternal happiness or the chance of a fast death when the Goblins break in. Whichever comes first."

When Coli had finished showing the defenders of the Amber Gate the highlights of their revolution, the God outlined his plans to them. As far as most of the population knew, the City was accessible from Time itself only through four portals. These were known to all as the Gates of Silver, Gold, Onyx, and Amber. The gates were ninety degrees apart on the great outer circumference of the City. Each stood on a huge plaza linked by wide avenues that led to the Palace of the Gods. In ordinary times the slaves and supplies that fueled the place came through these gates.

Beyond each was an adjacent world, stripped bare of life and wealth over the millennia. Many portals led to those four worlds, but from each of them only one portal led to the City. The Commandant showed his volunteer militia the flying columns of soldiers near his palace in readiness to rush immediately to any gate under attack.

As their God explained this, a young telepath detected the Goblins' first assault. She had volunteered to stand in the wide portal, hanging just short of a tumble into Time. She had been a porter, one who ferried goods, human and otherwise, on the short hop from the adjacent world into the City. A small party had gone through the portal as scouts a few minutes before their God appeared. The porter of the City's new husband was one of them.

She felt something in Time, probed and picked up the command NOW. She saw an image of a bomb, felt the Goblin imprint on a telepathic mind. Immediately she recognized a Zombie and fell flat on the ground while warning, INCOMING ATTACK. A dozen figures tumbled out of Time, leaping over the prone body of the porter. Their faces were painted red. Several had bloody heads strapped to their waists.

A barricade had been hastily constructed in front of the gate. From behind it, a hundred telepathic defenders reached out to smash the attackers, caught desperate enemy minds and the idea of bombs. As fast as attackers found their footing, defending telepaths paralyzed them. Gunfire cut them down before they could set off their explosives. It was over in seconds.

The Chancellor Coli stared down from the barricade, felt the God look through his eyes at the sprawled bodies, at the porter slowly picking herself up. A PROBE, the God told the defenders through Coli, NOTHING MORE. The porter began to broadcast her stunned shock at seeing her husband's head tied to the belt of someone lying on the pavement. GET HER AWAY FROM THERE, the Commandant ordered Coli. DO IT QUICKLY. The God was already headed away from the scene.

Minutes later another probe tried the Silver Gate. As he walked into Goblin Market, the God felt the attackers die, heard the explosion and felt the pain as one of them got off a satchel charge. The existence of the Goblins' Gate, a portal that opened directly into Goblin Market, was known in the City, but no one knew where it led.

The Market the God entered was nearly empty. Those

Riders and their Steeds seized at the Palace each lay in a separate pit, drugged and isolated with Scramblers. Zachberg, the Comptroller, a man the God had personally saved from these very pits, was in charge of a small number of keepers inside Goblin Market. The captured Zombies had been fed to the Wind which still powered the City. Brian Garvin's only regret was that there hadn't been enough of them, that the lights would shortly dim and the cold of Time creep inside.

The City contained greenhouses and hydroponic farms, but with the loss of power those had failed. The population would live on the dried and canned food stored up through the foresight of the Gods. The recycling mechanisms were becoming erratic and water had been rationed. Something would be needed to take the minds of the population off their discomforts. THE SCRAMBLERS NEEDED TO HOLD THE RIDERS ARE A DRAIN ON THE POWER, the Commandant told Zachberg as he ran up the stairs to the catwalks overlooking the Market.

DIVINITY? the Comptroller asked, knowing what would come next.

PREPARE THREE OF THEM FOR PUBLIC EXECUTION TOMORROW, ordered the Commandant. Then he passed through the portal that stood high over the Market and onto the world of the Swift Ones.

Shortly after that, Lex showed a direct, firsthand memory. Garvin Warchild stood in the coastal inn and turned over the Armies of the Four Seasons to her. She and the Guvnor had come out of Time at a portal downhill from Guitars.

Her arrival and the orders she carried were electric. The rebel troops had fallen back on the world of Guitars with no word from the Warchild, no sign that he was still alive. Rumors flourished; the revolt was coming unraveled. The image of Garvin alive and well went through thousands of minds in a matter of seconds.

WHO IS IN CHARGE HERE? was Lex's first question.

The answer was an image of Herself with her long hair tangled, her clothes filthy, stalking through a bombardment to rally a routing unit.

WHERE IS SHE?

IN THE REARGUARD WITH THE ARMY OF AUTUMN
AND WARCHILD CLUSTER. SHE IS DELAYING THE
ENEMY SO WE CAN ORGANIZE.

Lex turned to the Guvnor. "Bring her back. Bring them all
back." He saluted, leaped onto the Wind, and disappeared
through the portal. Lex told the guards, I WANT TO SEE
THE IMMORTALS.

A jeep was found to take her. A couple of dozen irregular
bikers wearing pirate bandannas formed an escort. By the
time they had driven halfway up the hill, the escort had swol-
len into a mob. Kids, most of them in the shreds of their
uniforms, followed her up to the stone and white-wood house
on the hill opposite Guitars. In the front yard stood a single
rosebush over a grave with a marker that read just, "Roger."
As Lex passed, something brushed her mind and she seemed
to hear a child's voice crying, "Where is Garvin?"

In the farmhouse dining room, Lex, crouching down, was
just able to see dim pinpoints of light on the floor and against
the wall away from the windows. On the table lay the empty
leather valise where Garvin had left it. The Talking Suitcase's
song, which she hadn't been able to pick up outside, was no
more than a whisper in her mind.

It was a song of journeys so long and hard that the voyagers
left bits of themselves behind on the way and returned so little
like the ones who had left that they were strangers. Lex
paused for a long moment, feeling some of the dead numbness
of her headlong flight on the back of the Wind begin to melt.

Unsure of whether the Immortal was aware of her, Lex
showed it her memory of pulling Garvin off the flaming pyre.
Something flashed in the web of light, the song ceased for a
moment and the entity on the floor asked, DID THE WAR-
CHILD SEND YOU TO ME?

Lex let its elusive touch go through her mind, take from her
the image of Nick and his memories of lying scared and hurt
beside the leather case. The song changed to one of Companions
lost and found again, of faces reappearing in the immensities of
Time. To Lex at that moment it seemed that all she ever wanted
to do was crouch near the heart of that song. Instead she said,
"There is one last task before any of us can rest."

Lex caught the snatch of a song of parents and children, of

lives curving back on themselves like Möbius strips. THEN THIS IS WHY THE OLD GODS CREATED ME, whispered the Immortal. AND YOU ARE TO BE MY FINAL BEARER. I AM GRATEFUL TO THE NEW GOD.

Lex felt no irony there, just an understanding of the twists of Time. Embarrassed, she showed him her short military career and said, "I think it must have been a joke. A joke of the Gods."

ALL BEINGS ARE THAT, ESPECIALLY THE IMMORTALS, it told her faintly. THEY CALL ME THE TALKING SUITCASE, YOU KNOW, and Lex smiled again after too long a while. Then she stood and crossed the room, picked up the leather satchel. When she touched the web of lights, Lex felt the cold of Time run through her hands and arms. But the lights seemed to weigh nothing and to flow back into the satchel like water. IT WAS THE GUVNOR WHO FIRST CALLED ME THAT, MANY GENERATIONS AGO, the Immortal whispered in her mind when it was back inside the leather satchel.

Lex didn't go to the Free City until the next day. Even if she hadn't been charged with command of the armies, even if she hadn't emerged from the house carrying the Suitcase, she would have been a celebrity as the one who had last seen the Warchild. In the front yard, she felt a mind like a frightened child's crying very softly and far away, GARVIN?

The minds of the army reached out to Lex; kids stared at her, shared their image with others. She stood near the Rose and Thorn and told them, WE ARE ORDERED TO MAKE OUR STAND HERE.

An Immortal's mind whispered, THIS IS WHERE WE'VE TAKEN ROOT. HERE WE WILL MAKE OUR STAND.

WHAT ELSE? WHERE HAS HE BEEN? Minds battered against Lex for the sight and sound of the Warchild. The Armies of Spring and Winter were posted downhill from Guitars. The Army of Summer, which had just fallen back to that world, was all around Lex and the farmhouse.

Lex formed the senior Companion commanders of the armies into a relay around her. As she gathered information from them, she dispensed images of Garvin that went out to the thousands of his followers. Lex showed them Garvin on the pyre, Garvin visiting his home, Garvin uncertain, and Garvin a god.

As she did that, Lex learned from the army about the world on which she stood. Perhaps created by Garvin in an idle moment, it had its own memories and history which it believed to be true. Previously unaware of the rest of Time, it now found itself a battlefield in a terrifying war. Fairly peaceful and prosperous, it had to provide food, shelter, clothing, and weapons for hundreds of thousands of wild kids.

THE INDUSTRIAL ECONOMIES ARE WRECKED, a corps commander told her. THE HOSPITAL SYSTEMS OF NORTH AMERICA AND EUROPE ARE FLOODED WITH OUR WOUNDED. WE APPEAR TO HAVE SEIZED THEIR SACRED CITY. Lex thought of the war-ravaged places she had seen on her way to and from Echbattan's world and nodded her understanding.

She visited Guitars the next afternoon. The parking lot at the foot of the hill was guarded by Companion troops. The constables of the Free City watched warily from across the bridge.

Lex had seen only Garvin's memory of his night in Guitars. In part she knew it was because she was viewing the place by day, but the city she saw looked faded and without magic. The gas lamps by morning light were just metal and glass and more than a few were broken. Cobblestones had been uprooted from the pavement, and the twisting streets climbed past dusty brick buildings with a lot of their windows gone. Fabric was stuffed in some of the holes. In one place a block of buildings had been burned out.

The very streets seemed to sing of young blood rising and young nerves snapping. Women sitting on their slumping front porches fanning themselves, young people on the street corners turning away as Lex and her escort passed, men sweeping up the litter of the night before, everyone showed images of young recruits, wide-eyed and naive, passing through Guitars on their way to fight for the Warchild. Then they showed the veterans returned from the front, the same kids in a lot of cases, telepaths with death in their eyes and no care as to who got caught in it.

A song hung over Guitars, sad and resigned. As she walked

uphill through the rising streets, Lex picked it out of the
minds of kids hanging around under a corner lamp post.

> *CHILDREN GONE ON THE FREEDOM TRAIL*
> *COME BACK CHAINED TO THE GUNS THEY*
> *BEAR.*
> *THAT'S IF THEY CAN RETURN AT ALL AND*
> *WAR DON'T LEAVE THEM WHERE THEY FALL.*

The people of the Free City refused to look at Lex, ostenta-
tiously turned their backs on her. But she understood that they
knew she and her Companions could turn them around and
force images of Garvin down their brain stems. They also
knew that Guitars was about to meet its doom. THERE HAS
BEEN SOME TROUBLE WITH OUR TROOPS. BUT IF
THE GOBLINS TAKE THE PLACE, THEY WILL EAT A
FEW SOJOURNERS THEMSELVES AND FEED THE
REST TO THE WINDS, a Companion staff officer told her.

From inside the Suitcase, in a soft whisper, came a counter
harmony to the song of Guitars:

> *CHILDREN WILL RETURN*
> *TO FIND OUR NAMES*
> *WRITTEN ON THE WIND.*

Lex found the mind she sought, stopped in front of a cafe
porch, and asked, MIGHT I COME UP?

"There is no way to stop you." Bethel sat on the bandstand
with a mandolin in her lap, a mug of tea on a piano stool next
to her. She looked up as Lex opened the screen door. "We saw
you on the mind of your army last night, Commander," she
said. "Saw what you showed them too. Now you've come to
see if everyone here is set to do their duty for your Warchild."

"I have something to show you," Lex said. Then from up in
the mountains she caught an image of a green face eating its
way into Garvin's stomach. The rear guard had started pouring through the portals ahead of the Goblins' advance.

Lex showed Bethel Truth what Garvin Warchild had shown
her: driven on by Goblins, Winds tore through worlds like
deliberate cyclones on their way to Guitars.

"Some are born to be raised up and some to be cast down," Bethel said, looking away. "And since he thinks he created us all, I guess he can dispose of us too."

Both of them felt the growing tumult around the portal up in the mountains. Lex caught an image of Herself, wild-eyed, pulling troops out of Time like a driven magician. Lex recognized the formation as the remnants of Sticks Battalion. Lex reached out to them on the relay and felt the Rider screaming in Herself's mind, felt the rear guard wild with the exhaustion and anger of battle. Then Herself looked downhill in the direction of Guitars and Lex felt as though they were staring right into each other's eyes.

"Now that one was here a few days ago," said Bethel. "She is going crazy fighting for Garvin Warchild. These last few months, my mind has gotten a lot sharper. I read people very well now. She's his sister and she thinks maybe she's carrying his child."

Lex broke contact with the relay and looked at Bethel Truth. "Oh, yes, Commander," said the singer, "I know what you want too. We are going to do our duty when the Wind comes down. Because that's why we were put here. All of us."

As Garvin fell into the Well of Stars, the voice in his ear whispered, "You took a long route on your way to see me, Garvin Warchild. You who were promised to me by your father long before he coupled with your mother." The voice tasted like autumn rain. The light of the stars sounded like distant horns. "It took you a long while to look for your mother. Yet I have kept her safe."

As the stars of the Well grew larger, they turned into lighted windows in tall apartment buildings. Garvin felt himself land softly on rubber soles and caught the scent of autumn rain. It was the kind that washes away the smell of a New York and replaces it for an evening with that of small towns and country roads, of damp leaves and the sea. A tugboat horn tooted twice somewhere on the Hudson and was answered by one long, mournful blast from a ship in the harbor.

For the moment Garvin forgot the one his uncle called the Lady, forgot Time and the Goblins. He found himself perched in shadow on a fire escape, unobserved above the streets of

New York. It wasn't quite the city he had known, but he was used to that. This one was both sleeker and more desperate, full of skyscrapers and beggars. Garvin sensed that he was different also, smart, quick to understand what others were thinking. Something cold and hard dwelt at the back of his skull. He could almost remember having a Rider and being the Warchild. But only as a kind of dream.

The building on which he stood was across an alley from a big apartment house. Looking over there, he caught sight of his mother in a lighted window, dressed to go out. She was lovely, he realized. Her smile had comforted him so often, her presence had allowed him to survive in the world where his father had left them. He had left her without so much as a word, but now Garvin was ready to leap the space between buildings and knock on her window.

Then he saw her cross the living room and open the door. Garvin could have learned to despise the guy who came in and kissed her, just as he had every other one who did. This one looked prosperous but not real rich. He handed Claire a wrapped present and gazed at her when she turned away to open it, as if he couldn't believe his good fortune.

They kissed again for a long while, then left Claire's apartment. Between then and the moment they came out the front door of the building, Garvin debated going down to the street and approaching Claire. He would say something, but he wasn't sure what. He had run out on her and wasn't sure how she felt.

The man hailed a cab as Garvin hesitated. He saw the smile on Claire's face as she slid into the back seat. He wanted to scream her name as they drove off into the night.

Later he leaped over the alley from fire escape to fire escape and looked into his mother's apartment. There was a picture in her bedroom where he remembered Claire keeping his father's photo when he was a kid. He had to look twice to realize it was a high school graduation picture of him.

Knowing that picture to be impossible, Garvin remembered Lex seeing her double. That made him begin to remember Time and the Well of Stars. As he did, he heard the cold rock under his feet and smelled the starlight above him. Garvin let

go of the fire escape railing very slowly and found himself
back facing the Well of Stars.

Crouched shivering on the bare stone, he asked the face
above him, "She's still alive somewhere?"

"Yes."

"And happy?"

"You saw that."

"I wanted to talk to her."

"But you realized the complications. She remembers you as
leaving the way your father did. Her memory is hazy, but she
remembers both of you fondly."

"Thank you for taking care of her." Garvin looked back
over the wasteland toward the worlds his father had created.
He felt his Rider again. "Tell me, why did you do what you
did with me? The Rider? The Republic? All the death and
suffering?"

The face in the stars smiled. "For that knowledge a payment is necessary."

"I don't have anything. What do you want, my firstborn?"

"Your child of my choosing."

"A kid. I don't have any. . . ." Then Garvin remembered his
father when they last met, asking him, "How dry have you
kept your own wick?" and shut up.

"It was an agreement both your grandfather and father were
happy to strike." Again Garvin's senses were scrambled. The
sound of running water stung his eyes and he heard the dark
of night. Then he saw a young man in hunting costume,
colder and more cruel than the Guvnor, but recognizably his
father. Black Jack Howard stood under the light of a full
moon in a circle in the grass, by a stream on the side of a hill.
His arrogance was cut by wonder and a fear he tried to hide as
he nodded his head in agreement.

"Your grandfather," the voice of the Lady told Garvin,
"wished the Goddess to unlock the chambers of his mind, to
make the vague premonitions he felt into true telepathy. I did
that knowing how it would end, because Lord Howard was
necessary to me. Later he fell in with Lady Tagent and her
circle. The child he produced with her daughter was the one I
claimed but not the one I needed most."

"That was my stepuncle. What about my father?"

"Your child of my choosing?"

'yield this unknown offspring,' he felt his Rider urge. 'it is a small price for knowledge.' And Garvin found his head nodding just as his paternal grandfather's had.

The face in the Well smiled sadly, softly. "Lord Howard learned from Lady Tagent to desire more. He wished to effect a passage beyond his world. This time he thought to steal the knowledge."

Garvin saw Lord Howard with a very young, very beautiful girl, Margaret Garvin his paternal grandmother. He led her by lanternlight to the circle in the grass on a night of no moon. Garvin flinched as his grandfather threw the woman down and took her. "He used his power on one who had served me well. Instead of the knowledge he sought, I opened the chambers of his mind further. He could no longer block the thoughts of others nor transmit his own."

Garvin saw Black Jack wearing only his shirt, with his hands to his forehead, screaming on the dirt street of an Irish village. He saw him beat in the head of a drover who laughed at him. That, Garvin knew, must have been the beginning of the madness of Black Jack Howard. "But from that, I gained a second child of my choosing. He stood before me three times."

Garvin saw Brian Garvin standing in the very glade where his own father had conceived him. It must have been just after his mother's funeral, and his father looked like a young man on the run. His father already had telepathy. Garvin felt him reach out and beg the Goddess, GRANT ME AN ESCAPE FROM THIS WORLD. LET ME HAVE THE KEY MY OWN FATHER SOUGHT.

Garvin heard the Goddess's reply: "Yield me the child of my choosing." He saw his father hesitate and then agree, then watched, as his father had, a single star in the overcast sky. He saw it float to earth as if it were on a leaf. It was the tiny flag that fit in Tantor the Elephant's trunk. Along with it came an image of Lady Tagent and her drawing room. The rest Garvin already knew; his father had gone to London and passed through the mirrored room to another plane.

"Thus, in one stroke I rid myself of a troublesome possibility in Lady Tagent and gained a powerful tool, your father. He stood before me once again."

Then Garvin saw his father wild-eyed, haunted looking. Behind him was a duplicate of the drawing room he had just left. But in this room the eyes of the peacock on its screen, the compass points of the antique globe, the jewel in the little flag the elephant held shone like the stars in a constellation. "Where is it that I have found myself?" asked young Brian Garvin, not a god, not even a gunman anymore, just a frightened mortal. "What is it that I am to do in this emptiness?"

Garvin, clinging to the rock, felt the Lady demand a great deed from his father. He saw his father nod agreement eagerly, felt the Goddess show him that he was like a stamp, that the worlds he imagined would become worlds as real as the one he had left. The Goddess also showed him that his intrusion had already attracted the Goblins looking for fuel for the Winds. His father's great task was to keep the Goblins away from the one true world.

Garvin felt her wipe his father's memory clean, leaving nothing but the idea of the great task embedded as deeply as the urge to breathe. As Brian Garvin turned away, the hedge of roses and thorns sprang up.

"One last time your father thought to stand before me." Garvin saw his father in front of the hedge, looking like a man who knew he had lost something but couldn't remember what. For a long while he stared at the Well of Stars, then finally shrugged, turned, and went away.

But Garvin knew that enough of that memory must have remained—the stars, the hedge, the presence of the Goddess —to have gotten into the very fabric of his father's creation. He had formed the Immortals and the Oracle out of his subconscious as he had bargained with the Goblins and spun worlds to protect his own world.

Garvin saw Time pass like a flickering light and he saw the world of the Republic created like thousands of others, saw it drawn a little away from Time by the Goddess. He saw the civilization his father had imagined wreck itself in war and pollution. And in the chaos that followed, the Lady experimented.

Telepaths who had been removed as children from that

world were returned to it. These were the ones remembered in the Republic as the wizards. The world was her laboratory, her breeding program. She had learned to touch mankind lightly. Even her least wrong touch could send whole races on paths of pain and confusion.

Generations came and went in the Republic. In that world of his father's imagining, tinged with the Goddess's own understanding, human folly continued but went down somewhat different paths. New technology appeared, the telepathic societies became more rigid. But in the midst of the population a certain number of humans arose, telepathic and with the kind of strength and understanding for which she searched.

As if from a great height, Garvin saw the Guvnor steal infant girls and plant them in the worlds of Time. The Goblins introduced Riders into Time and the Riders trained Zombies. Their harvest came closer and closer to the Republic while the Oracle and the Immortals struggled endlessly to stop them. In the Republic the Scarecrow was born, received his name, married Amre, was appointed guardian of the border district. And Garvin understood that this was the best that Her efforts had produced, that Scarecrow's compassion and gentleness were dearer to her than anything in Time.

Then Time and the Goblins and the hand of the Goddess all touched the Scarecrow at the same instant. Garvin saw him turn away from his desk on a fine spring day toward the skinny, barefoot kid in a long denim shirt.

Garvin saw himself in the Scarecrow's eyes, battered and scared, with a wild, strong telepathy just coming alive and a Rider stuck in his head. What Scarecrow was able to see was a human being in need of his protection and love. "You were the child at the moment of my choosing," said the quiet voice. "As it came about."

That's how the Warchild knew he wasn't chosen so much as settled on. As he considered that, from inside his mind he felt a question: 'all-powerful one, please tell me why this image touches me so.' His Rider showed her a huge beast plunging through the air, its huge paws coming down on the back of its prey, guided by a tiny clear spark in its brain.

Clinging to the rock with his hands and feet, Garvin looked into the Well of Stars angrily. "While you're at it, tell me why

I had to have this thing stuck in my skull. What is it? Who are you?"

"I will answer all your questions. My answer will fade. When I am done your Rider will trouble you no more. That will be my payment."

Garvin saw the lights of the Well expand and multiply, turn into galaxies, then narrow down to one large red star. "I was conceived long ago and far away as one-half of a single idea. That idea was as limitless as dreams. But the Dreamers who had spawned the idea were planet-bound."

Garvin watched as the race which dreamed evolved long and slowly on a hostile planet. Garvin saw them as triangles, light pink and covered with hairy tendrils along which something like static electricity seemed to play. To Garvin they seemed far less human than the Goblins. He watched as they struggled on the surface of their world against an implacable environment. The building of a tool took longer than humanity had existed. Their understanding of their universe was slowly and painfully bought.

Out of their striving and understanding, a common will emerged. At first no more than a consensus, a ground for agreement, it was finally able to exist by itself. Garvin saw the dense atmosphere stir for a few moments above an assembled mass of the dreaming triangles. It reminded him of the Winds.

Again, slowly and painfully, hitting and missing, finding and forgetting, the Dreamers evolved their hopes. The Winds became more common, able to exist outside the minds of the Dreamers for longer and longer. More and more of the efforts of the race went into their Winds. Their technology was never developed; the Dreamers went without nourishment. Winds were linked for longer and longer periods. Dreamers wasted away and died under their hostile sun while gazing at the distant stars. As they did, the Winds grew larger and more sentient.

At last they were able to break free of the atmosphere of their world. Garvin felt something between a Wind and the being he saw in the Well of Stars skimming the planets of the Dreamers' solar system. On their home worlds, Dreamers withered as their hopes grew. In the air above them their collective consciousness split in two. The Wind was their sense of adventure, their curiosity. The Well was the race's life wish.

The Wind floated off, left the home solar system, and visited neighboring stars. The Well remained with the Dreamers and comforted them as they grew weak and childlike. The two parts of the Dreamers' creation remained in contact with each other.

In its exploration, the Wind found another race, or rather two. On a small, fertile world there existed a species of predator, huge, horned, taloned, fast, and powerful, the crown of the top of the planetary pyramid. It normally would not evolve a great intelligence. And these beasts, except for a certain rudimentary telepathy, were limited. But within most of their brains existed parasites, weak but clever, mind fleas who coupled in the brief moments that they danced in the air between hosts. They were able to cheat death if they could leap to a new Steed before the old one died.

Garvin, clinging to the rock, felt his Rider writhe inside him. 'that was us before. before the goblins found us.' It seemed to be laughing and crying at the same moment.

SHUT UP AND SEE WHAT SHE'S SHOWING US.

The Rider quieted and they watched the Wind continue on its way, intending to return to the Riders and their original Steeds. They saw how the Wind never returned home. Powerful and naive, questing and trusting, the next race it found was the Goblins. Experienced pirates, plunderers of psychic energy, they broke up the Wind into manageable chunks and used them to power their starships. They stripped the Wind of all memory and followed its route back toward the Dreamers' home world.

Along the way the Goblins stopped at the Riders' world. They killed the predators and snapped up the Riders as they jumped from the skulls of the dying beasts. They too were stripped of their memory and kept alive in Goblin laboratories.

As Garvin saw that, he felt sympathy for the first time toward his Rider. He reached within himself and felt nothing. "The Rider will bother you no longer," the voice from the

Well of Stars said. "It gives you thanks for having saved its life as it has saved yours."

The thing which should have made Garvin glad made him hurt instead. Without the Rider he felt very alone and totally without protection. 'master, farewell,' a distant mind told him. And Garvin screamed, "What more do you want from me? I feel like a speck, a fly, a fucking lab rat. You give me the Rider, you take it away. Fine. You use my father, you use me. Great. All I want is for you to save the poor bastards who followed me. Can you do that?"

"You must fulfill a deed. One which you will soon forget and always bear in mind."

"Anything. Just get me out of here."

CHAPTER
Eleven

The Commandant held on to the mind of the young Steed, kept him calm and still, while a rope broke his neck. As the boy died at the end of the noose, the Rider in his brain tried to leap free. Without Goblin technology, it couldn't jump to a new host and instead expired, screaming with fright. In the moment before he died, the Steed caught a taste of freedom.

The God showed that to the crowd gathered to watch the hanging of the last of the prisoners. It was deep twilight in the City Out Of Time and the air stank of smoke, sweat, and excrement. EVEN IF THE FREEDOM THAT WE GAIN IS NO MORE THAN A SPECK, A SECOND, IT WILL HAVE BEEN WORTH IT. The crowd murmured, tired, hungry, strangling on bad air, but with him still.

HANG THIS ONE UP WITH THE OTHERS AS AN EXAMPLE TO OUR ENEMIES, the Commandant ordered Oublie, the city manager, who commanded at the Gate of Gold. She bowed in obedience, looked for a good spot on the fire-blackened gates to stick the corpse. The dead and injured from the last Zombie attack had just been dragged away. Oublie knew enough about the ecology of the City to be aware that they could hold out for only a short while more. She also knew that she was prepared to die there for the God.

The Commandant played his people like an instrument, touching their idealism, their awe, and their fear. THE DESPERATION OF THE LAST FEW ASSAULTS MEANS THAT THEY KNOW THE WARCHILD APPROACHES, he told them and turned away from the gate and the dead Steed. Deep inside, he thought, "I began as a terrorist and it seems I'll end as one."

Quickly, Brian Garvin made his way to the empty Goblin Market, went up the catwalks, and through the portal there. He knew that the assaults on the Four Gates were only diversions. The City itself was not the prize the Goblins sought. They were looking for the prime portal, the one back to the world from which Brian Garvin had come. They intended to reach it by cutting their way through his beloved Swift Ones on the park world. If the Goblins won there, then all that happened in the City meant nothing.

His favorite children felt his presence as soon as the God came through the portal from the Goblin Market. They stamped their feet enough to make the ground tremble. Brian Garvin saw trees burning on a distant hill where a Goblin scout ship had been smashed into the earth.

Those Swift Ones burned by laser fire before they could bend the air and wreck the ship lay near the portal for the God's inspection. They suffered like animals, not understanding their pain, but with bodies and minds choked by it. Here, Brian Garvin knew as he gently, firmly stopped their lives, was the important part of the siege. Nothing in the City Out Of Time touched him the way putting these out of their misery did.

To the Swift Ones, the God was a natural force. Spread out in open order, they followed him in their thousands as he strode over the overgrown parkland. In better days he had seen to it that good rough bread and fresh cheese, ripe vegetables and fruit were left out where the Swift Ones would find them. Now they were living off the land, eating mushrooms, catching fish. They didn't seem to mind. Dying didn't seem to bother them either, but it bothered their creator. THINGS

WILL BE BETTER, he told them, and they whooped and stamped, caused trees to shake and hills to tremble.

As he walked, Brian Garvin became one of them, brown, smooth-skinned, and long-legged. Looking up, he saw an unblinking star moving on a fast, straight path through the heavens. He didn't doubt that the great Goblin ship orbiting this world could see the herds of Swift Ones. But he was fairly sure they couldn't pick him out. In just the same way, he was sure that they knew the general location of the portal to the drawing room but not its exact spot.

Goblin technology was their great unknown, their face-down card. This world and the Swift Ones were Brian Garvin's revealed ace. The first worlds, the first people he had created after he had burst into Time, were horrors formed out of his own terror and loneliness. Those he had destroyed as soon as he saw them. This world was his first success and in some ways his only one. Here he had bred a race as one with its world. Here he had begun and here he would stand or fall.

Around him, Swift Ones started at a sound. One of them caught sight of something she didn't understand. Through her eyes the God saw a metal coil on a tree, recognized a sensor device. With her ears, he heard the air whistle. The rocket came in very low right then. The explosion blew him off his feet. The searing pain from injured Swift Ones almost turned the air to crystal. Grass and trees caught fire. Another rocket blew up wide of them. Brian Garvin saw the Goblin scout ship which had fired. It turned sharply on its side and almost fell out of the sky with the shock wave of the Swift Ones' agony.

He went for the crew: three of them. They sensed him and put on what he thought of as their war masks, the black-and-white mental images of their disdain. He was a stick man on the burning ground. NONE OF THAT, he said and probed for their breathing. The Goblins were older than the God and there were things about them he didn't understand. But he knew they feared for their lives and that was his advantage. Brian Garvin strangled them.

The one at the controls went into a sort of hibernation, a kind of fugue state. The copilot tried to keep the scout ship at full throttle, but the pain of the Swift Ones did them in. It curdled the air in front of the ship, brought them nose down into the ground, snuffed them out in an explosion. Brian Garvin bit his lip at the agony of the Swift Ones. Dozens of them lay dead, and he had to destroy as many more before he could continue.

Their God made them spread out into their family groups for the night. He himself moved fast to the portal with a herd of about fifty. As they escorted him, the Swift Ones spotted another sensor on a tree. Beating their hands together, they set the tree afire and continued on. The portal that led back to the drawing room lay in a hollow, an unremarkable site.

This was the heart of Brian Garvin's Eden, the center of the place he had built before he knew what he was doing and so knew just what he was doing. Oaks had grown up, grown old, and died around it. In a lifetime a man might come up his own front walk a thousand times and think it a lot. He had come this way a thousand times that number.

Too often for his own good, he realized when the ground under him blew up. For an instant Brian Garvin felt as if he were going to black out and thought that there were worse ways to die than here with his Swift Ones. Then he pulled himself back from the onrushing pit of unconsciousness and found that some of his chosen children could still move well enough to carry him.

So it was that a few moments later in the hall of the Gods' private chambers in the City Out Of Time, Tom felt a divine summons. TO THE DRAWING ROOM. BRING A TOURNIQUET. AND SOMETHING TO SOAK UP BLOOD. Tom grabbed a scarf and hurried down the hall, Mary after him with an armload of towels. At the door they hesitated.

"Your divinity said we were never to enter while you were inside."

IN HERE, DAMMIT. They pushed open the door and for a moment in the dim light saw three adult Swift Ones bearing what seemed to be a fourth one through the French windows. They looked again and saw that the one being carried was the gallant young Commandant, his mouth white with pain, one pants leg a mess of blood.

He delivered terse commands: STOP THE FLOW. Tom tied the scarf just above the knee. PUT ME DOWN. The Swift

Ones lowered him. DO NOT LET IT GET ON THE RUG. Mary had the towels under him. The couple watched the God's face relax, saw the butchered leg heal itself. The Swift Ones, two females and a male, realized they were indoors and snorted with alarm. Mary and Tom looked at them, innocent as horses and as beautiful. "Now, now," she said to one she recognized, "don't I remember you coming in for cookies when your head didn't even come up to the table?" The sound of her voice seemed familiar to them.

"I've never let them in here full grown before," the God said softly from the floor. "But these ones saved my life just now. Could you see to them, Mary?" She nodded and when she moved to the hall, they followed, padding after her to the kitchen.

As soon as they were gone, there came a rapping at the bronze doors at the end of the hall. The power that drove the Scramblers was almost gone. Minds from beyond the doors reported, THE SILVER GATE IS IN ENEMY HANDS, COMMANDANT.

The God laid his head back on the rug. He felt the heartbeat of the City falter for a beat or two. The secret of the Gods, the real secret, was that they were just one exhausted Irish gunman. "Say to them I'll be there in five minutes," Brian Garvin told Tom and shut his eyes.

"You will command the Army of Winter and your own Army of Autumn minus Sticks Battalion," Lex told Herself. The two stood with the Guvnor on the porch of the farmhouse opposite Guitars. Below them on the slopes, troops dug in frantically. "You will defend to the west of Guitars and uphill. Warchild Cluster will be around Guitars itself. The Guvnor will lead the mobile strike force. I will have the Armies of Spring and Summer and hold on to the east and downhill from the Free City." The face of the older woman fascinated Lex. It was pale from exhaustion, with black smudges under the eyes that had begun to look like bruises. She showed Herself and her Rider the plan devised by Garvin and his Rider.

Herself nodded, looked at the defense that Lex had laid down in the last couple of days. Garvin's Rider had come up with the outline, but it was left to Lex to get the tattered, hungry, dirty, clap-ridden Companions and troopers, mercenaries and camp followers to put the plan into operation.

Like Lex, the Armies of the Four Seasons had crossed Time, drawn only by hope and a vision of the Warchild. Suddenly they had found themselves in full retreat. On the way back to Guitars, a lot of their organization had collapsed. The rebels hadn't quite become a mob, but a lot of their formations were like the one directly below the farmhouse.

It consisted of the remains of a brigade of Greek soldiers who had been found by a telepathic reconnaissance unit lost, starving, wandering in a desert. All the Greek Companions had died when a single Wind fell on them at night. The reconnaissance team, holy women from a Zuni Indian tribe, now served as officers of the skeleton brigade. All that bound them together was their shared memory of the Warchild. All that kept them at work then was the image of Garvin promising Lex that he would return to Guitars or die trying.

"He told the Scarecrow the same thing," the Guvnor drawled, leaning against the porch rail. "But when Garvin got back to the Republic, the Scarecrow wasn't there to see it. When he started out, he was human enough. Not as bright as some, but a lad that I could understand. Now that he's grown into his godhood he's become more like his father. Still, he's better disposed toward me than his father ever was. Everything depends on what he learns at the Lady's house."

He saw Lex frown and smiled. "Pay no attention. Before the battle jitters. If I had a choice, I'd steady myself with a good boot-to-boot cavalry charge."

What he said about Garvin's changing bothered Lex. Then she heard a soft song that distracted her. The Talking Suitcase hummed faintly and images appeared of sailing ships becalmed at sea when the wind failed, of huge blimps springing leaks and falling out of the sky. The passengers on the ships and blimps were terrified Goblins. In the farmhouse yard, the Rose and Thorn took it up, almost too quietly to be understood. Lex caught the images and showed the song to the staff officers around her. A relay formed and took them up and down the mountains.

Herself said, "For a while Time has been getting very narrow and very thin. For long, my constant friend"—she indicated the Rider— "has had the feeling that the Goblins had just about charted and staked it out. Which is perhaps why we are all here."

Down the relay, like a response to the song of the Suitcase, came images of Echbattan formations advancing on portals. They were on the next world. "Tomorrow," the Guvnor said, "the Winds will be here tomorrow." He stepped off the porch and crossed the yard. At the rosebush he stopped and broke off three red flowers. Returning to the porch, he bowed low and gave one to Lex and the another to Herself. "I'll be at the airfield with my command," he said and stuck the third one in a collar button of his tunic.

From far down the Cumberlands, explosions echoed. "Could this be the last battle in Time?" Herself asked and also prepared to depart for her command. She placed her rose just below her throat and looked at Lex. "Do not worry," she said. "Your Garvin will return to you." Then, from across the river, a chord echoed and everyone in the army caught the song of Guitars:

> *WE WERE BORN TO TAME THE WHIRLWIND*
> *TO BRING IT FROM THE DARK TO LIGHT.*

She smiled, but Lex could not read the smile's meaning nor the mind lying behind it. When she reached out to touch Herself's consciousness, all she felt was an icy blade of anxiety. "Ah, my Rider is afraid," the Steed said and turned away.

That night a falling dream swept through the army. Young telepaths who had collapsed in the positions they would defend the next day felt themselves plunge face first. They tossed in their sleep and their exhausted troops caught the image of still black water reflecting stars and the moon.

Lex, dozing lightly, saw a face in the water at the bottom of a deep well. Silver and unhuman, as unreadable as Herself, the woman in the moon was about to speak when Lex got jerked awake. ZOMBIE CONTACT! ZOMBIE CONTACT! broadcast half a dozen points on the Great Relay.

The Guvnor, sitting in his flight jacket, his helmet, a bottle of brandy, and a glass on the table before him, saw the face, heard the silver, tasted the stars around it. An omen, he knew. "Lady," he breathed and stood up in Her honor. Then minds around him seized other minds. INCOMING ATTACK! Outside on the airfield kid pilots and crews ran in all directions and She vanished.

Herself recognized Garvin. Or rather, first her Rider recognized Garvin and in doing so woke her. "My life is yours," she heard him cry out, heard his words echo like telepathy. JUST LET NO ONE ELSE DIE.

His anguish moved Herself to tears. Then the inner presence seemed to bang in her mind like a caged beast, repeating over and over, 'i cannot find his rider,' and Garvin's cry was lost as the Armies of the Four Seasons woke up fighting.

Garvin felt as if he had been falling forever. He had tried to absorb all that he was shown. "Son of man," the Lady told him, "all of this will seem no more than a dream." She told him that after she had shown him her horrified understanding that beings like the Goblins existed, her psychic shock at the severing of the Wind. It didn't seem possible to Garvin that he could ever lose those memories.

He shared her wrenching pain. Garvin felt as though he lay paralyzed with grief over the dead world of the Dreamers for as long as the Lady had. But the Goblins knew of her existence and her location from the Winds and came to find her. Just before their arrival, she fled through the galaxy. Her place of refuge was a flaw in the fabric of the universe, a tumor ready to burst.

Feeling the black hole in her memory, Garvin was reminded of a portal. Reaching through it, the Goddess had found humanity on the other side. Earth spun like a top and intelligent life of a sort clung to it. Still in shock and grief, the entity which he thought of as the Lady reached out toward the minds of primitive humanity.

Garvin heard the light of tiny sparks in pitch-black that were his ancestors, smelled the awe of small frightened creatures as his race touched the Goddess. Many felt her and worshipped. Sparks became small flickering tongues of fire.

Always and everywhere, people existed who tried to seek her out, to find the secrets behind the mystery. Some of the fires grew brighter, flared, and died as individuals saw much more than they'd ever bargained for.

Over the generations a few reached her and were drawn, falling just as Garvin was doing, toward the Lady. Sometimes before they perished they left behind an impression like fingerprints, a mental image of their Earth with the Lady in the void. One or two even managed to survive and were returned. These were recast by the Lady, their minds, their memories, their brains and genes subtly changed.

From the Goblins she had learned caution. From humanity she learned the craftiness of a wild animal teaching its young to survive. Slowly, clumsily, she evolved a plan to take back the Winds from their captors. Her tool was humanity. Over millennia, the Goddess shaped members of the race to her purpose as humanity shaped her. She wove threads of sparks through the generations and saw them snap one by one. Somewhere behind her the Goblins grew closer. Then one of the sparks turned into a flame strong enough to pass between universes and not go out.

That was his father, Garvin realized. He saw tiny flickers like birthday candles in an abyss and knew he saw the formation of the worlds of Time. And that reminded him. He had screamed at her when he realized his Rider was gone. He begged her now, "The army, the ones who followed me. I have a plan to save them. Please help me make it work!"

Then Garvin saw the stars at the bottom of the Well grow larger. He realized that the lights were camp fires, were headlights, were airport flares. He was falling toward the Armies of the Four Seasons huddled on the slopes around Guitars. From the Free City itself, he caught a mighty chord.

WARCHILD'S COMING WILL END ALL WAR.

Lex heard the long train rolling out of the Free City as the shooting began. Guitars was sending the last of its children to safety. Some of the kids understood what was happening well enough to be upset. The City sang to them:

YOU ARE THE CHILDREN OF THE SUN.

As the train pulled away, a long artillery volley echoed off the hills. Lex reached out and caught the feel of her army, tense, expectant, brave, but fragile. A lot of them were sure they weren't going to live. HOME WAS YESTERDAY, she felt them telling each other as the Goblin shells came in. GROW OLD, WHY? They were willing to die if only the Warchild would make their sacrifice mean something.

The night before, Herself had turned over command of what was left of Sticks Battalion to Lex. They arrived that dawn as the battle began with Sung in charge. Lex, standing in the front yard, looked at her old command and they looked at her. The unit was down to less than company strength. I AM GLAD THAT YOU MADE IT HERE, she told them. PLEASE TAKE THE POSITIONS UPHILL OF THE HEAD-QUARTERS.

YES, COMMANDER. Sung's eyes were old, blank from seeing too much. Lex remembered him crying at the Valley of Bones. She doubted that he would cry again. A few of the cadets wore the bills of shakos around their necks. "One question?" asked Sung. Lex nodded.

"The Warchild got everyone with him killed back before you and Nick found him?"

"Yes."

"Why?"

"That's two questions. Take up your positions." All of them knew what her answer meant: Lex didn't know why but she still followed the Warchild's command. They turned uphill.

On the relay from downhill, Lex saw gray dawn become blinding light, felt scouts' eardrums ripped by the explosions. ZOMBIE-LED TROOPS ATTACKING ALL ALONG THE LINE, a divisional commander of the Army of Spring reported. Bullets smashed bones. Metal tore flesh. Kids just like her died and Lex knew this wasn't even the main assault.

Companion artillery opened up. In answer, out of the growing dawn came images of piles of rebel corpses. TOO MANY EVEN FOR GOBLINS TO EAT. The kids' bodies rotted in the sun. Their eyes were picked at by crows. She felt a tremor go through the army as Zombie minds grabbed at nontele-pathic rebels.

Lex understood the enemy plan. Zombie-led troops would go in against the rebel armies. Zombie minds would assault nontelepathic soldiers, hoping to draw Companion minds out to block them. YOUR WARCHILD DIED ON ECHBAT-TAN'S WORLD. An image followed of Garvin's head on a gladiator's belt, his face distorted with horror. It was a good fake. They knew what Garvin looked like and what his army feared most.

A recruit brigade in the Army of Winter started to panic. That brigade's Companion officers moved to block the Zom-bies. By revealing themselves, they drew the attention of more Zombies and several Riders. COMPANIONS, COME OUT AND DIE, they called. COME JOIN YOUR GREAT LEADER.

FALL THAT UNIT BACK, Lex ordered the downhill relay. It was better to give up ground than to let her Companions draw the Winds too soon. She turned to a mercenary scout, a black telepath in red sneakers and jump suit standing on the porch. He showed her what he had just seen on an adjacent world. A long line of trees bowed down; his twin brother fell dead just as they were about to scramble through a portal. WINDS TOOK HIM. Lex felt, as the kid had, the mind torn away that had been with his since before their birth. The kid's body heaved as if he were ready to scream and throw up at the same moment. I WANTED TO LET THEM TAKE ME TOO. BUT YOU NEEDED TO KNOW. THE GOBLINS ARE RIGHT NEXT DOOR.

Lex knew they were looking for portals through which they could lead their Winds. She ran her mind around the defenses. The Free City of Guitars the center of her position, her final reserve. Downhill and to the east of Guitars, the Armies of Winter and Spring had started giving ground slowly. Compan-ion minds blocked Zombies when necessary to protect their troops but didn't form a permanent relay.

Uphill and to the west, Herself's exhausted Armies of Au-tumn and Summer had yet to be engaged. Lex showed Herself what the scout had seen. WE HAVE EVERY PORTAL WE

KNOW OF UNDER GUARD was the reply from up above Guitars.

Lex touched the mind of the Guvnor, saw him reflected in the minds of the aircrews at the landing field. He stood beside a biplane, cigar in his mouth, loading a revolver. "If it happens that I'm forced down, five bullets are for the first Zombies who find me. One is for the old adieu." The kids around him, nontelepathic pilots, Companion navigators, nodded, wide-eyed, loaded their own weapons. REVVED UP AND WAITING, he told her.

She checked on the enemy advance. The Echbattan forces, led by their Zombies and Riders, came forward carefully. With them were mercenaries, older, less impressionable than the ones who had declared for Garvin. They were men and women who had learned to live on the lip of the Wind. Most had joined up only when the rebel armies started to fall back. But none of them were willing to risk their lives foolishly. They rolled forward slowly and hurled images of Companions falling dead as Winds swirled, of piles of corpses piled like a harvest. The intent was to take portals through which the Goblins would suddenly emerge with their Winds. The effect would be devastating.

Just before they reached the portals downhill from Guitars, Lex caught the song of the Suitcase and showed it to the army. It sang of Zombies and mercenaries walking past a pile of Companion corpses. In the song, Garvin leaped out of a pile of corpses and stood covered with blood, staring at the enemy with cold intent. FORM RELAY, she ordered and thousands of Companion minds swept the enemy lines.

The retreat stopped. Gunfire intensified. WARCHILD LIVES! Companions broadcast. And Lex sent out an image of Garvin breaking apart the Goblin Chain, scattering the pieces. Halfway through the morning, well downhill of Guitars, the enemy halted.

WINDS! The warning came from uphill. The one who gave it hesitated for a moment. Lex saw as that young Companion did the last long moment of his mortal life. He stared through trees at the mouth of a cave as his mind was drawn out of his body. At the same moment she caught that, Lex heard gunfire from up the mountains. A PORTAL WE DIDN'T KNOW

ABOUT, Herself reported. WINDS ARE IN MY LINES, AT LEAST A DOZEN OF THEM.

Lex felt the Army of Autumn shudder as Winds ran through the Companion relay. They had been used to falling back when the Winds appeared, taking losses but regrouping out of range. Now there was no retreat. They had to stand. The commanders of October and December corps fell dead. The relay snapped. The Army of Autumn started to come apart.

Lex signaled for the Guvnor and found he was already in the air. Over the gunfire, she heard the sound of engines, through the babel of minds, she felt Captain Tagent tell his pilots, CLOSE YOUR EYES AND THINK OF ENGLAND. In the eyes of the crews Lex saw the fleet, canvas and wood, flimsy as kites, wobbling in the air. Brightly painted barnstormers' biplanes, tiny two-seaters that looked like butterflies, planes used to fly mail over mountains, military aircraft decorated with a machine gun or two swooped down on the Winds.

The Guvnor stood, half in a plane and half hanging on to his Wind. COME WITH ME, he broadcast to the Winds. And as he did, he let them catch at his own Wind, let them feel its freedom. Gunfire tore apart a delicate blue biplane. Burning, it fell out of the air.

COME WITH ME, the Guvnor repeated and showed them a scrap of memory he had retained. It was of a world with air like fog and a race that dreamed. The Winds detached themselves from the relay on the ground and floated after the air fleet. A plane ripped one of its wings on a tree and smashed onto the ground. A navigator was taken by a Wind and died. The planes turned and started away. The Winds followed them.

Not wanting to expose themselves to gunfire, the Goblins had remained inside the caves. As the Winds got away, they broadcast images of the Cave of Winds, of the human minds always there to be consumed. RETURN, RETURN, they ordered. Zombies on the ground reached out and smashed pilots' minds. Gunfire caught aircraft. Canvas wings were sheared off. Lex saw the Guvnor's own plane bobble in the air, but all the Winds which had emerged from the caves flew off after the fantastic fleet.

The relay formed itself again. The Zombie forces which had come out of the caves fell back in panic rout. Troops along the upper slopes broadcast, FOR THE WARCHILD AND THE GUVNOR.

Assaults from downhill, raids from portals farther up the mountains went on all morning. The rebel positions held firm. Then just after noon a long groan came from downhill. Over the Companion relay, Lex saw treetops bend down on a front six miles wide. THE WINDS ARE HERE! HUNDREDS OF THEM. THE FIRST ATTACK WAS JUST A DIVERSION.

Panic threatened to make the rebel army crumble. But Lex knew that the Guvnor's air raid had worked. It had made the Goblins act in haste. The enemy had fewer resources than she had thought. Now was the moment for the last reserve. She reached toward Guitars. As she did, the Goblins sent a Wind down the relay right for her. Before the relay could break up, the Wind caught Lex. The hair on her head rose.

The Wind that had taken Doria was small and confused. The one she had felt on Echbattan's world was a toy. The Guvnor's Wind on which she had ridden was a pet. This Wind was huge and was on her like a shark. It had been fed for generations on criminals and defeated gladiators. From somewhere inside it, minds chanted, JOIN US, COMPLETE US. YOUR LIFE WILL BE FOREVER. RESISTANCE IS USELESS. YOUR BODY IS GOING TO BE FERTILIZER. LET YOUR SPIRIT LIVE.

Lex's mind came loose from her body. She unraveled in layers: Garvin and the Sticks Battalion, Nick and the Valley of Bones, the Bates Motel and the Goblin Chain. That last image had worked before against a Wind. But now it wasn't strong enough. The Wind unpeeled her childhood and Lex was beyond feeling.

She felt something like a child tug at her, saying, LEX, STAY AWAKE. LEX, DO NOT FALL ASLEEP. A tiny voice sang of young lives lost and found again. Together the Rose and Thorn and the Talking Suitcase pulled Lex back out of the mouth of the Wind.

Lex sneezed, shook her head, found that she was lying

face down on the front porch of the farmhouse. Staff officers lay where the Wind had knocked them. Some were unconscious. Others were dead. The Wind spiraled above her. Lex heard engines and the Guvnor's voice shouting, "Get Guitars on the line, will you? I can't hold this monster."

As she reached out for the Free City, Lex felt the ground shake from explosions and the air pulse with noise. In her mind thousands of minds screamed. All along the mountains, rebel troops fired wildly to save the Companion minds from being peeled away. Then as she reached for Guitars, the city found her:

WE WHO WERE BORN TO TAME THE WIND

The Companion relays were nothing compared to the Free City. Every Wind flowed away from the armies and headed right for Guitars itself.

WE ARE CHILDREN UNDER THE SUN.

As a thousand Winds converged, tens of thousand of minds lifted themselves up. They drew the Winds toward themselves. The Winds roared through the streets. Awnings fell, tree branches snapped, windows exploded, bodies fell dead. And Guitars sang:

THE WINDS ARE BROTHERS IN OUR HEARTS.

The Winds whirled over the Free City, feasting on the singers. Both sides paused while that happened. The minds reaching for other minds to crush, the pain of torn flesh and organs, the noise that destroyed the soul were stilled. Then the singers were all taken. The music of Guitars went out as if someone had pulled the plug on a radio.

To everyone on both sides, this seemed the Goblins' master stroke. The rebel army tottered, ready to fall apart. Guitars, at the center of the army, was dead. The Goblins formed the image of the Cave of Winds, the huge metal belly in the space station orbiting the Swift Ones' world. RETURN, the Goblins ordered, but the Winds over the Free City sang with a single mind:

OUR SONG WILL RISE AND MAKE US FREE

At first only the Goblins understood what was happening. And even they only thought that their herd had gobbled a feast it hadn't quite digested. COME BACK TO THE CAVE OF WINDS, hundreds of them coaxed. The Winds, conditioned to obey, hesitated between their Goblin masters and the minds they had just absorbed. The spirit of Guitars remained intact inside them. COME BACK, the Goblins almost pleaded.

Both armies stood, fascinated, as the Winds paused over Guitars. Then on the mountain just above the City a single mind broadcast an image. Companions and regulars, Select and Citizens, Goblins and Immortals, Riders and Zombies, all saw a hedge of heads with tiny eyes staring out from among the thorns and the Well of Stars, points of light in the dead black. For a moment no one breathed. Gunfire had died out; the Goblin attack had come to a halt. PURSUE THEM, the Goblins ordered.

THE SONG WILL RAISE US UP, sang the mind of Bethel Truth from inside her Wind. She recognized the mind that sent the images. AS SINGING MAKES US FREE, rang out the chorus. All the Winds began to drift up the mountains.

Then everyone tasted the cold shock of horns and heard the sparkle of sunlight in crystal. For an instant everyone was aware of hairy triangles with majestic wreaths crackling like lightning around them. The armies gaped and felt the questing part of the Dreamers captured by the Goblins, felt as the Lady had felt half of her soul hacked to pieces by the Goblins. They tasted hyperspace, smelled the explosion of galaxies as the Lady fled before the Goblins could find her world.

IN THE LADY'S NAME, I SUMMON THE WINDS, the mind on the mountain announced. The drift of the Winds uphill became faster. Then it stopped, spiraled around a lone figure who appeared out of nowhere and walked into the City. Only he and the Winds moved.

THAT IS GARVIN WARCHILD, the Goblins screamed. They showed an army of gray puppets storming the hill.

SHOOT HIM. SMASH HIS MIND. HIT HIM WITH EVERYTHING WE HAVE. As they gave that order, Riders all along the line caught images of a wild, free world where predators and symbiotic parasites roamed. The images wrenched the Riders' memories, interrupted for a moment the iron hold with which they held their Steeds. Along the battle line some Steeds, suddenly free, began to tear their own faces to get at the Riders inside them, to scream and fall on the ground. EXECUTE THEM, the Goblins ordered their shocked troops.

They reached out to their Zombies and commanded them, FIRE. RAKE THAT HILL. Guns went off raggedly, a cluster here, a solitary one there. An explosion overhead shook the farmhouse. Lex got up off the ground and shook her head. Her mouth was dry. The Talking Suitcase lay beside her. The Guvnor tended his wounds as his plane burned in the front yard.

Another shell exploded near the farmhouse porch and Lex jumped to her feet. UP, she ordered the Sticks Battalion. FIRE! Lex saw enemy troops not that far down the slope. She felt hesitation in the minds of the Zombies who commanded them. They had just killed a Steed as it writhed face down, choking on dust and blood from its bitten tongue. Its Rider had been their leader. Lex caught the Zombies' sense that the Goblins were about to cut and run.

SURRENDER AND FACE THE MERCY OF THE WAR-CHILD, she told the enemy as rebel troops began firing at them. GARVIN HAS RETURNED.

"And not a moment too soon, as befits a God," said the Guvnor. He sat on the porch with his left arm hanging uselessly at his side. All his attention was taken with holding on to his own Wind, which kept trying to break away and head for Guitars. "Wise on my part, never letting it graze on those singers. Never retrieve it if I had."

Lex realized that the downed plane was burning the Rose and Thorn. Beside her, the Suitcase sang very faintly of wood turned to ash and old gods yielding to new. When it told her quietly, AND NOW THROW ME IN TOO, she hesitated. It didn't repeat itself but fell dead silent. Then, finally, she obeyed.

The first to recognize the Warchild were the survivors of his old Cluster. They saw him striding down the hill with his tall crest and gold jewelry just as they had known him. He smiled as he saw them. FRIENDS, WILL YOU COME WALK WITH ME NOW? They rose up, shouting. I PROMISE YOU, THE END OF OUR PAIN LIES A SHORT WAY AHEAD.

Herself saw the Warchild as he went past. He didn't look at her but she felt his mind as he caught the battered relay of the Armies of the Four Seasons. DEATH TO THE GOBLINS, the Warchild told his followers. The clean mountain sunlight shone down on him as he showed them Zombies and their soldiers. ANY ONE OF THEM WHO SURRENDERS IS TO BE SPARED. BRING ANY STEEDS YOU FIND ALIVE TO ME.

The Rider inside Herself's head felt Garvin and was frantic. 'his rider is gone,' it kept repeating. Despite all that had happened, the sight of Garvin and the youth of him made Herself laugh aloud with delight. And all around him Winds made the trees bow low as he went to find Lex.

CHAPTER
Twelve

ENEMY IN THE MARKET! The God, as the hollow-eyed but indomitable Commandant, got that message from his Comptroller Zachberg right after the Gate of Gold blew up. He had supervised its destruction himself. The pile of rubble formed by the structure's collapse would close the portal to the Goblins, at least for a while.

But no sooner had he blocked that hole than he caught the panic of his exhausted defenders on the floor of the darkened slave market. Zombies up on the web of catwalks, desperate themselves, lashed out at those below. Brian Garvin knew that if Zombies were in the market they must have done it by cutting their way past his Swift Ones. If the Goblins had brought outsiders into the world which he and they shared as a secret, then the final assault was at hand.

"Oublie," he spoke aloud to his young city manager, "take the demolition team and block the other three gates in the same way I did this one." She, dirty, exhausted from breathing the bad air, sick from the fetid smell and half rations, nodded her obedience and moved away.

As he turned from the gate and jumped into a small car, the

last still operating in the City Out Of Time, Brian Garvin
heard a series of explosions from the Onyx Gate, caught the
pain of the defenders, their panic. PEOPLE OF THE CITY,
Zombie minds told his subjects, IT IS YOUR SO-CALLED
GOD ALONE THAT WE WANT. Images floated, bright and
comforting in the suffocating dark, of the City Out Of Time
returned to normal business.

"The enemy has a foothold inside the Onyx Gate. Take all
available reserves and crush them," the God ordered and drove
away. His route took him past Goblin Market, that mile-long
structure looming in the smoke-choked night. He felt the anguish of the defenders as Zombie minds battered theirs, caught
the ice-cold touch of Riders directing the assault.

The image they showed was of Goblins devouring the
Commandant aspect of the Gods of the City. JUST LET US
HAVE HIM AND THE MARKET AND THE CITY WILL
REOPEN. In the short while that his revolt had lasted, the
God hadn't been able to undo the terror an image like that
caused in his people. Seeing their God destroyed by Goblins,
they began to fall back.

ONLY A DESPERATE RIDER FACES DEATH IN THE
FRONT LINES. Brian Garvin showed a chain of terror—
frightened foot soldiers pushed by frantic Zombies who in
turn were prodded by horrified Riders on wild-eyed Steeds.
And behind them all, shoving them like coals into a raging
fire, were Goblins. And the Goblins kept looking over their
shoulders. Behind them the Warchild swirled and grew larger
and larger like an approaching cyclone.

That image unlocked the attackers' own fears. They knew
something had to be wrong for the Goblins and the Gods to be
at war. They had never seen anything like the Swift Ones or
their world. It gave them pause. On their hesitation, the defense caught its breath. FIRE, Zachberg ordered.

A blind volley fired in the dark, cut down several Zombies.
It also hit a Steed. SAVE ME, its Rider screamed. MY
MOUNT IS BLEEDING TO DEATH. Caught by its terror,
the other attackers fell back toward the portal.

TAKE AS MANY AS POSSIBLE PRISONER, the God
ordered as he sped past the Market. WE WILL FEED THEM

TO THE WIND, BREATHE BY THE AIR THEY PURIFY, SEE BY THE LIGHT THEY MAKE. "If any of us are still alive to need such amenities," the Commandant thought to himself as he reached his palace, leaped from the car, and headed up the great stairs.

Just then, from deep inside the building, he felt human minds riven with terror. Devoted Coli, his Chancellor, a man the God had found again and again on worlds he created mostly in order to find him, had just plunged a dagger into his own heart. As he ran through the Crystal Chamber past screaming Palace attendants, as he passed Coli dead outside the doors of the God's private chambers, the Commandant reached out and caught the minds that had seized his servant's.

Goblins would trust no human for their assault on the one true portal. Brian Garvin found them in the garden that lay outside the French windows of Lady Tagent's drawing room. He knew that Swift Ones must have died by the thousands before permitting the Goblins through.

His former partners had detected Brian Garvin at the same moment he found them. BROKEN AGREEMENTS, they announced. YOU WILL DIE. It was hard, the Commandant had realized, to teach the people of the City Out Of Time not to fear the Goblins when he himself felt an ice pick in the heart every time he looked at them. Fortunately, there was a part of him that knew no fear, and from that he had created a weapon. As he threw open the bronze doors and ran down the hall of his private chambers, the God was joined by Swift Ones he had stationed there.

They were hiding in the garden beyond the windows too. At their God's command, they leaped out at the Goblins from behind trees. The Goblins were armed with lasers but the Swift Ones smashed them with their hands and feet. The Goblins tried to put fear into their minds but the Swift Ones had been created without it.

Brian Garvin had no certainty that his son was on his way to the City or even that he was alive. His only hope was the Goblins' own desperation. Something had to be very wrong for them to be acting as they were. That was enough to keep him going. "Thomas," he yelled as he plunged into the draw-

ing room with his pistol drawn, "bring all the rope you can
find. I have some business with unwelcome guests."

Garvin, floating in Time, probed through a portal blocked
with earth and rocks, searching for the Swift Ones. He felt
nothing, but probed again. They had to be there. The heartbeat of Time was a pitiful, weak thing. Garvin remembered
that when he had first visited the City the pulse of Time had
almost been enough to knock him away.

Behind him he felt Lex, the Guvnor, and what remained of
Warchild Cluster. He had brought them and others with him
striding across Time. He knew that word of his victory wouldn't
have gotten here ahead of them. After Guitars, the enemy had
fled, scattering over dozens of worlds. Riders, stunned by what
they had seen, struggled with their Steeds, hid from searching
rebels. Zombies sought anonymity, tried to forget what they had
been taught, to erase the Goblin Chain from their memories. As
far as anyone knew, none of the Goblins at the battle itself had
survived the loss of their Winds.

Mopping-up operations were taking place back around Echbattan's world. The Warchild had left Guitars for his father's
city. The mission that drove him wasn't even one which he
consciously remembered. Somewhere at the back of his head,
stars rippled on water and a voice told him, "You are to send
your father to me."

Garvin sped over the days and nights from Guitars to the City
Out Of Time. Just as on the first occasion when he had visited
the City, Garvin approached it first over the dead worlds which
led to the gates. Zombies and Riders barred the way. Herself
stepped forward. THEY HAVE YET TO SEE WHAT BEFELL
THEIR MAIN ARMY AT GUITARS. IT WILL TAKE A
SHORT WHILE FOR ME TO SHOW THEM.

And so the Warchild left her with half his force to cut their
way through the besiegers. With the others, he circled the City
Out Of Time until he found the portal by which he had entered
on his first visit. Again and again he cast his mind through the
earth and rocks into the park world. To summon the Swift Ones,
he formed, as he had before, images of the drawing room, of the

globe and the peacock screen and Tantor the Elephant with its flag containing a piece of the Well of Stars.

Behind him, Garvin felt the Guvnor's Wind shift uncomfortably as if it had an unpleasant memory. It was night on the park world. The place seemed devastated, dead to Garvin's touch. Once more he sent out the image of the room, the table set for tea, the wood ready in the fireplace, the globe, the screen, little Tantor. And on the image of the elephant, he felt something stir.

First one mind, then two, then several at once, scattered, hesitant, the Swift Ones answered his call. Garvin felt them arise, no more than a dozen, most of them hurt, several of them dying. From all directions they assembled around the buried portal. At the Warchild's summons, they formed a circle and began to dance, stamping their feet down at the same moment, causing earth and rock to shift, the portal to slide open.

Garvin was first in, wriggling through the narrow way. Standing on the dead grass beside the Swift Ones, he joined them in their dance, his feet coming down as theirs did. The grass was burned, the air smelled of death, two of the Swift Ones were missing arms, all had seen the slaughter of their tribes. Still they danced with the son of their creator and destroyer.

Lex was the next one through. Then the Guvnor stood on that world, looking at a single bright star in the smoky night. Garvin felt him restrain the Wind. "It recognizes the stable where it was penned. A few of its fellows are up there still."

POWERING THE SATELLITE. As if it were something that he had learned a long while back and was in the process of forgetting, Garvin showed the Goblins breaking and harnessing the Winds. The one with the Guvnor responded, seemed to leap as if slapped. It whirled around the Companions and troops who were hauling themselves through the portal.

Then they were discovered. Garvin felt it a moment before it happened. DOWN, he ordered and everyone hit the ground. Except for the Swift Ones who stood, beautiful, noble, best loved of the Gods of the City, and were burned to ash by rays of light.

Garvin's rage seized him. It wasn't the wild fury he had

once had at the Roman Fields when he ordered thousands burned because of the death of a horse. This was colder and more specific. He found the laser operators and showed them what had happened to the Goblin army at Guitars. He showed them Goblins falling over each other as they fled without Winds to carry them. He showed Echbattan soldiers shooting their Zombie commanders and Riders screaming as Steeds leaped off cliffs.

It took only a few seconds. When the Warchild was done, the laser operators turned the weapons around. The lasers were set up at a command center in a lighted area near a charred stand of trees. They were only soldiers; Garvin's anger was not at them.

Behind the laser emplacement stood their Zombie officers, humans taken at childhood and brainwashed, some of them not much different from Lex. Several Steeds were at a table from which they directed operations. Garvin understood what had happened to them. He remembered with a certain fondness the Rider which had once inhabited his own skull. They were slaves almost as surely as their Steeds.

But in the light, broadcasting their contemptuous stick-figure images of humans, were several green forms. One of them had ears that twitched spasmodically. It was that one which directed the laser operators. LOWER, ordering them to scorch the earth around the portal where Garvin lay.

The operators swung around. Seeing that, Zombies fell flat. Riders pulled Steeds out of the way. The green ears twitched once as the Goblin stared at the laser. They twitched once again just as the head which held them was burned to a crisp.

Garvin and the rest of Warchild Cluster stood up. He saw flames in the distance where the Goblin command center burned. It was in the opposite direction from the one in which Garvin had once been led by the Swift Ones. That way had led to Goblin Market. Around the command center, he had seen dead Swift Ones. On the minds of Zombies and Riders was the idea that they guarded an important portal. Garvin thought he knew why it was important.

The Guvnor stood beside him, staring up into the sky. "My invisible friend seems to have gone to spread the word to the Cave of Winds."

"It will come back."

"If the Lady wills it."

"I'm going that way." Garvin pointed at the flames on the skyline. He indicated the other direction. "That way gives access to Goblin Market. Take most of the Cluster and clear the enemy out of there."

"Just the thing for me. Without the Wind, I'm a company commander, at best."

Garvin set off at a run. Lex followed him with a few dozen members of the cluster. She found the idea GOING TO FIND MY FATHER in his mind. Under that was something not quite an idea, more an inborn command like breathing. BRING HIM BACK ALIVE.

They ran past Swift Ones scorched to death and Zombies smashed into the ground. By the light of flaming trees, they saw craters full of wrecked machinery and whole tribes of burned corpses. Lex passed through the horror as if were a dream, but one which was about to end.

Garvin, right ahead of Lex, cast his mind forward, felt out the portal he had detected. He ran like an arrow, sure of his destination. What would happen afterward he didn't know or wonder about.

He caught the thought of his followers, heard it over their panting breaths: HOME WAS YESTERDAY. OVER SOON. GROW OLD, WHY? THEN REST. For him, just as for Lex and the others, there were no plans for after the Goblins and the Gods were gone. And death was as good a rest as any.

He ran along the path taken tens of thousands of times by his father. At the end of it was a portal where Garvin paused for a moment to organize his followers. He grabbed half a dozen armed soldiers and stepped forward. Lex and the other Companion telepaths did the same. Then they were in Time. The pulsing beat, almost too soft to be felt, skipped once, then skipped again.

The next portal was only seconds away. Garvin detected minds on guard on the other side, waiting, tense, unnerved by what they had just seen. They knew that Goblins and Gods were at each other's throats and mortals and Riders would live or fall as chance would have it. Garvin and his veteran troopers rolled out of Time, grabbing minds, spraying bullets.

The Steed commanding the defense took a bullet in the

face. He stared at Garvin with surprise as he died with the
Rider wailing inside him. All the ones who didn't die fled
from the presence of the Warchild and his terrible images of
their disaster at Guitars.

FOLLOW THEM. Companions spread out with their
troops. Garvin recognized the ruined garden littered with
corpses in which he paused. It was the same one he had seen
from the windows of his father's Palace. The flickering light
by which he saw it came from the French windows at the end
of a paved walk. Through them, he saw figures, round Goblin
heads and a single human form. As the Goblins closed in, the
man leaped, whirled in the dancing light.

Garvin headed that way, Lex and a few soldiers behind him.
Once or twice she had felt the idea that drove Garvin. FIND MY
FATHER. BRING HIM BACK ALIVE. The Zombies posted at
the windows had cut and run. GUARD OUR BACKS, Lex
ordered the soldiers. They turned, weapons ready.

FATHER! Garvin grabbed for the minds inside, felt his father's flicker at the same moment he saw the human figure
fall. He kicked open the windows. Three Goblins turned from
his father, who was on the floor, bleeding. Half a dozen Zombies and several young Swift Ones lay dead. The fire had been
raked out of the hearth and onto the rug. It burned not far
from Brian Garvin.

As he leaped into the room, Garvin showed the Goblins
how he had departed the world of Guitars. The portal he had
used was near a line of trees. From every one hung a Goblin.
As Garvin strode across the room toward them, the three
green figures backed toward the fireplace. One of them wore a
long black robe. Garvin showed them the Winds above Guitars after he had summoned them. Then he let the Goblins see
flags twist, leaves torn from trees as the Winds turned into
one mighty gale and streamed away across Time to the Lady.

He let the Goblins in the mirrored room feel the terror of
the ones caught outside Guitars. The Goblin's black robe
touched the flame. AN ARRANGEMENT, that one said. AN
ARRANGEMENT. It showed Garvin a gray stick figure sitting down with the Goblins. AN ARRANGEMENT SUCH
AS WE HAD. They began to spread out.

Lex, standing behind and to Garvin's right, saw that one of

them carried a hand weapon which it slowly raised. She caught the mind of that one. She showed it a brand-new Goblin Chain. Children awakened to the Warchild's call and caught the minds of Zombie servants who turned on the Zombies. That awakened the Steeds to revolt. They ran away with the Riders and left only the Goblins to face the Warchild's wrath. As the Goblin gaped, she turned its gun around. Its mouth twisted as it blew off the top of its own head.

The black robe caught fire. That Goblin whirled to douse it and Garvin jumped forward and kicked it where its scrotum might have been. Black Robe fell into the fireplace. The screech it gave tore at human ears. As it cried, the third Goblin jumped at the Warchild. And fell flat on its face with Brian Garvin's hand around one of its ankles.

From beyond the drawing room, Garvin heard a shot and a scream, felt human agony. GO. He gestured Lex toward the door. When she hesitated, he repeated, GO, and showed her an image of tiny Swift Ones cowering in a pantry at the end of the hall.

Lex ran out the door. Garvin turned his attention back to the room. His father was on his feet. He delivered a few swift kicks to the side of the third Goblin's head. Black Robe stopped screeching and went into suspended animation. The smell of its burning was foul. The flames that crept along the rug smoldered around the peacock screen.

Garvin Warchild looked at his father, who stared back unblinking. Brian Garvin was the Commandant. One of his arms was torn open. The bleeding, though, had stopped. He said, "You have given me my life, lad," and his eyes almost seemed to smile. "Fair exchange, since I gave you yours."

FIND YOUR FATHER. BRING HIM TO ME ALIVE. That command came into Garvin's mind automatically when he stood facing the man.

His father detected it too. "Yes, and in the small hours of morning, you will almost be able to remember who it was that told you that. I have something not unlike it." He moved so that he stood between Garvin and the flames. CREATE WORLDS IN THE IMAGE OF YOUR WORLD. KEEP YOUR WORLD SAFE AND A CHILD WILL APPEAR TO RELIEVE YOU AFTER YOUR LAST WATCH. He shook his head. "That sort of thing rolls around in my brain at odd moments."

"I'm taking you to the Republic, father."

"I see."

"You let them set up Goblin Market. You let Riders and Zombies run through Time." Garvin tried to summon the anger that had carried him this far. Instead he suddenly felt tired, drained.

"Lad, you are just starting out in the God business," his father told him. From down the hall came a shot and a screech and an image from Lex of half a dozen young Swift Ones hidden in one of Mary's pantries. "I did as I was commanded, though the orders themselves faded to a dream. You are the master of Goblin Market now, Warchild." He put an emphasis on the title.

FIND YOUR FATHER. BRING HIM TO ME ALIVE. As Garvin looked at the mirror, the firelight made the image of the room ripple. Neither his father nor he showed up in the glass. The ruined drawing room seemed empty. For an instant, Garvin felt himself falling forward into the Well of Stars.

"Be merciful if you can to any of my servants who survive. And care, if you would, for those little Swift Ones your girlfriend just found. I believe they are the very last ones left." His father turned toward the mirror.

"You're not leaving," Garvin said. He had his father trapped between himself and the flames that still burned outside the fireplace.

"To every generation its deed, as they said in Dublin in Easter of 1916. Good luck on yours, my lad," and Brian Garvin, his bad arm tucked in, leaped over the flames and through the mirror beyond them out beyond Time, beyond life, into Eternity. At the moment he was gone, Garvin felt the heartbeat of Time stop. Then it began again and Garvin realized it was his own heartbeat. As he understood that, the fire on the floor went out and the mirrored room was restored.

EPILOGUE

The first order the Warchild gave after he inherited Time was that the City and Goblin Market should be abandoned. The last dying Wind that powered it had joined the ones that had fueled the Goblins' satellite and sailed back to the Lady.

Without Winds, the City was dead. Without the slave trade, the City was without purpose. The Gates of Gold, Silver, Amber, and Onyx had been wrecked. Whispers echoed on the empty catwalks, the abandoned holding pits of Goblin Market. The floor of the Crystal Chamber of the Palace was knee-deep in shattered glass. The empty cold of Time seeped in and the lights on the high ceilings were dark. The air grew more stale with every breath taken as the survivors of the City packed the possessions they could carry and filed out of their home, led by the Companions.

Besides the shattered Crystal Chamber the palace itself was in ruins. Blood soaked the carpet of the receiving room where the beautiful Oublie and a few others had made a last stand and been torn to pieces by Goblins. The bronze doors leading to the private apartments of the Gods had been blown off their hinges. Bullet holes and the gouges made by blades marked the walls of the corridor that led past the bedroom and study down to the dark, empty kitchen where Mary had fed Swift Ones and Gods and where she and Tom had laid down their lives to save the last children. Even the door of the drawing room was splintered.

But the drawing room was like a magic bubble. The air inside it was a little chilly, but flames danced in the fireplace to chase that away. It was there they found Garvin, staring into the mirror at his missing reflection. They made no sound, coming from the Swift Ones' world through the French windows behind him. And neither of them showed up in the glass. He felt their presence and turned to see the Guvnor and Herself.

"Time for me to be going, old boy. She Who Must Be Obeyed summons me." The Guvnor reached out his good arm to shake Garvin's hand, his mind skipping away from contact with his nephew's mind.

"And it seems she wishes to see me." Herself stepped forward. Dressed now in a green coverall with a single red rose at its collar, her hair tied behind her, she seemed to him more beautiful than ever. Realizing that twisted Garvin inside. She caught his reaction and started to smile gently, to step forward and kiss him on the cheek and tell him that all which had happened with them had happened to many before.

She wanted to show him that the events before the Goblins' fall had as little to do with them as dreams do in bright sunlight. But feeling what he felt and thinking to amuse him, she let him see the blank terror of the parasite in her mind. "Ah, could it be She wishes to take my Rider and breed it with yours? This one is afraid to leave me."

As she spoke, Garvin caught a dying memory of having clung to a barren rock, staring up at the Well of Stars. He remembered a promise he had made but couldn't remember why he had made it. The phrase YOUR CHILD OF MY CHOOSING jumped into his mind. Herself flushed, broke mental contact, and didn't touch him, though her smile remained in place.

The Guvnor fingered the flower in his buttonhole. To fill the empty pause, he asked, "Now that you've come into the property, what are your plans?"

"I want to undo . . . to make it simpler. Too much exploitation between worlds . . ." Garvin wasn't sure what he meant. But he showed them an image of worlds rolling together.

"Just before you appeared, I felt that Time was running down, closing in around me. Don't much like the feel of that. Good luck, nephew. I go to the place I can never remember. I return to the Goddess."

Garvin nodded, started forward to embrace them, then stopped. "Rule well, Garvin," Herself said. "I will see you again." She blew him a kiss and disappeared through the French windows with the Guvnor.

Garvin felt her Rider's touch. He knew what his own Rider would have thought about this. It would tell him not to trust Herself, or the Guvnor, to act right then and prevent troublesome heirs from arising. He knew all that now without the parasite. He wondered if that meant he was fit to rule. Thousands of worlds, billions of people awaited him. Garvin wanted to run away as he never had wanted it before.

Turning toward the mirror, Garvin thought he could see something move, not a reflection but something in the glass itself. He heard the beating of wings and remembered Scarecrow showing him the flight of wild geese. He put out a hand and saw it pass right through the glass. Cold went up his arm and into his heart. He gasped and drew the hand back.

The little park visible only from the God's Palace had also restored itself. It was there that Lex saw the Guvnor and Herself pass out of the mirrored room and walk toward the portal. "Farewell," the Guvnor said and raised his hand in salute as he passed by. "You directed the best battle I ever saw. Time and Garvin will be safe in your hands." Herself just nodded and smiled in Lex's direction.

They had fought well and bravely, but if they were leaving for good, Lex wasn't sorry to see them go. The way of Garvin's family was something she didn't want to think about. Seeing the red roses they wore reminded Lex of the one she had been given. She felt in her pockets, found it crushed but still alive, and stuck it in a buttonhole of her shirt. From somewhere, a mind whispered, THE OLD GOD PASSES. A NEW GOD'S REIGN BEGINS.

With Garvin, Lex could remember moments when she had seen him mortal and vulnerable. Those made it possible for her to think of them having a life together. But when his face flickered before her, when at night she caught his dreams of ice and stars, she felt he was as unhuman as his father and the Goblins ever had been.

A half dozen young Swift Ones clustered around her, reached into her pocket for cookies. Ranging from babies who could barely walk to half-grown kids, they were bright-eyed, seemingly untouched by what they had seen. When they laughed it was like crystals tinkling.

Lex led them up to the French windows. Inside, she saw Garvin staring into the mirror. "Garvin," she called. He turned and for a second Lex caught something in the glass behind him. He smiled and Lex felt his joy at seeing her. They stood for a while in each other's arms and turned away from the mirror. Then, with small Swift Ones darting around them, they left the room without looking back.